More praise for

Birds of Paradise

"This Jordanian-American author writes about food so enticingly that her books should be published on sheets of phyllo dough. *Birds of Paradise* contains her most mouthwatering writing ever, but it's no light after-dinner treat. This is a full-course meal, a rich, complex and memorable story that will leave you lingering gratefully at her table."
—Ron Charles, *Washington Post*

"Brilliant. . . . *Birds of Paradise* is likely to add further luster to [Abu-Jaber's] literary reputation. . . . With her evocative prose and accomplished style, Diana Abu-Jaber's *Birds of Paradise* explores with wisdom and insight the emotional fallout of a shattering family crisis. Yet in this profoundly moving novel, she also manages to unearth the inherent, cathartic beauty of family and individual survival in this complex and perilous new century."   —Cecie O'Bryon England,
Washington Times

"Abu-Jaber makes us wonder about more than what will happen to one girl with a guilty secret. What, after all, does it mean to be a family? Is love really 'exchangeable, malleable'? We can't help turning pages full of stunning prose to find out."
—Sara Nelson, *O, The Oprah Magazine*

"A beautiful and complex examination of a mother-daughter relationship."   —Jennifer Haupt, *Psychology Today*

"Miami comes alive in *Birds of Paradise*, a lush new novel. . . . From the verdant streets of Coral Gables to the back lots of Little Haiti and the seedy underbelly of Miami Beach, the metropolis is floridly, meticulously detailed."   —Cristina García
New York Times Book Review

"Abu-Jaber . . . employs her descriptive talents in bringing Miami to steamy, pulsing life, but it is *Birds of Paradise*'s neither predictable nor merely haphazard momentum and its rich cast of characters that make us feel we're in deliciously capable hands."   —Bliss Broyard, *Elle*

"Few writers entwine food and memory as well as Diana Abu-Jaber."
—Emily Witt, *Marie Claire*

"Gorgeous. . . . [Abu-Jaber] writes with a precise, almost poetic distillation of feeling, heightened in contrast to the ripe, exuberant landscape and the unsettled feelings of a family in limbo. . . . To put it in Abu-Jaber's terms: If the book were a pastry, it would be savory and complex, layered with richness, with a flicker of sweetness that lingers on the tongue."   —Amy Driscoll, *Miami Herald*

"A meticulous, deeply moving portrayal of imperfect human beings struggling to do right. . . . Glorious descriptions, both of nature and Avis's mouthwatering pastry, offset yet intensify the jagged emotions of the Muirs."   —*Kirkus Reviews*

"The Muirs' absorbing story builds to a thoroughly satisfying climax."
—Sue Corbett, *People* magazine (four stars)

"With *Birds of Paradise*, Abu-Jaber has made an amazing, gigantic leap into rare air, that hazy stratosphere we jokingly call The Big Time. Her novel is that worthy, and that beautiful."
—Christine Selk, *Oregonian*

"If such a thing were possible with books, I would have licked the plate."   —Sarah Norris, *Chapter 16*

"Abu-Jaber is a brilliant storyteller and this is the kind of novel that appeals on many levels: plot-oriented, well-written, moving, and dealing with a family breakdown that transcends class."
—*Frisbee: A Book Journal*

"It's impossible to read the work of Diana Abu-Jaber without at least an occasional lump in the throat. . . . Abu-Jaber is able to achingly express each family member's regrets, hopes, and fears."
—Agnes Torres Al-Shibibi, *Seattle Times*

"Whether it's the creation of evanescent confections or the drug-ridden life of the streets, award-winning writer Abu-Jaber (*Origin*) impressively describes vastly different worlds with equal expertise. . . . A literary family drama with extra appeal to foodies."
—Joy Humphrey, *Library Journal*

"*Birds of Paradise* is that best kind of novel, one that finds a serious writer honing and developing her gift with each new work. It offers new readers an opportunity to catch up with this important American novelist just as she comes into the fullness of her powers."
—Chauncey Mabe, *Open Page*

"Abu-Jaber's effortless prose, fully fleshed characters, and a setting that reflects the adversity in her protagonists' lives come together in a satisfying and timely story." —*Publishers Weekly*

"Abu-Jaber's appeal is universal, multi-cultural and joyful, a tangled world experienced through the prism of family, a microcosm of humanity's most damning flaws and finest moments. Diana Abu-Jaber's language of the heart transcends borders, a refreshing wash of hope in a time of need." —*Curled Up with a Good Book*

"[Abu-Jaber's] prose is often lyrical. . . . But *Birds of Paradise* has satisfying substance, too, for anyone hungry to read about the many ways that modern families lose and love."
—Colette Bancroft, *St. Petersburg Times*

"Carefully concocted, Diana Abu-Jaber's *Birds of Paradise* is a feast that is easily one of the year's best novels—food or no."
—David Chambers, *Super Chef*

"Diana Abu-Jaber's fourth novel charms with delectable prose, vividly unique characterizations, and an exquisitely-rendered Miami setting. . . . Our hearts and our appetites are stimulated by this extraordinary quest to the heart of family connections." —Glenda Bailey-Mershon, *Women and Books*

"The counterpoint of protagonist Avis Muir's finicky pastries and her Haitian neighbor's mysterious home remedies bracket the heart of Diana Abu-Jaber's novel the way outer petals frame its titular blooms." —Bethanne Patrick, *Star Tribune*

"Intimate and evocative. . . . Hungry yet? Read the novel and you will be. Not just for the many fragrant and fragile pastries that float through its pages, but for the landscape of the story as well. . . . What really sets *Birds of Paradise* apart is Abu-Jaber's genius for immersing the reader in a sense of place. From the manicured Eden of Coral Gables, to the amped-up narcissism of South Beach, to the rough, hot streets of Little Havana, you feel and smell and taste Miami. . . . It's in Felice's chapters that *Birds of Paradise* comes to full and sizzling life." —Veronique de Turenne, *Chicago Tribune*

Birds of
Paradise

Also by Diana Abu-Jaber

ORIGIN

THE LANGUAGE OF BAKLAVA

CRESCENT

ARABIAN JAZZ

W. W. NORTON & COMPANY | NEW YORK LONDON

Birds of Paradise

A NOVEL

Diana Abu-Jaber

Copyright © 2011 by Diana Abu-Jaber

Printed in the United States of America
First published as a Norton paperback 2012

For information about permission to reproduce
selections from this book, write to Permissions,
W. W. Norton & Company, Inc.,
500 Fifth Avenue, New York, NY 10110

For information about special discounts for bulk purchases,
please contact W. W. Norton Special Sales at
specialsales@wwnorton.com or 800-233-4830

Manufacturing by RR Donnelley, Harrisonburg
Book design by Barbara M. Bachman
Production manager: Anna Oler

LIBRARY OF CONGRESS
CATALOGING-IN-PUBLICATION DATA

Abu-Jaber, Diana.

Birds of paradise : a novel / Diana Abu-Jaber. — 1st ed.

        p. cm.

ISBN 978-0-393-06461-2 (hardcover)

1. Runaway teenagers—Fiction. 2. Teenage girls—Fiction.
3. Families—Fiction. 4. Parent and teenager—Fiction.
5. Brothers and sisters—Fiction. 6. Miami (Fla.)—Fiction.
7. Domestic fiction. 8. Psychological fiction. I. Title.

PS3551.B895B57 2011

813'.54—dc22

                                            2011014575

ISBN 978-0-393-34259-8 pbk.

W. W. Norton & Company, Inc.
500 Fifth Avenue, New York, N.Y. 10110

www.wwnorton.com

W. W. Norton & Company Ltd.
Castle House, 75/76 Wells Street, London W1T 3QT

1 2 3 4 5 6 7 8 9 0

For Scotty and Gracie

Birds of
Paradise

A COOKIE, AVIS TOLD HER CHILDREN, IS A SOUL. She held up the wafer, its edges shimmering with ruby-dark sugar. "You think it looks like a tiny thing, right? Just a little nothing. But then you take a bite."

Four-year-old Felice lifted her face. Avis fanned her daughter's eyes closed with her fingertips and placed it in Felice's mouth. Felice opened her sheer eyes. Lamb slid his orange length against her ankles. Avis handed a cookie to eight-year-old Stanley, who held it up to his nose. "Does that taste good?" she asked. Felice nodded and opened her mouth again.

"It smells like flowers," Stanley said.

"*Yes.*" Avis paused, a cookie balanced on her spatula. "That's the rosewater. Good palate, darling."

"Mermaids eat roses," Felice said. "Then they melt."

THIS MORNING'S PASTRY poses challenges. To assemble the tiny mosaic disks of chocolate flake and candied ginger, Avis must execute a number of discrete, ritualistic steps: scraping the chocolate with a fine grater, rolling the dough cylinder in large-grain sanding sugar, and assembling the ingredients atop each hand-cut disk of dough in a pointillist collage. Her husband wavers near the counter, watching. "They're like something Marie Antoinette would wear around her neck. When she still had one."

"I thought she was more interested in cake," Avis says, she tilts her narrow shoulders, veers around him to stack dishes in the sink.

"But really—look at this." Brian holds one on the palm of his hand; it twinkles with the kitchen light. "Shame to eat them."

Avis had shopped for the ingredients two days earlier, driving to Fort Lauderdale, to an Italian import store, to buy the rock sugar and flour. The outlying regions of downtown Miami, Hallandale, Hollywood, seemed esoteric, scribbled over—inscrutable as an ancient desert. She was offended by the ads painted on the sides of warehouses, hawking lamps and furniture, medical treatments and ice cream, a thirty-foot naked man reclining, selling God-knows-what.

Yesterday she crystallized the ginger, then mixed the ingredients slowly, not to disturb the dough. But even after one full day's work, there were still more steps to complete this morning, including baking and cooling. Avis had hurried, not wanting Brian to notice how much labor has gone into this. Her assistant won't be in for another hour and there's a tower in the sink, open bins of pastry flour, the hair dryer on the counter (just a blast of cool air, to ward off the humidity, before slipping the cookies into tins). Brian slips one of the half-dollar-sized pastries into his mouth. Avis knows it will dissolve mid-chew, fleeting as a wink. "Have I had these before? Do you sell them?"

"Not for years." Avis can't help boasting a little, "Last time I made these, Neiman's sold them for $4.95 apiece in their case."

Brian eyes the three remaining on his plate. "We should stick them in a safe."

Avis admits, "A little labor-intensive." *Gingembre en cristal* was Felice's favorite cookie; Stanley's were homely, proletarian Toll Houses. Avis remembers toiling over the delicate ginger coins for Felice's tenth birthday, only for her daughter to thank her politely and then refuse to eat them. She'd said, "I just like the way they look."

Avis had felt singed by the rejection. Yet there was also a pang of admiration: the purity of Felice's desires—preferring beauty to sugar!

Avis had started baking because there was never anything to eat when she was a child. Her mother—head lowered over Dante, Hegel, C. S. Lewis, reading Voltaire, Bakhtin, Avicenna, in French, Russian, Arabic—would murmur, "Go get yourself something." Avis would hang on the refrigerator door, staring at cans of tomato juice, sticks of butter, bags of coffee. She went for days at a time eating only jam and slices of bread. The women at the Redbird Bakery on the next block gave her free muffins and scones whenever she came in. Her mother was busy: she taught and wrote about private and cultural representations of Heaven, the phoenix, the transformation of base materials into gold. Instead of reading storybooks, Avis stood in the kitchen studying the pictures in cookbooks, a more immediate form of alchemy.

Avis asked about the identity of her father when she was ten: Geraldine waved her off, saying, "Oh, who keeps track?" When Avis persisted, she shook her head: "No, no—don't be tedious, dear."

The first time Avis knelt on a chair and stirred eggs into flour to make a vanilla cake, she had an inkling of how higher orders of meaning encircle the chaos of life. Where philosophy, she already intuited, created only thought—no beds made, no children fed—in other rooms there were good things like measuring spoons, thermometers, and recipes, with their lovely, interwoven systems and codes. Avis labored over her pastries: her ingredient base grew, combining worlds: preserved lemons from Morocco in a Provençal tart; Syrian olive oil in Neapolitan *cantuccini;* salt combed from English marshes and filaments of Kashmiri saffron secreted within a Swedish cream. By the time Avis was in college, her baking had evolved to a level of exquisite accomplishment: each pastry as unique as a snowflake, just as fleeting on the tongue: pellucid jams colored cobalt and lavender, biscuits light as eiderdown.

Brian edges in front of the sink, trying to stay out of her way. "Like you don't have enough to worry about today."

"Yes, yes." She glances at him: he's holding the counter as if it were keeping him steady. He's in the kitchen, she knows, because they'd fought earlier—or had what passes for a fight between them— the dart of words: Why are you still doing this? I just don't think . . .

I'm aware of what you think.

Now he looms, big as an obstacle. Not sure where to put himself. She doesn't like having people in her kitchen, but she does feel a lilt toward him, grateful that he hasn't run out yet. They're trying to stop fighting, but can't quite leave each other alone.

"That kid never ate anything anyway," he says darkly.

Avis begins the cautious and deliberate transfer of cookies to tin, using just the tips of her fingers. "Yes, and I'm crazy to go meet her."

"Now you're angry again."

"No I'm not." Avis places the cookies in concentric rings on parchment layers inside the tin. "I know just what my husband thinks, thank you very much, and I'm not angry. I'm fine."

Brian crosses his arms, the suit fabric bunching in fine soft ripples. She knows he can't stop himself. "But, please, *admit it*. It's what? The first time all *year* we hear from that girl? Light of our lives. You're already exhausted, at your wits' end. Finally you'll see her—*if* she comes. I don't get why you knock yourself out even *more*—making some impossible dessert that—I'm sorry, but she probably won't even eat. Am I wrong?"

Avis touches the sides of the tin. Her ribs feel compressed, like a whalebone corset. "No. No. You're right."

He stares at her, a weight in his gaze. He turns and his eyes fall on the Audubon calendar hanging near the door—the only ornamentation in Avis's kitchen. The month of August, Snowy Egret. He looks away.

Avis sees this and smiles. Her hands are steady and cool as she lays down another round of parchment. "Felice never liked cakes," she says. "Even for birthdays."

He tucks in his chin, silent.

Avis finishes the layer and fits the lid on the tin, inhales the kitchen's gingered air. Flour and yolk and cream are all coarse—of the earth. But sugar and air and vanilla are elements of the firmament. Avis used to tell her kids: Sweets should be an evanescence: cakes and pies represent minutes, cookies and *mille-feuilles* are seconds, meringues are moments. "I actually haven't made these since she left," Avis says. If a voice could be inspected under a lens, the first tiny crack of the day would be detectable. "I thought these might be—" She's gone too far—pretending to be braver than she can manage right now—and there's no good way to complete the sentence.

"Never mind," Brian murmurs. "It'll be fine today." He touches the ridge at the back of her neck, just under her twist of hair. But she is so light-boned, he feels clumsy and lifts his hand. "I have to get to work," he says like it's an apology.

She lifts her head, offering him a temple to kiss goodbye.

THE SUN IS RIPER, more golden and potent as Avis stands in the driveway, trying not to show impatience as her assistant roots through her purse, hunting for her keys—first, without looking, just feeling, then plopping the bag on the hood of her car and examining its contents. From over the tiled eave of her house comes a bird cry, so close, deep, and staccato it startles Avis. It's a new song that she's been hearing over the past few mornings. Chortling followed by a long whistle, like a dove's three-note gurgle, then a low-level, agitated squeak—a funny extended song. Catbird? It starts sweetly, then sharpens and escalates: Brian's complained about the noise waking him, threatens to call Animal Control.

"Listen to that."

"What?" Nina pulls out her handful of keys. "Hooray already."

"You didn't hear that?" Avis asks as she slides into the car. "The loud, angry one? The bird?"

Nina pulls her door shut, adjusts the rearview mirror. She laughs through her nose. "A loud angry bird? Okay, let's focus. Now, we're going to the usual place?"

"Please." Avis stares out the window, trying to find the bird. The flickering bamboo along the perimeter of the drive seems to correspond to her own internal state, a flickering grief or rawness, left over from that morning's argument with Brian. "You're just causing yourself pain," he'd said, several times. "It's like you're doing it deliberately."

Did she love him still? *Persist* in loving him, her mother would have said. "Oh, don't marry a lawyer, my dear," she'd cried. "They're horrible. They're venal. At least accountants say what they are. They make no bones about it."

Was it possible to still love someone when she fantasizes about solitude? She can see the state of separateness so clearly: a house without Brian. A cottage with a fireplace and thatched roof, a morning sky like opal; every inch of the place a kitchen, a bakery. Where would she sleep if she didn't have Brian to make the bed for? Would she sleep at all? She's read that the unhappiest, loneliest writers write the sweetest poems. Still, she loves their house, a wonderful old Spanish-style with plaster moldings, fireplace framed with blue mosaic, rooms that flow like river water into each other, a generous, high-ceilinged living room that opens into a dining room, an office, a Florida room, all imbued with subtle lights from a row of French doors that lead to the backyard and pool. She could never give up her house or kitchen.

Nina and Avis pull out onto Vizcaya. They pass through the vault of old black olive trees, the pale houses in ocher, terracotta, and sienna—light-stained, rippling tile rooftops. The neighborhood is filled with key-shaped doors, arches, brick drives, Moorish tiles, round windows, sly turrets and gables, windows in triangles and trapezoids glinting from hidden corners. And this is a restrained, middle-to-upper area. Just a few blocks to the south, Coral Gables unfurls into immense estates, manicured lawns, private docks, the winter homes of czars. Avis has taken strolls past the study of Thomas Edison, an orchard where barefooted Alexander Graham Bell picked mangoes, beyond languid botanical gardens that hug the shore, copses of banyan trees with their preternatural dangling limbs and silvery flesh.

At a cocktail party she'd overheard a realtor referring to Avis's neighborhood as "the ghetto of the Gables."

"What is that supposed to mean?" she'd edged into the conversation while cutting a baguette on a sharp bias. "A *ghetto*?"

The realtor, a woman with a long, corded neck, had seemed to barely register Avis, glancing at her hands on the cutting board. Avis wasn't the caterer—she merely disliked the way the hostess ripped her loaves into chunks. "It's silly," the woman had answered, mainly addressing the man across from her. "Just, you know, four bedrooms instead of eight, balconies but no tennis courts, no servants' quarters. That sort of thing."

Avis had coolly revealed her address to the realtor and the woman had replied, "Goodness. Well, at least you're to the west of LeJeune."

The scent of jasmine drifts into the windows. Songbird season is over. No more gardenias: hurricane season. The trees have grown dense as rooftops; the plumeria hold their flower-tipped branches up like brides with golden corsages. Avis sits hunched forward, clinging to her tin: she can feel the metal chill through her blouse, all the way to the pit of her stomach. She'd forgotten to eat again. She flips down the mirror in the car visor, batting at her hair—lately it's started thinning but there's still enough to twirl into a twist—a smear of chocolate on her cheek. She rubs at it, then slaps the visor back. Her breath gets shallower as they drive, and there seems to be a lump forming in her throat. By the time they've reached the Alton Road exit ramp, heading up the spine of the beach to their meeting place, her arms feel rubbery with fear. A small unwelcome voice returns to the back of her head: *Please forgive me, please forgive me.*

Avis stiffens as they pull over at the corner, pressing herself into the seat. Five months ago: Avis had received one of her daughter's random calls to meet, and off she'd gone to the appointed place—always against Brian's wishes—clutching money, a shopping bag of gifts—expensive shampoo, a new sweater, and an iPod—and sat alone for over two hours, suffering miserably through suspense and, finally, disappointment. Today she brings nothing but a wallet stuffed with crisp fifties and the tin of cookies.

Nina waits a moment, engine idling, watching Avis's profile. After a few long moments, she says, "Hang on." Nina pulls out her thermos, pours an inch of inky coffee in the bottom of two waxed paper cups—*cortaditos*. She touches her cup to Avis's, toasts, *"Salud, amor, y pesetas."* Avis can barely return Nina's smile. She closes her eyes to drink. The richly black liquid tastes of smoke, like the pot of Turkish coffee she stood over throughout her childhood, stirring and watching and stirring. When Avis brought it to her mother, she would take a sip, close her eyes, and mutter, "It takes like dirt."

Avis would apologize and her mother would say, "No, it's good dirt."

Avis's eyes feel hot: she tucks her empty cup on the dash and touches Nina's hand, mute and overgrateful. Nina shakes her hand loose, waving at Avis. "You get going."

The car door opens: the day is mild, the air crystalline, rendering all details in hyper-real clarity. Avis realizes she's shaking, her teeth chattering. She clings to the edge of the car as if it's an airplane hatch. She shakes her head. "I can't."

SHE'D FELT DISORIENTATION strong as vertigo after they'd first moved to Miami—as if her magnetic poles had been switched. The drivers were appalling, punching their horns, running reds, cutting each other off like sworn enemies. There were certain shops and restaurants one would not wish to enter unless one spoke Spanish—and not at her halting, college intermediate level, either. There were whole neighborhoods and sections of town where she felt scrutinized and sized up. How many times had she waited by counters while salespeople went in search of "the one" who spoke English? One of Brian's new business associates took the two of them out for "traditional Cuban cuisine" to an immense old restaurant on Calle Ocho, a warren of rooms filled with speckled old mirrors and gilt frames. He rattled off an order in Spanish, and barely five minutes later, the waiter returned with heaped-up plates of ground beef and cubed pork and fish in a blanket of white gravy. While Brian and the other man leaned forward into a discussion of easement disputes, his wife raised a penciled eyebrow at Avis. "This isn't real Cuban food," she muttered. "It's for the tourists. Hector brings Americans here because he thinks they'll like it better."

Avis insisted that the food was fine, but the salty, greasy meat unsettled her stomach. The waiter ignored everyone at their table but Hector.

Brian gleaned from his new bosses that to lead a civilized life in Miami, one had to buy in the Gables: apparently Coconut Grove was for artists and related "marginals," Kendall for Colombians, Doral for Venezuelans, Hialeah for Cubans, Pinecrest for multichild suburban dullards, and beyond the (frightening, inscrutable) downtown, there were ominous "ethnic" regions with names like Overtown, Liberty City, and sad Little Haiti. PI&B helped Brian and Avis find and finance their gracious home ($104,000—an astronomical sum to Avis, nineteen years ago), and when Felice was born, Avis pushed her stroller through the streets, trying to get her bearings. She crossed neighborhoods filled with pillowy silence, where landscapers roamed around waving herbicide wands, where the rare matron walking her borzoi might offer an arch, provisional "Good morning." Five blocks from their front door there were houses on the historic register, manses with titles, "Villa Tempesta," "The San Esteban," ivy-circled palm trees, secret gated communities, limestone entrances flanked by stone unicorns. And, everywhere, polished sedans with blacked-out windows, gliding by like ghosts.

One day, after a year and a half of living in Miami, she was again out pushing Felice on their daily walk. At the end of one block, some women gathered around the stroller. *"Qué linda! Hola, muñeca!"* the women cooed, patting Felice's thighs, *"Hola, gordita,"* while Felice frowned into the sunlight: a gorgeous child. They were nannies and housekeepers: they lived in cottages behind their employers' homes— some of these servants' quarters bigger than Avis's house. Avis smiled uneasily, nodding, straining for bits of comprehension. One of the women had a smooth, young face, her hair gathered in a glossy chignon at the nape of her neck. Avis remembers the woman's curiosity—the way she seemed to regard Avis as a sort of exotic creature. Despite Felice's pale skin and lighter eyes, Luma did not assume, like the others, that Avis was her nanny.

She became Avis's first assistant—initially, more of a babysitter for the children—once they started school, she began helping Avis in the kitchen—washing dishes, crushing walnuts, chopping cherries, scraping vanilla beans, measuring and sifting flour. After she left, claiming snidely there would be less work at the Au Bon Pain, Avis went through a series of assistants. They talked to the children in Spanish; they helped Avis with the infinite tasks of running a home bakery. Some became her friends—though rarely confidantes. This was, as far as Avis could divine, the way people did it in Miami: they were friendly but reserved, confined mainly to the close orbits of relatives. While Avis's kitchen was increasingly taken over by her bakery, the assistants brought in home-cooked dishes—*picadillo, moros y cristianos, ropa vieja, pastelitos*—beef crumbled or shredded, fried nearly crispy and tossed with dark spices, served with rice or bread or stuffed into flaking, downy pies that, Avis knew, had to be made with lard. They took Avis shopping, taught the kids torchy, breathless Cuban love songs like *Bésame Mucho* and *Adoración*. Avis had no extended family, no old ties to the area: they explained Miami to her, the intricacies of the Cuban community, the warring clans that owned the city, the class nuances of the Gables neighborhoods—the "Platinum Triangle," the "bohemian North End." Rarely did anyone work for her for more than a year or two—they left to get married or have their own children: or they tired of Avis's imperious, Gallic approach to baking. Or Avis fired them, tired of "Cuban time," "Miami time." The entitled pouting and eye-rolling of formerly wealthy or spoiled women.

ON THE CORNER OF ALTON and Lincoln Roads, Avis feels wobbly, as if the ground is stirring very slightly beneath her feet. "You okay?" Nina calls through the passenger window.

Avis is barely aware of having moved from the car. She turns to Nina and lifts her lips into a smile, then turns back. As she starts down Lincoln Road, she tries not to hold the bakery box too high.

The pedestrian mall is fluted with trees, a late-summer flush over the simple, old Art Deco buildings. A ruffle of awnings and brick red table umbrellas, planters spilling over with arthurium, ginger, hibiscus, blooms in decadent colors, vermillion, magenta, sapphire. Grand date palms line the center of the walkway, their emerald fronds like starbursts and water fountains. Orchids and bromeliads tumble from crates hanging over store displays or secreted in the branches of trees. Avis hunches her shoulders and lowers her head—she doesn't have the reserves to take in this exuberance. The stores and shoppers appear blurry, then break into clarity as she gets closer, as if moving along the sides of a fishbowl. There are shopkeepers rinsing their storefronts with garden hoses and waiters setting out chairs; shirtless men strut along the sidewalk; elderly women in pearls and black cashmere window-shop beside young girls who each in some way remind Avis of Felice. Couples push double and triple baby strollers, some of the mothers are also extravagantly pregnant. Avis believes that these women deliberately avert their eyes.

Four—almost five—years of erratic visits—perhaps twelve visits in all. No, Avis corrects herself; she has not lost track after all. There have been eight visits to date, no more no less. She has seen her daughter exactly eight times since she turned thirteen.

By the door of a restaurant, a girl with long beige hair steps forward, pushing a menu at Avis. "We're offering out-of-towner specials," she chimes, then seems to detect something on Avis's face and directs herself to the next pedestrian.

At last, Avis reaches the outdoor café table where she will await Felice. It takes all of her effort to stay clear-headed and calm. She notes that the usual waiter is there, an olive-skinned man with drowsy eyes, who once exclaimed, "She is here at last!" when Felice arrived an hour late. Avis sits at a table, feeling fluish, gripping the tin of precious cookies. Will Felice eat these? Avis charges such exorbitant prices for her little pastries that her son told her it was "shameful." But she doesn't take the shortcuts of professional bakeries—nothing is rushed, each batch is constructed of pure ingredients, no factory lard or chemical fillers or cheap flour. She thinks of herself as an artisan, each of her pastries as delicately constructed as a piece of stained glass. And she has discovered that the more she charges, the more the customers want.

She orders an iced tea and tells the waiter she needs more time with the menu. He returns with a basket of rolls, a tin of purple jam, a round, peach-colored plumeria blossom among the rolls. Avis sits back, scanning each face in the stream of shoppers. She tries to avoid her watch but catches a glimpse, involuntarily, when she lifts her water glass: 12:08. She lays one hand on top of the other on the tin and tries to steady them.

Felice is often late.

She sips her sweating iced tea and watches the passersby: everyone is so young. So many girls, their small chins tilted toward the light like sunflowers. A child walks by, perhaps six or seven years old, her narrow back sprightly, her hair tucked into a black velvet headband; she is holding her mother's hand.

The waiter wafts through her line of vision—a gigalo-ish face, outlandishly seductive eyes. She looks down.

12:13. She is angry with herself for peeking—not meaning to—doing it habitually—she twists the watch face around on her wrist so it taps against the café table. Felice isn't usually more than a half hour late. But there was that one time. An hour. Anything is possible.

The ice in her glass begins to melt. The waiter removes it and puts down a fresh glass of ice and tea. "Do you know what you want yet?" He scans the other tables as if he's at a party, waiting for someone more interesting to appear.

Sunlight edges around the table umbrella and she can feel the heat on her forearm: they must use such small umbrellas to keep people from lingering. "No—I'd like to wait for my—for my other party to arrive." Her voice is professionally uninflected; she looks directly at him, sits back into shadow: I too have worked the front of the house.

But Avis also feels a minor soughing at the center of her chest as the waiter turns on his heel. The air seems to bow straight through her skin, her body raw. She moves the cookie tin from her lap to the table, not caring if the waiter thinks she's a weird lost woman clutching her treasure. Nothing matters. She stares at her hands, crosshatched with scrapings of this morning's flour work, sinewy with veins and knuckles, overdeveloped, like her calves and ankles, from standing and kneading and stirring. The tin is her talisman. She no longer focuses on the crowds: she sees herself and her daughter everywhere, like memory echoes from the past, bouncing along the sidewalks. All those pairs hovering outside store windows, a hand glissading down the back of a head of hair, an armload of shopping bags—oh, that was once her and Felice. For years and years, that's how it was—even her son knew it—that somehow, without any conscious decision, Avis had assumed that daughters belonged to mothers, and sons to their fathers. Before she'd ever had kids or even met her husband, she'd imagined baking with a daughter. Showing her how to crack an egg one-handed, between her fingers, the way to distill essences from berries, the proper way to tie an apron.

Avis curls in her lips, bites down with just enough pressure to keep from crying. She thinks of Felice at twelve—just before she had gotten so angry.

Felice had wanted to go to a party at Lola Rodriguez's house—just a few blocks away, right in the Gables. They knew Lola—she was one of Felice's cadre—unserious, sweet-natured girls, all of them just beginning to be vain about their smooth hair and skin and nails. When they were together—Lola, Felice, Betty, Coco, Marisa, Yeni, Bella—Avis had a general impression of splashes of laughter, colorful dresses, and thin, tan arms. These girls were accustomed to elaborate entertainments—pool parties, birthday parties; in a few more years most of them would plan wedding-like *quinceañeras*, their fancy white dresses like poufs of Bavarian cream. Brian and Avis did their best to keep up—taking the kids to water parks and museums, summertime hegiras to Europe, and the costly winter pilgrimages to Disney World, its coiling lines and raw sunshine. But sometimes she would notice Felice standing apart from the others, especially as she grew older—her eyes grave, even when she was laughing—a kind of fretful concentration about her.

A few days past Thanksgiving, six years ago. Avis had been working so steadily kneading bread dough that she hadn't noticed how late it was until a blue glistening in the window distracted her: the Calvadoses' Christmas lights had come on, floating the outline of a house on the black night. Brian didn't get home until after seven and Stanley was at a friend's house. Usually Felice would've stopped in the kitchen after school for whatever treat her mother was testing (back then, she was forever developing new offerings for her clients). Avis checked the cooling rack: a tray of raspberry éclairs in glossy chocolate coats.

Avis moved through the house, switching on lights, wondering if Felice had stayed late at school. In the hallway outside her daughter's room, her hand on a light switch, Avis stopped: there were tiny, gasping, imploring sounds coming from within. They sounded so unearthly that everything seemed to hover there, as if the night and stars had leaked into the house and hovered in this dark, sparkling hallway. After listening for a moment, Avis knocked gently, bringing her ear close to the door. "Felice? Darling? Are you there? Can I come in?"

The tiny noises ceased and it was quiet for such a long time that Avis began to wonder if she was hearing things. Finally she heard something muffled and low, and after another pause, she turned the old glass doorknob. She could barely make out Felice on the bed. Her head was propped on the pillow, her hair curling and waving like a sea anemone, her arms flung to either side, she looked half-drowned, ineffably lovely. "Watch your eyes." Instead of the overhead, Avis switched on the softer desk lamp so the room glowed with a sea-green penumbra. "Hey." She sat on the edge of the bed. "What's going on? You didn't say hi. I've got éclairs, and there's still some mousse with the salted caramel."

"Hi Mommy," Felice said in a dazed, unnatural voice. "I feel so tired. I don't know what it is. I'm just so tired."

Avis felt her daughter's forehead, then helped her get undressed and slide under the covers: the child fell asleep instantly.

Felice stayed in bed all night and all the next day: she lay so still it didn't even seem like sleep to Avis, but a kind of stony, mortal sinking. Stanley boiled a whole chicken, browned carrots, onions, and turnips, and brought Felice the fragrant broth, but she barely managed a few spoonfuls. Avis and Brian had terse, whispered conferences outside Felice's bedroom door. Brian was convinced that Felice was merely overtired: "Soccer practice, gymnastics camp, birthday parties practically every week. And these mountains of homework! She needs a vacation just to be a regular kid."

Then Avis learned through the school's phone grapevine that there'd been a suicide at Gables Middle. The girl was thirteen, a grade ahead of Felice, but Avis had heard that suicides could send ripples of shock throughout a school: the administrators offered counseling services to students. She went into the bedroom to ask her daughter if she'd known the girl. "Who?" Felice stared up from her pillow: her eyes had a pearly luster. "Who is that?"

Even after she'd spent three days in bed, Avis didn't want to take Felice to a doctor: she didn't think it would help. She didn't have much of a fever—or any clear physical symptoms, apart from lassitude. It almost seemed as if she needed some sort of *bruja,* as Nina would say, a witch or sorcerer, to break the feverish spell. She tried to talk to Felice, to be easy and comforting, hoping that conversation might help restore her. But Felice's unresponsiveness was so frightening she gave up. Instead Avis retreated to the kitchen, trying to concoct something to tempt Felice, as if coaxing her away from a ledge. She made chocolate truffles with essence of Earl Grey; Brie *gougères*; sable cookies; *baba au rhum*. Felice refused everything. Throat constricted, Avis watched Stanley withdraw from Felice's room each day, his soup bowls emptied.

Eventually she did reemerge, but the light in her face seemed different: she'd gone from clarity to a gray gem. Even her voice was different, textured. There was a new satiny quality about her, like grief, that made her seem older—her loveliness elevated into something unearthly. Geraldine—Avis's mother—would have said that Felice had stepped through some sort of enchantment, and that it had altered her. Part of the spell remained inside her. Avis could see its remnants—a sly, feline indifference: the impatience to return to her enchantment. Things escalated after that, the atmosphere in the house became inexplicably combative. Avis remembers her daughter's distraught expression, unable to comprehend why her father was forcing her—*forcing her*—to return from a party before midnight.

"Humor me," Brian had said, lingering in their daughter's bedroom door. "I only have a few more years to pretend to make the rules."

Avis knew this would be meaningless to their daughter, that Felice believed that the only true time was the present: she was twelve and she would always be twelve, sprawled across her bed, sobbing. They had elected to be old, they were meant to be old. Nothing would change: Felice was meant to be young, and she was sad and would always feel that way.

Felice used to be such an easy, pliant child. "Of course she's easy," Brian used to joke with their friends. "All you have to do is give your child everything."

After her "illness," as Avis thought of that time, she noticed the sharpening of Felice's personality—a willful recalcitrance, bouts of spoiled, pettish behavior. It was unpredictable. A kind of furtiveness spirited across her daughter's face. Once, she broke into tears when Avis made her change an outfit. "It's like you think you *own* me. You don't even really love me."

Brian, of course, said Avis was imagining things. "She's a preteen girl. This is what they do."

The night of the party, there'd been a storm of tears. Brian, home late from work, bowed over a stack of paperwork. Avis thought he was being particularly rigid about a 10 p.m. curfew, and she was tempted to dissent. Their daughter wept passionately, her lashes dark and pointed. "I can't believe you people," Felice had cried, her voice ragged as if something were sawing away inside her.

"Maybe you'd rather not go at all?" Brian threatened, arms crossed, standing in her doorway. Looking back, Avis is jealous of these young parents who could still offer and withhold freedom. Avis spoke with Brian privately in their bedroom. A compromise was brokered.

So Felice went to the party. She smiled at them before leaving—it seemed that all was forgiven—they'd agreed on a curfew of 11:30. When Avis kissed Felice, she detected a trace of dried tears on her daughter's face and moved to brush it away, then checked herself, saying instead, "You look so pretty."

Felice had given her a tremulous smile that pierced Avis. "Thank you, Mommy. You do too." She waved on her way out the door.

That evening, Felice didn't come home.

AVIS STIRS THE MURK of sugar in the bottom of her glass. She watches it rise a few inches into the amber liquid, then settle back. If this place were half-decent, she muses, they'd have given her simple syrup.

She fingers her watch, refusing to look at it. Felice has been over an hour late in the past, hasn't she? Surely. She has also not come at all, on one or two occasions.

The waiter is hovering near her left elbow and Avis finds she has taken an intense dislike to this man, his demonic appearances and disappearances, the way he places the refilled basket before her, murmuring, "Fresh bread."

The cell phone rings and Avis nearly upsets her drink, which the waiter (why is he still there?) catches. It might be Felice, she thinks, though her daughter never uses the prepaid cell phone she gave her three years ago (too late, too late . . . Felice had started asking for her own phone when she'd turned ten, but Brian had ruled she was too young). Avis checks the screen and her pulse slows with disappointment: *Nina—Cell*. The time stamp on the screen: 2:02.

"Do you know what you'd like, ma'am?" the waiter asks.

Avis experiences a surge of rage so cool and hard it feels as if her body is filled with ice. She could stand and quietly crush the waiter's windpipe with her thumbs, sit down and finish sipping her gritty tea. She smiles at him, her face metallic. "Not right now, thank you," her voice a tiny hammer on iron.

She can't quite let herself get at that night—the first night—that Felice didn't come home. She knows police were involved, and 3 a.m. drives, and calls to other parents—she can't recall the sequence. Then, after the terrible empty hours of waiting, like a miracle, there was Felice emerging from Del Fishbein's BMW. It was the morning after the party, the sun a blister on the horizon. The birds were chucking, creaking, whirring; they sounded like monkeys and lizards and rubbing tree limbs.

And there was that boy with Felice—what was his name? Casey? Shawn?

But it wasn't the boy, Felice insisted. She'd gotten tired of the party, she said. She'd asked Casey—or Connor—to walk her home, but they'd stopped to look at the water in the dark. *Water?* Avis realized she was talking about the canals that intersected the Gables: slow, fat manatees sometimes rose to the water's surface and ibises littered the banks like stars.

See, Felice had wondered if they could see the manatees in the dark, she tried to explain to her mother in her reasonable voice. She and Avis stood in the middle of the yard in the dawn, as if Felice simply couldn't wait to get inside the house to explain herself, both of them still in the clothes they'd been wearing the night before. Felice's hands held out in explanation, "I wanted to see if they slept or where they would be, you know? And we cut across the Fishbeins' yard and there were, like, a hundred million of them! They were playing all together in the canal—the manatees!" Avis glanced at the boy; he stood, sleepy-eyed, behind Felice, hands jammed in his pockets. He squinted, the grass on the front lawn seemed to be too bright for him.

Avis's daughter's eyes were overwide; she was speaking too loudly. She'd told her mother that she and this Shawn—who was just a friend, nothing else (he looked away, over one narrow shoulder, blinking at the bright lawns. He was fourteen at most, Avis calculated)—had sat on the banks of the Fishbeins' yard, just above the stone steps to the water, watching this display in the dark. "And it was just, you know, it was all like warm and soft"—Felice had put her hands up to her face, calming a bit—"and we fell asleep. And the next thing we knew, Mrs. Fishbein was out there in her nightie. 'Your mother's going crazy!' " Felice mimicked.

Avis listened with tears standing in her eyes. Brian was too furious to come out of the house. He didn't trust himself to speak. Still, they didn't actually punish Felice: perhaps they should have? Brian wanted to ground her but Avis talked him out of it, saying, That's the problem—we tried to control her, so she rebelled.

Avis didn't know what to make of her daughter's fantastic story. Was she on drugs? Avis stood next to her and ran her fingers through Felice's silky hair. Her daughter's breath and hair smelled clean—not a hint of beer or cigarettes.

Felice seemed to ground herself—coming straight home from school, sleeping for hours over the weekend. Stanley moved through the house silently, as if around a convalescent. Gradually they all relaxed, and things seemed mostly normal again. Three months later, when Felice was thirteen, she went to another party. She'd laughed on her way out the door, swearing she'd be home by ten latest, kissing her father and saying, mock-serious, "Don't worry, Daddy." She was missing for three nights in a row.

Avis remembers the three nights and days without her daughter—the sheer panic of driving around, searching. At home, she couldn't sleep more than ten minutes at a time; instead she stood at her marble slab rolling pie crusts that shattered and crumpled, filling the freezer with crusts lined with flour and parchment, stacked in towers. When Felice finally reappeared in the driveway, it felt like taking a breath after being buried alive. Avis recalls how Felice stared out of the backseat of the cruiser, fixing her parents with a sharp, red gaze. She hadn't meant to come home that time—not ever. The police had found her with some older kids in a nightclub on Hollywood Beach. She was wearing clothes Avis had never seen before—a mesh blouse that adhered to her skin and a pair of faded jeans cinched with a belt of leather petals like a daisy chain. Avis wept while a white-haired officer with a weathered, kindly face stood in their front door talking to her and Brian about social services and family counseling, and their daughter stared out of the police car, over their heads. She begged Felice to tell them why she'd stayed away. Felice stared as if she wasn't there at all.

Avis had wished desperately at that moment that she'd grown up with a proper mother—a real one—who would've shown her what to do—not the shadow figure, muttering over books and papers, two pencils tucked into her hair. Avis's mother had raised her in a state of benign neglect, and would scarcely have noticed if Avis had stayed out all night for a week or a month. After the police had taken their statements, the officers left and Felice followed her parents back into the house. Avis had closed the front door, and Brian grabbed Felice by one of her winglike arms and swatted her, hard, twice with the flat of his palm against the seat of her jeans.

Avis gulped a high, startled suck of air, and watched her daughter's face broaden, as if she were about to burst into tears, and then tighten, masklike, into something unfamiliar. Avis didn't blame Brian exactly—or at least not in the way he assumed she did—not for the spanking. It seemed possible in fact, at times like that, that she really did still love him. She blamed him only for making it so plain to all of them—the gesture so furious and despairing—how ineffectual they were. Felice had started leaving them already: neither one knew how to stop it, neither knew why it was happening.

AVIS LOOKS PAST the waiter's shoulder. About to surrender the table, she takes a last look at the crowded sidewalk. In that moment, taking in the flux of hair and eyes and talking, the hands and dresses, all at once, a rush of pure, incandescent relief. It floods her body, melting away her bones. There: emerging from the crowd, that brisk, unmistakable, long-boned walk, tall and slim, the fingers curling absently against her sides.

Avis releases the cookie tin and places her hand on the iron chair arms, letting her breath deepen, pushing up, uncurling from her tight hunch. *At last.* Another electrical cascade of release as she moves forward. At the same moment, the waiter appears, interposing himself between Felice and Avis. "Know what you want yet?"

She flinches. For a moment, the day seems to tilt: Avis sees green and silver leaves, a lace of cirrus clouds, a bit of linen-colored umbrella. Her breath and pulse knock in her cranium. Avis lifts her arms, moving toward the girl, but Felice looks so shocked that Avis halts midway, her arms frozen in the air. The girl's eyes are wide; whites show around the irises—Avis sucks in a tiny sip of air, trying to smile, because (of course!) it seems that this is not Felice after all, but just another lovely wraith of a girl, a stranger minding her own business. Avis's lips tremble as she smiles; she says, "Oh, I just—I beg your pardon. I thought you were my daughter . . . I'm so—I'm—" But the girl turns her body in a smooth, evasive manuever, flipping her hair through her fingers, reentering the procession of shoppers.

Avis watches her go: blood rushes to her face, stinging as if she'd been slapped. She snaps, "You aren't even that pretty."

Two bronzed women, dark, sprayed hair piled on their heads, look up as Avis sinks back to her table. She notices the waiter watching her from several tables away, and returns his stare until he looks away.

AVIS HAD AN IDEA of how things were going to be, of her and her daughter, their fingers in a *pâte sucrée,* rolling, cutting out the shapes of cupids and sea horses and dragons. But Felice was uninterested. The blithe girl ran around the house, light-spirited as a firefly, calling her friends, lying out by the pool, or playing video games. It was Stanley who came into the kitchen to help Avis shell walnuts and separate eggs.

Her own mother had openly disapproved when Avis had announced that, instead of college, she wanted to attend the culinary institute to become a pastry chef.

"That's a girls' slum," Geraldine had said. "All that sugar and decoration. Just a blue-collar job with a frilly apron. You'll never get half the respect or the pay of a real chef. If you can't be bothered with an education, at least learn to *cook*."

Years later, Avis sat on the couch, her own daughter's head in her lap, hair spilling like ink over her leg. They'd had a daylong immersion in shopping at the mall in Pinecrest, then tea cakes (crude, coarsely frosted) at the French-Cuban bakery on the Miracle Mile. Avis combed Felice's hair with her fingers, murmuring, "Who's my beautiful girl?"

Felice smiled at her mother, barely shifting her attention from the TV cartoons.

Stanley emerged from the kitchen; his arms like twigs in the oversized oven mitts. At twelve, his hair was glossy, his small face pale with thought. Oh, Avis loved him too, but she'd had other plans for her son: she tried to direct his attention toward his father—a *lawyer*—she murmured the word to him like an incantation. But Stanley persisted in the kitchen, performing the small yet demanding apprentice's tasks she set for him—removing the skin from piles of almonds, grating snowy hills of lemon zest, the nightly sweeping of the kitchen floor and sponging of metal shelves. He didn't seem to mind: every day after school, he'd lean over the counter, watching her experiment with combinations—shifting flavors like the beads in a kaleidoscope—burnt sugar, hibiscus, rum, espresso, pear: dessert as a metaphor for something unresolvable. It was nothing like the slapdashery of cooking. Baking, to Avis, was no less precise than chemistry: an exquisite transfiguration. Every night, she lingered in the kitchen, analyzing her work, jotting notes, describing the way ingredients nestled: a slim layer of black chocolate hidden at the bottom of a praline tart, the essence of lavender stirred into a bowl of preserved wild blueberries. Stanley listened to his mother think out loud: he asked her questions and made suggestions—like mounding lemon meringue between layers of crisp pecan wafers—such a success that her corporate customers ordered it for banquets and company retreats.

On the day Avis is thinking of, she sat in the den where they watched TV, letting her hand swim over the silk of her daughter's hair, imagining a dessert *pistou* of blackberry, *crème fraîche*, and nutmeg, in which floated tiny vanilla croutons. Felice was her audience, Avis's picky eater—difficult to please. Her "favorites" changed capriciously and at times, it seemed, deliberately, so that after Avis set out what once had been, in Felice's words, "the best ever"—say, a miniature *roulade Pavlova* with billows of cream and fresh kumquat—Felice would announce that she was now "tired" of kumquats.

Felice sat up as Stanley approached. Avis had noted that Felice was always pleased to eat whatever her big brother offered. Stanley wasn't looking at Felice, though, but at Avis. "It's a *castagnaccio*—I found some stuff about it online. And I tried a few things . . ." His voice tapered off modestly. He held out a plate with a low, suede-gold cake. Avis had struggled to conjure up a lighter chestnut cake: she realized that—while they'd been shopping—Stanley had reconfigured the laborious recipe. She cut a sliver for Felice and herself and they ate with their fingers while Stanley watched.

The cake had a delicate, nearly vaporous texture that released a startling flavor. There was something, some ingredient, that tugged at the chestnut and lemon and opened the taste on her tongue—the chimera, as Avis thought of it—the secret in the maze of ingredients.

"Mmmm, Stanley—so good." Felice was already cutting another piece.

Avis took another bite as Stanley waited. She could barely grasp her own response, the plummeting sensation that seemed to plunge through her. Why couldn't the boy stay out of her kitchen? She wanted him to be more than a food worker. He didn't realize what punishing work it could be—hot, monotonous, hazardous: it was true manual labor, but magazines and TV dressed it up in glamour. She wanted him to use his mind, not his back. "What is it?" she asked quietly. "A savory herb. Basil?"

"Some basil and some rosemary." He averted his gaze, still too tentative to smile—as if he were afraid he'd done wrong. Felice was watching her.

Avis nodded, eyes closed. She wanted to praise his ingenuity, to say how proud she was. Why did that simple act elude her? She opened her mouth, struggling for words; she had said finally, "It's fine, but it isn't quite right."

He took the rest of the cake back to the kitchen and disposed of it.

Five years later, after Felice was gone, Stanley built a raised bed in the backyard and grew herbs and vegetables. He worked in grocery stores. He cooked dinner for his parents—vegetable stews and roasted chicken—trying to make sure Avis in particular ate something beside cookies and tarts. He avoided sugar. He stopped baking.

THE CELL RINGS AGAIN: Nina. There is the time stamp: she has to read it twice before she understands: 2:53. She's been waiting for three hours.

Avis lays her hands and phone flat on the iron-grid table, gazing forward like a woman at a séance, staring past the streetlamp post and the gang of stick-shouldered boys with skateboards and the enormous black-and-white mural for Abercrombie & Fitch. When she recognizes the dark bounce of Nina's hair, she feels mostly numb. Nina is overbearing, even caustic and punitive, but she has never said—like several others, "Oh well! They all eventually leave home, anyway, don't they?" (Once, at a dinner party, a snow bird from Cincinnati, upon hearing about Felice running away, remarked dryly, "Lucky you.")

Avis can see her assistant composing herself, chin lifting. Nina approaches the table with one hand on her chest. "I'm so sorry, dear," she says softly. "When you didn't answer the phone, I just—I thought I'd better . . ."

"Oh, she didn't come, I guess." A tiny smile on her lips. "Oh well."

"Ah, sweetie." Nina touches her shoulder, but Avis stands.

"No, it's . . . No—no. It's nothing." Avis glances around for the waiter. "I should have—I don't know." Evidently she'd outlasted his shift. She can't remember if she'd paid for the tea. Avis refuses to say that perhaps her daughter forgot, she got busy. These were the things she'd said last time while Nina looked at her with those kind, terrible eyes. Brian refuses to go to these meetings at all. We don't negotiate with terrorists, he says, voice bone-dry, desiccated by anger. So it's been nearly five years since he's last seen his daughter. Stanley hasn't seen his sister in that time either, as far as she knows. And ten months, now, for Avis. Not so bad in comparison with five years. Really, not bad.

Ten months, she reflects as she follows Nina. For some reason this is all she can hold in her head, like the refrain to a song. Ten months, as they pass the French bakery franchise, ten months, as they cross the street by the theater. They enter the parking structure, the air dim as a chapel's. Perhaps if she clings to this clot of thought, it will hold her. Not so bad. She climbs into Nina's big, empty car. Beyond the open ramparts of the garage, Avis sees the sky lowering, the damp air growing heavier. She will try not to wonder where Felice is: where she goes when it rains. She can't be that far away.

Felice

OH FUCK THEM, WHAT DO THEY KNOW?

Felice is sick of the Green House, its stink of cat pee and old pot and cooking oil, and a kind of rot—as if losing youth or hope or just some idea of a future would have a smell. All the kids and bums and "musicians" who wander in and out of that place carry that odor somewhere on their clothes or hair. This morning when Felice wakes on the couch in the back bedroom, her stomach tightens and buckles at the smell.

She props herself up, surveying the room: two kids on the floor, another sleeping sitting up at her feet, his skinny neck tipped back against the cushion, mouth sloped open and a thread of saliva escaping from one corner—a skinhead in black jeans and lace-up boots. She's awakened before to find other kids who've stumbled into the same room or corner as her: most of them are just looking for the comfort of another body: someone to crash next to, to feel a little safer through the night.

Some of them sit in circles at night, like around a campfire, in the immense, trashed living room (there's even a big fireplace where they cook things sometimes, but eventually the room fills with smoke and they have to stop). Mostly they're kids like Felice—a lot of them even younger—some like eleven and twelve years old. There are a few old people too—guys in their thirties—and those are the worst with all the psychologizing and talk, talk, talk. That's all those guys like to do, suck on their wet joints, eyes watering, discussing their stupid ideas of how to take down the government or break into the mansions out on Star Island or Key Biscayne or South Gables. And Felice knows that some of them grew up in palatial homes on South Hibiscus Drive with private docks and gates and servants, and that many of the worst and dirtiest and smelliest kids will inherit enormous trust funds in five or ten years.

Not Felice.

She moves slowly, slipping on her backless sneakers, lifting her feet one at a time over the first skinhead, slumped on the floor beside the couch. But then she does something stupid—she knows it's stupid even as she does it, yet she can't resist lifting the half-pack of cigarettes from the lap of the propped-up sleeper. She doesn't even smoke anymore, but it's taken her longer to break the habit of stealing— every now and then she slips back into it—and smokes are useful and tradable among the street-poor. She might've gotten away with it too, but she's hasty and the flimsy pack crackles in her hand. Instantly the skinhead seizes her hand—fingers, actually—crushing them together. Felice sucks a yelp back, furious with herself for getting caught.

"Look at you." The skinhead's name is Axe. These guys all have names like that—"Raver," "Dread." They hang out together—a tribe of thirty or forty massively stupid and destructive boys—Felice can't keep track—their names and faces interchangeable. "So what the fuck is going on up in here?"

Pain knifes through the small bones in her fingers; it's like one of those paper finger traps—the more she struggles, the more tightly he squeezes. "No." She deliberately keeps her voice low. "Please, just . . . please, please . . ."

He pulls her closer, smiling to reveal gray translucence covering his teeth; she inhales an acrid effluvium—as if he's been drinking vinegar. "You're so fucking polite—*please, please,*" he minces. "Don't you know not to steal, girlface? Someone might fucking tear your hand off."

Felice does some brisk calculations: it's possible he'll just hassle her awhile if she plays along. But playing along carries its own risks. At that moment of hesitation, he gives a wild bark of laughter, grabs her free hand, and fake-bites it. She feels his teeth graze her knuckles, the slime of his tongue: she yanks her hand away. "My boyfriend won't like that!" she says breathlessly, resisting the urge to wipe off her hand. Her heart pounds in her voice, but she keeps going. "He's super jealous. He doesn't like men touching me." She used the word "men" deliberately, as a kind of flattery: she doesn't know if Axe is smart enough to call her bluff or if he'll just view this as a challenge. He seems to connect with some thought that lifts his features. His shredded lips part, and again, she sees the gray gleam. "What fucking bullshit boyfriend is that now?" he asks loudly enough that one of the other skinheads stirs and groans.

"Emerson," she says quickly.

He scrutinizes her face for a long moment. "Emerson doesn't have any girlfriends." But his voice lowers. "Especially not *you*." He releases her crushed hand. The cigarette pack bounces on the floor as she folds her hand against her chest, a furtive slide along her eyes. She backs away, stepping over a fat skinhead sacked out on the floor, his throat vibrating with a snore. She picks open the door and doesn't look back as she slips out of the room.

Her mouth is dry, her stomach cramped with hunger, though she's used to that old pain. She stops in the kitchen—more cigarette butts reeking in the sink, empty bottles with their own sour yeast stink—a few shriveled oranges in the fridge: she grabs one, unearths her board from its hiding place in one of the cavernous pieces of furniture—a carved mahogany armoire—too cumbersome to cart off and sell or someone would've done so years ago.

The outdoors kids told Felice that a wealthy family used to live in the Green House, back when rich people moved out to the beach to party. Supposedly it was one of the first houses ever constructed on the beach. The owners left it to their kids, it got passed down for, like, generations. It used to be full of priceless art and chandeliers. But then eventually, there was just one old lady living there—the Green House kids called her "Myra." Hanging in the front entry was an oil painting of a fat, pink-cheeked lady in a blue dress. The canvas was streaked with grime, but it was still up there in its gold frame bristling with curlicues and rosettes, and might even be worth something. The kids said Myra had lived there all alone and one day the skate punks and street rats who'd been noticing the weeds and the St. Augustine grass getting wild in the big front yard and the scabby cats and the increasing chirr of bugs—they just tried the front door and the handle turned.

"She was probably about three-quarters crazy, sitting there, bunched up in that same old blue dress, watching TV right on that couch," Douglas told her. He was seventeen with a narrow, handsome face and ghastly, rotten yellow teeth. "She saw those guys come in and she started screeching, Hey you kids get outta here! Get outta here!" He gulped with laughter, displaying those teeth.

"When was this? How long ago?" Felice asked. She was fifteen years old then, already skeptical of most stories like this.

"Fuck. I don't know. Like back in the 1970s or something?"

"So what happened?" Felice folded her arms over her chest. "After the kids came in and she yelled and all?"

He smirked. "They ignored her. What was she gonna do? They moved in. She didn't even have a phone anymore. She didn't know anyone and no one wanted to know about her. I mean none of the neighbors or anybody. She was so fat, she couldn't get out of her chair or anything."

"Damn." Felice stared at a big bald gray spot in the middle of the ratty Persian carpet. "Poor lady."

It seemed to be a true story. More or less. The details changed depending on who told it. Some kids said that Myra lived upstairs on the third floor—where Felice liked to sleep—while the street rats lived downstairs. They said they brought in like squirrels and cats and slaughtered them on the hardwood floor in the living room, just for fun. They said there were all kinds of gangs that moved in and out, a meth lab in one of the parlors. Everything. Every surface of the house was scarred and rutted and burned as if a wagon train trail had rolled through. Even the police ignored it.

"What happened to Myra?" Felice asked.

"Oh." Douglas shrugged. "They killed her." He laughed his big galumphing laugh again. "No. They tried to be nice to her at first. They brought her food and shit. But they didn't know what an old lady likes to eat. She probably needs stuff you don't chew or something. And she just kept yelling at them to get the fuck out and shit. So after a while they killed her."

Other kids said that wasn't true at all. That social services finally showed up and carted her away and the kids just stayed, like they were her actual grandkids. But they all talked about hearing "Myra's ghost" in certain rooms at night and some of them liked to touch the corner of her painting, "for good luck," so that corner was smudged mossy and black. Felice liked that painting—old Myra with her sour purse-strings mouth, but something sweeter in her eyes—like a mother's eyes.

Every time Felice comes back to the Green House, the painting looks less and less human and she finds fewer kids who've even heard of Myra. Once, she'd asked one of the thirty-year-olds about her, a spooky guy with matted hair and whirly blue eyes named Cartusia who slept up in the stifling attic. Some of the kids said that he'd inherited money, that he was the reason the Green House still had any electricity or running water. When Felice asked him, he'd hummed and smiled and said only, "Myra's my mother."

SHE SLAMS OPEN THE FRONT door and, once again, Felice is free of the Green House. She drops her board and pushes off; the board is the best place for her to be, her head empty and clear and the only thing is tilting and steering, the air brushing her face and the street rumbling through the wheels under her feet. She will never go back there again. This time for real. Her eighteenth birthday is coming: time for things to be different.

She has to make a plan, she thinks. And she has to get money.

The air is sweeter than usual today, a rich, undulant, lanolin, heavy with ocean minerals; she's not so anxious to work. Felice kicks and rolls to the raised, wooden boardwalk behind the mid-beach hotels; she passes joggers, strollers, people in workout clothes taking their power walks; some of them squint at her, hating skateboarders. She drifts past a homeless guy she knows named Ronnie. He looks, at first, with his long hair and cutoff jeans, like a regular person. But then you notice his too-dark tan, the way his eyes seem too pale for his skin, his face weathered, a desert nomad's.

"Hey man," she says, rolling by, slow as fog.

His eyes flicker at her, a dimensionless khaki color.

After rounding a bevy of plump women in petaled bathing caps, she stops to watch some children and a young woman playing in the skirt of the water. The woman could be a college-age nanny, but she has the same yellow hair as the children. The water is almost hot in August, and the children shriek and kick up a froth; their transparent laughter barely reaches Felice. She stands there, board under one arm, watching the play, feeling alone and sad and hopeful, when someone says, "Hi? Felice?"

"Felix," she says automatically, annoyed. "Oh." It's one of the skinheads from the House—Emerson. She swallows her breath and steps back. "Hi." Her voice sounds like an eight-year-old's.

Emerson's hair is so pale and close-cropped she can make out his scalp in the sunlight, prickling with sweat. The color in his face is high and pink, as if he'd been running. His mouth is small, possibly cold, but he's so strong and healthy that he emits a natural attractiveness. She's a bit afraid of him. On more than one occasion, she's noticed his translucent eyes following her across the room: perhaps why she said his name to Axe. He places his hand on top of his head, then removes it. She remembers now—when he first appeared at the House, the other shaved boys made fun of his measured pace and demeanor. They sat around in the living room once, flicking cigarette butts at Emerson in improvised torment, until he burst up from his place on the carpet, upending the mahogany coffee table crammed with half-emptied beer bottles, crashing the whole foaming mess to the floor. He grabbed one of them—a vicious boy named Damon—

and knocked his head against the floor so it made a hollow thump. For a while, the boy laid there without moving, eyes open, staring. Emerson tossed a cigarette butt at him and walked out. The next day the boy had an egg-sized lump on the side of his head. They treated Emerson differently after that.

Now Emerson stands in front of her, an obstacle, pink and glistening, his sheen of hair sparkles, and his gray T-shirt with the faded rock band is sweated onto his big chest. "I thought that was you," he says.

Felice grips her skateboard and glances back toward the children in the surf. "Yeah, hey," she says. "Who told you my old name?"

"I like Felice." He smiles and his lower lip droops in a soft, unguarded way. "All those kids at the Green House—they know something about everyone."

Felice snorts. "More like nothing about everyone."

"Well, I just heard something about you and me."

"Oh yeah?" Something trembles in the small of her back as if the temperature just dropped. She stares at him, determined not to look away. "Like what?"

He slides his hands into his pockets and his big, loose shorts slip. "Like, we're getting it on, supposedly. Like, that's according to *you*."

"Someone told you that?" She widens her eyes; a pulse leaps in her temple.

"Axe and Dink."

"What did you say?"

He turns to gaze at the little kids and huffs a laugh. "I guess I said it was true."

Instead of feeling grateful, though, Felice is irritated: the way he's standing there, those see-through eyes floating over her, like they really are together. "Fine. Whatever. I hate all those guys, I'm not going back there." She doesn't care what he thinks, hoping only to avoid the humiliation of explaining herself.

"What? Who you talking about?"

"The fucking Gross House. It's disgusting. I can't believe I ever stayed there."

Emerson runs his hand over the brush of his hair. He swipes back and forth, color climbing into his face. "It's nice—I think. It's decent. You can hang. There's cool people. People bring beer and food."

"It's gross," she snaps. "Everyone steals everything—they're all so annoying. And loud and stupid. And it's fucking *hot*. Like a fucking jungle swamp."

He chuckles, letting his hand fall off his head. "I know."

"And the *toilet*—"

"I know."

Felice drops her board to the pavement and rests one foot on it. "Hey man, I gotta be going now. I got stuff to get to."

"Like what?" Emerson studies her face with interest.

"Like, I don't know." She almost says: Like, I got to go meet my mother and beg her for money. "I gotta see if I can scrounge work." Also true. She pushes off on a slow spin, but he follows on foot. "Where do you work?"

"Off Seventeenth."

"You're a model, aren't you? I knew it."

She rolls her eyes and steers around a couple of men in business suits who turn when Emerson says *model*. "I'm not a *model*-model," she drawls. "Obviously. I don't stay in their little palaces. I model, like, tattoos. Or other crap—watches and sandals and shit."

There's a section toward the north end of Lummus Park called the Cove where Felice and Berry and Reynaldo and some of the other kids go. They'll lie out or sit near the beach entrance with Frappuccinos and sometimes a gig will come along. Sometimes they won't feel like doing anything. It gets so hot out there, the sun melting the thick bright air into orange honey, she just wants to curl up and sleep out her life. Exactly what Micah, one of the modeling scouts, is always harping on: *You want to throw it all away? That's great, that's your own damn choice.*

When she was still at home, Felice ran around with boys and tried pot and stayed out late: she'd thought she was wild—but she'd had no idea what wild was. She knows that now. By the time she got to the beach, she was dried up inside like a cicada husk. The thing that happened to Hannah had done that to her. It was like there was nothing left of her; she slept outdoors all the time back then, with her legs cinched in a knot against her chest, like she'd dried in that position and one stiff breeze off the water would sweep her away.

Sometimes she can't help it and she sees Hannah in the east field, sweeping her hand through the grass, saying, "Basically, your choices are you can be smart or pathetic. And you can be good or truly evil."

"Then I want to be smart and good." Felice sat cross-legged in the grass.

"Possible, but that hardly ever happens in nature."

"So what are you?"

She smiled a long, slow, tipping smile. "Smart and evil. Like my dad. And my mother is pathetic but good. That happens to mothers a lot. Which is why you should never be one."

"Not my mom," Felice said. "She's the least pathetic person I know."

Hannah just kept looking at her with that subtle smile, her lips bitten and dark and her eyes like seawater.

Now Felice is almost eighteen, and she's tried so hard to turn into something new. But every day there's dancing and drugs spread hand to hand—silver pipes, tabs that melt away on the tongue, medical-looking hypodermics, capsules and all the names, letters—E, H, MDA . . . And Felice knows she's lucky because she's afraid of needles—fear like a part of her circulatory system—a source of shame and protection. She needs money now if she's really going to get out of the Green House. So perhaps one of the stores on Lincoln Road, one of the blaring European boutiques, will need a website model, or possibly some people from Benetton, or Ton Sur Ton, or Boden will come out on the beach combing for their scruffier "real life" catalog models, and she'll land a gig that pays $750, maybe a thousand bucks a day for a couple of days.

Maybe her mother will give her some cash. Maybe she'll let herself ask this time.

"Really, I gotta get going," she says to Emerson, though she stays at a slow roll.

"Can I come?"

She feels irritated again. "You want to come?"

He smiles again—the expression so restrained it's almost conspiratorial—and says, "Yeah. Please. I'd really like that."

SHE'S NOT WILLING to admit that they're together—even for a walk. He's too big and odd and ungainly. So she stays onboard, skates at a crawl—which would've driven her crazy in the past. She abruptly cuts away from the crowds, veering right, passing the edifices of Eden Roc and the Fontainebleau, turning south on Collins' coral-pink sidewalk. Across the street, the narrow blue cut of Indian Creek glows with a crinkled sheen. Felice tries to roll ahead of Emerson, but he's surprisingly good at keeping up and apparently doesn't mind breaking into a trot if she pushes it. "So like do you have a last name?" She doesn't look at him when she asks, because nearly everything she says seems to make him smile, which seems like a sign of weakness or supplication. Instead she just stares down the pink sidewalk, the nostalgic white beach apartments on one side, an eternity of SUVs on the other.

"Officially or what?" He smiles and she looks away, glaring. "Lindemann, I guess. I don't really use it so much. It's not like my stage name or anything."

"Uh-huh," she says, rolling her eyes. Everyone in the whole world is in a band or trying to start one up. "So, fine, what is your stage name?" She sighs.

He speeds up, jogs backwards in front of Felice. "I'm just thinking something—just—shorter? Easier for announcers to say. Like, Lind. You know, like, Emerson Lind? And it doesn't sound so *achtung* that way, you know, so *I'll be back*." He lowers his voice into a Schwarzenegger impression. Then, in the same round, guttural accent, he says, "Yah, der he is, ladies und gentlemen, Emerson Lindemann."

Felice can't help a burst of laughter. "What are you even talking about? What announcers?"

For a second, Emerson keeps smiling but doesn't say anything, a red mottling appears in his skin (she feels sorry for him, he's such a transparent, white-guy color). "I forgot I didn't tell you yet." He falls back to keep pace beside her. "I always feel like all of us from the House already know about each other." He doesn't seem to be willing to look at her now; instead he's fixed on the sidewalk. He smiles again, more intensely, and Felice realizes that at least some of the smiling is nerves and she softens toward him a bit. "I-I'm in training," he says in a lowered voice. "I'm going to enter strongman competitions."

"You what now?"

"They're these big contests—of strength. It's always on TV—like a sporting event. You can make a lot of money if you get known. Caber toss, stone put? Started with the Scots. The Highland games?"

Felice slants a frowning glance at him.

"These days there's usually a truck pull and a tire flip."

Now, with her board rumbling easily along the cement, Felice gives him a long, frank look. "Are you kidding? You mean, like, those guys who drag around tree trunks and junk? That stuff?"

They pass two girls and a Pomeranian jittering like a windup toy. "I'm not saying I'm gonna walk right out there and pick up trophies. I know I don't have the muscle mass yet. But I'm close. Training hard, almost every day. I jog and walk the boardwalk twice a day."

"And I thought you'd followed me here," she says, joking yet privately disappointed.

"They let me into the Gold's on Fourteenth. Herman and Ileana—they're trainers there. They've been helping me out. They say I've got natural explosive power. We're keeping it totally pure—no juicing, no additives. I'm working out three, four hours a day—arms, back, grip strength, everything. The manager said if I pick up a trophy at the regionals this spring he'll sponsor me. He says I could go national."

Felice closes her eyes, just enjoying hearing about the future. It's not like the kind of dreaming all those waste products at the House or the yuppie losers out on Cocowalk are always doing—fame and money—everyone hanging around at Mansion or Nikki Beach or Cro-bar, like dancing and shit was going to transform them into Paris or Lindsay or Britney. Famous girls were always hanging around, wearing their fedoras, giggling in a knot of stoned celebutante friends, kids waving cell cameras at them, so you felt like you really were one of them already. Except the truly famous girls stuck to the clubs' VIP lounges and woke up in their suites at the Delano, and the beach kids woke up back on the sand or even worse places than that.

Felice quits kicking, lets her board slow, and closes her eyes again. Daring herself, she keeps them closed and lifts one hand; her fingers pat a series of curling palm fronds—tap, tap, tap, tap. She lets the board roll to a stop, cants back her head, evaluating him through lowered lids. "Prove it."

"Prove it what? You mean, like what—"

"That you're all strong, like you say."

He lifts and drops his hands: Felice notes the way his shoulders flare behind his shirt. "I could take you to the gym . . ."

She presses her lips together skeptically and kicks off on her board again. "Ever you say, Chief." They pass a bank of police cars parked half on the curb. Cops standing around in tight black uniforms, hands on their hips, narrowly eyeing Emerson and Felice. Once they're well down the block, she tosses her head so her hair flips across her back. "No, fuck the gym. You strong guys supposedly drag anchors and crap around, right? Can't you, like, break a branch in half with your bare hands or something?"

"Depends on the branch."

"Okay." She jumps off her board abruptly and stomps the end, flipping it into her hand. "So go pick up that car over there, how about?" She gestures to a Hummer that looks like it's been dipped in black lacquer.

"*That* car? It weighs like five tons," Emerson says. "Plus it'll totally have a car alarm." He gazes at her, her haughty chin. "Wait." He heads toward the line of parallel parked cars and picks a rusting lime-green Impala convertible. "All right," he says grimly. He stands in front of the car, rubs his hands together, huffing a little as if hyperventilating, and drops into a squat. "All right, all right," he mutters.

Felice watches in silence as Emerson bends and the big muscles in his back fan out, and she sees—even before he's fully gripped the car—that he really can do it, and then he's lifting the front end of the car, one, two feet off the ground, up, holding it in place, then he or the car is making a deep, shuddering moan, lowering quickly. He lets go and the car falls, its frame bouncing with a crash. He turns, his face red. "Okay?" Then, gasping, "That—right there—called a power clean."

Felice wasn't aware of her hand drifting to her mouth, a flash of adrenaline.

He recovers sufficiently to smile, his face red. "You see that? Now you know. If that car there ran over you, I could save you. Nobody else could do that."

Felice thinks of saying, Yeah, as long as it wasn't a Hummer. Instead she nods. "Yeah, I guess."

HE LIKES TO TALK, this Emerson, unlike pretty much any boy she's ever met. The punks and skinheads Emerson hangs out with get drunk and loud, their shouting and cursing like smashing windows. Emerson talks like a boy who's been stranded in his thoughts—coherent yet odd, twisted into abstract designs.

"Just, the way I look at it is I think the mind is like a muscle, too," he's saying, ducking under the crimson spray of a bottlebrush tree. They circle an elderly couple, shuffling, facing the ground, hand in hand. "You just got to train it—like any other part of your body. I mean, like, you have to, if you ever want the other muscles to respond."

"You mean, like—" Felice scowls at the sidewalk. Somehow Emerson got her to get off her board and go on foot—her least favorite form of locomotion. She won't let him carry her board. "Like, your actual brain is a muscle? Can you move it?"

Emerson stops on the sidewalk, then starts again. "I like that. I don't know the answer, but I like the idea of it. Moving your brain. But no, I mean, more like, the *mind,* consciousness, thought."

"How could thoughts be a *muscle*?"

He slides his hands into his pockets. "I *know,* but they are. And also, your muscles are a mind. Muscles feel stuff and think stuff and sense, all of that, and they, like communicate with the main mind and tell it stuff. So everything in you, every part of you is *mind* in the end."

"And your mind is a muscle," she repeats in a low inflection, not quite a question.

"That's right."

She glances uncertainly at Emerson's smiling, preoccupied profile. Felice can't tell if he's a little bit scary and mental, or maybe a lot smarter than she'd thought. Back at the House, she'd seen him roaring with his stupid friends, ripping open beers and smashing cans on his head. "Where do you get this crap?" She is carefully dismissive.

He shrugs. "Everywhere. All that lifting gives you time to think about how things work. That's when I do my best thinking. Picking up heavy stuff and putting it back down again? After a while it's boring."

Felice and Emerson enter the busier commercial area of South Beach: passing rows of pastel apartment buildings, hotels like old toys, glimpses of azure ocean floating in the distance, the sidewalk filled with tourists. Doddering elderly, like shipwreck survivors. "So . . . so," Felice fumbles to redirect things, unwilling to try to keep up with Emerson in his *mind* terrain. ". . . So, if you're thinking about all this smart crap, then why do you hang around with a bunch of skinhead losers?"

The hand returns to the top of his head. "Skinheads?"

"Duh, like Peckham, Earl, Moe," she goes on in a pitiless, dry voice, surprised that she even cares. "Axe, Derek . . ."

Emerson frowns. "Naah. Skinheads are a bunch of jackasses—I'm not into that."

Her laugh is bright. "Well duh that's kind of exactly what you look like with your head all shaved—those guys in their stupid wife-beaters and tats and piercings and shit. Like a bunch of Hitler Youth assholes."

He laughs too. "*Heil*. Right, *heil*."

"You do!"

"Yeah, *Heil Hitler*, man," he whoops. Two sunburnt tourists slide their eyes in his direction as they pass; one old woman in a floral top and skirt gives him a bright, venomous stare, her face hard as a walnut. "Whoa!" Emerson sputters.

Felice cringes. She'd thought the old woman was going to spit at them. "Why don't you shut the fuck up, man?" she snaps.

He quiets then, his smile diminished, and shrugs.

"I don't know if you're stupid or crazy or whatever you are."

"Both maybe. I'm whatever," he says lightly, but his head is ducked.

"Such stupid shit. Stupid fucking-ass thing to say. What are you, twelve years old?"

He doesn't say anything. She wonders then if she should be more cautious: something comes back to her—something about Emerson being "away." It occurs to Felice that Emerson was frequently absent from the Green House. Whenever he reappeared, the other skinheads made remarks about him *escaping*, escaping *that place*.

They cross the wide busy mess of Seventeenth Street, scrolls of driveways and entrances, pass girls in platform espadrilles, baby doll shirts, shirtless boys with cargo shorts like Emerson's hanging loose around their hips; a couple pushing toddlers in a wide stroller; two ladies with big, ridged breast implants, Botox-sleek foreheads. Felice studies the women critically as they approach—one looks like she's had a face-lift, a faintly demonic rise to the outer corners of the eyebrows; both of them are wearing halters and kick-pleat miniskirts; one has a quilted Chanel purse on a chain sinking into her shoulder.

They cast intent glances at Felice as they pass and Felice looks away. Youth beats money.

"Look, I'm sorry," Emerson says as they pass another clutch of tourists; a squat boy goes by on a skateboard wearing a T-shirt that says *Lost in Margaritaville* and nods at Felice, noticing her board. "Really. I'm not a skinhead. I'm not like that. I'm not a Hitler-guy or anything. I guess some of those guys might be, but they're morons. I was just goofing around." His voice lowers. "Stupid."

"Fine," Felice pulls the wind-pasted hair from her face. "Get a grip."

They cross Lincoln Road where Felice recalls—swift drop— she's supposed to meet her mother today. *Fuck*. Felice had called her, hadn't she? What time was *that* supposed to happen? Noon? She tries to make out the time on a neon clock in one of the shop-windows, but it's in the shape of a flamingo, impossible to read. They cross Sixteenth and almost get hit by a stretch jeep pulling into Lowe's; a gang of teenyboppers standing in a Bentley convert-ible shriek at them, their voices like shredded ribbons. "I so hate this place," Emerson says.

"It's fun," Felice says defensively. She shields her eyes, then relents: "It's more fun if you don't live here."

He glances at her. "Yeah."

They head back to the smooth brick boardwalk, cutting between hotels, the white cabanas and silver bellhop carts, past cheap jew-elry vendors, soap bubbles spiriting over the walkway, to their right, sprinklings of salsa music, oiled bodies on massage tables. Prisms hang in a silvery mist from the hotel fountains. To their left, walls of jasmine and sea grape trees, the beach perimeter plumed and sway-ing with sawgrass and sea oats. They turn into the Fifteenth Street entrance, set off by keystone pillars, white ropes protecting the sparse patches of sea grass. In the distance, beyond the royal palms, blue umbrellas and awnings flap in the breeze; the sand is already scorch-ing. She can feel it kicking up under her flip-flops. There are kids sprawled on towels all over the sand, listening to radios, drinking beer; a Frisbee arcs through the pale blue.

Turning north toward the Cove, they run into Reynaldo and Berry. They're lying in a drifting spot of shade under a stand of palms, stretched out on smuggled hotel beach towels, a gold interlocked *DH* embroidered on the edge. Both of them are so diminutive, with the same blue-black eyes, they look like brother and sister. Sometimes they get hired to do gigs together—they did a series of TV commercials in Spanish for a local car dealer and Reynaldo had to teach Berry how to pronounce everything so she sounded like an authentic *chica,* not a Jewish girl from Rutherford. They probably spent most of the night there after the beach patrol slacked off. Berry gazes at them languidly, her hair spilling past her shoulders to her elbows. Scents of coconut and apricot drift over from one of the hotel spas. She props herself up on the towel, knobby legs glistening with oil. "Babe," she says, "what's going on?"

Reynaldo is yawning hugely; he shakes back his long black hair, catches it up in one hand, finger-combing. "Felix, you should've gone with us last night. You'll never believe—we went to Tantra. Guess who was there. Calvin Klein. He looks like he's made out of wax. Didn't he?" He looks at Berry, who lies back on the towel and nods. "Just a teeny white man made of wax. He had slave boys with him. He took us to the Raleigh, then he wanted to go on his yucky boat." He gives a horrified shudder. "Eugghh!"

Berry smiles again, eyes closed. "I don't mind boats."

"I do." Reynaldo finally seems to notice Emerson. He looks at Felice. "Miss Kitty Cat, what's going on? Where'd you get this big nasty thing?"

Emerson stares over Reynaldo's head.

"That's not nice," Berry says placidly.

"I'm not a nice boy. I don't care."

Felice and Berry are narrow enough to share the board and Reynaldo and Emerson take the towels. Reynaldo produces a thick, half-smoked joint from his pocket, along with a silver lighter. He flicks it open and lights the joint, dragging delicately, then hands it to Felice. She tokes the earthy, grassy smoke, looks up through her exhale to watch a series of tourists filter onto the beach holding Starbucks cups like ritual offerings. A row of frat boys with beat-up surfboards. A young woman with a fat pug on a studded leash. The pug genuflects in the beach grass while the girl checks her cell phone: they stroll away, leaving the glistening droppings. Four girls come down the walkway as far as the line of sand, then stop. They are groomed and painted, hair ironed to surgical linearity, brows waxed clean. Not especially pretty, just beautifully kept. *College girls,* Felice thinks scornfully. She gazes after them.

Emerson refuses the joint, saying that he's in training—he has to keep his *mind* clear—and Reynaldo starts to mock him again for being Mr. Muscle, but Berry and Felice both tell him to shut up. The pot tastes rancid and she doesn't like the burn on the back of her throat. "No more." She waves it away.

"Oh, bullshit, darling," Reynaldo says. "That'll be the day." He turns away from her and takes another drag. Reynaldo's neck and shoulders have a silky drape, his skin—like Berry's—is tanned almond-dark and even in this light it's hard to discern the coils of a mahogany-colored serpent that spirals over the upper quadrant of his chest, down the bicep, to the crook of an elbow. He and Berry have posed for *Tattoo* and *Skin Art* magazines, done party ads for local clubs, and worked as party-fillers. Felice thinks they've hired themselves out for other purposes at these events (they're always broke, cadging drugs and drinks), but if she doesn't ask, she doesn't have to know. "Little Miss Innocent," the outdoor kids call her. Berry smiles at her again, her mouth long, angular, and dimpled. "They're doing go-sees for V.S. today over on Washington. You wanna go?"

"Like I've got the boobs for that." Felice crosses her arms.

"Shut up. Like you never heard of airbrush," Reynaldo says.

They seem to live on virtually nothing, yet Berry and Reynaldo are the most pretty and stylish of all the outdoor kids. Keep your little ear to the big ground, Reynaldo always tells her. They're the ones Felice has admired, the ones she likes to be near. After Felice ran away, she tried to look older, more like a model. Like she belonged there. Out

on the beach or in the clubs, it was all models and tourists. The kids
who looked scared, their skinny shoulders tucked up, eyes searching,
they were the ones who ended up with "boyfriends," older guys who
always needed money. At first Felice wore makeup and was careful
with her hair and clothing. But she quickly realized that the outdoor
kids saw prettiness as a kind of weakness—just the opposite of the
way it was in school. In the rougher places like the Green House, her
prettiness seemed excessive: she noticed kids watching her like she
had cash spilling out of her pockets. They called her "Face" or "Girlface," and stole her skateboard and clothes; one night some older girls
pushed her down in a church parking lot, pulling her hair and tearing
at her clothes until Felice screamed, swung back with all her might,
kicking and shoving, slapping one girl across the eye and cheekbone,
knocking the other one to the ground, breaking her nose.

Reynaldo and Berry showed her how to use her looks without attracting too much attention. The trick was to wear stovepipe
jeans and T-shirts, nothing fancy or frilly, no jewelry, high heels, or
purses. Black was best. "It's the West Coast thing." Berry showed off
a chunky pair of black platforms. "It's Seattle."

Now Emerson sits with his feet gathered up, arms around his
knees; neither he nor Reynaldo has anything to say to each other.
After a few minutes, Emerson stands, whacks the sand off the back of
his shorts and his palms. "I better get a move on."

Who says that? Felice thinks—he sounds like a dad.

Reynaldo says something over his shoulder to Berry, possibly,
"Nasty redneck." Berry laughs, her mild, musical chuckle, her eyes
filmed. Felice glances at Berry and there's a bad moment where she
wonders—as she has lately—if Berry and Reynaldo are all that wonderful. She gets to her feet.

"Where you going, Kitty?" Reynaldo asks, shielding his eyes with
the flat of his palm. "That boy's too ugly for you."

"Don't go, Felix," Berry says. "Why?"

Emerson is already trudging away, head lowered. Felice hesitates,
she looks past him, down the beach: tourists mill over the sand, the

air sepia-toned: a sense of heat and distance cast over everything. This is the end place—where people go to get erased. "I don't think there's any work coming today," Felice says.

"Good. Thank God." Berry lets her head droop back against the towel. She closes her eyes and looks so lifeless that Felice just grabs her board and goes after Emerson.

FELICE AND EMERSON walk along the surf. Emerson seems to understand that her presence at his side at this moment is something of a miracle, and he must not say a word against Reynaldo or Berry. Her board gets heavy after a while, so she hands it to him.

They pass topless girls in thongs, men in slacks and lace-up shoes, Jax with his pet iguana and straw hat; old guys covered in silvery flat chest and back hair sitting in lawn chairs with laptops or shouting into cells, trying to be heard above the surf. Just a few boys with dark, Caribbean faces and glassy hair are out in the water. The lifeguards drowse in their wooden shelters. Most people slumber or stare, beached on the sand under slices of umbrella shade—there's hardly anyone near the waterline—and Felice plods through the wet, compacted sand in a state of relative contentment: it's been ages since she's touched the water. Occasionally Emerson will pick up and dispose of an empty coffee cup, broken comb, broken sunglasses—detritus swept in from cruise ships or left behind by sunbathers. Felice is barely able to contain her impatience with this pointless activity—appalled at the grossness of touching a sodden diaper.

They cut up the beach to a food stand. Emerson tells her to get anything—really. By now, her hunger pain has vaporized—as often happens, so she just orders a Diet Coke. Emerson gets her a cheeseburger anyway; he gets himself four burgers and an enormous chocolate shake. They find a place on the sand and this time Felice lets him squeeze partially onto the board, his body damp and hot beside hers. She eats slowly, but she is hungrier than she'd realized, studying the burger after each bite. Usually she subsists on cans of tuna, oranges, chocolate bars, and rum and Cokes. Sometimes she lets herself think about her mother's crisp little pizzas, the salty pretzels, the croissants stuffed with Nutella and a thin layer of marzipan. After the burger, Emerson peels the orange Felice took from the Green House, pushes his thumbs into the center, and they split it. It's shriveled but still sweet. She sips the diet soda but it burns the roots of her teeth, under her gums. She hasn't seen a dentist since she left her parents' home and sometimes she feels sharp spikes inside her molars. She tosses the soda and starts drinking Emerson's milkshake.

"When's the last time you ate?"

"What?" she asks crossly, frowning at two dimply, middle-aged women strolling past in bikinis.

Emerson eats another burger in a few bites, like a cookie. Then he gazes back at the stand. "I should be in the gym right now."

"Hell, don't let me stop you." Instantly defensive. Why does she care? The burger sits in her stomach: she feels drugged and groggy and wipes a line of sweat from her hairline.

"I didn't mean anything about you—I *like* being here. I don't want to be anywhere else. Like, at all."

"I know," she says moodily. After a few more sips of milkshake, she starts to feel better. Felice squints at the water, which shimmers in bands of deep turquoise and cerulean. "It's pretty nice here," she offers.

"Oh. Well," Emerson says. "I wasn't thinking about the place, really."

She slides a look at him, then stares at her feet in the sand.

He looks out at the water with her a moment. Without moving his eyes, he says, "I could take care of you, if you wanted."

It feels like the blood in her veins speeds up. "What're you talking about?" She tries to laugh. "What's that supposed to mean?"

He stays trained on the water, his face studious—something about him reminds her, oddly, of her brother. He isn't turning out to be anything like the person she'd assumed he was. "I'm not trying to offend you or anything or say you aren't doing great yourself. I'm just saying . . ." He shrugs.

"What?"

"Well, like—" He permits himself a half-glance in her direction. "What do you want to do with yourself, I mean."

"I dunno. Be a model." She can't look at him as she says this.

"A model? Fuck." He keeps staring at the water. "You're too pretty. You're beautiful." He lowers his voice reverentially. "But mostly you're too smart. Way too smart. If you want to do something like that—I don't know—be an actress."

Felice is silent, studying her wadded-up wrapper. He doesn't know about the punishment. Emerson goes to get them more burgers, and when he comes back he's animated with a new plan. "Listen, Felice," he says quickly, "I've got some money saved up—nine hundred dollars—"

Her spine straightens. *What?*

He smiles.

"Well, what the fuck?" she says quietly. "Where'd you get all that money?"

He brushes his hand over his head several times before looking up. "I'm pretty good at working, and, like, saving up. I bounce and mix drinks at a couple clubs." He interlaces his fingers, straightening and closing, studying them. Everything about him so intent and serious. Like one of the old Jewish men set up on their folding chairs on their apartment balconies. Felice can see the ghost of his eighty-year-old self on his face—pouches and worry lines. She feels, weirdly, drawn to this, to his funny soberness. Every other kid she knows would've spent that money, dropped it on drugs, a new board, some shitty, stupid thing. She brushes elbows with wealth every week in the clubs; she even, on occasion, has picked up better gigs—like the swimsuit special for Australian *Elle* or the Nordstrom spring junior catalog— that paid $2,000 for a day's work. But she currently has $7.50 in her pocket and she's never so much as opened a checking account. Nine hundred seems like a staggering amount, especially for someone like Emerson—just a street kid—to have actually saved up.

A rose flush rises under his skin. He flashes another tentative look at her—smiling and not-smiling. Then he pulls something out of his side pocket, some striated shells, some shaped like little turbans. He puts them in Felice's hand: miniature lightning whelk, sand dollar, and a ruffled conch. She admires them a moment, feels a smile come to her lips, then she drops them on the sand. "So?"

Emerson looks at the shells. "There's this guy, Yann Hanran— he's one of the really, really big-time strongmen? I met him at the Dixie Gym. He said he'd train me. I mean, he's a real coach—not just some, you know . . . Like, just a really excellent guy. His gym is out in Portland."

Felice's stomach tightens: all this sincerity and weirdness. Her feelings oscillate toward and away from Emerson. "You're going to move to California to go to a gym?" She nips at the side of a nail, wishing for a cigarette.

"Not California—*Oregon*."

"So what, whatever, it's retarded. You're not going to *Oregon*— there's nothing even out there."

"Why not?" Emerson bounces a little on his haunches, shaking the skateboard. "Why not, why not?" It's a bit of the frenetic energy she remembers from seeing him with the other shaved boys at the Green House. She inches away, calves flexing, ready to spring to her feet. "We can move wherever we want to," he says. "*Why not?* Seriously. Let's go see stuff."

His shirt is wilting, collapsing like a tissue onto his skin. Sweat streaks his forehead, his skin looks tenderized—reminding her of the "white natives" she'd seen on a long-ago vacation with her family to Trinidad. Her father said they had lived on Trinidad for generations, migrating there from northern climates. But they all seemed to suffer from the sun; their skin gleaming red.

Felice has her mother's sparkling, near-black hair, and a lighter version of her biscuit-colored skin. As far as she knows, they're German and English, a little Scottish on her father's side. Apparently there is also a grandmother in there from some biblical place, Bethlehem or Nazareth. Her mother had shown her the photo of a dreamy girl, elbow-propped on her bed. Avis turned the photo over, reading her name.

"Lamise," her mother had said her name tentatively: the black-and-white snapshot was tucked in an envelope with old family photos. Felice held the photo by the edges.

Her mother wasn't sure of her identity. "Maybe my great-grandmother. Or maybe a great-aunt. You know how Grandma is about the past . . ." Avis smiled, referring to her own mother. Avis had the impression that Lamise had married into the family.

Felice couldn't stop staring at the photo: Lamise's soft expression was lost in a dream; she seemed to communicate with hidden traceries in the air. Felice saw clearly her mother's face and her own face—right there—as if superimposed on top of each other's. This old image seemed to describe all sorts of inner sensations, to show Felice the sorts of things her own face couldn't reveal. She'd returned the photo to her mother, but later she'd crept back into her mother's bedroom closet, taken the photo out of its box, and hidden it in her own dresser drawer.

EVEN THOUGH IT'S EXCITING to hear someone talk about leaving—Miami is still the only home Felice has ever known. It's never seriously occurred to her to really leave: the rest of the world, even New York and Paris, seems so dismal and drab, so far away. "I'm sorry." She gathers her knees toward her chest, mirroring Emerson. "But that's crazy. Moving to Oregon."

"Why?"

" 'Cause it is, okay? You gonna move to the other end of the earth, just to go to a *gym*? We got fifty million gyms right here, right on South Beach. And, *Oregon*? It's like, practically the North Pole."

Emerson's face brightens. "But it isn't really. That's just what they say to keep outsiders from coming there and wrecking it. I've been studying it on the Internet. Yann says it's got the prettiest summer and fall of anywhere. It'd be so cool—real seasons."

Felice looks back down the beach, over the miasma of shimmering bodies, slanting umbrellas, sunglasses. Even with his old-soul face, there's something about Emerson, his excitement, that makes her tired. It's not fair, how everyone else always gets to be the kid. She stands abruptly and glares at Emerson. "Off the deck."

"What?" He stands slowly. "What I say?"

Felice stomps up her skateboard and turns away from Emerson, starts walking.

"What? All I said was there's seasons."

"There's seasons in Oregon—big fucking deal!" she roars, wheeling on him. He actually flinches, which she likes. "You know what your problem is? It's you don't know when to shut the fuck up." She walks faster: she doesn't know exactly why she's so angry. Maybe something to do with imagining Emerson fitting in so perfectly in a place called Oregon—or Nebraska—or Cali-fucking-fornia. All those places like those creepy towns in North Florida they used to stop in on their way to visit her grandmother. Everyone in those places as pale as Felice's father and brother. She remembers their pink-rimmed gazes over their soda straws. The way everyone in the restaurant would study her. Her mother used to say: *You're just so lovely:* people want to look at you; they're a little afraid of beauty.

"You know," Emerson goes on, doggedly keeping up with her. "Portland is full of skateboarders. And all sorts of special trails and like parks—places where they hang out."

"Big deal," she mutters, watching her language as they pass three old ladies in skirted swimsuits. "This is just for getting around," she says, though she is still on foot, carrying the board. "Not a *lifestyle* or some crap like that." Still, as they push through the hot sand—higher on the beach now, dodging garbage and beer cans—too much for Emerson to collect—she finds she likes the idea of a land of skateboarders and parks full of trails. "What else is there?" she asks irritably.

"All kinds of stuff! Like—like everyone there loves good coffee—"

She snorts. "Yay—a bunch of Starbucks yups."

"No, no—better coffee than Starbucks—cooler." His blunt hands circle in the air. "Like—European—or something?"

"Uck."

"And special beer-making places. There's a store there that just sells cupcakes—that's all! And nice bakeries, and gardens and—and the people are super-super friendly. They've got statues of rabbits and beavers downtown!"

"Awesome," she drones. She grew up in the greatest bakery in the world: nothing can impress her. "Sounds like South Beach, practically." Though it doesn't, really. Especially not the people and the statues. Felice and Emerson walk in silence. The faint give of the sand feels good under Felice's feet as the sun's shifted and sand has cooled a bit. They walk out onto one of the boardwalk benches and sit side by side listening to the white rumble of the surf. Enormous container ships ease past on the horizon; overhead, a yellow plane tows a banner: *2Nite At Nile!*

Emerson looks at her once, quickly, a glance full of a furtive hope that Felice tries to ignore. He takes a deep breath. "There's a river that goes through the city, and lots of nice bridges, and a mountain— Mount something. And the farmers—they come into the city and sell, like, flowers and carrots and eggs and—all kinds of farm stuff. I just really really like the idea of it all. The fresh stuff. I don't know," he adds a bit hopelessly.

Normally Felice would be groaning at the corniness, but on the hot beach afternoon, air stale with suntan lotion, she actually feels a twist of longing. "Peaches," she says, remembering her parents' table. "Probably plums."

Emerson stares at her now. "Felice, listen—listen—if you would— if you'd consider it . . . We could go out there together, you know? I've got this money. And I—I wouldn't expect like—like—anything." He glares at his knees, his face and neck turning crimson, but he keeps going. (Sort of brave—Felice thinks.) "I—I know you don't like me *in that way.* Whatever. I don't even care. I mean, it would be just so fun—I think it would—to have you there."

Felice doesn't say anything. She just lets the salt spray rise over her legs, its gauzy vapor coating her skin. She's disoriented by Emerson's offer, a bit dazzled that this boy, whom she's never really noticed before, has evidently imagined a whole world around her. She lets her head drop back, arms braced against the bench slats. Is there a time when she gets to hope for things again? Turning eighteen could be the moment you turn into a new person—from a kid to a grownup. Does the grownup have to keep paying for things that the kid did? "I dunno," she says finally. "How could I?" She squints into the salty ocean sky. "When are you going to go, do you think? Supposedly."

"We could go any minute of any day. We can go right now if you want!"

Felice snorts and bounces her fist off the big, wooden curve of his upper arm.

THEY WALK BACK TO Collins then, which the yups have slowly been abandoning in favor of Lincoln Road. There used to be all sorts of forbidding little overpriced designer stores which, Felice has noticed, have started giving way to big mall-type places. And the more cranes and construction-site dump trucks that have clogged the streets, the more the people seem to change. There are still the elderly, trembling over walkers. There are still the crazy people, the wailers and lurchers, reeking drunks and meth-heads, the cadaverous, their skin shrunken to their bones. There are still people carrying animals—boas and cockatoos, Italian greyhounds, white roosters, fluffy coin-eyed monkeys, kittens in sailor suits. There are still middle-aged couples kissing on the street, still girls leading boys—or other girls—on leashes, exquisitely muscled, skin sparkling. But, increasingly, there are robust, generic "young people," who might've grown up next door to Felice in the Gables or in Akron, Ohio, swarming to Sephora and Old Navy, elbowing away the ecosystem of marginalia.

All connected somehow with the drone of construction, rumbling up from the waterfront.

Felice checks out a few of the prettier, sylphlike girls they pass. Even the models look different, weirder, with broad, bony foreheads and no eyebrows. It occurs to her that it might already be too late to become a "real" model. Over the past few years, her arms have started to look sinewy and there's a hardness setting in along her jaw-line. And the razor-eyed scouts and art directors miss nothing. The last few gigs she's taken—holiday catalogs—the photographers tilted her face up into the lights, begging her to relax her jaw, soften her pupils.

She and Emerson settle at the outdoor bar at El Tiki, a normally deserted place that only gets crowded after the cruise ships dock. Emerson buys her a margarita in a bowl-sized glass. He points out a rotating glass case of desserts, offers to get her something, but she says, "Ech. Look at the fondant on the layer cakes." Besides, there's a package of strawberry Twizzlers Emerson bought her at the 7-Eleven, now stashed in her rucksack. They joke around with each other, Felice twisting back and forth on her chair. She registers the dim, smiling faces around them at the bar—college kids from other cities. Emerson isn't bad-looking, she decides as he tells her boyhood stories about swiping mangoes from the neighbors' trees in Fort Lauderdale and selling them to spring-breakers.

"Yeah, so when we gonna go to Oregon?" she cracks during a pause in their conversation. And Emerson's head lifts; he's off on his ideas for a car, supplies, a place where they can stay when they get there. He seems to be improvising some of it on the spot—but much seems premeditated. ("This guy I know—Johnny—he comes to the beach every March, but he lives in Lawrence—which is maybe half-way. He said I could always crash at his place if I start traveling.") She listens, chiming in with her own suggestions ("We could stop in Wyoming on the way, and look at, like ranches")—all of it a kind of sport.

She can't remember the last time she's felt this good. Felice knows—it's there like a bruise in the back of her mind—she can't really go to Oregon, just as she knows the punishment doesn't "run out." And yet they linger at the bar through another round of drinks, talking. Emerson tells her about his terror of his childhood doctor and vaccinations. Felice volunteers a story about getting chicken pox, which fills her with strands of feelings she'd thought she'd shed a long time ago—the lost, unearthly sensations of being sick at home. As they talk, she gazes into the hotel courtyard beside the bar: a jumble of blue-glazed terracotta pots, sprawling aloes and ginger and birds-of-paradise, an assortment of cats skulking around the perimeters. The daylight has mellowed into pre-evening and in the distance, there is the mournful note of an ocean liner leaving port: a blue stain on the air.

Now Felice and Emerson fall into a syncopation, they talk as if they're catching up—rushing to fill in gaps—together watching the gradual, particulate shift of the light. Felice feels a wistful happiness: getting something that is not exactly what she'd expected. A sense of lowering the guard, of risking something, and of gently forgetting something important, though she couldn't say exactly what.

Brian

IT KEEPS COMING BACK: THIS MORNING'S FIGHT with Avis. She'd become distraught over what she'd called his "coolness." He'd merely used the usual gentle logic to discourage her from going to meet Felice. "Setting yourself up," he'd chided. Avis had lapsed into such a bright, cold stare he wondered if she actually saw him at all. Later, he heard her crying through the bathroom door.

The Dixie Highway sun bounces hard off of car hoods and fills the interior of his SUV with the scent of footballs and shoe leather. And now this. It comes over him at unpredictable moments. A not unpleasant sensation, a bit like fainting: the sense that the solid matter of his body is spontaneously reverting to a gas, joining the fumes and exhaust contrails burning all around him.

Brian squeezes his eyes shut, but a blaring in his right ear jolts him. He swivels in time to see a wrathful face in a white ragtop convertible come too close to his passenger side. The driver thrusts out his finger; Brian catches a burst of some ferocious rap recording in the background (and those startling whiffs of old songs that pop up like snatches of perfume in a crowd). *"Fuck you asshole."* Barely muted by the car window. *"Go the fuck back to Jersey."* A girl cranes forward from the passenger side, hair long and dark as his daughter's, snapping in the wind. He forces himself to slow down, eases to a creep along with the other drivers all glazed on their phones, and the young men, barefoot and shirtless on motorcycles. He makes it without further incident into the covered parking for the Ekers Building, but something seems to have shifted within his chest. He smooths his tie, notes Jerry Howard's black BMW M6; Javier Mercado's baby blue Jag convertible, and, on the other side of the cement pylon, the smart gray trunk of Esmeralda Muñoz's Mercedes coupe. He tracks this private competition—prefers not to be first (though certainly not, say, the eighth) among the cars to slip into these privileged air-conditioned spaces.

He leans on the side of the Benz as he climbs out, then slams the door shut. For some reason he thinks again of Avis crying in the shower. No. Not that.

The open-air marble walkway from the garage to the building: a spell of heavy air and brine, views of towering royal palms that line the walk. Rufus leans into the glass door, giving Brian that shrewd, evaluative glance, before dropping his eyes and mumbling to the floor, "G'mornin, Mr. Muir." Rufus has been there for two years. For the first eight months, Brian stopped, smiled, and said, "Please, Rufus, just *Brian*." For nearly sixteen years, Rufus's predecessor, Pavel, used to smile and say in his dignified way, "Hello, Brian, how are you?" One day Pavel never showed up for work. There were a couple of lackadaisical temporary doormen. And then there was Rufus. After a while, Brian gave up on Rufus. Now, every morning, that beat of sourness, just as he enters the building and begins his day. One morning Esmeralda happened to arrive at the same time and as they walked in together ("G'mornin' Mr. Muir, G'mornin' Ms. Muñoz") she picked up on Brian's discomfort and said, "Why does it bother you? He's just being respectful."

Personal assistant to Jack Parkhurst, Esmeralda is nearly seven years older than Brian, from one of those cultures where everyone is so conscious of class and family and respect, etc. "Old World."

He walks through the door that Rufus holds for him, neither man looking at the other. And there is the memory of Avis weeping again. *No.*

The trick, he reminds himself, is to discipline the mind. It's what one does during the toughest times that proves one's mettle. Arguing before a zoning board, negotiating fees with county commissioners, placating citizen action committees. This is the true reason to work, he thinks: to train oneself. His son understood this almost intuitively. But his daughter. Spiraling disappointment. Across the lobby, Celia and Esmeralda are chattering in front of the elevators: they'll be speaking Spanish, they'll stop, politely, as he approaches, and ask in English, "And how are you, today?" At first he hangs back, not eager to talk to anyone this morning. But then he notices that Fernanda Cruz has come in from the Biscayne Boulevard entrance and, impulsively, quickens his step.

The elevator doors slip open. "Wait, wait," he calls. He bounds across the lobby and into the elevator. "Going up? How is everyone this morning?"

"How are you, Brian?" Celia asks, a sweet glance from the corner of her eyes.

"Hey Brian." Fernanda gives that little wave.

He nods at both of them, glancing at Fernanda—new manager of the Investor Relations division. She's been using one of the offices down the hall from Brian—a corridor nicknamed "the bullpen"—while her own wing is being remodeled.

For eighteen years, Brian had looked down that hall into Hal Irvington's office as Irvington sat hunched, forehead lowered to his interlocking fingers, his mournful gaze locked on *The Wall St. Journal Investor's Edition*. Then, for a year it stood empty. One day Brian looked up, expecting the usual darkened window, instead discovering this lily of a shoulder, this lightly downturned mouth, a fringe of lashes. Every day for the past two weeks, Brian has looked up from his screen, eyes ticking to the right, down the hall, to see Fernanda Cruz's white shoulder delineated from her neck by a dark curtain of hair, the first three knuckles of her right hand resting on her telephone set, all set off by the modernist glint of the swooping office window.

She's been at Parkhurst, Irvington & Benstock for five or six months and Brian finds he's forming a steadfast affection. She waves at him on her way in or out of the office, a clipped, girlish gesture. It's what sets her apart from the usual parade of brazen Miami beauties: that wave. She seems sweet and retiring—a throwback to some earlier ideal. Now Celia and Esmeralda stand side by side, backs against the elevator wall like sentries, while Fernanda stands close to the door, near the buttons; her hair spills forward, partially obscuring the side of her face.

Brian says to the general assembly, "Could boil an egg out there—just wave it through the air."

Celia and Fernanda laugh deferentially. Esmeralda adjusts her coral button earrings, slides her finger along the curve of her ear. Her smile deepens but doesn't quite touch her eyes. He notices her glance tick from Fernanda back to him again, an icy glimmering. "How is that new office working out for you, darling?" she asks her.

Fernanda flicks her hair back across her shoulders. Her face brightens. "It's weird over there. Must be three times the size of my regular office. It's like a cave."

A cave! Brian studies the laces in his shoes.

"It's a little lonely," she adds. "Up there."

"You know you can always come talk to me," he blurts. Brian catches a look between Celia and Esmeralda. He glances at Fernanda then; the elevator light touches her hair: gossamer strands of blue light on black hair. He thinks of how he used to slide his fingers along the nape of Avis's neck, warm hair slipping between his fingers. He picks up some familiar strand of honeysuckle. Then Fernanda sniffles and rubs under her nose, the roseate tinge of the rim of her nostrils, with the back of one knuckle.

The elevator button for 28 flashes, the doors swipe open. *"Ciao, chica,"* Celia says to Fernanda. "And Brian—" Esmeralda's voice drops. "Take care of yourself."

He smiles from the upper reaches of the elevator. As soon as the doors wisp shut, he says to Fernanda, "Really—I'm always down the hall. Anytime." Anytime what? He falters, uncertain if he's finished the sentence.

"You're kind." She smiles. "I just like to complain for the ladies." Now he laughs, though he isn't sure what she means.

The doors open on 32. She whisks off the elevator ahead of him.

A blade of calf appearing in the slit of her coal-colored skirt. Brian follows her out, then hangs back, unwilling to follow her all the way to their wing.

Lately it requires more energy and concentration for Brian to face his lineup of client meetings and phone-ins, and the obligatory weekly rendezvous on the links at the Doral or over drinks at the Highland or poker—that eternal round of scotch, cigars, and playing cards—at Old Benstock's manse on Santa Maria Street by the golf course. Everything takes more energy these days. Brian decides Fernanda has enough of a head start. He's walking toward the bullpen when there's the whoosh of the executive restroom door: Javier Mercado, PI&B's sales czar, as he laughingly refers to himself, appears before Brian, shooting his white cuffs. "There he is." His teeth are startling against his deep tan. "There's my man! What're you doing right now? You got a minute. C'mon, bud." He slaps one hand on top of Brian's lightly padded shoulder and steers him around. "Walk with me a little, yeah? I wanna ask you something."

Brian looks longingly over his shoulder, the sanctuary of his desk.

"*Vámos! No problema*—I know you're busy, man. We're all busy until we're dead, right?"

Unlike many developers who contract out to other specialists, PI&B is so vast their staff includes architects, landscapers, surveyors, as well as a legal department, which Brian heads, and a wing of sales agents—Javier's domain—to move units once the condos go up. At times it seems to Brian that he and Javier are very nearly adversaries. Most of Brian's legal colleagues wouldn't be caught dead consorting with real estate agents. As the last man on the "development food chain"—as Parkhurst dubs it—Javier is all about sales, speed, and profit. Brian presides over the beginnings of things—talking to environmental engineers, zoning boards, and county commissioners, patiently sifting through contracts, moving slowly, scanning the horizon for problems. It was well after law school that he heard corporate lawyers referred to as *the handmaidens of the deal*.

Javier cries at the partners' obscene jokes, always has cash for big tips. Brian keeps to himself, but Javier spins legends about his *compañero*'s oracular, "Vulcan-like" powers of reason. "See that dude?" Javier says to buyers, tipping a thumb at Brian, "Dude is like CIA, ice-cold intelligentsia." He himself spends afternoons schmoozing poolside at the Biltmore while Brian logs hours in meetings with the regional planning councils, their Blackberries and legal pads lining the tables. Now Javier drops his voice to a private, closing-the-deal tone: "What about that little Fernanda? You check her out?"

A project manager at Lennar—her previous employer—had regaled Brian and Javier one afternoon with a string of rumors about Fernanda. Brian knew how it was: executives entertained themselves: private fantasies spun into whispered allegations. He tries to act amused, but now he feels defensive about Fernanda and ends up over-doing it, wagging his head. "Heh-eh-eh . . ." Trailing off, he tries for a hapless shrug. His shoulders feel heavy. "She's something all right."

Hap Avery and Dean Hayes burst out of Accounting talking intensely about a Heat game. Avery salutes Brian and Javier and says, "Hey." Hayes nods. "Hello, Jav." He brings his palms together and bows slightly. "Counselor."

Javier and Brian stop speaking until they're well beyond the others. Javier stops Brian just as they reach the glass door to the East Wing. "So . . . what? You're really not interested in her? Or you just don't go for that Jewish thing?" Jack Parkhurst once said that he'd hired Brian as much for his "moral compass" as for his research acumen: a comment Javier never tires of kidding him about.

His fingers loosen in his pockets. "She's Jewish?"

"You know—Juban. Fernanda Levy Cruz? What do you think?" He peers through the glass door marking off the land of the bullpen. "That cute little fixed nose. That Russki hair."

Another flash of annoyance. Proprietary, indignant, he says, "How's Odalis doing?"

Javier gives Brian an immense smile. "My wife? What, are you kidding? I'm not going to actually *do* anything." He pulls the glass door open and heads in, Brian close behind him. "Besides," he says, clearly aiming for Fernanda's office, "that's there and this is *here*."

Brian falls back, dwindles to a halt. He rubs the inner corners of his eyes: his pupils feel soft—is that possible? A sign of heart disease? There's a diffuse ache in the center of his chest left over from the morning commute. He opens his office door: even the back of his hand looks old.

A stack of invitations and contractual materials are heaped on his desk. Brian's desk is a piece of smoky green glass with one drawer adorned by a coral-shaped handle. Each morning, Hector places mail on the corner of Brian's desk beside the screen, its wafer of light. Brian sits down with his coffee and releases a preliminary daily sigh that signals his immersion in contract review. This is the moment he craves: the vitality of his body stirring, his imagination focused on problems and solutions. He feels hints of the time when he met Avis and fell into a sublime entrancement. He bent over her bedraggled Economics 102 text in the tutoring center and the airy scent of her hair, the dented lower lip of her smile, turned him aphasic: all higher thought abandoned him. She passed her final somehow, then agreed to dinner with him.

Brian checks voice mail: there's the usual barrage from his ambitious associate Tony Malio giving Brian the rundown on development locations and the status of new project plans. "The Little Haiti Corps people are back again—blowing hot air. Just rescheduled our sitdown with them—again. Probably looking to leverage more buyout. Keep you posted." Brian jots "Little Haiti," then shakes open the paper, but his attention keeps floating over the top of the page. Peering down the hall, he spots the patent leather gleam of Javier's head as he arches over Fernanda's desk. It's hard to see through the sliding blebs of reflections in the glass wall—the curve in the glass imparting a whimsy to passersby—but it appears that Fernanda tilts her head—into laughter?

Brian squeezes the bridge of his nose between his thumb and forefinger. The newspaper lies on his desk, his other hand flat on the paper. For a moment, it seems that he can feel something insectival rattling around inside his body.

Juban.

This term, which he has heard bandied about Miami for years, now strikes him as somehow distasteful, impertinent even. He can clearly make out Javier's gestures: the whisk of hand through air as he laughs. Brian imagines Javier sliding his eyes in Brian's direction, whispering, "Our office Anglo." The thought causes him to shove himself away from his desk, his legs lifting his weight from his chair. He pushes through his office door. Passing the corridor's glass wall, he spots the skeleton of the Metro Building going up just two blocks from the Ekers Building, one hastily constructed story at a time. These days, Miami is a skyline of towering developers' cranes operating in varying degrees of legality. Beyond that, filling the view, floats the striated, Caribbean blue of Biscayne Bay. By noon each day, three-quarters of each window glow like mercury.

As he moves down the glassy corridor, more reflections flicker before him; they glide sideways then and Javier is leaning out, holding open the door to Fernanda's office. "The man himself! We were just talking about you."

The air around him shimmers for an instant, like heat rising off blacktop. Brian closes his eyes, opens them, follows Javier into the office. "Here he is—here's the man," Javier says again. "Resident legal evil genius."

Brian gives Javier a thin smile. "Don't you have units to go sell?"

"You looking to invest?"

He realizes peripherally that Fernanda does not seem to be amused. There's a pliancy to her shoulders, a pretty girl's receding from attention. This had been one of Felice's habits as she began to edge toward young womanhood. Fernanda's eyes are sable black, so dark they seem to float slightly apart from the rest of her features. She has a funny, petal-shaped mouth—too much humor—or cunning—to be considered a real beauty. He smiles broadly. "I haven't wanted to bother you while you were settling in—Investor Relations must be in chaos with the remodel."

"We are." She reveals a row of even white teeth. "It's been insane, trying to stay on top of anything—I feel lost without my little nest."

"Look at her smile," Javier comments. "She was just being polite to me before. She didn't give me any kind of smile like *that*. Where you been keeping that smile?"

To Brian's gratification, Fernanda's smile hardens in place. "I know it's silly."

"*Ya,* what's silly?" Javier ticks back his head. "Good Cuban girl needs *su familia.*"

Watching them, Brian feels a jealous pang: it's the trace of collusion he seems to sense in the air around him—not only between Cubans but between the hip young African-American women buying tabouli and the languid Arab men at the counter at Daily Bread, between the Italian models at South Beach and the Swedish au pair girls sauntering around Cocowalk. Javier says that Brian suffers from Anglo paranoia. So many people seem to know something that they're not sharing with Brian. Everyone flirting, accents magnetically attracted to accents: everyone dusky, sexy, Spanish-speaking. Brian slips his hand to the back of his neck, trying to collect his wits, wishing for Javier's dragonfly quickness. "I can understand—" he begins, just as the door flashes and Agathe pokes her head in, a bolt of gray pageboy swings forward.

"Mr. Muir? I'm terribly sorry—someone's been waiting on line 2?"

Irked, Brian twists toward her, about to bark, *So take a message—* but Fernanda is listening. He flips a hand in Javier's direction. "Duty calls."

"YEAH, HI, UM, THIS IS NIEVES?" a young voice says.

"Excuse me?"

"*Nieves.* Stanley's girlfriend?"

There's a minor ringing in his ears. "Um. I—I don't—" He plunks back into his office chair. "I'm sorry—*who* is this?"

"Oh." There's a long pause. Then: "Did he not *tell* you about me?"

"I don't know." Brian places one hand on his desk. "He might have. What can I do for you?"

"It's concerning—well—I just thought—I just wanted to make contact, you know? Only you don't know about me. So, okay. This is weird now."

"Excuse me, I—" He pats his keyboard very lightly with his open hand. Over his shoulder there are dark files of clouds reflected in the interior glass wall; it looks as if he is caught between cloud banks. "Is there something I can help you with?"

"I think I goofed here."

Another pause. This time he can hear a swipe like a hand being squashed over the receiver, muffled voices in the background. "Hey—hello—is Stanley there?" He raises his voice. "I'd like to speak to my son."

A muffled squeak. "I'm sorry—what?"

"I want to speak to Stanley."

"Ha—me too." Her voice is lightly serrated. "I can't believe he— well, I'm embarrassed now. I'm sorry for troubling you."

"That's all right, dear. Why don't you have Stan call me when he gets in?"

There's a pause in which she seems to be weighing her answer. "Look, it's—everything's okay," she says at last. "We'll get back to you." Then she hangs up.

BRIAN'S CALLS TO STANLEY'S cell and office number go unanswered; he leaves messages at both: *Call your father.* Stanley is a bit of a local celebrity: the girl was probably some sort of crank. Brian sits back and stares at the bay that fills his windows. He thinks of a time, an hour like a silver-blue membrane, that covered him and his infant son, tucked into the crook of his arm, sitting in the creaking leather rocker. They were still in Ithaca and Stanley was six months old when Avis went back to work at the Demitasse Pâtisserie. She had to be at work each morning by 4:30, so Brian took over the early feedings with Stanley, then dropped him at day care on the way to his own job. Those recalled mornings possess a quality of translucence: Stanley's bare shoulders, his curved fingers touching Brian's lips, his gray eyes fixed on his father over the curve of the bottle. They breathed together into the slow drinking, Stanley's body flung across Brian's legs, his tiny arm flung back, his hand rhythmically crushing and releasing a lock of his own hair. Brian memorized the globe of his son's forehead, the silk of his eyebrows, the frog-crouch of his legs. Avis was always bringing work home: their counters, refrigerator, and freezer were filled with boxes of danishes, layer cakes, and cookies, the kitchen was crowded with cake pans and rollers and an enormous, hunched-over Hobart; the whole house had the pink scent of sugar. He read to Stanley (reaching for the book with groping, swimmer's fingers) about a witch who baked a gingerbread house to lure children. Brian felt as if he and Stanley were the children in this story and Avis the good witch who baked the house they all lived in.

Brian couldn't imagine that things would ever be otherwise. But then somehow he lost his job. Dan, one of the partners at the firm in Syracuse, kindly made a few calls on his behalf, and Brian was able to tell Avis he'd been made a better offer, pure opportunity—perfect for their growing family. It was the truth: he just didn't tell her that he'd been "laid off." Didn't mention that Dan had first expressed the feeling during an early performance review that Brian wasn't sufficiently "tuned in" to their office "culture." With her baker's hours and physical work, she slept instantly and deeply and had no idea that Brian no longer slept well at night, his dreams laced with shreds of morning meetings, the dread of unmanageable research, massive client folders, the creak of his hated office chair. He'd finally drop off around two each night, then drag himself stupefied and shivering from the bed when the alarm went off at five.

Fortunately, business at Parkhurst, Irvington & Benstock was exploding, the *WSJ* filled with their ads luring land investors to South Florida. Back then, Miami seemed to drowse in a heat stupor; the highways were wide, gray, and quiet. The Everglades encroached on the roads—Brian could smell the swamp air and sulfurous mangroves—and every winter, black motes of vultures spun high overhead like genies. The city was lonely then, populated mostly by old folks. God's waiting room. Yet, to his surprise, Brian loved the sun-soaked landscape.

His father, a litigation expert, had told Brian he was a fool to take the job—that he was trading earning potential for the security of a retainer. "You'll be a kept man," he insisted. "You're too young to be playing it so safe. Hang up a shingle, take divorces. A little malpractice—just to get going. You'll bag ten times as much inside of two years and have all the security you please. It's billable hours, Bry, that's all it comes down to. The hours."—his father scratched at the loose skin under his neck—"What's in Miami? The dying and the dead."

Still, Parkhurst offered Brian enough that Avis could afford to start her at-home business. PI&B were her first clients: she supplied the Austrian chef at their executive dining hall with linzer tortes, *lebkuchen,* strudel, Black Forest cakes. Gradually other corporations and local businesses began to request her goods for retreats, conferences, and boardroom lunches. At the same time, Brian found he enjoyed working for a big developer. They hired brilliant architects and contractors; their buildings became part of the sharp, pale skyline. Brian believed he and Avis were helping to build an actual city—food and shelter—inside and outside. Unlike New York or Boston, Miami was a place you could go to and really create something new. Best of all, its boom-or-bust energy, a penchant for dreaming: a dream of a city in a dream of a state.

Avis hired assistants; they hosted dinner parties, bought a 34-foot Sea Ray, a twelfth-floor getaway on Marco Island. There were season tickets, box tickets: they joined the board of the Fairchild Garden; contributed to the Deering Estate.

Avis and Brian had lived in Miami for about ten years when the father of one of Stanley's classmates invited Brian to an art opening. Brian wondered if there was something prohibitive in the nature of practicing law—he found it difficult and frequently stressful to connect with other men—at least to the point of real friendship. But there was something easy and agreeable about Albert. A publicity rep for the Miami Symphony, he was the sort of cultivated person Brian had tried to emulate as a student. Albert talked about opera and dance and "performance." He saw hidden meanings in films and books— what he called the "layers" in things; he brought up the uses of symbolism in theater and music.

The opening was in one of the neighborhoods on the northwest outskirts of downtown—territory Brian had never ventured into before. The local denizens kept muscular, flat-headed dogs tied to ropes in the yards and each house was ringed by a chain-link fence. Albert parked on the street and they walked by a group of men with bandannas tied on their heads. One yelled at Brian, "Yo, *suit*! What up, homes?" The "gallery" turned out to be a private home—the owner, a Haitian-American collector—had bought and connected several little cottages, making a rambling, warren-like space, every wall covered with canvases. Brian had expected to be bored, but he was electrified by the work: seven- and ten-foot-high canvases of nudes—their faces torn at and broken with slashes of paint, their eyes like open wounds. They stopped in front of one canvas—an image of a woman with a rippling chest and blotted black eyes.

"What do you think about that?" Albert asked.

Brian was startled, disoriented by how deeply the work affected him. There didn't seem to be any meaningful way for him to put words to what he was experiencing.

Albert stood next to him, nodding. "Strong, isn't it? The image has depth and dimensions. Makes you feel there's an actual presence here. Maybe even like she's angry with us."

"I suppose so—that's it," Brian said.

"I think that challenging work—it kind of takes your words away."

Albert nudged his glasses with a knuckle. "Not everyone really lets the experience in—I mean, like you are now. People love to try to talk over everything." Albert engaged a woman in a sinuous dress in bantering conversation and rattled off the names of prominent Haitian and Cuban artists: Brian had heard of none. Apparently the artist whose work they were viewing was from a town called Gonaïves, on the northern coast of Haiti. "Of course there's plenty for this artist to be angry about," Albert said. "Before he became famous, he had to rely on missionaries for art supplies. He would go without food so that he could buy paints. And the political situation there, well . . ."

When Brian and Albert left the gallery, Brian was buoyed by the images he'd seen—the deep slashes through the paint, the skin rippling with sinew, and sudden, unearthly glimpses of bone. He felt vividly how his young son would love this sort of thing—the outlaw gallery and humble neighborhood.

It had grown darker. Brian looked around at the still street: a streetlamp burned out at the corner, the shrunken houses and ragged patches of grass, gray in the low light. On the way to the car, he heard voices—people gathered in a front yard, a burst of laughter, the quiet slap and tick of dominoes. There was a scrabbling movement along the gutter: rats? At the end of the block, something fetid and black pooled in the center of the street. A gray scarf of smoke rose from a bonfire—children tossing in sticks and bits of trash: the air was thick and watery, as if the convergence of shared history had a visible weight. It occurred to Brian that the people on this street were from the same island the artist had come from. He stared at the reflections sparkling in the passenger window and didn't speak for the rest of the ride back.

BRIAN PUSHES AWAY from the desk. The phone is silent for once, emails blink on the screen. He regards the crowded sky high above the horizon, filled with thunderheads and a silken light the same shade of gray as the lining of his grandfather's coat. The forecasters are merrily predicting an "active season." His thoughts leap to the house, the weight in the halls, the unlit rooms he'll come home to if— as he expects—Avis returns without having seen Felice. He checks his watch: 12:37. He closes his eyes with a brief fervent wish that his wife isn't waiting alone at some café table.

His window faces south and east. If only he had strong enough binoculars he might be able to locate his family. The city spreads its cantons over endless miles. Little Haiti must be somewhere behind him: one of those places where you should never run out of gas. And Haiti itself is somewhere before him, beyond the barrier island of Miami Beach, a slender nation tucked within the horizon, Edenic and rife with turmoil and poverty. There but for the grace of God, his father liked to say. As if his own life had descended to him straight from heaven itself.

Now the gray light evinces the lowering of Stanley's stern gaze, his disapproval: how he would scorn this latest condo project! Brian can almost hear his son's voice, taking up his favorite topics—the preservation of neighborhood fabric, cultural history and community. Brian admires his son, but sometimes he reminds Brian, oddly, of his righteous old dad. He turns from window to desk—his two poles— with a sense of facing something. He picks up his handset, preferring its shape to the cold chip of the cell, and makes a call. "Tony—yeah— tell me again where we're at with Little Haiti?"

Avis

AVIS LOOKS WITH BLANK EYES AT THE ONRUSH-
ing freeway. The air smells of tar and cement, as if the city has turned
into a smoking construction pit. She curls into herself, trying not to
touch the sides of the car, trying not to speak or brush up against
anything.

Miami seems as frightening to Avis now as it had when they'd first
arrived—a lawless land where cabbies kidnapped young coeds on
spring break, German tourists were shot in broad daylight, gangs of
young black and brown men roved around in their thin white tanks,
long baggy jeans, hands jammed in their pockets. There were "home
invasions," in which thieves would simply rampage into houses and
murder the inhabitants at their dinner tables. She'd seen a fistfight
break out at the local video store, twice watched police run across
neighbors' lawns with guns drawn, and—too many times to count—
she's had to slam on her brakes to avoid a careening drunken driver—
her heart seized up, throbbing in her chest. One day Avis cut short a
phone conversation because of a racket outside. She went out to the
front lawn to see a police helicopter hovering almost directly over her
house: some neighbors told her that a "fugitive" was on the loose: she
and the children stayed inside, doors locked for hours, waiting for
an all-clear. After Felice had left, Avis had to stop watching the local
news because it was too awful, more than she could stand. Her teenage daughter was out there.

How is she supposed to endure this, she wonders, nearly in a
trance. They meet only at Felice's whim, on Felice's terms. The psy-
chotherapist, the police counselor, the family social services coun-

selor said, No: don't agree to these conditions. "You're giving her too much control and no incentive to come to you," the girl at the runaway crisis line told her. Brian seemed to have instinctively understood this principle—coolly, systematically shutting down all attempts at seeing Felice within months of her final disappearance. But two months ago, Avis was standing in the produce section at Publix when a woman approached her. Her round face was clear, just a wrinkle at the corner of each eye: she took Avis's hand and studied her for a moment before saying in cadenced English, "I heard you go to see your baby whenever she calls. I would do exactly same thing as you. Exactly."

She squeezed Avis's hand and Avis realized that this was Marina, the housekeeper for Mrs. Grigorian, down the street from them. Avis stared at bunches of guavas, hunched as if her center had caved in.

Nina clears her throat and Avis realizes they are already done with the freeway and are now taking Coral Way to beat the Dixie backup. "Do you have anything in the house for dinner? Do you need me to stop—we get some rice and chicken, *empanadas* or some *postres*?" Nina insists on certain Cuban interpretations in her own cooking, uses lard in her pan Cubano and boils condensed milk in the can for *dulce de leche*.

"No, we're fine," Avis mumbles. She presses the window button and accidentally hits the lock instead. "*Postres,* why would I want *postres*? Do you not know what I do for a living?"

"You need more air?" Nina reaches for the climate control panel.

"No, please, nothing."

They make a left on Douglas and stop at the intersection with Bird. The traffic is torturously slow with the erratic, newly-arriveds—immigrants and tourists—prone to rolling to a distracted stop mid-lane. As they wait, about eight cars from the light, a homeless person materializes between the cars near the intersection, wafting up the street toward them, flashing his wrecked, hand-lettered sign on a panel of cardboard box: *Please help. I have wife and kid and no—* He turns toward a white Cadillac several cars ahead before Avis can finish reading. Cadillac stuffs some bills into his jar. He turns back and begins drifting back toward them, a tall black man so emaciated Avis can see the fine bones of his scapula, the ribboned, muscles of his forearms; he looks burnt down to a shadow, a cinder in the blast of August sunlight.

Avis picks up her handbag.

"Oh no," Nina says. "Please don't."

"Oh, for heaven sakes," Avis mutters, rummaging in her bag. "I only want to give him a buck."

"Too late," Nina says, because the light's changed, but they have to wait for the usual procession of yellow and red light-runners in the cross street. When they finally move, it's only to inch up a few spaces before the light turns again, so they're now a car length away from the man and his sign: *job or hous. Im good person—*

"Please, *querida.* I really do understand, but it's better if you give the money to a homeless shelter or some sort of something . . ."

Avis ignores her, digging out her wallet, in which, she discovers, she has no small bills, only the fifties for Felice. The man is now making a beeline for them, his eyes round and hollow. Avis goes for the window button and instead hits the lock again. "Shit. How do you open this thing?"

"*Ay, mujer,* why do you have to be so—"

"I want to help this guy out a little. What's the big deal?" Now the man is standing on the other side of the window, peering in.

"He's some scam artist. These guys, they make tons of money."

"Well, then it's a crappy job and he's earned every penny!" Avis's voice rises, stretching thin. Anger throbs in her temples as she grabs her door handle.

"What are you *doing?*" Nina taps the accelerator, trying to scoot ahead, but now a row of skate punks and pedestrians is crossing in front of the car. The man on the other side of the window strolls alongside the car as they move a few feet. "That's dangerous!"

Avis opens the car door and hands the man some fifties. His eyes roll from the cash to her face and she can see a fine, inflamed crimson web beneath his irises. "*O Bondye mwen bon sou latè.*" His voice is grainy and low, it sounds like crushed sugar. *"Mèsi, pitit fi. Bondye beni ou."*

Flooded by a jolt of pleasure, she also hands him the silver cookie tin: he accepts, thunderstruck. "Cookies," she says. *"Pâtisserie."* His sign is tucked under his arm and his hands shake with tremors that rattle the tin like a snare drum. He tugs at the lid and for a moment Avis fears he isn't strong enough to open it.

The light changes, Nina steps on it, and Avis slams the door shut. "I cannot believe you," Nina says angrily. "What a waste."

"Why? Because I wanted to help someone?" She turns in her seat in time to see him pry the tin open, cars swerving around him as he peers inside.

"That won't help him—he's just gonna go get drugs or some booze."

"Good. I hope he enjoys it. I hope he has one moment of pleasure on this crappy earth."

"I doubt he even has enough teeth to chew those cookies," Nina adds bitterly. "He won't know what to do with that sort of food. Let him go up to Overtown and get food."

Avis is infuriated. "How is this any of your business?"

Nina starts to speak, stops, then, with her eyes narrowed, she says, "That *negro viejo*—he has nothing to do with your daughter!"

Avis's lips part.

"Because they're both outdoors—on the streets. Come on, don't act dumb. Just because you gave to him doesn't make things better for her. You do these stupid things like you think one is like the other."

Avis feels another throb in her temples. Her fingers curl into her empty hands.

When they pull into Avis's driveway twelve blocks later, Nina is calmer and she tries to mollify Avis, speaking in her modulated voice. *"Ven, cariña,* hey, I'm sorry." She touches her employer's wrist. "I shouldn't have tried to stop you. You were right—it—none of it was really my business."

But the anger has a chemical grip on her. Avis shoulders her way out of the car door, then throws it shut without a backwards glance.

Nina gets out of the car. "Please, Avis, can we just talk?" Avis keeps going, skipping the flagstone path and striding across the lawn. "It's okay if you want to be angry," Nina pleads. "But do you have to be this angry?"

Avis turns the key in the door. "Aren't we still friends?" Nina calls, hands on her hips.

Avis steps inside and closes the door.

DURING THE YEAR OF Felice's runaway attempts, Avis and Brian created their own protocol: call the Gables police, the sheriff's department, the highway patrol. Contact the local FBI, the missing children help lines, her school. Place notices in the *Herald* and local newsletters. Send alerts to the National Runaway Switchboard. And they searched. They spent hours in their cars crawling through the streets of Coral Gables, Coconut Grove, Kendall, Hialeah, staring into yards and windows, spying on other people's lives and families. Avis approached strangers in the street with photographs—which horrified Brian. He told her: *That isn't safe.* And: *You're upsetting people.* Some of the worst fights of their marriage were over those snapshots. Avis accusing him of caring more about appearances than about their own daughter. Brian said: We have to draw a line.

After two or three or four nights away, Felice would either come home by herself or the police would deliver her, followed by humiliating and protracted visits from social service counselors. But there were long, comparatively peaceful periods between these vanishings, during which Felice seemed to "return" to herself. As if she'd split into two separate girls. She settled back into school. She would be well-mannered; she helped Stanley with the dishes; she chattered with her father about soccer practice; she confided in her mother about her friends—but never about running away, why she kept leaving. Where she went when she was gone.

She tricked them—Avis thinks—every single time. They'd relax the curfew, relax their vigilance, enjoy a week, a few months, without incident. And just when Avis would tell herself (she wanted to believe it so badly) that their nightmare was ending—it would happen again.

Two months after Felice's thirteenth birthday, Avis woke in the vinyl rocker in the den with dread like a slickness covering her skin. She knew, even as she was waking, that things weren't right because she was in the vinyl chair—it sweated and stuck to her skin; it was where she waited and slept whenever Felice was missing. It was an uncomfortable chair so it helped her stay up late and wake early and it was a punishment place—for failing to keep her daughter at home.

Brian materialized out of the powdery dark, a pale face in gray pajamas, like a figure in a nightmare. The house felt hollow to Avis, despite the presence of husband and son. It seemed that some menace was lurking in the hidden corners, something worse than mere emptiness. "Darling," he whispered. "Please. Bed."

"Where is she?" Avis asked, almost conversationally. She stared at the blackly glinting night outside: she'd left the windows unshuttered just in case she might catch a hint of someone in the street, a single footfall, a child's breath.

"You have to rest," Brian said. "This isn't helping anything."

"She's never stayed away this long before." Avis's voice sounded wrong.

"She'll come back—she always does."

Avis looked at her husband: it was like nothing she'd ever felt before—almost crystalline in its hardness and acuity. Grains in her blood, between her internal organs: her voice full of slivers as she said, "She's only thirteen years old."

Brian tried to put his arms around her, but Avis straightened up, turning deliberately toward the windows. She'd slept for an hour at most—the wall clock said 3 a.m. But Avis was trained to these black morning bakery hours. She went to the kitchen, shook out an apron, and pried the lid from one of the thigh-high canisters of flour. Deep, fluting emotions were a form of weakness. She'd seen the softening in her work over the years, she'd started making the lazy, homey treats like apple crumble, chocolate muffins, butterscotch pudding, and lemon bars. They were fast and cheap and they pleased her children. But she'd trained at one of the best pastry programs in the country. Her teachers were French. She'd learned the classical method of rolling fondant, of making real buttercream with its spun-candy base and beating the precise fraction of egg into the *pâte à choux*. She knew how to blow sugar into glassine nests and birds and fountains, how to construct seven-tiered wedding cakes draped with sugar curtains copied from the tapestries at Versailles. When the other students interned at the Four Seasons, the French Laundry, and Dean & Deluca, Avis had apprenticed with a botanical illustrator in the department of horticulture at Cornell, learning to steady her hand and eye, to work with the tip of the brush, to dissect and replicate in tinted royal icing and multihued glazes the tiniest pieces of stamen, pistil, and rhizome. She studied Audubon and Redoute. At the end of her apprenticeship, her mentor, who pronounced the work "extraordinary and heartbreaking," arranged an exhibition of Avis's pastries at the school. "Remembering the Lost Country" was a series of cakes decorated in perfectly rendered sugar olive branches, cross sections of figs, and frosting replicas of lemon leaves. Her mother attended and pronounced the effect *amusant*.

It was this training, the discipline, her instructors' crisply starched linen hats and jackets, which she summoned in that seesawing darkness. She was ill, unbalanced from lack of sleep and food, and raw from crying. Avis yanked the apron strings twice around her waist: she ate a dry scone. She asked Brian, "Please, would you keep the boy out of here?" Then she dusted her pastry slab with jets of flour and began the daylong process of making *mille-feuilles*. She drove the flour and sugar before her on the slab, drew its vapors into her lungs, knowing that this work—the most challenging and imperial of pastry creation—might have the power to save her.

Avis remembers that time as a feeling, the sensation of entering a long tunnel: her dreams, when she slept, were night-curved; they wound around her. The police had urged them to "carry on" with their lives. Her reimmersion into classical baking stopped her from obsessing over her daughter's possible whereabouts, whether she was hurt or hungry or in danger. Her peripheral vision burned away cleanly, like the edges of a *crème brûlée*. She built her business, garnered awards, had her photograph in magazines, was approached by publishers asking for her cookbook. She could charge almost any price and customers seemed to consider it a privilege to pay it. For a year, then two and three, she couldn't quite see her husband, son, or assistants. It was like being a deep-sea diver—the cold pressure on her body, her hands waving through frigid darkness.

Sometimes, while she worked, she revisited memories of the prelapsarian days with Felice, of shopping and talking. After a morning of strolling through the open-air mall, they went to the café and settled down to cups of *consommé* and airy popovers with strawberry butter. Felice sat across from Avis, a black velvet choker around her neck, her attention drawn to the young women who entered the tearoom wearing expensive, formfitting clothes. Mother and daughter would discuss the outfits—which styles would look the most becoming on Felice. Avis's mother was amused by their old-fashioned domesticity. She told Avis, "You're teaching the girl to be an *odalisque*!"

After Felice had gone, Avis would admit to herself—much to her shame—that there were occasions when she felt as if she hadn't known her daughter as she should have. Among the happiest memories were more difficult, even confounding recollections: changes that had come over Felice after the time she'd taken to her bed. How she stopped laughing. How the light had seemed to go out in her face. Depression? Drugs? One night at the dinner table, Avis asked if Felice was feeling all right.

"I don't know," she'd said. That was her answer. Avis turns it around and around, this memory. She has considered that tiny exchange many times over the years; each time she does is like running her fingertip along a blade, testing to see if it still draws blood. Because she didn't ask Felice anything more. She put her daughter to bed and placed a cool washcloth on her head and read to her from

The Magic Garden, but she never asked her what was the *matter.* Why didn't she—Avis asks herself now. Why didn't I ask her?

Neither she nor Brian knew what to do with this wordless, unsmiling girl. When she began running away, Brian responded by becoming more rigid, moving up her bedtime, insisting they eat breakfast and dinner together, insisting she continue her violin lessons long after the point she'd lost interest. Brian had great faith in discipline—as if Felice could be saved by principles alone.

SHE STANDS STILL in the kitchen; her head is heavy and a damp warmth starts in the quick of her spine, spreading up through her skin, capillaries dilating. Typically the meetings with Felice turn her jittery, nerves jangling in her body for hours afterward. Now, however, she must physically fight the craving to crawl back into bed. Avis holds on to the wide counter that runs along the north wall: it feels as if microscopic earthquakes run through her arms and legs, and she seems to hear blood move in a rumbling twist through her head. This corner, with its window overlooking the necklace plant and the old avocado and overgrown garden out back, was where Stanley liked to sit while she was working. He was so sensitive as a child. He had too many questions, and he watched her too closely, as if certain that she would try to run away from him. The way she used to watch her own mother escaping into her books. He gave away his toys: once, he came home from school without his shirt and belt. He worried like an old man over people. When he was five, he walked into the kitchen, his voice rusty from crying, and told his mother that Andrew, a boy in his class, was eating rotten cakes.

That was Avis's term for Ding Dongs, Yodels, Ho Hos, Zingers—any of the artificial desserts that lined supermarket walls. Stanley had always intuitively grasped the difference between such things and, say, a vanilla mousse *roulade.* He admitted to giving his pastries to Andrew. A year later, he wanted Avis to provision him with enough éclairs for his school. In junior high, he began to scowl at her assistants, complaining that they didn't knead or measure properly—and it was true, they were sloppy. He often appeared in the kitchen, taking notes, making caramel, at times when he should have been in class.

When he moved out to attend—and drop out of—college, and then to open his market, she began to feel differently about him. She missed him: not in the way she pined for Felice, but quietly, a steadily building sensation. Mostly they talk only when Brian calls him, then she'll come on the line, her voice furtive and supplicant: conscious of old transgressions. The phone seems to breathe with a kind of crinkling static—the long pauses between them. These days, he is busy and successful. She is proud of him, of course, though there is something in her that holds aloof from the notion of a market—the gulf between a shopkeeper and an artisan.

She places her hand on the phone, breathes deeply, trying to think of a reason for calling him. "Not now," she tells herself sternly. "Not until you've done some solid work." She will not let herself cry. Crying cracks you open. Better to cry over pointless things, she thinks, like burning the butter, than things that matter. Or things you can't pin down. "Justify your existence a little." Her voice is eerie in the still kitchen. Justify your existence—that sounds good and hard, like something Stanley might say to her.

Avis goes to her desk: there's a fat folder of work orders for *macarons* and petits fours for corporate banquets and graduations—tiresome, debilitating, pointless cakes! She lowers her face into the blankness of her palms. It comes to her, clear as thought: a familiar repetitive rasp that swoops into a human register. A woman crying or laughing, but in an eerily regulated way. She lifts her face from her hands, gazing around. Rising like a sleepwalker, she moves through the house, tracking the sound, then opens the French doors at the rear of the dining room. Their backyard was built for children— a grassy expanse containing shaggy old gardens, a kidney-shaped pool, a green rope hammock—bordered by a copse of coconut palms and cycads, dense bamboo, a young palmyra palm, and the rambling avocado. A mild wind has come up, rustling the foliage. The weird repeating noise is louder outside but less objectionable. Avis circles the pool and walks to the limit of their property, to the palms. She pushes the fronds back and peeps between the wicklike trunks. Their backyard looks into the Mastersons' on the right, the Regaleses' directly behind, and on the left, the Calvadoses'. The Calvados had retired to Savannah and rented their house to a professor at UM and his family, but the man had confided to Avis last fall that they were sick of the heat and hurricanes and planned to return to Asheville.

It occurs to Avis, as she pushes aside more fronds, that it's been a long time since she's been in her own backyard. She steps onto the knuckly base of the Calvadoses' avocado tree and, looking through the palms into their yard, she sees an array of brilliant orchids, vibrant and implausible as daubs of paint, knobby roots hanging from the eaves of the house in halved coconut husks. A rope clothesline stretches from the corner of the house (Gables code infraction) lipped with hinged and straight wooden pins, displaying white underwear, shirts, and an ecru dress, wash-worn and translucent in the sun. The musty smell of the orchids reaches her along with that of a gardenia— sweetness with a sharp, peppery center. Avis is mesmerized by the lines of the glowing dress, the rustling undulance of the trees. She steps deeper into the shrubbery and palms, nearly into the neighbors' yard, and then she spots the big cage.

It's near the rear of the house, maybe six feet high, a bronze bird-cage with a domed top—beautiful and baroque yet roughly wrought. Inside, hunkered down, casting back and forth, a wet black shadow. It shifts to and fro, sidestepping. It lifts its head, so Avis catches a flash of beak, and makes its grating prehistoric noise. Its feathers ruffle up, then sleek back into a blue-black reflection. Its rasping elides into eerie human noise—somewhere between a sob and laugh—then rises to a piercing frequency that sails through Avis's body. The bird breaks off, goes back into that hunkered, mad, side-stepping motion, lifts its feathers, smooths them, and begins to render a pitch-perfect imitation of a little boy shrieking, sounding to Avis like, *Non! Non! Donnez-moi! Donnez-moi!* Avis flinches, rankled by the screaming.

Who keeps such a bird in a cage? Big as a monkey. Huge and slick and oily.

She pushes aside the reedy palms and steps into the Calvadoses' backyard. The shrieking bird breaks off, apparently shocked into silence by this figure bursting from the trees, then reverts to a frenetic shuffling motion. "Uh, uh, uh, uh!" it cries, as if stumped. It's hard to see the creature clearly through the curving bars of its cage, but Avis notices a bit of bright orange on the beak: a mynah. "Uh! Uh! Uh! Uh!" it goes on, scrabbling and sobbing, a small, desolate minotaur.

Avis strides past the cage, her mind compressed into something murderous. How long has she been listening to this racket anyway? The noise is enough to drive anyone mad . . . she moves along the side of the house, noting the blistered paint, warped windowsills, frowsy, intricate weeds popping up between the bricks of the walkway. She doesn't remember the house looking so unkempt when the professor was living there.

As she walks to the front of the house, however, it occurs to Avis that this is not the socially accepted way to approach a stranger's home. If anyone is home—perhaps washing dishes, looking out the back window—they might well notice her creeping around in her apron and clogs. Avis stops in the neighbors' front yard. Had she been about to walk right up and knock on that door? In that instant, all she can imagine is how horrified Brian would be, his concern with the opinions of others, and how he loves to remind her: "You might not want to deal with the public, but I *do*." Unnerved, Avis touches her hair, proceeds to the sidewalk in front of the house, makes a right, and walks all the way down the block to Salzedo as if she's just out for a stroll. She makes a left on Salzedo, another left onto Viscaya, and goes home.

THE NOISE CYCLES through a repertoire. There are the sounds of the child's cries, sharp as chips of ice. Then, somehow more intolerably, the sounds of a woman's tremulous laughter that transform into sobbing, then back to laughter: thick, raw sounds. Avis squints into the light.

Propped on a small easel she uses for orders and ingredient lists is a request for a *gâteau Saint-Honoré* bearing the legend *Together, Toujours* in scrolling Edwardian script. She attempts to calm herself with her work. It's a nicely time-consuming cake, though Avis finds it distasteful to deface her pastries with these slogans—even *Happy Birthday*—using fine creations as billboards. Today's order, from a Cutler Road matriarch, is an anniversary commandment—*till death do us* . . . Avis embarks on the journey of the cake which will require both the work of *pâte feuilletée* and the *pâte à choux,* a carefully timed caramel, a *crème patissière,* as well as a *crème Chantilly.* She has barely begun the long folding and kneading for the puff—her fingers already reddened from the chilled slab—when the bird noise seems to reach a new crescendo. Avis kneads, then overkneads—the sound like a finger rubbing at a sore spot, a fiery shrieking: *Fie! Fie! Fie! Fiiiiiiiiie!*

What was it Brian was always talking about? Strategy, organization, plan of attack? "Plan of attack," she says out loud, staring at the windows. "Plan, plan, plan."

She goes to the computer on her little desk, switches to New Document, and begins writing:

Dear Neighbor:
Welcome to the neighborhood. Obviously ours is a "close-knit" neighborhood—there isn't a lot of space between our houses! While I'm certain you mean no harm, I have to tell you, when you put your parrot outside in the morning, it begins making a lot of noise. Surely the bird is just lonely for you—you probably work away from home. I, on the other hand, like many others—have a home business. There is no such "escape" for me. I need some peace and quiet in order to concentrate, and the bird makes this impossible for me. Its voice is piercing—it can be heard in every room of our house, even with all the doors and

*windows shut. It is a hideous assault—it starts before dawn
and screeches without cease. If you don't do something immediately to silence the creature, we will be FORCED to contact the
authorities and . . .*

The noise beats on outside her window, a remorseless, piercing caw.
Avis stops and glares at the screen, fingers trembling, she writes:

Damn DAMNDAMNITALLTOHELL

She prints out the letter, gets up, goes into the bathroom, splashes
cold water on her face. Avis returns to the desk and reads what she's
written: she sounds so crazy that it frightens her.

AVIS PUTS ASIDE the *Saint-Honoré* and decides to embark on a
new pastry. She's assembling ingredients when the phone rings in
the next room. She ignores it as she arranges her new *mise en place.*
This recipe is constructed on a foundation of hazelnuts—roasted,
then roughed in a towel to help remove skins. These are ground into
a *gianduja* paste with shaved chocolate, which she would normally
prepare in her food processor, but today she would rather smash it
together by hand, using a meat tenderizer on a chopping block. She
pounds away and only stops when she hears something that turns out
to be Nina's voice on the answering machine:

". . . *Ven,* Avis, you ignoring me? *Contesta el telefono!* I know you're
there. Ay, you know what—you're totally impossible to work for . . ."

Avis starts pounding again. Her assistants never last more than a
year or two before something like this happens. They go stale, she
thinks: everything needs to be turned over. Composted.

She feels invigorated, punitive and steely as she moves through
the steps of the recipe. It was from one of her mother's relatives, perhaps even Avis's grandmother—black bittersweets—a kind of cookie
requiring slow melting in a double boiler, then baking, layering, and

torching, hours of work simply to result in nine dark squares of chocolate and *gianduja* tucked within pieces of *pâte sucrée*. The chocolate
is a hard, intense flavor against the rich hazelnut and the wisps of
sweet crust—a startling cookie. Geraldine theorized that the cookie
must have been invented to give to enemies: something exquisitely
delicious with a tiny yield. The irony, from Avis's professional per-
spective was that while one might torment enemies with too little, it
also exacted an enormous labor for such a small revenge.

The luxuriously laborious process takes Avis into late afternoon:
ignoring the flicker of pain in her lower back, intent on her anger
(she imagines going next door, offering cookies, making a gentle
complaint, and all the ways her neighbor will be mortified). Eventually Avis arranges the bittersweets on a footed silver tray delicately
limned in tarnish, stretches plastic wrap over this, then walks out
her front door.

Their neighbor's back door is perhaps sixty feet away on a diagonal line across the backyard. But Avis climbs in the car, tray of cookies beside her, makes a left on Viscaya, a left on Salzedo, a left on
Camillo, pulls up in front of 378, and parks.

The bird cry pierces the closed windows of the car: it seems to have
assumed a higher, shrieking, Dopplerized frequency, sawing into the
very bones of her cranium. Avis holds the tray aloft on one back-bent
hand—the way they whisked out the pastry trays at the Demitasse.
On the tray, propped beside the cookies, is a handwritten note on one
of her catering cards bordered by vines and blossoms: *Welcome to the
neighborhood!* The shriek heightens vertiginously, migrainously, as
she walks up the red-bricked driveway. The house itself is a canary-
yellow stucco with old flat white roof tiles; royal blue awnings extend
over the windows and blue Moorish tiles line the concrete step.
There's no car in the neighbors' driveway, not even a battered Tercel
or Quattro for domestic help. Avis decides to leave her plate and card
on the front step and flee: she feels a rush of adrenaline, an impish
sense of trespassing. Geckos skitter like sprites across the walkway as
she approaches. She hesitates, imagines this neighbor coming home

to a plate of nibbled cookies, chocolate webbed footprints. There's no protected place to leave the cookies on the wide stone hip of the front entry. She stands before the front door, agonizing. Finally she grasps the brass circle on the door and gives it three raps.

No answer. She waits, squinting into the dark mantle of trees on this block. Two more raps. She turns to go when the front door hisses open. Startled, Avis turns back. The parrot noise ceases, and stillness, an unearthly afternoon silence, rises from the earth. A slight woman with dark brown skin stands in the doorway. She's wearing an old-fashioned cotton garment with rickrack around the neck and hem—the sort of thing that used to be called a housedress. Her face is neutral, open, almost drowsy—as if she had just awakened from a nap—but her mouth is firm. She doesn't speak or smile: she stands there waiting, her eyes two glimmering black dashes.

"I . . . made . . . these . . ." Avis hazards. "Hello."

The woman doesn't look at the plate. She stares at Avis. Avis senses a rising, palm-dampening fever. Half of Miami doesn't speak English. She tries a word or two of her humiliating Spanish, "Yo . . . estoy . . . una . . . vecino . . . um, vecina . . ." Nothing.

Now the woman seems impatient, eager to return to her nap. She steps back, the door narrows a fraction of an inch, and Avis notes that she doesn't feel the vapor of air-conditioning that exudes from most homes in the Gables. Her gaze flits up: the louvered windows of the house are tilted open. In late August, no less. Open invitation to mold. She holds up the plate again. "This is for you. *Para usted?* To say welcome to the neighborhood. *Saludad.* Also, I want to tell you that in the morning? When you leave it outside—your parrot—*su . . .* um . . . *pajaro? es . . . un poco . . .*" She makes circular, feathery gestures with her hands. "Your bird is too loud."

The woman's faint right eyebrow appears to lift.

"So. Well." Now Avis feels impossibly foolish, certain the woman doesn't speak English. She must be the housekeeper after all—sleeping on the job. Probably an illegal. "These cookies . . . for the people who live here," she says slowly, lifting the plate practically into the woman's chest. But she does not take them. Finally Avis relents and places the tray on the entryway at the woman's feet. Let the lizards have them! She dusts off her skirt as she straightens up. The woman's eyes are wider now, though her lower face remains immobile. "Whoever it belongs to—that goddamn bird," Avis says, "is driving me out of my mind." She gives the woman a brisk wave and walks off the step.

Brian

THE BACK OF GAVIN HENNIGAN'S BENZ IS DUSKY with late-afternoon light, a miraculously dry August day. The near-evening could have been plucked from any number of near-evenings from Brian's college life—riding around with friends, a beer held beneath the dash. He feels good—it's been a while since he's felt pressure at the center of his chest or had to sweat his way awake through the lonely middle-of-the-night.

Still, concerns flitter over him, embedded in the light racing through the car windows: a tricky application for a variance, half-written contracts, permeable wording. They used to be judicious, PI&B—especially compared with other developers—they were strategic and deliberate in the way they picked sites and new projects, but over the past five years (he gazes over the bay at a creamy 38-foot Hinckley): poor workmanship, substandard materials. Lately, PI&B has focused on tear-downs—on the Beach, in the Grove, the Gables, and downtown—throwing up buildings one after another. Parkhurst and his clients rush into board meetings clutching MLS printouts, sweating through the armpits of their jackets. '05's been the wildest yet—even now in the thick of hurricane season. Exciting if you can stand the exposure. After Hurricane Andrew, and last year, an iron lashing from Hurricane Charley, he'd thought investors would cool off on South Florida. Increasingly Brian feels that living in Florida is an act of both rebellion and willful perversity—like rebuilding a house on the train tracks. The city blocks that PI&B develops acquire such exorbitant price tags that Brian feels, at times, there is no connection between work and reality.

When Brian was in law school (those solemn, solitary days, illuminated only by the glow of future hopes), he was serious and earnest in his pursuit of principles, and he embraced the contractual ideal of *ad idem*—meeting of minds. He had classmates who claimed to be already jaded—who knew, they said, that law—especially corporate law—had virtually nothing to do with "justice." Some rolled their eyes when they said the word. "Only a moron," his then roommate Dennis Litton had stated, "believes in justice anymore. It's like believing in the Easter Rabbit."

Now Brian rubs his fingers over the ridge of his brow. His eyes rest on the mooring field, boats like white stars on blue waves. Javier, next to Brian in the back, shifts his body uncomfortably. "Hey, man," he says, "what's going on this weekend?"

This will segue into a dissection of all things Miami Dolphins: the prospect is slightly unbearable. Brian's felt distracted lately, prone to staring out the window after his phone calls have ended. He glances at the billowing sky over the causeway. "*Nada*. How about you? What's on with you and Odalis?"

Javier doesn't look at Brian as he says, "Same old, same old, same old, same old . . ." He exhales heavily, as if a layer of cigarette smoke drifted on his breath. (Brian's noticed the scent of spearmint and tobacco in the restroom stalls—Odalis made Javier quit last year.) He pricks up a smile then, a bright slice of teeth, saying, "What about that genius of yours? Make his first million yet?"

"Owes it more like."

"I miss that boy—do I have to make an appointment to see him now?"

"Get in line. His mother and I do."

A thin whistle through his teeth. "Ya. Working too hard. It's not good for him. Tell him to come see me—I'll hook him up. Got a great little unit coming open on mid-beach. He could turn it around in a few weeks, double his money."

"What're you men talking about back there?" Conrad Strauss calls over the seat back. "No making money till we get to lunch."

Light flashes at Brian between the dark slots of palm trees along Government Cut. He eases thumb and forefinger over his eyes. "Got to get him to pick up the phone first."

"I still say we should get out fishing again," Javier says moodily, as if it's a point of contention. "Why not? Javito's about to head upstate for school. Let's hit Pine Island."

"Again . . ." Brian watches the big derricks lined up like soldiers along the cruise ship channel; beyond them, boats adrift on white ruffles. "I'd settle for a lousy call back from that kid. Time to time." He doesn't mention the earlier call from the strange girl.

"So we go to Homestead and grab him." Javier turns to his own window.

They drive on to Miami Beach, past an array of towering edifices and scaffoldings flanking the bayside—two of them new PI&B constructions. Once past the massive projects, the beach scale returns— squat, geometric, funky Art Deco hotels, chalk-white office buildings with orange-tiled roofs, homes with Mediterranean archways and columns, all slide by. The men turn right on Washington toward the bottom of South Beach—an area that used to be the worst of the worst—slums and junkies and thieves. Now, all is beautifully revitalized: gleaming buildings, wooden walkways through plumes of beach grass, and the ocean just beyond. Brian surveys it with satisfaction; at the back of his mind, there is simultaneously a glade, verdant, arboreal, and filled with tilting butterflies, and, beyond this, one thin, nearly invisible, thread of despair.

SECOND WEDNESDAY LUNCH happens at a padded bar booth at Joe's Stone Crab. There's the usual jockeying for places. No one orders the crab. Gavin sips a highball, listlessly watching the neckline of their server's blouse. Chantelle, one of the few female servers, lowers herself upright, from the knees. She's waited on their table for two years while the executives parsed new project sites. When the men get bored with each other and start bantering with her, Chantelle banters back in her soft, grave voice. Brian knows she wants to become a pediatric nurse, that she lives with her family in the South Bay Estates neighborhood. More than he knows about his own daughter.

The restaurant is packed: Swedish tourists laden with shopping bags throng the bar, heels ringing on the terracotta. The men stare at the tall blondes, their skirts like bits of fluff, tasseled purses sag from their elbows. Conrad points at some sort of photocopied schematic unfolded on the table, already butter-stained. "Four *thousand* units. Is that beautiful? Breaking ground spring '06."

"This spring? That's insane," Gavin says, voice reverberating with admiration. "Instant City."

Fred Wales, City of Miami Zoning Board, shakes hands with Brian, drags over one of the heavy wooden chairs and sits on it backwards, his arms resting on top of the chair back. "So, Prevlin Group?"

Chantelle arrives with a tray of thick-bottomed glasses. Conrad holds a sprig of mint to one side with the backs of his fingers and takes a gulp. "Oh, thank God," he says.

"Ambitious—those Prevlin boys," Brian allows, staring at the upside-down schematic. "The scope of this thing." The men watch him: along with his vaunted powers of analysis, he has a reputation as a bit of an industry seer—Parkhurst asks him to weigh in on all his big projects—particularly what communities look promising for gentrification. Brian had predicted the revitalization of Hollywood, and drawn his attention to the early rustle of activity in Wynwood; at conferences, other developers corner him by the buffet table and throw out the names of neighborhoods. "They might just pull this off."

Conrad lifts his cool, Presbyterian eyes, grins at Brian. He experiences a prickling uneasiness, like being dragged lightly against a brick wall. "Those boys are only getting started." Conrad folds up the photocopy.

"What's the point?" Javier tugs at his collar. "Redlands're a bunch of farms. Downtown, we're gonna outsell them within the quarter—

no question. People are lining up for preconstruction prices—half-mil for studios. Who's gonna move to Homestead?"

"Ha," Conrad says, stirring his drink with his finger. "That's where everyone's gonna go. People can't afford Miami, but they can afford the swamp." He licks his finger.

"With a jumbo mortgage."

"We have a wise old saying in South Florida," Brian intones. There's a murmur of laughter around the table. "Show me the money."

Waiters in black tuxes and bow ties mill around the table ferrying trays of glasses, bamboo and sugarcane stirrers, a swirl of Spanish under the strands of Sinatra. The mayor's chief of staff comes to greet Brian en route to the grand dining room, and Javier glimpses the tubby governor and entourage on their way out. A couple of the Lennar people stop by the table, one thumps Brian on the back so he can hear hollow thuds. "Whadya call a group of lawyers at the bottom of the sea?" Sydney Eckles, a site contractor, grabs Brian's arm.

Brian gives a patient half-smile to the wrought iron chandelier. "Really? You just heard that one, Sydney?"

"A good start!" Sydney hoots with laughter.

"Really, Eckles—long as you been around? Best you can do?"

He stops and straightens as Chantelle appears; two waiters place the trays on folding stands. Brian admires her queenly profile, the way she lowers each plate, giving it a slight turn to center their steaks.

BRIAN FORBIDS HIMSELF certain memories. Like the times Felice waited up past her bedtime for him to come home from work—three, four, and five years old. Her face seemed to go pale with joy when he opened the door, *Daddy*. He'd loved her profoundly: there were times he worried he loved her more than even Stanley (it wasn't true). He'd taken her to her first day of kindergarten and he'd stayed at the curb, watching, long after she'd gone in. He'd loitered outside on a bench, kicked at the grass, stared at the doors of the school until one of the teachers came out and told him—gently chiding—that Felice was playing happily. For years, he'd read her bedtime stories, her small, warm head resting against the cove of his chest: once, he'd read to her from a library book that had turned out to be more sophisticated than he'd expected. He worried she was bored—especially after a long meditation on children playing in a field—but his six-year-old daughter had looked up from her pillow, saying, "That's you, Daddy. You catch us." *No.* He couldn't think of that without feeling his throat tighten. The children were small and Brian and Avis still young, holding each other inside shining nets, in equipoise. Early spring nights where they sat together on the hood of the car eating ice cream, watching for the red pulse of a passing space station. Is that what a happy family looks like? He would have sworn it was. A family like any happy family. He wanted only to keep them whole and entire: to provide. But perhaps that's where the problem was? The drive to pour oneself out, into the providing?

Chantelle nods at Brian as she returns to clear some platters. She bears away Gavin's nearly unmarred steak with an air of mournful dignity. Brian hopes that she will take it home later for dinner. At one time the lunches had seemed useful—instead of chewing over the same old cases with other lawyers at La Loggia, these get-togethers gave him a chance to collect intelligence from a cross section of architects, bankers, elected officials. But Brian became impatient—it was all developer gossip, analysis of their next car and boat purchases, rubbing elbows with, frankly, subordinates and the semi-educated—agents, appraisers, and engineers. The indigenous population, as Javier puts it. One day Chantelle appeared, a trainee server for their table: *Affirmative action hire,* he thought. Her face a young, frightened translucence. Brian spoke to her while she studied the older server. She was the same age as Felice. He learned that Chantelle was on summer staff, still a student at Gables High: she'd been in some of Felice's classes in middle school. When he said Felice's name, her eyes ticked to his face "Everyone knew Felice, sure." She stopped. "Are you her dad?"

Brian closed his eyes and a white star of light bloomed behind his eyelids. He smiled as Chantelle asked, "Did she become a model? That's what I heard."

It doesn't matter that much to Brian if they talk to each other— simply catching sight of her is enough. These moments of contact with Chantelle are small indulgences. They rarely mentioned Felice after that first meeting, but suddenly he had a marker, a buoy in darkness. He never misses summertime lunches at Joe's. If Chantelle is out sick, he feels bereft. When she moves to his side of the table, he says, "How you doing today, sweetheart?"

"Just fine, Mr. Muir." She doesn't pause in her clearing.

"I guess you'll be heading back to school soon."

A faint smile. "I just started fall semester. But I've got morning and evening classes, so I can stay on lunch service."

"Fall semester?"

"I started at Miami-Dade."

"Ohh, yes . . ." She's eighteen now. Beginning college.

Brian catches Conrad saying to Harold Wisen, relationship manager at First Trust, "Hear we're cracking Little Haiti?"

Chantelle hands her tray to a busboy and turns.

Harold, in the visitor's seat, leans across Gavin—who now seems to be napping with his eyes open. "No shit? It's going through? Who's doing the financing? You guys must be getting that property for nothing."

"It's part of the *Design District,* friends," Javier interjects, simultaneously joking and serious, eyeing Brian, "Remember? Making the downtown bloom?"

Brian glances at Chantelle's impassive profile as she clears Conrad's plate. He should help Javier shut Conrad down before he blabs too much. Chantelle picks up the last piece of cutlery, her back straight as a carpenter's level, her expression formal.

Conrad laughs and closes his eyes to drink. "Right, right—we're saying the block's in the *Design District*—neat, huh? Northeast Fifty-sixth Street!"

Gavin says mournfully, "Aguardiente Group never got that zoning nailed down. They don't like talking to the neighbors. But our man bagged it." He nods at Brian. "High-density and mixed-use, right?"

"That zoning board." Brian can't resist the boast. "They were out for my blood."

"Always," Javier says. His wingman.

Brian gives a good dash of salt to the remains of his New York strip. "Northeast Fifty-sixth. I went to an art opening there. It looked like a combat zone. There was this weird old space, closer to the west. I think it used to be someone's house."

"Residential." Conrad checks the bottom of his drained highball glass, then looks around hopefully. "Suburban. As in suburban warfare. Ha."

"That area, they'll be begging for high density. You're doing them a favor," Harold says. "So you *are* all set with that financing?"

"Gentrify me, oh baby!" Conrad breathes, lifting the glass from his server's hand.

"Shit, man." Javier has a look of furious concentration, staring around the table. "Build on the outskirts—there's the Everglades. Suburbs is all freakin NIMBY. And try to be nice and fix up the core? They're hollering gentrification. Where the hell you supposed to put people?"

"Hey, you don't have to tell me," Harold says dolefully.

"Follow the money, baby," Conrad says.

Brian draws himself up and looks around at the table. "We're doing good work here and there isn't a goddamned thing to apologize for. Building houses is God's work. Look at those missionaries in— where do they go? Guatemala? Putting up those shacks for people."

"Yeah, the only difference is that ours have a security system downstairs," Javier says, laughing. Brian can't tell if he's agreeing or mocking him.

"He's right, actually," Harold says. "It is God's work. I believe it."

The men nod and there's a good moment of values lining up with financial goals. Brian lowers his eyes to his steak.

"Of course some Little Haiti citizens' action group has just popped up—breathing down our necks," Gavin says.

"Day late, dollar short." Conrad is almost humming. "They got their payout. Let them try to fight us now."

"It won't look very pretty if they do," Brian says. Something about Conrad always makes Brian want to push him down a flight of stairs.

Javier has a narrow, skeptical look. "What's behind it? Anyone heard anything?"

"Stryker?" Gavin murmurs. A competing developer: Brian knows the name. A small-timer, which makes sabotage tactics more likely.

"Oh baloney," Conrad brays. "Styker doesn't know his elbow from his ass from anything . . ." He drunkenly waves the intimation away.

And the others are already distracted, draining their glasses: they don't want to talk about the actual projects; that's old news. They like to think about the next deal and the one after that. "Well, onward soldiers." Brian throws his cloth napkin on the table, accidentally spraying it with bread crumbs moments after Chantelle whisked the tabletop. "Oh God. Sorry." He tries to brush at the crumbs with his hand, spreading them everywhere. Chantelle places a restraining hand on the forearm of his jacket. "Please, sir."

He sits still, face stiff, as she brushes up all the crumbs and rights the cloth.

THE MEN'S LOBBY HAS a comforting lushness: potted palms, the lighting angled and discreet, an inviting spot for the men to make their ruminative strolls. He pushes through the doors to the inner sanctum. Entering this dim room with its splash of reflection is like catching a glimpse of a ghost. He holds his hands under the faucet, then combs them back over what's left of his hair. He stares hard at himself. There are blue shadows under his eyes, in-dwellings. What do you call one lawyer at the bottom of the sea?

Chantelle has graduated high school. He touches the mirror.

Chantelle has started college. Community college. He'd hoped his own kids would attend Cornell. She'd had to walk several blocks out of a poorer neighborhood to attend Gables High. He feels proud of her.

His own mother had seemed the reserve of all love. But there was a thread of delicacy in her: he felt it within himself—a sensitivity to the world, a snappable filament. She suffered, stranded in a family of men, eating sweets, her body softening, losing the bones in her face, her afternoons spent sleeping or hunched in tears, a kind of pure surrender. At times, over the last few months, Brian too has felt visited by that old grief, the allure of surrender.

What. What should he and Avis have done? Put their girl's face on a milk carton?

Missing: Felice Muir, Age 13.

Kidnapped by herself.

Motivation: Unknown.

What child does such a thing as that? Could she have been that unhappy? The temptation was to blame each other: Her mother's daughter. Avis pointed to Brian's absence from their life. They fought about what to do. Open a bank account for her? Rent an apartment? She refused everything they tried to offer. "She can always come home," Brian finally said, his voice ragged with exasperation. "She *knows* where we live."

Felice seemed so tiny and delicate at birth, it had taken them weeks to attempt bathing her. Avis was terrified of dropping the baby, so Brian held her: he remembered the moment that he'd dipped her tiny body, white and curved as a lotus, into the basin. Her newborn eyes widened and fastened on his—a look that pierced him. He felt he would lay down his life for his daughter. But things were never easy between Brian and Felice. She became aware of her own beauty, fussing over her clothes and hair, it seemed, from the moment she recognized her own reflection. She showed no interest in the ball games he attended with Stanley, not even in backyard games of catch and badminton. Brian caught his own stern expression flickering over her head as she looked into the mirror.

Still, there were many good moments: the hunt for shells on Sani-bel Beach, long weekends in the Keys, the spring break when Felice stood at the end of the pier beside Brian and her brother. He'd bought them each their own Zebco reels and she waited patiently for the line to nod, eventually landing more than Brian or Stanley. Those long, warm afternoons of blue diamond skies, soaking a line, the flashing twists of fish, those belong to Brian and his children.

There was one night in particular: the four of them in a vacation rental on Pompano Beach, a fifties-era unit in the beach grass. He remembers a burning white circle of moon and the night, scooped out, almost cobalt behind it. There was some excitement on the beach, voices under their window. A little girl banged on their door, still open at nearly midnight, and called through the screen frame, "They're hatching!"

Stanley and Felice rushed from their beds, Brian and Avis fol-lowed, laughing. They huddled around a staked, taped-off section of beach, waiting with a small crowd as the sand trembled, gray under the moonlight. It bubbled, then shed from the backs and flippers of emergent baby turtles. They watched the tiny creatures—tens, hun-dreds—struggle over the sand to the shoreline, flippers beating blind and determined. Brian watched his children watching, craning for-ward, pacing the sea turtles, fanning away any little stones or shells. In that warm, salty night, he felt as if the texture of time itself were thickening, settling over them, as if they would be held together in the froth of air, its silky threads attaching and keeping them safe, everlast-ing family.

THE RINGING ON THE other end steadies Brian as he drifts near the foyer by the entrance. He turns to face into the wall. "Hi, hello dear."

She says, "Brian," and then, "How is your meeting? Did you eat?" Her voice is stiff. Still angry about their earlier fight? Then it comes to him: Felice didn't show. He'd been almost certain this would happen again. The receiver feels hot and a fringe of sweat breaks out above his temples. The phone slides a little in the damp of his palms. He rests his forehead against the wall. "Oh darling," he whispers, "what can we—what—" But there's a rumble of voices behind the doors, and then the whole table of men emerges from the bar. Gavin nods to Brian as he lumbers through the front lobby. Javier parks himself right next to Brian and leans against the wall. Something tightens in Brian's gut; he turns into the receiver and asks Avis, "How you holding up?"

"Just fine, dear. Don't . . . I'm fine."

Javier interlaces his fingers and straightens his arms behind his back, then tips his head from side to side, popping the vertebrae in his neck.

Brian wants to tell her about Chantelle, ask what she thinks Felice is doing with her absconded life, but this seems, now, deliberately cruel. "You know—is that bird still making a racket? How's the noise level?"

"Brian," she says more quietly. "Don't worry about that."

"Well, it affects the whole neighborhood." His voice grows professional. "There are nuisance laws. It's why we live in the Gables. Civil codes."

"You know what, let's not talk about the bird." She sounds almost like a phone-menu voice, like the automated answering service at Citibank.

Javier hums, whisper-sings not quite under his breath.

"Well. Damn thing."

"Brian. I'm sure you're right."

"Well . . . I don't mean to . . ." His voice seems to echo back at him. "I'm not trying to be *right*." Brian lowers his voice into the phone, cups it with his other hand. "Dear? Are you there? Can we— let's talk again later . . . They're waiting for me."

"I'm sure they are."

"Now, why are you so—what is it? *Is* it that bird?"

"Brian, it's nothing."

"It's nothing," he echoes. "Well, I have to take you at your word."

Long pause, then, "Yes—consider it an oral contract, okay?"

He winces, places his hand on his head. "Okay, well. I guess I'll call later, okay?"

No signal. He snaps the phone cover closed. Indicted, found guilty. He crosses his arms and blots his hands on his sleeves.

"How's the wife?" Javier jingles the change in his pockets.

Brian makes a waving-off gesture, but Javier claps a hand on Brian's shoulder and says, "Hey man, really."

"What?"

"Honestly, how's things. How's the *niño*? He doing okay?"

Little boy. The same thing Javier calls his twenty-two- and twenty-five-year-old sons. "As far as I can divine." Brian laughs softly; he can't meet Javier's eyes. Javier talks to his children every day—his married daughters live down the street from him. He never asks about Felice.

"I meant what I said before. You know what we should do? We should take Javito and Juanchi and Stanny out bonefishing on the boat again, like the old days."

The old days. They went fishing exactly once. Juan hooked a rock and snapped his line. Stanley was so sun-scorched the skin across his nose and forehead turned purple. Still, it was a good trip—they drank beer with lime—even fifteen-year-old Stanley—and ended up going out for grilled mahi since they hadn't caught anything. "I don't know, Jav—Stan works through the weekends these days. He's doesn't get a lot of time off."

"See, that's your problem—you guys working nonstop like robots. Is that what life's for? You really want to work so much you don't enjoy the being alive part?"

Brian smiles through an internal sag: Javier sees no divisions between himself and his kids. He eyes the rectangular suit backs of his exiting associates, gauges the tenor of their laughter. They're not laughing at him: he knows this. As an attorney, there's little he finds more tiresome than paranoia. What's that joke? Just because you're paranoid doesn't mean they aren't laughing at you? He touches his eyes with his fingertips. When he looks up again, he notices Javier watching him. "Where were you today, man?"

"What're you talking about?"

"No, no." Javier looks around impatiently. "I know you, man. You *weren't there*. Not in the car, not at lunch. You were"—he flits his fingers in the air—"all gone."

Brian is struck by his certainty: *does* Javier know him? A fishtail of fear slips through him. "It's been a hard time. With Avis. This year, it's . . ."

"I knew it." Javier's hands drop loosely against his sides. "When is it not the woman? I get it. But you got to draw that line, right? It's interfering with your superb concentration, man. Maybe you're fooling the others, *hombre,* you're not fooling your old partner here. Take that beautiful girl out to dinner. Enjoy each other. You're letting things get to you. Listen to me—you can't let them get you. Keep it light, right?"

"Light," Brian repeats, checking his Blackberry. "Yeah—I don't know if that's on the agenda."

Javier slaps him on the shoulder. "Sure it is, buddy. Easiest thing in the world."

BACK AT HIS DESK, Brian jots notes to himself: *research—NE 56th? Ask Agathe to look up precedents. Neighborhood Associations.* He's got an idea for the in-house newsletter's "Legal Eye" column—Considerations of the Ethical Developer: Established Neighborhood Fabric Vis-à-Vis New Development. Brian types bullet points on the computer: Quality of Life; Family and Friend Connections; Sense of History and Stability; Connection to Place. Parkhurst loves it when Brian "talks ethics," which Jack believes is more compelling coming from legal counsel than from "some fairy PR guy." "Proof we're not one hundred percent bastard," Parkhurst cracked. Now that Brian has a staff of associates, paralegals, and clerks, he has more time to construct a conscience for PI&B. His argument with Avis lingers, a sooty dankness in the office, behind his eyes. Brake noise and car horns slice through the window. His hand slips over the mouse when a fragrance reaches him. It's familiar, yet he can't place it: barely sweet, like funeral orchids, the earth of geraniums. For some reason he thinks again of Felice—sprawled on the living room floor, mouth pursed, removing toenail polish, her narrow back hunched over her work, purple-stained cotton balls all around, black hair scooped over one shoulder. An entire summer of polish remover and stained cotton balls. That sweetish acetone reek. "Doesn't it bother you?" he'd asked Avis—always so particular about keeping the house "clear." "Of course." She'd held up her own trimmed hands. "But she's that kind of girl."

A voice behind him says, "Brian? Am I disturbing you?"

Fernanda is leaning in his office door. He sits back in his chair open-eyed. She enters, takes the leather guest chair, and lets the seat glide back, then forward. "I'm sorry to interrupt." Her voice a soft undertow. "I wanted to thank you for helping me earlier."

"Helping?"

Her smile tilts, half-bitten. "Well, Javier," she says. "He keeps 'dropping by.'" She curls her fingers into quotation marks. "And there's nowhere to hide in these glass offices up here. I don't know how you guys get anything done in these fish tanks."

"Christ, that Javier," he says, feeling disloyal. "A little too hands-on, sometimes."

"That's one way to put it." She leans over and picks up the framed photo on his desk. "Aha." She tilts it, a sliver of light in her palms. He has a funny impulse to reach forward, slide it gently from her fingers. "Is this your family?"

Javier took it. The photo shows Brian with his arm around Avis's shoulders, and Stanley, inches away, holding up a fish, tail lifted, he'd just caught in the Sebastian Inlet. It was a year after Felice had run away for good, the summer before Stanley left for college. A good trip. Still, the three of them look gaunt, their smiles vaporous—all photos post-Felice looked like this. "Yeah," Brian says. "That's them." *Them?*

"They're charming. How old is your son?"

Brian clears his throat. "Well, he's twenty-three now. I guess he was almost eighteen in that shot."

"And this is your wife? She's lovely."

Brian lowers his eyes: Avis *is* lovely. Her face now not so different from when they first met: the ice tones beneath her brow, the soft corners of her lips, her skin lit like a Baroque portrait. Fernanda replaces the photo but her hand lingers a moment, hovering over his desk. He notices a dot of silver glinting at her clavicle. "I love that you have them here." She doesn't look at him but at the photograph.

When the phone rings, he glances at the phone, line two, Agathe. He presses *Off.*

Fernanda lifts her chin, puts her hands on the chair arms. "I should let you get back to it."

"No, please don't." He lifts his hand. "It'll stop." He waves at the phone. "I mean—it's probably just one of the clerks. Research reports. I can get those later."

"Oh, is that all?" She smiles archly. "Isn't that, like, your job?"

He rubs the back of his neck, squeezes it, smiling and disoriented. The city is full of such young women: they exist in a world separate and apart from his. They speak to him in a deferential way, as if he were a kindly old uncle. He recalls then the first instant of seeing Avis—seated in a college seminar—the back of her hand curled under her chin. He inhales, startled by a hit of the agitation and confusion of twenty-five years ago, as if time could dilate and collapse into a crystallized . . .

His BlackBerry starts to buzz, vibrating an obscene spin on his desk.

"Let me let you . . ." She's pushing out of her chair. "Somebody really wants you."

He stands also as he grabs the phone. "Give me two seconds. It's just—Agathe knows I'm not answering." He keeps one hand in midair, as if holding Fernanda in place, presses the speaker phone on with his other. "This is Muir." In his peripheral vision, he sees Fernanda give a wave and back out of the office. Brian opens his hand—*Stay!*

He lets go a sigh then, rakes one hand through his hair, settling back in the chair, watching through the glass as a city worker installs a new billboard: *Can you say Beer-veza? Se habla CHILL?* Image of a bottle of beer and an edge of lime.

"Dad?" Laughter. "That your Donald Rumsfeld impersonation?"

Brian sits up. "You got me," he says, withered. "Want to hear Karl Rove?"

"Got your calls—what's up? I've got a hundred cases of plantains I've got to cope with here." Stanley has managed, once again, to flip their positions, so he is the harried overseer and Brian's the needy old dad.

"No, no, nothing—it's just—" Now he feels uncertain—is it even worth mentioning that strange girl? "Have you heard this singer on the radio? I think her name is Nelly? I noticed this. Is it that there are *two* Nellys and one is a rapper and one is a regular singer?"

"Dad—" Stanley breaks off; there's some scuffling and a thin stream of voices in the background.

"Are they singing? Is that considered *singing*?" Suddenly he wants to know. Stanley is the authority on all such matters by virtue of being young: musicians give steel drum demonstrations in his parking lot; he has a sale bin at the front of the store, *Music of Indigenous Uprising.*

"I don't know, Dad." Another pause in which Stanley might be muttering instructions to someone. "Sure, yeah, it's singing, why not?"

"Oh." Brian falls silent. Even though Brian's son is often remote and very busy, he's also dutiful: the child they could count on. Brian presses, angling to keep his son on a little longer: "It just sounds like a mess."

"It's protest—like reggae," Stanley says peevishly. "They're angry. It's a sign of sanity."

"Yeah. Probably." Brian sighs.

"Dad, is—are you okay?" More voices blur in the background, a small shuffling crash and distant laughter. Always this mesh of noise at the market.

"No, no, yeah. I'm fine," Brian waves one hand in his empty office. "Um. Your mother was—she was going to meet with Felice today."

"Oh."

Brian rubs at the underside of his jaw for a moment: *mistake*.

Stan asks, "Why does she bother?"

"I'm sorry?" Brian massages his knuckles into an aching spot between his ribs. At four, Stanley was smitten, practically in tears at the sight of his newborn sister. Even in those first hours, before Felice's beauty was apparent—her iridescent eyes, the numina of her skin—Stanley was devoted. He held his sister in his lap, her tiny hands fused into fists, her face purplish with crying. He kissed her head and murmured into her damp hair.

"No, nothing."

"Yeah. Well, hey son, I got this call . . ." Staring out the window, he sees a rope of lightning flash over the skyline.

"You got what?"

"This *girl*—" Brian chuckles, embarrassed. "She called my cell and said she's your girlfriend?" He chuckles again, wishing he could stop. "She told me not to worry."

"Shit."

"Stan?" Brian presses the phone to his right ear. "What's the deal?"

"Gimme a minute here. Fuck." He hears his son's voice muffled, away from the phone, shouting something like *Nevis!* Then, "Fuck."

"Stanley, what the hell is going on?"

"It's just—she's my goddamn girlfriend."

Brian lifts an eyebrow—the last girl Stanley was seeing was not someone that a person would apply the word "goddamn" to in a million years. "What happened to—"

"*Nieves!*" Stanley is shouting, away from the phone again. He returns. "I'm sorry about that, Dad. I can't control her."

"So you know her?"

A long hot sigh. "Yeah. She must've gotten your number from my cell phone. She does stuff like that."

"Stan. This is someone—you're seeing? You're involved with?"

Pause. "Dad, listen. Can you just sort of—can you pretend like you never got that call?"

"Stan—really. What's up?"

"Nothing. Just. We've had some money issues."

"Money issues."

"Nothing really. Goddamn Citizen's finally denied our claim for the refrigerated cases."

"Oh, jeez." Last summer, Hurricane Charley took out the electricity—both mainframe and backup generator—at Freshly Grown, and three of their industrial freezers were ruined, along with extensive wind damage to the exterior of the building. The case investigator, a crimson-faced woman, kept dropping in at the store, writing reports and gazing at Stan. Brian knew his son had encouraged her—inviting her to wine and cheese tastings and baking sessions at the store; he'd given her an "appreciation basket" filled with organic pears and apples and chocolates from Vermont. Stanley can be a bit obtuse that way, Brian thinks—so focused on business that he never realizes there are other motives at work. She'd strung the investigation out for months, continually remembering some new piece of "evidence" she needed to collect or some bit of damage that needed to be photographed. She'd been encouraging about their chances, but then Stan demurred from her invitation to a home-cooked dinner.

"I had a bad feeling about that one." Brian tips the remote at the office climate controls.

"Yeah, so did we all," Stanley says morosely. He'd refused to let his father intercede in the case: Brian swallows the impulse to point that out. "And then there was all that water damage. And we've been dealing with the shoplifting thing."

"It's the local kids, isn't it?" Brian thinks but does not say, *Those Mexicans.*

"Actually, it seems to be in-house. One—or more—of my trusty staff—someone with access to the books, inventory sheets."

"Oh, Stan." Brian rubs his temples, then lifts his head. "Does that girl—that—Neeva? She have access?"

"Dad, no. It's not Nieves."

"How do you know? You said she was crazy. She *sounded*—"

"Dad, trust me."

"Why was she calling me in the first place? She made it sound like there's something—"

"What?" Stanley's tone is abrupt—tinged with the anger Brian remembers from Stanley's high school years.

Brian inhales, considers pushing back, asserting his paternal rights. "Well."

"Nieves just has some issues right now," Stanley says. "It's nothing for you to worry about. Really."

"Hey—whatever you say." He feels an ache at the back of his throat. The desire to set things right. The inability to do so. He can't get his mind to clear: the old bits of memory are there: a fog of late days at work, entire months where he didn't cross paths with his son, saw his wife only when she lay across the bed, released into a long twist of sleep. They were living in a state of hibernation—that's what it'd felt like at the time. Outside of work, every encounter and every conversation felt like a swipe of sandpaper. Now Brian suspects that what he did was worse than neglect—it was abandonment—precisely when his son needed him most. He'd thought he was gently leaving him alone—that it was what he assumed adolescence required. Brian's hand lingers a moment after he's hung up; he sits very still, his body humming with the frequency of far-off traffic.

BRIAN AND STANLEY NEVER found their way back to that early closeness, the time of the gingerbread house. Felice was born, a Miami angel: it was as if the perfumed air and sifting fronds had pervaded his and Avis's genes and given them this unbearably lovely, worthless child. Is that what he really believes? Brian rubs at his jaw. Yes: *worthless*. His son's presence had a heaviness, an unasked question. There was usually a dusting of flour in Stanley's hair, along the ridges of his knuckles. If Brian offered to take him fishing, Stanley was always game. They went on day excursions to Key Largo, Lauderdale-By-The-Sea. But he'd head right back to the kitchen when they got home, saying, "I'd better check on the starter," or slap on the hot water and start loading the heap of pots and pans into the washer.

Neither of them had interest in organized sports. Brian grieved over this: sports gave men a way to talk to one another: a language to smooth one's path through life. Brian had suffered without that language. He'd imagined taking his son to soccer practice, baseball tryouts; he'd planned to cultivate an interest in whatever activity his son took up. He hadn't counted on the son he got. After Felice left home, Stanley moved outdoors as well. He started an herb garden, then expanded, building raised beds with clean blond planks of wood, planting stringbeans, eggplant, and Brussels sprouts. He dug up swathes of the backyard for leafy greens and purples and reds, and grew a type of lettuce that was filigreed in blood-red, as if a circulatory system ran through it.

He rarely spoke to his parents—perhaps he'd blamed them for Felice's disappearance. Brian recalls one early evening, home from work, when he'd gone to the kitchen for a snack (they no longer ate together) and he found Stanley with his arms immersed in suds, the air smudged with mist. Stanley looked almost beatific, his eyes like glass, as if he'd been at prayer. Brian hesitated just as Stanley turned.

"Hey—uh—just thought I'd grab myself something."

"Let me." Stanley withdrew from the sink, shaking off his hands. "I haven't been to the store yet—there isn't much." By the time he was seventeen, Stanley had taken on the grocery shopping and food preparation. He made them stews, pastas, salads filled with the crisp vegetables from his garden. Brian was surprised that such tomatoes and onions grew in the dirt behind his house—that his son would know what to do with them. Stanley heated some refried beans, dropped a scoop of butter into a skillet and let it foam. He cracked eggs into a bowl, whisked in a dollop of heavy cream. "So, Dad." Stanley spilled the eggs into the sizzling butter. "Something I'd wanted to talk to you about."

Brian pulled up one of the tall stools by the counter. "All ears. What's up?"

Stanley gave him a bright, alert glance. "Nothing bad. It's just—you know I got into UM, right?"

Brian nodded, avoiding Stanley's eyes. Brian had attended Brown and Cornell Law. As had his own father. But Stanley's grades were mediocre, his attendance sporadic. And Avis wanted to keep him close; neither Brian nor Avis had encouraged Stanley to apply out of state or given him advice on other schools. It was this—the lack of ambition for his son—that deviled Brian even more than their lack of time together. "Yeah—it's great, Stan. I'm proud of you," Brian said. "That's a very solid school."

"Well, I hope you'll still be—because the thing is, I decided I don't actually want to go to college."

Brian stiffened. "Oh?"

"I mean—I think I really want to start a business." Stanley stirred the eggs, the wooden spoon tilted in his hand, a steady oval of motion. "I don't need school."

Brian's eyes ticked up at the kitchen: Brazilian hardwood floors, counters reflecting tiny, embedded ceiling lights, sleek white porcelain cake pedestals with thick glass covers. They'd poured nearly $200,000 into the remodel, retrofitting Avis's kitchen to professional grade. Stanley thinks *this* is what it means—what running a business is. "The grocery store?" Brian tried to sound sincere and neutral.

"I *know* I want to start a business." Stanley's voice grew hotter as he stirred. "I've got investors lined up. My friend Jason Perez says he's in—and Mrs. Gregerson, my old boss at Winn Dixie? She's very interested."

"Well, you know, the business school at UM—"

"Dad, wait—just listen. The whole organic lifestyle thing is everywhere these days, right? There are entire stores that are just organic food and vegetarian. Really committed to natural, alternative approaches."

Brian's eyes were now trained on the stirring. They'd had this conversation—in pieces—over the years. Stanley took a class in History and Deconstruction in ninth grade—the stuff they taught in schools! He'd started reading Noam Chomsky, Theodor Adorno, Ralph Nader for crying out loud. Stuff Brian didn't even want to read in *college*. The more Stanley read, the more intense he became. Brian tried to reassure himself it was just part of the evolution of adolescence. When Stanley started on *Diet for a Small Planet,* he became insufferable—quoting statistics on the environmental damage caused by a meat-based diet, giving diatribes on the imperialist legacy of the big-food industry, the plight of grape pickers in California, coffee growers in Sumatra, sugarcane haulers in Cuba. At seventeen, Stanley was fired from his job as a bag boy at Milam's for smuggling discarded cheeses, crackers past their sell-by dates, and dented cans to homeless shelters and missions. Brian had been mortified. He drove to the store and told the manager that Stanley's sister had disappeared a few months earlier and that Stanley had been struggling. The man watched Brian with a doubtful, grave frown, straightening the tie under his apron. Finally he agreed not to press charges as long as Stanley never reentered the store. Brian found himself repeatedly offering the same explanation to a series of teachers and employers.

The eggs looked molten, ivory-yellow wavelets closing behind the sharp lines of the spoon. "I don't like school, Dad. It's never been right for me—you know that. I'm not like you that way."

Meaning what? Intellectual? Cold? Out of touch? Brian drew a slow, tense breath.

"I mean, I wish I were, but I'm not—I don't get the school thing. But I *do* know business."

"I thought businesses were all part of the corporate hegemony," Brian said softly, trying to stave off the sharpness he felt. Stanley gave him another of his bright looks: Brian realized his son was terribly anxious.

"Well—yeah, usually they are. But my deal would be different. The employees would all be part-owners. It's basically the co-op model but grown up. With better food and more variety. You don't have to be a member or volunteer or buy, like, the spotted, moth-eaten fruit. The co-op sells this vegan cheese that tastes like tires. Forget it. You just pay the money and our produce will be just as pretty as the stuff at Publix. There's nothing even close to it around here, Dad!" he said in a passionate burst, his eyes shining with the kitchen lights. "I've researched this. Tons of people want to eat clean and healthy but they don't want to go into places like co-ops—they're too small . . ."

"And grubby, and depressing." Brian crossed his arms, his suit jacket pleating into the inner creases of his elbows.

"Sure, yeah. I guess they can be."

"So . . ." Brian felt the archness enter his voice—the way he'd circle in a summary statement at a hearing. "All these Miami doctors and attorneys, driving their Lexuses and Maseratis—they'll have a place to buy the nice healthy food they've always wanted."

"Yeah, exactly. We'll go mainstream with it." Stanley looked so pleased, his smile so wide and bright, Brian almost didn't have the heart to keep going. But he had to—there was a crucial point to be made. "So you're identifying a need and positioning yourself to fill it?"

"That's right."

"But if you do that . . ." Brian brought his fingertips together, let them slide the length of his fingers, interlacing. "Don't you, of necessity, end up hurting the majority of people? Meaning the poor and lower middle classes? The ones who couldn't afford the beautiful, clean food in a nice store like yours—and who'd be too anxious—too *intimidated*—to go into a place like that in the first place?"

Stanley lifted the pan from the stove. "Well, it wouldn't be *that* nice."

"Then you wouldn't get the deep pockets—all those dressed-up big spenders! Because people like that *do* want a gorgeous environment. Which is it, son? Steal from the rich or give to the poor? Because you can't have both at the same time—not legally. Remember Milam's?"

"It's not stealing *or* giving, it's—it's all legit, it's—" Distracted, Stanley scraped the eggs onto a plate beside the beans. They sent up a plume of butter steam. He slipped the plate before Brian with a spoonful of homemade salsa. "It's a whole other idea of things, Dad. It's a community."

"You mean a commune, I think. It's a beautiful idea, communism—for saints and angels."

"No—I mean *community*." Stanley dropped the pan and spatula into the sink. "Same idea as family—or a neighborhood. I know you must get it. Community has to come first, or there's nothing."

Brian picked up his fork. "Listen, Stan, Jesus. Just get your degree. College gives you a chance to live a little, think things over, meet people. You think you don't need it, but you'll always regret it if you don't, believe me."

"Dad, I can tell you right now exactly how I'm going to feel about this later—I don't want it and I don't need it."

"You *do*." Brian's tone was preemptory. Irritated, he forked up some eggs. At first he didn't taste them, but gradually he did: the curds were light, bearing traces of salt, pepper, and butter. He felt almost, but not exactly, as if he were sad. He inhaled deeply and exhaled. He stopped talking for a moment and ate. His son had made this. Even then, seven years ago, Brian was beginning to sense the size of his debt to Stanley—the permanence of it. Even before Felice was all they could think or talk about, he'd given up spending time with Stanley. It was easier to let Avis raise the children and Brian would bring home money—just as it was done in all sorts of families for generations.

Why couldn't he soften toward his son then? Instead he finished eating and put his fork on his plate and said, "You're going to college, Stan. You're too young to make this decision, so I'm making it for you. Case closed."

The sun in his window is flat and pitiless. There's an ache at the center of his chest that seems to have to do with both of his children.

We were watching the wrong child, he thinks, a sensation of some vital organ deep within dragged across a grater.

WAITING FOR THE ELEVATOR, Brian catches the flutter of Spanish just before the door opens: Esmeralda is there, speaking with Hector, the mailroom boy. *"Mandale saludos a tu madre de parte mia."* They glance at Brian.

"Thanks, I will," Hector says as he wheels out his mail cart. "Hello, Mr. Muir."

Esmeralda checks her watch. "Brian—you're leaving at a decent hour for once?"

Brian feels a streak of mild irritation: Javier sometimes intimates that deals take place in these corridors in Spanish. So Brian tries to act unconcerned—as if he *almost* understands. *Could* speak if he so desired. "You don't have to do that, you know."

"What?"

"You know." He smiles. "Switch to English for my sake."

Esmeralda stares at the closing elevator doors. "I've found that Ameri—that English speakers—think you're talking about them when you speak Spanish—even though you're usually not."

"You're American too, you know."

"I'm well aware of that, Brian." She lifts her eyebrows. "I'm even proud of it, believe it or not."

They lapse into silence, mesmerized by the digital display of floors: 25, 24, 23 . . .

"You know, Brian," Esmeralda says softly, still staring into the glassy black doors. "You might want to be a little more cautious."

His jaw loosens. "Because I said you're American?"

"No, Brian." She glares at him, folds her arms in her silk blazer over her imposing chest. She has the skinniness of incipient old age— her stockings have a fold at each ankle—but at sixty-five, she has held on to her good bones and posture.

17, 16, 15 . . .

"*Because,* you really might want to ask yourself if it's worth it." Her tone has softened into something unendurable, like pity, as she raises her presumptuous, irritating nose. He turns back to face the digital display.

"I honestly don't know—"

"Fernanda," she cuts in. "I'm talking about Fernanda."

10, 9 . . .

He sighs, squeezing the fingers of his left hand with his right. Is that a tremor? Is he actually developing a tremor? Deep in his body, he feels something shift, as if his bowels were loosening.

"That's a certain type of girl."

6, 5 . . .

He stares at her. "Oh, now, Esme."

"You're in over your head with that one."

The elevator doors swish open to the marble lobby. "Just so you know." Esmeralda strides out into the watery light, one hand curled up behind her back to wave at Brian as she goes. He remains in the elevator, watching. Twenty years ago he and Esmeralda had carried on an energetic flirtation. He'd been distracted by her topaz eyes, her tiny feet and waist, the way her upper lip curled back when she smiled, creating a minuscule dimple. But they were both married, and Brian wasn't actually interested in taking things any further. He'd even wondered if there was something wrong with him for not going after Esmeralda, pursuing her the way he heard upper management pursued affairs. And in all those years of secretaries, escorts, interns, the rumored private trysting apartments supposedly shared among the vice presidents, the junkets and conferences and the trading-in of spouses for ever-younger models, Brian had never seriously entertained the idea of having an affair.

She's jealous: he winces and smiles. He strides across the lobby, briefcase swinging; he feels rising indignation on behalf of both himself and Fernanda. *These . . . Cuban women*—he thinks—*with their village minds.*

Rufus steps forward and holds the door. Brian walks through, so preoccupied, he barely notices the man. Rufus says something. He turns. "What was that?"

Rufus's face is like a piece of carved mahogany. "Didn't say nothing, Mr. Muir."

Brian holds his shoulders squared all the way to the car. His hand shakes as he turns the key in the ignition and he checks his rearview at least a dozen times as he backs out. What is wrong with him? He needs to have that pressure in his lower abdomen checked out. If only he still believed in doctors. He cranks his big steering wheel, pouring his car into the stream of traffic—the speed demons and sudden-stoppers and befuddled elderly—the deep madness of Miami embodied in its drivers. The sky is backlit with high, dense clouds, a fast-approaching system. He passes the dinosaur crouching outside the Museum of Science. In the middle of the traffic, creeping and stopping and loitering for miles along the Dixie, he turns on the radio. The Miami skyline, pale as a leisure suit, glistens in his rearview. It's only 5:50 but the sky darkens, gathering clouds. Brian creeps ahead one car length as he tries, once again, to listen to the angry chanting of rap. It may take him an hour and a half to travel the seven miles back to the Gables. There's a rumble he assumes is a jet. Then another—this one so close he flinches, the floor of the car vibrating.

He drives under a canopy of poinciana and spiky palmettos growing up along the highway, then passes a wreck taking up the right-hand lane, and finally the traffic begins to move. Brian muttering along with the music as if there's nothing wrong at all.

Felice

FELICE AND EMERSON STRETCH OUT ON A BIT OF lawn in Flamingo Park by a stand of fragrant, inky trees, the night overhead tinted lilac by the city lights. First Emerson lies back, then he holds out his arms and she laughs but she lies down and rests her head on his chest, the fabric of his T-shirt warm and smelling of outdoors air. At first he holds as still as if she were a sparrow that'd miraculously lighted on him, only gradually relaxing. Felice thinks they will just lie there for a while, her hand riding the rise of his chest, listing to the chirp and creaking of geckos and the watery swish of cars. She remembers being six years old, sprawled in the stiff, sun-warmed grass—not quite asleep or awake—while Stanley picked the tiny strawberries in his garden. "Hey, hey, hey," Emerson murmurs into her hair, soothing her. She hears the clip and snap and thump of people getting into their cars in the parking lot—off to the clubs. There's a burst of French nearby, then some German from another direction. She doesn't even notice when she hears Spanish. Her best friends Lola, Bella, Yeni all spoke Spanish at home. She feels, as she listens to the rush of air through his chest, that it's been years since she's experienced the luxury of falling asleep, instead of passing out from exhaustion or drinking or both. It has felt, for such a long time, as if there was always something to watch out for.

ON THE DAY FELICE ran away, she brought almost nothing with her: a cosmetics bag, a tube of her mother's expensive sunscreen, a bottle of water, the sweater her brother had given her. Nothing to eat. It was cool and dry, an early March morning; still dark. Her parents had learned to watch her at night: they weren't expecting her to get up early. She watched for police cruisers and stayed on the back streets, walking from the Gables through the chain-link Shenandoah neighborhoods, then crossed U.S. 1, weaving through lanes of stopped traffic, into Coconut Grove. There were so many roller bladers, baby carriages, and dog walkers on Bayshore, she risked strolling along the big thoroughfare, taking in the view of white Biscayne Bay. It took hours to walk and by the time she'd made her way into downtown, the morning commuters were clogging the narrow street and the air was ripe with exhaust. Felice was sweat-soaked before she was even halfway across the Venetian Causeway, but before her were plains of silvery water and the mirage horizon of high-rises. She had a feeling like struck sparks flitting through her body: anticipation and scraped-away dread and grief, and clear drops of joy.

Felice hadn't wanted to move to the beach. But an older girl at a Gables party talked to her about it in a low, serious voice—you could so totally be a model. She'd heard it all her life; this girl had actually done it. She had a trapezoidal jaw and listless eyes: a strange ugly-beauty that made you stare. Felice had seen her on covers, her concave stomach and shoulders and peach-pit mouth. She said: Go do it, now, while you're young. Felice was scared and crazy enough to think it would work—she would leave the thing behind in another time; she would be changed and lifted out of her life.

After she got to the beach, she napped in a wooden booth at the back of an Internet café, and that night Felice partied with the kids out on the sand. This became her regular practice—stealing naps in cafés, partying on the beach, along with spring-breakers, drunks, transvestites, homeless kids, bums, skate punks, illegals—everyone rooting through each other's coolers, setting huge, illegal bonfires, trashing the beach grasses and dunes. Someone always had Quaaludes or Ecstasy, or tabs of acid, which she particularly enjoyed. She fell in with a group of tough, pretty Mexican girls who worked as chambermaids: they had hard brown arms and shoulders from bed-making and vacuuming. Sometimes they let Felice sleep in an empty room at night; but the air-conditioned spaces were so clean and silent she felt as if she didn't sleep there so much as float, drifting on the slab of her body. Hilda, a tiny, dark girl, gave Felice her skateboard just before she moved to Orlando. Hilda said: Skateboarding is wearing wings—which Felice found was especially true when she was high. Felice and the girls used to drop acid together—the girls favored it mainly for the extra kick of speed. They dared each other to run through the sizzling edges of the bonfire. Once, Felice got to her feet and walked into the fire. The low flames rippled and bent around her feet like water, sealing up behind her. The beach rats faded beyond the scrim of heat. She dashed across the burning wood and the bottoms of her flip-flops melted. After that, the beach patrol started to crack down; they arrested the kids who were too strung out to run away—some had to spend two months in jail—and that was the end of bonfires for a while.

BACK THEN, SHE SLEPT outdoors all the time, legs cinched in a knot against her chest, like she'd dried up in that position, and one stiff breeze off the water would sweep her away. Felice saw outdoors kids everywhere. That's what Reynaldo called them: "Like some pets are made for inside—little fluffy cats—but some you just gotta let run around outdoors." Reynaldo's dad kicked him out of the house. The police had their own name for kids like him—*thrown-aways*. Laughing, Reynaldo chanted his father's words, *bestia, perro, serpiente, maricón* . . . "I called him a Colombian redneck. Asshole. He came after me with a machete. Lucky he was so fat—he couldn't move fast enough to kill me."

There were times she found herself about to confess to Reynaldo what had happened in school. But she believed silence might be part of the punishment—that telling would somehow lighten it. Anyway, the outdoor kids didn't tell so much about where they came from—not unless they could make it a joke, like Reynaldo did.

Felice met Alma at one of the bonfire parties at the beach. Alma wanted to be a model and she said Felice could come live with her and they could be models together. It had seemed like a good plan. Alma lived with her mother in a tiny ground-floor apartment, so Felice slept in a battered recliner in the living room. Then the phone started ringing with modeling requests for Felice: Alma scowled and chewed at her nails while Felice chatted with booking agents.

Alma's friend Bethany came around the apartment whenever she needed a shower or some food. Bethany was maybe fourteen years old: her face had a feral, foxy quality, her eyes full of glinting light, as if she could see in the dark. There was a thread of grime like a shadow along her jaw, her nails were lined with dirt. She talked about something she called her "baby" that Alma said was code for crack cocaine. Bethany ate candy mostly, clutched in her pointed, tiny hands, her face pinched in a nearsighted squint. She was pin-thin— the size of an eight-year-old—and had a stream of "clients."

Felice couldn't stand Bethany—her small teeth or her chatter. She couldn't stand her furtive manner—the way her gaze roamed around, as if she were looking for something to steal. Lots of outdoor kids were like that: after a year on her own, Felice was also beginning to sense some of those qualities in herself. But Alma thought Bethany was "hilarious," with her stories about seducible police, executives with fetishes, tourists with poisonous breath. There were her detailed, depressing dreams, and the way her voice sped up, clicking spit or stretched out like something unraveling, depending on the drug.

Alma's mother cleaned houses in the afternoons, then worked a night shift in an imaging lab at Miami Beach Community, so Alma and Felice usually had the place to themselves. One night around 2 a.m., the girls were sitting around drinking Diet Cokes, watching a dumb reality show about people starving on a tropical island. There was a bang on the window and Felice jumped; she turned to see Bethany's grubby face pressed to the glass. She wished Alma would tell her to get lost. Instead Alma giggled. "Oh my God—Bethany is insane." They went outside: Bethany was so stoned she swayed from side to side, rippling with laughter. "I gotta take a leak, you guys!" she brayed.

It was a late-summer night, the warm air was filled with bugs like ruby dots in the darkness. Felice wished she weren't there. She never would have hung out with anyone like Bethany in school. Though sometimes the girl's slanted smile, the forced, splintered quality of her laughter, reminded Felice of Hannah, and a wave of dizzying sickness and guilt rushed over her.

"Go for it!" Alma sat on one of the squat cement posts that lined the building's front entrance. "We're all outside in nature. That's what animals do." Alma propped herself with a straightened arm and her brown hair swayed in a curve down her back. When Felice first met Alma, she was working as a temp in several of the Miami Beach modeling agencies and she had all sorts of friends and "contacts." But Felice gradually came to understand Alma was just desperate for people to like her.

"You think I won't?" Bethany's laughter made her look old, wrinkles cracking around her eyes. She plopped down on the patch of grass in hysterics, kicking her legs, panties around her knees, peeing on herself and into the grass. Like a baby. Alma told Felice that Bethany hadn't even known what her period was—she'd come to her, shaking and tear-streaked, and Alma'd had to explain everything, show her how to use a tampon, give her aspirin. "She left blood all over the toilet seat," Alma said, rolling her eyes. "My mom shit a total brick."

That night, Bethany (now smelling of pee) wanted to go out and Alma immediately agreed. Felice wasn't sure if she was even allowed in the apartment without Alma. Alma's mother put up with having Felice underfoot, but she muttered about her daughter's "user-loser friends."

First they went to The Sinker, then to Gerk's, places where they wouldn't be carded. The bars seemed interchangeable to Felice: starchy triangles of light suspended over pool tables, jukeboxes, waves of rancid grease, nicotine, and old beer. The men leaning against the bar automatically looked the girls over. Their eyes lingered on Felice, then slipped to Bethany. At the second bar, a man with an oily gray ponytail reached for Bethany, pulling her close; Felice watched Bethany turn pliable and childlike, pressed against the side of the man's gut, her hands resting on his half-buttoned guayabera. The man tongued his cigar from the front to the corner of his mouth. *"Esta es mia!"*

After he'd bought them rum and Cokes, the girls moved on to another bar Bethany knew about, closer to the beach. It was in the basement of an apartment building and the only marker was a little acid blue lightbulb above the door. Felice didn't like the look of the place. Alma said, "So leave if you want to, you big wuss."

This place was the worst one yet—its sour old reek mingled with something chemical, as if it were built on a toxic waste dump. The bar had a flinty light, like that of an office in a nightmare, and except for a few hazy forms at the bar, it was deserted. Even Alma mumbled, "Fuck, Bethany—the fuck kind of place is this?"

The bartender nodded, his white cap of hair dimly visible. He had some sort of tattoo that crept up his temple, extending halfway onto his forehead. Bethany went over to one of the men leaning against the back wall. A few minutes later, Felice, Alma, and Bethany sat at a table in the corner with a dusting of white powder on a ceramic plate like the ones in her mother's kitchen. They weren't even going to hide it. No one—not even the bartender—seemed to pay any attention. The man crouched over the powder, chopping it up with a butter knife and scraping it into lines on the plate. Felice thought they looked like mathematical symbols—equal signs and minuses—a coded warning. He handed Alma a rolled-up twenty. His name was Gary. He had one clear green eye, and one murky green one that lazed in the wrong direction. Felice didn't like his fawning manner or the way he put his hand on Bethany's head while she snorted, as if holding her underwater. Most of the kids Felice knew couldn't afford real cocaine. Felice snorted less than half a line, gulped back the chemical drip from her sinuses. "I'm good."

Gary smiled, his teeth big as chalk. "You don't like my present? That's not crack, you know—that's the real shit. You think it's full of baking soda and Ivory soap?" He turned to Alma and Bethany. "I don't see any soap bubbles coming out of the princess's nose? Do you see bubbles coming out of her nose?"

Gary watched as Alma and Bethany finished the powder. Bethany straightened up, shivering and sucking air through her teeth. She waved her hands. "Mmm!" Alma rubbed her nose fiercely with the flat of her hand. "Everybody happy?" Gary asked. The girls collected their bags as if they were leaving a restaurant, and trooped out of the bar into the soft night. Felice still tasted the acrid drip. She wasn't sure if she had a buzz or if it was sheer relief that made the air seem so feathery. *"Finally,"* she blurted. "God—did you ever think we'd get away from that slime ball?"

Alma elbowed her and Felice realized that Gary had followed them out. He caught up to Bethany and put his hand on the nape of her neck. "What about my tip?" Felice grimaced at Alma, trying to stave off a beat of fear, but Alma'd had the most to drink: she rolled forward, unsteady on her feet; head swinging as if too heavy for her neck. After just a few blocks, Alma sat down on some cement stairs leading up to another apartment building and grabbed the edge of the step with both hands. Her head tipped forward. Felice sensed the weight increasing in the front of her own temples, as if she'd snorted lead dust. She waved to Bethany and said she'd have to help Alma get home. Bethany twisted around under the man's hand, her eyes small and hard, before Gary jerked her forward.

Felice stood there watching Bethany stumble up the street beside the man. Alma was already passed out, her upper half slumped at the waist, so her face rested on her knees and her arms dangled to her ankles. Felice would've been content to curl up on that step beside Alma. They were on a quiet residential street, dead-ending at the lip of the beach: everyone was indoors, peacefully asleep. But Felice couldn't stop seeing Bethany's face—contracted, mottled crimson, as if fright could seize up under the skin. After a minute of dread and profound indecision, Felice started up the street after her. She went cursing Bethany under her breath, walking at first, then trotting. She spotted them at the opposite end of the block as she rounded the corner. They were hard to see in the dark; the man was pressing Bethany into a shadow against the side of a building, pinning her with his body. As Felice came closer, she saw Bethany's head turned flat against the bricks. Uncertainty wobbled inside Felice: bat wings seemed to pulse in the air. One or two cars swished past. It was a wide public street but no one was out, the whole island weirdly deserted.

Barely two weeks earlier, she and Alma had been walking along Ocean Drive when a rumbling growl had stopped them. They craned back, shielding their eyes, watching a helicopter slide over their heads and out over the water. It stopped about half a mile out, hovering in place like a dragonfly. Squinting, Felice saw a rope or ladder flung from the side and dark forms—people!—being lifted, seemingly plucked directly from the sparkling waves. Tourists gathered on the sidewalk to watch, commenting on the scene. The silhouetted event, from that distance, seemed almost balletic. People around them started clapping, then someone made a comment about *spearfishing for Haitians,* and a few people laughed. Felice couldn't move her eyes away: she saw sparkling shadows for an hour afterward.

Now Bethany shifted her face, her eyes looked fixed and unlit. But then a quickness, a kind of whip-crack, slit the air. Perhaps it was just the shock of seeing Felice there at all. Bethany's mouth opened wide, a black circle. She shrieked and shoved Gary with enough force so he stumbled backwards, laughing with shock. Then Felice saw his face darken. "What the fuck! Little cunt. You fucking little—" He seized her upper arm. Bethany's hand flickered so quickly Felice almost missed the jab to his windpipe. Gary wheezed, doubled over, grabbing his throat. Bethany leapt off the curb, running, but it seemed to Felice that time wrinkled, expanding and contracting: now it slowed again, throwing details into relief: Felice saw the arc of Bethany's neck, the scorched ends of her hair, her wrinkled fingertips. She saw how the toe of Bethany's shoe snagged on a piece of broken pavement, throwing her, chin and palms slamming on the sidewalk, smearing blood. Gary scrambled after her; lunging at Bethany, he snatched at her ankle. She kicked free, smashing his fingers. He screamed and lunged and caught her again, dragged her backwards over the sidewalk. "Fucking—cunt . . ." His voice a rasp.

Felice opened her mouth but couldn't make any sounds. There was no noise anywhere but Gary's strangled wheeze. His bad eye seemed fixed on her and she felt as if she were caught in some paralyzing beam. Then Bethany started trying to kick again, her body electrified, one foot flying into his face; she let loose a tremendous, night-whitening blast of a scream.

Felice didn't remember running, only that when she came around the corner she spotted, just ahead, a girl in a pencil skirt and silk blouse crouching over Alma. The girl straightened as Felice ran toward her and started moving away. "No, no, no—it's not me!" Felice gabbled, pleading. "There's a man—he's hurting my friend—they're right over there, around the corner—we've got to call—"

"Sorry." The woman held up her hands, warding off Felice. She cut across the street. "I can't—I'm—I just can't . . ."

Can't what? Felice stared as the woman scurried off, as if *Felice* were the danger. She wanted to run after that woman, to shout, You don't *do* that! You don't *leave* people!

But it was exactly what Felice had almost done. It's what she would have done if she weren't somehow more afraid of going backwards. Nobody cared about girls like Bethany. Felice thought of the meth-head kids, their teeth burnt away to silvery stubs, eyes like crusts, as if you could see the rot of the drug eating them from the inside out. She thought of the kids who drink to unconsciousness, kids who break into homes and drink rubbing alcohol, Listerine, if there's no booze. Melinda, her arms and legs furrowed with scar tissue from slitting herself with a box cutter. She loved the feeling of it, she'd said, as much as she loved crack. One day her arm—then her whole body swelled, turned hot, an angry bluish-red: by the time they got her to an emergency room it was too late.

Felice went to Alma who was still doubled over on the step. Felice shook her with all her might, but she flopped around. Something clattered out of her pocket to the steps—a cell phone. Felice picked it up, hands trembling, and stared hard at the numbers. Her mother had given her a cell the year before, but she'd let the battery run down, had forgotten it at a bar. The numbers on the metal wafer glowed in her hand: who could she call? The police were unpredictable and dangerous; she didn't have any friends besides Alma. The girls she'd known in school would have crumpled, gone up like puffs of smoke over something like this. Night air rushed through her: Please don't let me be like that anymore. The numbered keyboard looked like beads of light under her fingers: she heard her mother's voice, it was as if Felice had summoned her from the air. There was a tidal movement within her body, her voice crying, *"Mommy . . ."*

Her mother was saying, "Felice . . . Is it *you?*"

She clutched the phone; edged around the corner: so dark it was hard to see what was going on at the end of the block. She thought she saw Bethany and the man. Felice crept toward her, keeping close to the buildings, outside the penumbra of the streetlamps. The light was dismal, a sort of absence in the air. She could just make them out: the man was on top of Bethany. Felice wanted to tell her mother what was happening, but she couldn't speak. She clung to the cement face of a building, her thoughts cut to pieces.

The phone fell out of her hands, an object on the sidewalk that spoke with a miniature version of her mother's voice. She backed away, staring. Behind her, another sound crept up, a metronomic beating: Felice lifted her head to see a lone car stop at the intersection. White with a tattered convertible top, its windows were black, as if the interior was filled with smoke, and a growling thud bounced up the street. The chambermaids had warned Felice to stay clear of cars like this: Haitian gangbangers, Miami Kings, the MS-13 guys down from California. "They'd steal a girl like you," Hilda had said, "and sell you. Make you into a slave, somewhere far away, and no one would ever hear from you again." As Felice approached, the music crept over her—a dire, unintelligible voice chanting warnings. The engine roared so loudly it strummed across her bones. She slapped her hands on the tinted glass of the driver's window. It lowered a few inches and she made out black eyes, a small black tattoo at the outer corner of one eye. "Please—please . . ."

"Qué te pasa, qué quieres?"

There was something about the eyes that struck her as a kind of perfection: she couldn't look away. *"Un hombre—quiere matar a mi amiga*—please—he's got a knife I think—*tiene un cuchillo."*

"Fuck, man! No fucking way." This came from the backseat. *"No coño, vámonos de aquí ahora, vete, coño, vámonos!"*

There was a quiver of motion within the car and for a terrible second Felice thought he was about to pull away. A light rain had started like static. She put her hands on the partially lowered window: she didn't care if he buzzed it back up; she wouldn't let go. She'd caught an accent in his Spanish. Haitian? She'd known a Cuban-Haitian boy in her school—Andres. Once, he'd walked up to Felice in his low baggy shorts and polo shirt and asked her, You know what they call the color of those eyes? She'd shrugged. "Violet," he'd said in his lilting voice. "Those are violet."

The perfect black eyes kept staring back at her: in that moment, Felice began to feel that he knew about her, that he knew that all of this was part of her obligation. After several seconds of that gaze, fine and clear as a sheet of glass, the eyes turned toward the corner where she'd pointed. Felice held still. She could no longer hear Bethany's cries, only the booming from the car.

The eyes flicked back to her: the driver said, "We take care of it. You get out of here."

Felice stepped backwards, watching as four young men with cinnamon-colored skin climbed out of the car, moving casually as if they were going to a party. One man reaching behind to the back of his waistband. She turned and walked straight up the road without looking back. She walked all the way to the Cove, where the beach rats and outdoor kids hung out. She knew she'd be safe there. It was possible that Bethany would get away. And Alma would eventually stumble home to her mother. For one night, at least, Felice hoped the judgment was over. Sometimes the most important thing was just staying safe, and knowing and being among the right kinds of people—so you didn't get anyone into trouble. That was the most important thing of all—not getting anyone else into trouble.

FELICE CONTINUED DROPPING ACID, loving the delicious, curling sensation of the drug sinking into her system, the sense that she was afloat within her own body. She and Berry lay side by side on the sand, giggling and listening to the trickle of the ocean. Their hands swam back and forth in front of their eyes, leaving contrails. The girls whispered, murmuring, *"Wishh, wishh, wishhh . . ."* It all seemed hilarious: Felice enjoyed the shifting, transitory feelings.

They slept out on the beach, but Felice's life improved with her new friend. They'd met in a crowded hall on a go-see for Gap and shared Berry's caramel Frappuccino. Berry had grown up in North Jersey in a three-story pale blue house with black shutters and gables and gingerbread trim (Felice had seen the photograph) and she knew all sorts of valuable things. Berry and Reynaldo came with their own problems of course, like their bulimia. Reynaldo's habit (or profession) of following men out of the bars. So you never knew what he'd look like the next morning, covered in bruises that turned black, bruises the size of eggplants on his chest and neck, and once his eye bulged and leaked blood and he had to have part of his eyelid sewn back on.

But they were also smart. Berry, for example, taught her to shoplift at nicer places, like the Lord & Taylor or the Saks Fifth Avenue at Bal Harbour. Berry and Felice were careful not to return to the same store, never to steal more than an item or two at a time. The salesgirl would ring up new jeans, a silk tank top, and baby doll dress—snipping off the alarm tags—then suddenly Berry would decide that she needed to try everything on again: she'd sneak out of the dressing room while

Felice sent the clerks all over the store on errands for matching belts and handbags and scarves.

"They *expect* you to shoplift at Swim N' Stuff and the secondhand places—those guys're just waiting to catch you," Berry explained. "Not as much at Lord & Taylor."

The staff in these palatial stores did seem resolutely disinterested, swanning around, all lethargic elegance. Felice sometimes had the impression that they were in on a grand collusion—the sales staff masquerading as wealthy women, Berry and Felice masquerading as shoppers.

Each night around 1 a.m. they'd walk over to one of the cavernous places like Mansion dressed in new jeans and heels that they kept in a locker at the Nineteenth Avenue Y. First Berry, then Felice ducked under the velvet rope, flashing silver leather wristbands that Mauricio—the head bouncer—had given them. They never paid for cover or drinks. Felice wasn't modeling much—but that was even better, Berry told her—she was *pre-discovered.* Overhead, images of singers and volcanic landscapes and smoking cars splayed across fifty-foot screens; the space rang with an industrial, metallic din, and the girls' throats ached from screaming into each other's ears. The best part of those places was that only silver wristbands were allowed on certain floors. It was as if the desires of the earth had been boiled down and Felice and Berry were part of it—the *best thing* anyone could ever be. They danced on the mobbed gleaming floor, while regular people could dance only on the stairs and upper levels, staring down at them.

It was fun to go to shoots when she was fourteen and be a sort-of model (the only real ones appeared in certain magazines—on the *covers*). People gave her clothes from new designers and paid her with hundred-dollar bills, all for letting them do stupid things to her hair and face. But she hadn't counted on how much she would hate modeling. The soul-suck of standing around, of sets and steaming lights and fussy stylists and the photographers barking commands: More *life* in the eyes—no—*intelligent* life. Give me *something!* And that one designer—his horrible, thick, old-fashioned clothes—rayons and orlons that stuck to her skin, crackling with static. He walked onto the set in the middle of shooting (Felice was supposed to look like she was pumping gas), grabbed the flesh of her upper arm, and announced that she was "heinous." She couldn't be a real model, because she was 130 pounds and only five feet nine. Both the New York scouts wanted her to lose at least ten pounds. She refused to even try. Her life was precarious and she didn't like the confusion she felt about dieting and just not having enough to eat. The scouts also wanted to take endless Polaroids of her, to fly her to New York or Milan, to paint streaks in her hair, and make her go live in one of those retards' palaces off of Collins—three-bedroom apartments packed with ten other skinny, starving, tall girls. Bulimia ballrooms. It was just another version of the life she'd left behind in school: pretty spoiled girls and too much money. She started to dream about Bethany, about the seraphic eyes watching her from the driver's seat, the one night she'd passed through judgment. Felice didn't want to lose that moment.

SHE WAKES TO an ivory sky; over the water to the east, a plane tows a banner advertising the dance party at Automatic Slim's. The air feels mossy, the sun rising in layers of new light, and Felice slowly sits up, her bones stiff. She inclines toward Emerson and examines his sleeping face. His size and his manner make him seem older than he is. Asleep, he has a boy's face with a softly curving mouth and pale, almost transparent eyelashes and brows. She admires the fact of his strength: it strikes her as a kind of luxury.

If only, Felice thinks. If only I wanted to kiss him.

"Hey." Emerson is awake, gazing at her from the grass.

"Hi," she says moodily: she can't help it.

"What're you thinking about?"

She scowls, then tears up a handful of coarse grass and sprinkles it over Emerson's head like confetti. "What. Is. It. With. You?"

He grins and bats away the grass. "I'm *starving*. It's seriously time for food."

Emerson says they can get breakfast at his friend Derek's place. She thinks again—a strand of anxiety—that she has to get work. But as they start up Michigan Avenue, Felice realizes that it feels good to let someone steer the course of the day. What else would she be doing? Smoking on the beach? She'll just stop for coffee, maybe a cigarette—then she'll get going. It's early and the air is soft as sea foam. As they walk, Emerson talks about his parents. "Jim—my dad—he was Mr. Activist Guy. But originally he was an engineer—he worked on the rockets at Cape Canaveral. Then he, like, became a hippie and moved to Fort Lauderdale. Totally a dad by accident. My mom too, pretty much. Neither of them was so into it."

"Did you love them and all?" Felice feels as if, walking this way, hands in pockets, staring at the pebbly sidewalk, Emerson carrying her board, that she could ask or tell him anything.

He shifts the board to his other arm and the back of his hand brushes hers. "Well, yeah," he says finally. "We fought a lot, but I guess we loved each other—me and Jim and Mandy, and my brother Tosh."

"I have a brother too," Felice says. "Stan."

"Yeah? Did you used to fight?"

"Not really—not so much back before. But he got pretty pissed at me—I'm sure he hates me by now." She smiles.

"Not exactly your fault you got born."

"Well, he didn't exactly beg to have a little sister, either." But that's not what she'd meant. Scuffling her sneakers in the white dust, she feels protective of Stanley, who'd seemed to Felice—even back when he was fifteen and she was eleven—heroic and slightly removed, reading about stuff like feeding the poor and cleaning the environment. "So, if you all loved each other," she says, barely able to stop herself from adding, *so fucking much,* "so then why are you, like, living in the gutter and all?"

"I'm not living in the gutter." Emerson laughs—a fine, clear tone. He puts one hand in his pocket and carries the board loosely in his other arm. "I don't know. I just wanted to try living not in a house for a while. Or, well, not in the same house my family was in. And not at a college either. Jim says that college is just another arm of the military-industrial complex."

"Pfft!" Felice curls her upper lip. "What isn't?" That came directly from Stanley.

"What about you then? Why are you staying in a place like the Green House?"

'Oh." She shrugs heavily, aware of Emerson's scrutiny. "No reason. Same as you." She walks with her arms crossed.

Emerson is still considering—his eyes lifted as if reading something on the air. "I guess—for us it all kind of fell apart. Jim and Mandy never got married in the first place, so . . . They said it's too hard on kids if you have to go through a divorce and all. So. Pretty thoughtful." His smile is private, directed at the ground; Felice looks away, uncertain if he's serious.

"They made it too easy—in a way—to fall apart. I mean, next thing we know, Dad's kind of living with Sandra—this other lady with a baby son—over in Plantation. And Mom moved to Denver to take jewelry design classes."

"They moved away from *you*? That really sucks."

Emerson's expression is mild. "Well, they were pretty decent about the whole deal. They talked to us tons about it before they went. I had some impulse control problems, I guess. I'd get a little wild. Jim still stopped by the old house sometimes and gave me and Tosh some cash for groceries and stuff. Of course Tosh would always spend it on weed mostly." He smiles at her again, that flickering, uncertain expression, but now he's looking at her.

"Fuck," she says softly. She lets her knuckles graze his, their fingers intertwine for a few moments before she lets go. They walk several more blocks, silenced by traffic noise, and negotiate a chaotic intersection. Then they pass a residential hedge tall as a gate and the traffic howl diminishes and the street opens to tall, wide trees like those in the Gables. Felice has never been in this neighborhood before—sticking to places she knows—crowded, touristy spots on the beach and a few secret street rat places—avoiding the police and kids from school. She feels exposed and anxious walking up this stately street: there are houses with circular drives, velvety emerald lawns, and children's bicycles on the lawns. "So where's your brother now?"

"Tosh?" Emerson half shrugs. "I don't totally know. He works as some kind of assistant in a medical lab at MIT. I'm too much of a waste product for him. He's really into, like, motivation and incentives and excellence and shit."

"And pot." Felice smirks and Emerson nods and laughs. He pulls a ragged frond from a banana tree and fans her with it, the dry edges flapping against her hair. She swats it back at him, laughing.

DEREK LIVES IN A big house, mid-beach, behind an ornate iron gate on Pine Tree Drive. Felice admires the place, its vaulted ceiling and big fir beams, an entry filled with flat rugs and beaded vases and wooden sculptures that look vaguely African to Felice. She immediately recognizes the young, beefy boy with the shaved head who answers the door. "Wow." She touches a curved lintel as they enter the main room. "You *live* here? I thought you lived at the Green House."

Derek looks around the expansive room with distaste. "My so-called dad lives here when he's not out with his ho. I'm not supposed to even be here when he's not. But, like when *is* he here?" He knocks on a waist-high silver sculpture of a elephant with human arms and legs. It writhes on its wood base on the floor. "Conk-conk. You wouldn't believe what this fucker cost. Steve-o got it like in Pakistan." He picks up a small dark carving of a woman's body with a bird's head, a sharp, open beak. "Here"—he thrusts it at Felice—"it's for you—take it."

"It's your *dad's,* dumbass," she says, scowling, and replaces it on an empty bookshelf.

"Whatev." Derek picks up a half-dollar-sized flat silver heart with a dagger through its center, then an old watch that was positioned in an artistic display of timepieces. He slips them into his pocket. "I'll sell all this crap eventually. He always gets more."

They follow him through the room into a bright doorway. It's been years since Felice has been inside a nice kitchen—granite counters crowned with chrome appliances, clean glints of untouched things. Like the kitchens of her school friends' mothers. Her own mother's kitchen had a big convection oven and fans—the counters glowed but her appliances looked battered and industrial. Felice sniffs, half hoping for the flour vapor of her home, but the air here is flat and empty. Her hands tremble as if with reawakened muscle memory: she tugs on the heavy fridge door—its tomblike chamber spilling milky light. Expensive, nearly empty shelves: film canisters, six cobalt bottles of water, a package of bacon and carton of eggs. "What a waste," she mutters.

Derek and Emerson prowl around, rummaging through the cupboards, pulling out jam, peanut butter, macaroni, Oreos. They fry all the bacon and eggs, stirring in ingredients—olives, onions, cocktail franks—apparently at random. When it's done, the boys half stand, half sit on tall stools pulled up to the counter; Felice sits across from them, knobby elbows on the counter, and watches them eat hunched over their plates, a bar of light cutting across the kitchen from a blue-veined window in the back wall. Felice nibbles a strip or two of Emerson's bacon—refusing the eggy mess—imagining, with some pleasure, her mother's revulsion at such food. Her mother didn't entirely approve of food anyway. Felice thinks of her poking at a steak with her fork, saying, *It's sodden.* The food is gone within minutes. Emerson makes an attempt at stacking dishes, but Derek waves them down. "Leave it, the maid's around somewhere."

He leads them out a back door to the polished slate patio and a racked assortment of iron weights, dumbbells, and two padded benches. The boys peel off their T-shirts: both of them are big and broad, but Emerson's back and biceps are defined, anatomical. Derek points a remote, turning up the volume on a portable player; music pulses, drumming the air, a Teutonic frenzy. "Rammstein!" he crows at Felice. " '*Du hast*,' ha!"

Felice slides into a painted Adirondack chair under an umbrella and watches the guys clatter on and off the benches. They laugh and clap: Derek shouts, "You got it! You got it!" slapping his hands together while Emerson swings the weights up and into his chest. Felice is used to boys showing off for her, but she notices a sort of concentrated seriousness of purpose in Emerson, as if he is focused on a point buried inside his own body. Derek drops the weights, clanking loudly, groaning while he lifts the bar, then hectoring Emerson, standing over him at the head of the weight bench, arms outstretched, ready to catch the bar. Emerson lifts in near-total silence, his neck flattening and his veins bulging in dark seams beneath the surface of his skin. Derek's sets taper off but Emerson keeps going, sliding one, then another set of thick plates on the bar. Mesmerized by the rivulets of sweat trickling along his brow and neck, Felice loses track of the amount of weight Emerson is lifting. The sun climbs to a steeper, hotter angle, approaching 90 degrees—but Emerson continues with single-mindedness.

As she watches Emerson in his silent exertions her thoughts feel sharp, her emotions honed on a hard edge. Felice hasn't seen this sort of focus since the days when her friend Hilda flew down parking ramps on her board, hair whipping, her arms aloft, pulling out nose grinds, rails, flips, drop-and-grabs. Emerson in movement is like a new sort of beauty: she'd always thought of beauty as a kind of passivity. Felice has never pursued anything so passionately herself. She grew up taking admiration for granted—eyes all turning toward her—soaking the air with a goldenrod-colored aura. She didn't have to do a thing to be loved: by her family, their friends, the teachers at school.

Derek dutifully assists Emerson, jotting down weights and reps, racking his weights, helping him to chalk his hands. Emerson switches from barbell to dumbbell, through overhand and underhand grips, shoulders, biceps, triceps, deltoids, pectorals. He's flushed all over, glowing, panting, hair glittering, swigging from a pitcher of water Felice refills from the tall blue bottles in the refrigerator. Felice watches the whole session—two continuous hours of methodical training—her long, thin legs drawn up beside her on the chair, her black hair flared across her back. Emerson finishes his workout by gulping the water straight from the pitcher, then dumping the rest over his head. He waves at Felice as if too tired for words, then wanders to the outdoor shower around the side of the house. His sweat-soaked shorts flap over the edge of the wood stall. She hears the hiss of the water and wonders what he would do if she joined him. Then Derek appears. He sprawls in the chair across from hers, dragging an arm across his forehead. "Awesome, right?"

"I guess."

"You hungry yet? You want something?" he asks. "Or you one of those air fern-type girls?"

Felice shakes her head, eyeing the shower mist.

Derek grins at her, shoulders jutting, straight arms, palms flat against the seat of his chair. "I've seen you around the Green House, right?"

Felice looks away, lifting her chin. "If I had a house like this, I'd be home all the time."

He bobs his head. "Hey, you can come over, like, whenever."

"What does your dad do?"

"He's a psycho-the-rapist." Derek's smile reveals a crooked incisor and bicuspid. "He talks, talks, talks, then he gives his clients nice painkillers. He says it's 'therapeutic.' " He makes air quotes with his fingers. "We're all best friends with the shipping department at Merck around here."

Felice glances over his shoulder at the shower again; frilly green shrubs and bougainvillea surround the yard. A single palm branch arches above a white rope hammock almost hidden among the trees.

"You can even live here, if you want. For real."

She crosses her arms, the long bones pressing against each other. "We've got another plan."

"Yeah? What?"

She can't help herself: she wants to tell someone. "We're going to Oregon. Maybe."

Derek doesn't say anything for a moment, studying her, his eyes still and small. "Oh yeah? Since when?"

"He's going to train at a special gym out there. I'm going with him." She thinks: I'm going to do it.

"Right."

"We are."

"*Oregon?* Do you have any idea how far that is?" A leaf shadow bobs over his face. "How're you gonna go?"

"We've got some money."

"Yeah? How much?"

"Plenty." She hesitates. "Almost a grand."

He sagely gazes over her head, evidently digesting this information. There are premature lines running from the sides of his nose to the corners of his mouth, a divot between his eyebrows. He's no older than Emerson, but his skin looks weathered as sandstone. Finally he says, slowly, judiciously. "That's enough to get you there—maybe—depending—but not much else."

Felice shrugs, sensing he's right—a band of anxiety encircling her ribs—because now she feels invested in the plan—but she won't let him see this. "We've got other . . . sources."

"Uh-huh. Like?"

She examines the cuticle of her index finger. "My brother Stanley maybe. He owns Freshly Grown."

"Pff! No he doesn't."

She lifts her chin and peers at him through lowered lids.

Derek's grin disappears. "No fucking way. The *store?* In Homestead? Are you shitting me? My dad is, like, obsessed with that place. We get all our protein mixes and eggs and stuff like that there. No, really, I gotta admit, that place rules." He angles his face to one side. "You just mean he runs the place, right? He doesn't actually *own* it?"

"He owns it all right. Came up with it, started the whole thing out of nothing," she boasts.

Derek's face softens with a pleased wonderment. "Wow," he says.

"That is too cool. I gotta say, I love that place. Do you hang out there a lot?"

"I don't know." She doesn't want to admit she's never actually been to the store. Stanley opened it after she left; her mother told her about it. She knew he would: he used to talk about his market as if it already existed. Stanley always did exactly what he said he was going to do—he was different that way from everyone else.

"So he must be pretty fucking loaded now, right? I mean, he could blow old Capitalist-Stevie here away."

Felice doesn't respond. She pulls the backs of her ankles in close to her butt and rests her chin on the flat of one of her knees. She thinks of Stanley's colored pencil drawings of theoretical businesses: a café, a bookshop, and, always, a grocery store. When she was ten and he was fourteen, he was already working as a bag boy at Publix, reading what their father called "hippie books." He talked about stuff like citrus canker, the Big Sugar mafia, and genetically modified foods and organisms. He got his store manager to order organic butter after Stanley'd read (in the *Berkeley Wellness* newsletter) about the high concentration of pesticides in dairy. Then, for weeks, the expensive stuff (twice as much as regular) sat in the case, untouched. So Stanley used his own savings to buy the remaining inventory and stashed it in his mother's cold storage. He took some butter to his school principal and spoke passionately about the health benefits of organic dairy: they bought a case for the cafeteria. He ordered more butter directly from the dairy co-operative and sold some to the Cuban-French bakery in the Gables, then sold some more from a big cooler at the Coconut Grove farmers' market. He started making a profit and people came back to him, asking for milk and ice cream. The experience changed Stanley—he was sometimes a little weird and pompous and intense before, but somehow, he began to seem cool and worldly.

Their mother, however, said she couldn't afford to use his ingredients in her business. They'd fought about it. Stanley said that Avis had never really supported him. Avis asked if it wasn't hypocritical of Stanley to talk about healthy eating while he was pushing butter. And

Stanley replied that he'd learned from the master, that her entire business was based on the cultivation of expensive heart attacks.

Derek sits back in his chair, gnawing meditatively on the corner of a thumbnail. He lifts his eyebrows. "How come Sonny's never mentioned this plan to me?"

"Emerson?" Felice feels a pulse of satisfaction: she busies herself with raking back streaks of loose hair. "I don't know. Maybe he didn't have time."

Derek interlocks his fingers over his stomach and narrows his eyes at Felice. "He tells me everything. We go back, man, like before you were fucking born."

"We're the same age."

"Fine," Derek utters in an exasperated whisper, looking over one shoulder. He swings back, his face tight. "Listen—I already know what you think of me."

"You *do*?" Felice can't suppress her smirk.

"Yeah, I *do*. I know you think I'm an ugly faker loser. And like I hang out with street kids and I've got this great big fucking dandy mansion where I can get drugged and beaten and generally fucked up as much as I care to let myself be . . ."

Felice blinks, dropping her eyes to her knees, reflexively gathering her calves up to one side.

"Okay—sorry—sorry." He lifts one hand, fingers spread. "Not to freak you out, like, oh, I'm so messed up. Just to say that you might think that kind of shit about me, but we're not so different, Felice. I mean, yeah, you've got this hair and these legs and this *face* and you could be living in a for-real mansion, up in like, Palm Beach, if you worked it a little and went to the right yacht parties—or at least pulling down some obscene fucking amount of green as a model or something—if you weren't such a lazy piece of shit."

The bones in her face loosen. She hears a whining in her right ear.

"Come on—don't give me that stupid look. You know it already. Don't act astonished. You're so pretty you're practically a different freaking species. And yeah, how exactly did you accomplish that?

Well, fuck you—you didn't. You were l-u-c-k-y. Your daddy fucked your mommy and your genes lined up in a nice pattern. Well, hooray for you. I'm rich, sort of, and you're stupid-gorgeous, and Sonny over there? He is insanely smart and honest, and in every way known to man, he is so much better than you or me. He beats his ass working. He is gonna go everywhere. I know. He started from absolute nothing—less than nothing—no parents, no money, begging for freaking food out on the *street,* okay? And here's my point—" Derek slides forward, his stomach folding and his elbows digging into his knees. "It's fine if you want to screw around with him and torture him out of his mind. Dump him. All the usual girl bullshit. But I want to emphasize that you gotta stay the fuck out of his way. Right? Because he does not need some scrawny bitch dragging him around to hell and back, messing up his training, fucking up his plans. Okay? *Capisce?*"

Felice releases her breath in a thin stream, almost a laugh.

"We cool?"

"Jesus—get the fuck away from me."

"What? We can be friends—you don't have to get messed up about it."

Emerson emerges from his shower, a bath towel wrapped around his waist, and says to Derek, "Hey man, let me borrow some clothes?"

"What's wrong with your own crappy clothes, asshole?" Derek stands and kicks the sweaty pile of shorts and T.

Emerson darts a glance at Felice. "I'm not going back to the Green House anymore."

"Oh, right, the big plan," Derek drawls. Still, he comes back with some clothes and Emerson turns away modestly, pulling shorts on under his towel. He drags over another Adirondack chair and sits across from Felice, their knees almost touching, his borrowed T-shirt draped over one shoulder like a waiter's towel. Felice is angry, but now she has to stay, to stake her claim on Emerson. She felt a burst of competitive adrenaline after Derek's dumb little speech, recognizing some element of truth in it. Emerson sits back, showing off his sloping chest and arms, gleaming with drops of shower spray. He smiles at Felice, one arm resting along the back of his seat, a cavelike space between his forearm and chest. She notes the even lift of his smile; a note of lilac soap drifts from his skin. She moves to perch on the flat arm of Emerson's chair and places her hand experimentally over his: a kind of startle runs through his body. He lifts one thumb, claiming her fingers.

The sky grows overcast with mounting summer thunderheads but there's no rain, just a dense, hot curtain of air. The afternoon is pure languor. Derek lights a crackling joint, which Emerson waves away— Felice leans toward the joint, then smiles coolly at Derek. "Better not."

"So your brother owns Freshly Grown?" Derek says, as if none of the earlier conversation happened, his expression once again meditative. "He actually *owns* it."

Felice looks away.

"I wonder if he'd like to expand his operations, carry some, like, new product . . ."

"Jesus."

"That store has got major clientele. Man—all those old hippies, fuck."

"Forget it," Felice snaps.

Emerson's gaze turns from Derek to Felice. Derek gives Emerson a lift of the brow, then disappears into the house to make his calls to "associates." "So what's all that?" Emerson asks. "What's Freshly Grown?"

Felice crosses her arms in a scissor over her chest. "Why do you even hang out with that guy? Such an asshole."

"What?" Emerson turns toward the house. "Derek? Nah. He's just, like, a businessman." He explains that Derek sells drugs to other people who sell drugs—all kinds, amphetamines, cocaine, pot, but mostly he specializes in MDMA, "otherwise known as Ecstasy," because, Emerson continues gravely, "he believes in it."

Felice shakes her head, studying the bouncing, calligraphic flight of a black wasp. "Whatever."

"That's not even to mention," Emerson goes on, "how he's kept me alive on a number of occasions."

Felice stares at the wasp, refusing to say anything more about Derek. There's something drugged about the stillness of the air: she can't hear any road noise at all, just a white insect whir, a slush of fronds in the breeze. She unfolds, takes his hand, and leads him deeper into the palms, to the rope hammock. She's so narrow she's able to slip, eel-like, under his arm, and they swing, cradled in the braided rope, so quiet Felice can almost imagine it's just the current of their breathing that's moving them. She closes one hand around the curve of his wrist. For a while, neither of them speaks. She's wet with sweat, glued to Emerson's side. Overhead, a shelf of clouds has started to cover the sun.

"You feel like maple syrup," he says.

Felice hoists herself up in the braid, slips a leg over Emerson's, her hand swims over his chest. She kisses his shoulder, then his neck, and watches the blood rise beneath the surface of the skin. She kisses the outer rim of his jaw, the edge of his smile. She kisses his mouth, which is wonderfully soft, and her hand travels over the towel before he catches her hand. "Wait, Felice."

She nuzzles the warm space behind his ear. "Wait for what?"

He puts her hand on his chest; it slides back down to his hip where he stops it. "You don't have to do this."

"As if." She pulls in her chin. "You're such a freak. Do you think I ever do anything I don't want to?"

"Still." He's so serious it's annoying.

She kisses him again. She feels his body warming with response. She finds that she's giving herself over as well—just a bit, but more than ever happened before: in the clubs, on the dance floor, kissing whoever swirled an arm around her neck, and, often, moving into the plush, blurry hours that followed: feeling nothing. Now, hanging in the swing among tendrils of purple orchids, dots of moisture in the air like a sparse, suspended rain, it's an infinity away from the rest of the world. Her hand roves over the cotton covering Emerson's thigh and again he stops her. "It's just sort of soon. Like, I don't want to wreck it."

"You're so stupid. What a stupid movie thing to say." Something about him is making her chest flutter with suppressed laughter. "You're such a big fat baby."

He holds her wrist, captured, up by his shoulder. "How many men have you been with?"

"Since when do you get to ask me that?"

He puts his hands up, lowers his head. "Sorry."

"And 'been with'? *Been with?* What are you now, Mr. Talking Bible?"

"No."

There's a low, thin grumbling in the eastern sky and a mass of clouds flash. Something hums past Felice's ear. It occurs to her that her face is all sweaty. She hasn't eaten enough and her breath must be tart: maybe she shouldn't assume that Emerson finds her alluring. She twists away from him grumpily, onto her back, rocking the hammock.

"What? Where you going now?" he asks.

She closes her eyes, mentally toting: Frank, Ronald, Jorge, Raffy . . . who else? Anyone? Oh, what was his name? Wayne? Oh and that yucky Doyle. "Six," she says grimly. "How about you, Mr. Bible? How many girls have *you* had fornication with?"

"Two."

"Two? Jeez." She fans at a mosquito. "That's lame."

"Not to me it wasn't."

"What, were you all *in love* or something?" She drags out the words, then looks over her shoulder at him.

"Well, a little maybe." He gives her a subtle smile. "Nothing big."

"Brother."

"Are you jealous?"

"Eww!" she erupts. "Oh my God. You are just so queer and gross." But she doesn't leave the hammock. She remains, pressed shoulder to shoulder, side by side. It's like catching a glimpse of something distant, to feel her body spark with attraction, and even better, to not have to act on it. They rock drowsily. The air smells of the ferns and dirt and stone, the before-rain. Her mother used to open the front door and ask, Smell the rain? She'd hold a conch shell to Felice's ear and say, Hear the ocean? And Felice did, both her hands gripping the base of the whorl.

Without warning, Hannah Joseph comes into her mind. Felice turns her head as if she could brush the thoughts away, but it's too late. She remembers how Hannah hated everything about Miami— even some of the best things, like the hooked-nosed white ibises roaming around in the grass and the flowers that blew up into winter foliage—a tree or bush opening overnight into flower like perfumed flames. All of it bothered Hannah, who'd walked around with her arms folded against her chest, complaining, "It isn't like this in Connecticut. The grass is softer there. And the trees are normal and *leafy*." At first everyone wanted to be like her. Felice and Bella and Yeni, the most popular girls, replicated even the way Hannah folded her arms.

Felice remembers Hannah saying, *This isn't even like America!*

That's what she'd say, in the cafeteria, at recess, in class. "You guys don't realize how not-American you are . . ." she'd begin. Even the teachers would chuckle, a cowed, embarrassed look on their faces.

Pressing the heels of her palms against her closed eyes, Felice waits until the image of Hannah fades into the gray dissolve behind her eyes.

GRADUALLY THE RUMBLING comes closer and the humidity builds until Felice and Emerson are caught in a powdery, confectionery shower. They climb out of the hammock and run through the door to the kitchen. Derek is sitting at the table with a pad covered with columns of numbers. "Where you two been?" Derek mutters, not looking up.

Emerson walks past him into the guest bath, then returns with a big towel. He seats Felice at the table, chair turned out, and begins to run the towel along her arms and legs, rumpling it around her scalp. Felice doesn't move while he does this, her back straight and head lifted. Even Derek is silent; he puts down his pen, as if a ceremony of some sort is taking place. No one has touched her like this since she was eight or so years old: she feels a fine, prickling heat on her skin as he finishes.

There's a muffled snort: Derek, his tipped smile. "Nice."

She turns away, infuriated—just another street kid, wrecking everything; acting as if some sort of performance has been staged for his pleasure. She wants Emerson to smash him, but he hangs back as if abashed. She stands. "I'm getting the fuck out of here. And you two homos can go fuck yourselves."

"Woo-hoo!" Derek leers. "Nice mouth." Emerson shoves him so hard his chair scrapes back a few inches. Derek grabs the arms of his chair. "The fuck, man?"

Felice goes to the living room, seizes her deck and her bag as Emerson runs after her. "Felice, what?" He follows her out the front door. "Hey, talk to me."

It's still sprinkling; her clothes wither with moisture. She tosses back the damp cables of her hair, ducks a branch of sea grape tree, then opens the iron gate. "You could've just *told* me you were gay."

"Felice. Jesus. I'm not gay."

Felice stops and slaps her deck on the street. "Then that just makes it worse, doesn't it?" She's yelling. She can't help it. The feelings seem to come from outside of her body, possessing her, tightening her lungs, her rage like a screw tightening in her temples. So angry she's crying, the tears nearly springing from the corners of her eyes. It doesn't make sense; it's like some feathery thing beating the air around her, all betrayal and humiliation. He puts his big, dumb hand on her, which enrages her more. She trips as she tries to kick away on her board, her vision speeding, unraveling. She trips again and nearly falls. Emerson follows her.

"Of course I want to—I want—Jesus . . . Please just listen for two seconds." He trots in fronts of her, momentarily stopping her. She glares at his blond lashes and red cheeks. She thinks: Why do I even care?

"I want to be *with* you. Of course I want . . . you know. But I also want more than that. I don't want to just . . . screw around." Now he's blushing, his face a dark, bruised color. "We're more than that, Felice— we're for real. I'll take care of you and we'll watch each other's backs."

Felice can barely hear him, thinking, Fuck you, fuck you, fuck you . . . a tattoo in her head. She doesn't want to hear any more. She forces herself to lower her voice, to contain herself enough to say, "That's just wonderful for you, Emerson."

"Please, just, let's try to—"

"No." Her voice is scalding. Thoughts open in her mind, a thin white band, widening: he wants her to go backwards, to do things in that stupid, weak way. She will never be that way again. "No, *Emerson*. You aren't listening right. I think you're a big fake loser and Derek is a scumbag. Okay? Do you hear me yet? Are you getting that? That whole thing about Portland and strongman stuff—it's never going to happen. We both know the reality. Just stay the fuck away from me." She turns her back on his stricken face. Gets on her board and kicks away as hard as she can. A big silence behind her. She's so furious she can't tell the difference between the vibrations of her board and the powerful quaking that's broken inside her body. As she rides, the unwanted image comes back to her: a girl's face—streaked, hollowed out by shadow—she seemed to be crouching on the sidewalk. Even though Felice knows that isn't right, it's the way she remembers it.

FELICE FIRST NOTICED the starry spill of the girl's hair when she appeared in French, the way it trembled with light when she answered questions or gave a toss of her head. The girl always had her hand up and knew more French than the rest of them—including Madame Cruz—actually correcting the teacher's accent—"That's *tre-s*"—gently crushing the *r* in the back of her throat. *"Not 'trres,'"* a Catalan roll off the tip of her tongue. The rest of the class tittered but the girl stared at Madame Cruz because, Felice realized, she was simply right.

Hannah was a year and a half older than Felice, in ninth, but the eighth and ninth graders took electives together. Felice ran into her in the hallway. It was easy for her to be bold—she was so pretty everyone wanted to be Felice's friend. But Hannah was shy and self-possessed and even a little stuck-up, which attracted Felice. Not as easy to conquer as the other kids. Felice started sitting in the front of French class as well. Afterward the two girls walked to lunch together and Felice asked questions which Hannah answered in a low voice—hard to hear over the din in the corridors, her head lowered, books hugged to her chest.

"Where did you come from?"

"Litchfield."

Felice lifted her eyebrows: almost everyone in her school had started from someplace else—usually their parents' country.

Hannah said, "Before Litchfield, other places."

"What do your parents do?"

"My dad's a surgeon. My mom is an ophthalmologist."

"Why did you move here?"

Hannah scrutinized Felice a moment before she replied, "Dad thought it was too white. In Litchfield."

Hannah's hair was lighter than Felice's but her skin was dark, a deep, rosy tan. She had a softly curved nose and a sloping chin that almost spoiled her looks. But there were her lucid green eyes, pale as windowpanes, startling and ghostly in all that dark skin. After a week of hallway conversations, the girl entrusted Felice with the information that her real name wasn't actually Hannah Joseph but Hanan Yusef. That she hadn't been born in the States—her parents had moved them from Jerusalem when Hannah was two. That her father had changed her name when they moved to Miami because he was sick of putting up with anti-Arab bullshit.

A frisson ran through Felice's arms and spine. Thrilled, she asked, "But don't you hate that? Hanan sounds beautiful. Don't you hate having a fake American name?"

"No, I was glad," Hannah said curtly, and looked away.

Bella, Marisa, and Yeni made room for Hannah in their coterie, a little infatuated with her. "She just has this way about her," Jacqueline said. "Yeah, like, she knows what's cool and what isn't without even trying," Court said.

Felice also sensed an adult weariness about the girl—her comments adroit, funny, often bleak. She seemed to have a kind of cold insight verging on telepathy into people—especially adults—their lives like transparencies before her eyes. "Dottie over there?" she whispered to Felice. "She wants to get with Charleton Baker." Felice cracked up, a hand cupped over her mouth. "No way!" Charleton was sweet and tall—a thyroid case, as Hannah put it. But he was twelve, stringy and chronically broken-voiced. She realized that a doting light came into the social studies teacher's powdered face whenever she called on him: Dottie Horkheimer's smile deepened and she looked, fleetingly, pretty. Knowing something forbidden about Ms. Horkheimer made social studies bearable.

All that fall, through Hannah's funny, scorching way of looking at things, school itself seemed more tolerable. Hannah seemed to know a lot about other kids: she warned Felice that her friend Coco was a fake, jealous of Felice's looks, that she whispered behind her back. Felice and her friends had known each other since kindergarten. As soon as Hannah told her this, Felice thought it must be true: she began to distance herself from Coco. Later she realized she wasn't sure if it was true, or if it just seemed so because of the supremely certain way that Hannah said things.

Felice and Hannah fell into rituals of endless email and phone calls—messages raveling together, switching from one to the other at whim. By October, they snuck out of P.E. on a regular basis. They sprawled in the east field and watched the boys' soccer team running wind sprints and snapping through calisthenics. Hannah would gossip with Felice about teachers and other kids for a while, but then she'd start to say things like, "Isn't it weird that everyone has to die? Like, everyone on this field right now? Someday they'll all be dead. Everyone in this whole school. Gone."

"I guess." Felice squinted so spangles of colored light glittered inside her eyelashes. Off in the distance, there were moving vistas of palms, their enormous shaggy fronds seemed to swim and undulate against the sky. Felice loved listening to Hannah say her crazy stuff. She had decided never to introduce her to her mother. Avis would come out—she always did—with plates of cherry cookies, their chocolate icing like lacquer, or lemon cream scones coruscated with sugar crystals—her friends fought for the morsels of her miniature éclairs. "Your mother is a *god*," Bella once moaned.

Hannah didn't like to talk about her parents either. "My dad is a big boring freak and for some reason my mom married him." She flopped back in the grass, swishing her arms back and forth, the way Felice had seen kids make snow angels on TV. "I hate Arabs. I hate Israelis. I hate soldiers. I hate Saddam Hussein. I hate George Bush. I hate politics, I hate words that begin with *p*. So don't ask me about any of it."

"Fine," Felice said, laughing and rolling her eyes. "I wasn't *going* to."

Felice could see the shapes of old shadows moving over Hannah's eyes. Odd references came up all the time. A truck overturned a block away from the school and a brackish chemical exhaust hung in the air: Hannah said, "That smells exactly like a sulfur bomb." Another time, when a jet clapped a sonic boom over the school, Hannah collapsed into a hunch on the floor, her face stark with shock. She recovered, brushing aside the teacher's concern, but later went home without speaking to Felice.

Hannah made fun of Felice's other friends behind their backs. She mimicked Yeni's prissy Venezuelan accent, Bella's slack, sweetly bovine expression. They sensed her disdain, as well as the way she claimed Felice all for herself, edging out a world in which she and Felice were the only ones who mattered: Felice was flattered and pleased. This was a new kind of friend.

SEVERAL BLOCKS LATER, Emerson and Derek receding into distance, Felice starts to relax. The streets widen and hiss with traffic, the air rain-pearled. There's a burst of squawking in the air and she looks up to see a passing flock of sapphire-colored macaws with orange bellies. Stanley said they were the prettiest animals with the ugliest voices. He'd told her how, after big hurricanes, wild birds escaped from the aviaries and zoos and from the metal cages people kept in their backyards. They returned to nature. "They'll nip off your finger with that beak—like scissors. Snip!" he said. Felice was seven when Andrew hit, but she didn't remember much of it beyond the fun of nightly picnics from their cooler and reading by flashlight and bathing in the swimming pool.

Felice admires the long blue tails of the birds just before they vanish into the trees. That's the way to be, she thinks, kicking hard on her board, letting the wind stream through her hair—no plans, no fear, no expectations: never to be held in live captivity.

Avis

SHE DREAMS OF A LITTLE BOY: HIS HAIR SLOWLY rising and falling as he runs in long, slow arcs, up to kick the ball, the air filled with bright cries:

I've got it! I've got the ball!

Avis opens her eyes. For a moment, she waits, spooled in the sweetness of an after-dream. It seems to continue unfolding around her, her son still eight years old.

Consciousness emerges then, and Avis realizes she can still hear the cries, the child's voice. Gradually she notices the hard repeating beat. The mynah. She lingers in bed with her eyes closed, marveling at the mimicry—the miracle of it—a bird, capturing the parabola of laughter so exactly. Who is the little boy, Avis wonders, this parrot listened to?

Glancing at the clock, she realizes, with a deep dismay, that it's 6:30: she's overslept by two hours: too late to fulfill the standing order for palmiers at the Anacapri and La Granada restaurants—she'll probably lose their business. Usually she wakes on her own with no problem. She hears Brian's familiar pace between bathroom and bedroom. Why didn't he wake her? He hums and mutters, runs a brush through his hair. Because she'd been stood up, she thinks grimly. He felt sorry for her. Avis rises, ties back her hair; ignores the strands that slide free in her fingers, ignores its lighter mass. She brews strong black tea with cream and honey and goes to her desk in what she still thinks of as Stanley's room, to email the restaurants. She struggles to construct an apology as the mynah shrieks through the window.

Newly showered, Brian smiles at Avis as he moves past the door.

She still enjoys the sight of her husband undressed, his slightly bowlegged stance, the softening pouch of his middle, his penis, its innocent, leftward slump. Once Stanley was out of the house, she sometimes lured Brian back to bed in the morning, enjoying the coolness of his washed skin against her kitchen warmth. But she hasn't been much interested in a while. She sighs, then twists around at the desk chair. "Do you hear that?"

Brian ruffles the back of his hair with a towel. "You mean the damn bird?"

"It always sounds a little different each time."

He combs his hair before the full-length mirror, presenting his back and tidy buttocks. "Not to me it doesn't."

She rarely sees Brian in the morning—she's usually in the middle of rushing out orders of fresh baguettes and scones. Avis abandons the desk and prepares Brian a plate of croissants, salted butter, a bowl of blackberry preserves she gets in trade from a local jams and jellies lady. Then she sits at the table with him, one hand knotting closed the placket of her chef's jacket, the other hand running the length of Lamb's slinking back.

"Parkhurst. Ugh. Wants to wrap up the contract on the Design District deal," he mumbles, studying his BlackBerry. "He's obsessed with that deal."

"Design District's supposed to be the hot place," she says, watching him stare at the tiny screen. "I have a restaurant client there— their lines are out the door."

"Except it's not the Design District—not even close. I keep telling them." He looks up at her. "I'm sorry—you were saying something— what were you saying?"

Avis considers the view through the French doors: in that pause, she feels herself telescoping backwards, out of their life. She watches him touch the rim of his plate with the edge of his knife, observes the striations of his knuckles, the ropy veins in the backs of his hands. She estimates that it's been nearly six months since they last made love. The longest they've ever gone. Perhaps it has something to do with her mother's passing last year. She wonders—the thought softly bursting in on her—if he's in love with someone else.

He pauses before getting up. "That bird," he says darkly. She becomes once again conscious of the parrot's cry, now the quavering singsong of a madwoman. "This is ridiculous," he says. "How's anybody supposed to get any work done?"

"Most people around here commute to work."

"*You* don't." He takes his plate to the kitchen sink. She hears him rummaging around. "I swear I'm going to call code enforcement."

"Oh, I don't know." Her hand slips to the base of her throat.

Brian stands in the doorway holding a banana. "But you've been struggling." He stops short, the catch in his statement like a little gap between them, encompassing her stumblings and mistakes over the past year: miscalculating ingredient amounts for breads she's made hundreds of times; forgetting orders, singeing entire sheets of the most delicate, time-consuming pastries: she's mournfully discarded entire batches. Long sheaths of nothingness open in Avis's days, inertia: she reports to the kitchen, picks up a spoon, then, quickly, it's the end of the day and she's done nothing. Sometimes the days dissolve between her fingers. They haven't spoken of these things openly.

Avis named her business Paradise Pastry because she imagined cathedrals. She thought about the stonemasons, glassblowers, sculptors—who gave lifetimes to the creation of beauty. Every sugar crust she rolled, every simple *tarte Tatin* was a bit of a church. She consecrated herself to it: later, it became her tribute to her daughter and the unknown into which she'd disappeared. She had her cathedral to enter, to console her. Her friend Jean-Françoise, chef at Le Petit Choux, said that her pastries would be transcendent, if only she weren't American.

BRIAN FLIPS OPEN his briefcase on the dining room table and places a waxed bag next to the sheaf of folders and his BlackBerry. "You remember the thing Barry told us . . ." One of the post-Felice fam-

ily counselors—an earnest man with a habit of stroking his ponytail
throughout the sessions.

"He told us a lot of things."

"He said sometimes our partners know us even better than we
know ourselves."

Through the French doors, Avis watches wet black branches lit with
buds, the Precambrian curves of the palm fronds. "Oh. Right. Okay."

He doesn't move for a moment. She turns and notices with a pang
that he's sneaked a bag of Florentine cookies into his briefcase. He
says, "We can talk about it again later."

"I've been thinking about the kids so much these days."

"Stanley's fantastic—he makes that place hop—no question
about it."

"Well, I just hope . . ." She watches Brian; it's like speaking in
code. "I want him to be happy is all. Do you think he is?"

"Well, I think he's got a new girlfriend. He called me yesterday,"
Brian says softly. He seems to be about to say more but stops.

Avis's hand moves to her chest. "What happened to that other
one?" During his high school years, Avis had watched Stanley cycle
through one date after another—pretty, ephemeral young ladies like
fireflies.

"Who knows—that lady killer," Brian says, smiling. Avis remembers Brian at twenty-eight: narrow sea-blue eyes. Irish-handsome, her
mother had said—untrustworthy. Brian's good looks settled into a sort
of normalness—he put on weight, his face broadened, and he started
to look like everyone else: she found this calming. She doesn't really
want to ask about Stanley so much as she wants to ask about their own
marriage—how happy are *we*? It seems they've lost the ability to speak
to each other in such plain and direct words. "He's always so busy,"
she murmurs, examining the white flour crust under her nails.

"Hurricane season—it's a scramble for them. They've got to lay in
supplies."

"Does Stan know that her birthday is next week?" She doesn't
look at Brian.

"Whose?"

She approximates a smile. "Her eighteenth. D-Day. I was thinking maybe we should do something—like a memorial—to commemorate it."

Brian gives her a genuine smile. "She's not dying. Far as we know. You ask me, if anything we ought to celebrate that she's an adult now—free to torment whomever she likes."

MINUTES AFTER SHE HEARS Brian's car rolling from the driveway, Avis goes to the French doors. The parrot is warbling, back to the watery contralto, a low, inflected pulse that reminds her of her mother's collection of scratched up LPs—Edith Piaf, Billie Holiday. She opens the door and slips outside to the flagstone patio. The sound draws her into the fringe of the bamboo and coconut palms. Avis can't account for her change of heart. It reminds her of how Florida had slowly opened to her twenty years ago, how she began to see the differences in lizards, and petals, and tree trunks: bark swirling in a spiral; spreading gray roots like the tendrils of a beard; one peeling like paper; one fine-grained as skin. Avis peers through the branches, pushing them aside so they release scents of grass and lime. This is the time of year when mangoes hang from the boughs, soft as hips, each tree with its own flavor. An amber butterfly floats over the neighbor's clothesline. Avis realizes that a wave of shadow at the far end of the yard is the woman she spoke to the other day. She stands with her arms lifted, pinning a pair of men's boxer shorts to the clothesline, a basket of laundry beside her, a wooden clothespin in her teeth.

As the woman shuffles forward, Avis notices something at the woman's feet: it's the bird, about a foot high, oil-black with a blue sheen, a crimson spot on its beak. It toddles behind the woman and emits a chortling, purling sound like Avis's cat. Avis stands still, her hands on the trees, scarcely breathing. The woman wears an emerald-colored head scarf knotted at the back of her head and another house-dress, this one in a celadon color, ethereal against the darkness of her skin. About halfway through her basket of clothes the woman pauses.

She takes the clothespins from her mouth and whistles. The bird twitches its wings and tail feathers. She whistles again and the bird responds with a burst of song.

HER MOTHER HAD WARNED HER: You aren't suited to the kitchen—you're too anxious: you'll go mad from the isolation, the repetition. Can you stand to make croissants every day? What if you poison someone? Lose a walnut shell and someone chokes to death?

To placate her mother, she enrolled in college—the same school her mother had attended—in a hilly, gorge-cut town. She spent all her time in Risley Hall, drowsing over Dickens, Brontë, Eliot, Woolf, the decrepit sunlight coming into the late-afternoon glass. Half attending to the lectures of her professors. Like the wonderful old Russian who spoke about Victorian novels and their "primitive coloration," who set her imagination off in other directions for weeks. It seemed as if the life of the mind precluded the life of the body: poets were ascetic, hollowed-out by thinking; her professors seemed almost deliberately ugly—especially the women. Though her mother couldn't help the lovely black drift of her own hair and eyes, she restricted herself to the bitterest little cups of coffee and lived on the biscotti Avis made for her—bone dry, barely enough sugar to matter.

Brian was her tutor. He'd taken her on after three other grad students at the study center had given up. He stuck with Avis, going over *oligopolies* and *externalities,* and never said, "But it's so *simple . . .*" like the others.

He had a satisfying wholeness about him, American good looks like a baseball player's—level shoulders, a pale shock of hair. A good mind and ethical nature: little gave him more pleasure than learning laws and governance—"It shows you the shape of your society." But what drew the deepest sliver of her self toward him, toward love, was the weakness in his chin, his slightly disoriented air, like an injury he allowed only Avis to see. Brian was the opposite of her mother. There wasn't a whiff of mystery about him: he was solid, entirely himself. Avis still cooked in those days and she invited him to her minuscule studio. She set a hibachi up on the fire escape and grilled him a marbled, crimson rib eye, crusty with salt and pepper, its interior brilliant with juices. Some garlicky green beans with pine nuts, rich red wine, mushrooms and onions sautéed in a nut-brown butter. She'd intuited his indifference to chocolate, so dessert was a velvety vanilla bean cake with a toasted almond frosting. It was a dark art: she knew what she was doing every step of the way, but she wanted him. She wanted children with him. By the end of the meal, he sat half sprawled beside her on the couch, crushing the hem of her skirt. He pulled her down on top of him, wouldn't let her clear away the dishes: she heard his pulse through the thick wool of his sweater. He loved her, he'd said, his breath redolent of vanilla and almond. He loved her one hundred percent.

She'd smiled—guiltily conscious of having unbalanced him. "But do you love me 105 percent? How about 173 percent?"

He'd turned red and said, "Yes." Then added politely, "Though those percentages aren't possible."

She told him then she hated school. She took him to the Moosewood Café, the Morritz Bakery, she showed him the way they folded cranberries into their *Vacherin*. She made him seven-layered strawberry *pavé* cakes. When she confessed, with a deep blush, her wish to attend the culinary institute, he encouraged her to apply. Told her there were loans and scholarships, that he would help her research these things. Excited and anxious, she felt an unraveling in herself, the disconnected threads reaching toward Brian.

THERE IS, IN THE BACK of Avis's mind, the thought that now she'll need to hire a new assistant. But for some reason she isn't in a rush to do so. Delivery trucks rumble to and from the front step every day— two are refrigerated vans which pick up her pastries to ferry throughout the city—the others arrive with specialty items for her baking: lilac honey, a fine-milled pastry flour, a gelatin from Provence. The sound of an assistant speaking Spanish with a delivery driver limned the edges of her day. As she piped rosettes, docked a sheet of dough, or doused a tart with sanding sugar, another world occurred on the doorstep. Now Avis answers the door herself and leads surprised delivery people into the front entrance, across the living room, and through the heavy swinging door to her kitchen. She almost enjoys the contact with the outside world. On Monday, there is a Colombian man who delivers free-range eggs and unpasteurized milk that glows like satin. Tuesdays, a woman from Lima bring special concoctions of candied lilacs and fruit peels and *gelées,* and later a young boy comes with a box filled with dried starfruit and bananas and fresh tea, mint, and sage from his father's botanical garden in the Redlands. She asks and forgets everyone's names, but next week, she thinks, she'll ask again. Some deliveries—like those from her son's market—come every week, others—like the fig balsamic vinegar— were special-ordered to accompany a single chocolate strawberry ice cream cake.

On Wednesday, Avis stands at the window, peering through the latticework of leaves and spines at the neighbor pinning up her washing. The doorbell chimes startle her. She drapes a towel over a rising brioche dough, feeling newly capable, a tick of expectation as she goes to answer. When she opens the door, at first all she sees through the screen is a glint in someone's hand. Pushing open the screen door, she realizes it's Eduardo, one of Stanley's delivery people, holding Avis's antique silver tray. "This was propped against your front door."

When she'd left the tray at the neighbor's feet the other day it was etched with tarnish all along the swirls and the central silver coin. Now it gleams. Avis marvels, turning it over. Someone has polished every crevice, rubbed at every impossible edge and crook; not a speck on it. Eduardo carries his cooler into the kitchen, stacks tubs of strawberry purée in the freezer. There are almonds for her *macarons,* vanilla pods, raw cocoa. She follows him in, props the tray against the wall, staring at the gleam. After he finishes unloading, Eduardo stands, about to lift the cooler, then stops in place, looking out the back window. "Is she Haitian?"

Avis turns. Their backyard is framed in the wide window above the sink. "I don't actually know." She can see the woman shaking out a wet pink skirt. "We haven't really talked."

"Did you notice those?" He gestures up.

Avis is momentarily dazed by the bleached sky: a hawk of some sort floats by, wings glinting and flat. Something twinkles at the near corner of the neighbor's yard, nearly hidden among the branches. "What is that?" Avis puts on her kitchen readers. She sees it now: small creatures fashioned out of straw and grass—a mouse and two small birds, swaying, suspended by invisible strings.

Eduardo stands beside her at the sink. He smells slightly sour, like physical labor. "Voodoo," he says. "They're some kind of little offerings."

"Really? Voodoo?" She lifts the stem of her glasses. Once, while delivering some cakes with Carlita, another assistant, Avis spotted a dark knob of some sort in the street. She stared, unable to identify it until she was nearly standing over it: a dog's paw, cleanly severed mid-leg. Carlita had grabbed her and pulled her away, muttering a Hail Mary under her breath.

"It's just another religion," he says dismissively, and turns back to study the kitchen. "So cool here. This place reminds me of Hansel and Gretel."

Avis continues to stare at the bouncing straw mouse. "I wouldn't let a gumdrop or candy cane within twenty feet of my kitchen."

"Well, you're not that kind of witch." Eduardo squats over the cooler, stuffing plastic bags back into it and slapping the top shut again. He backs out of the kitchen holding his cooler; at the front, he opens the screen door with his shoulder. "According to Stan, you're the real deal," he says, starting down the front steps. "A real sugar artist."

She stands in the doorway. "I'm just a worker bee."

Eduardo opens the truck and slides in the cooler. "He says you're a genius."

"Stanley?" Her voice is quiet. "Really did he say that?" She averts her eyes. "About me?"

He shrugs. "You know, with the Haitians, there's a pretty interesting relationship to sugarcane—if you're interested. It's sacred to them." He opens the van door and props his arm on it. "But it's pretty horrible. They have to harvest it for other people and they starve. You and her should talk about sugar some time."

When Avis returns to the house, the air inside feels like the bottom of a well. She browses through her work folder, stuffed with orders on slips and receipts: *Monday—cinn. palmiers—the Morris Group. PI&B—mocha cr. puffs, 5 Saint-Honorés. Winslow Co. retreat 20 plum tarts* . . . She tries to plan the day's baking schedule but she keeps putting down her pen, returning to the French doors, cracking them, leaning out into the damp air. How still it is in the hottest part of the day! Just a minor insect whir, a few random bird notes—everything deadened by molten heat. She returns to the kitchen: the woman and her bird have gone in for the day. Why doesn't she feel relieved?

FOR TWO DAYS, Avis sneaks out of the kitchen after she's set out dough for the first rising, to climb into the densest section of overgrowth, among webs and rotting avocados and palmetto bugs—muck, spores, and tiny-legged things falling into her hair or down the back of her shirt. From there, she watches the neighbor pull what seem to be weeds, bundling them neatly in the lap of her apron. The woman wears a bib apron like the sort Avis's grandmother wore—white, tied with strings behind the neck and waist. Under this, she wears a variety of simple housedresses in honeyed colors, turquoise, sea green, lavender, and pale rose, usually some sort of kerchief tied over her hair. From a distance, she looks delicate as a girl, but Avis suspects she is just a bit younger than herself. While she gardens or hangs laundry, she sings or murmurs to the mynah who waddles nearby and occasionally attempts to climb the fabric of her dresses.

She speaks in a rapid, staccato language that Avis think must be Creole: the bird often responds in exactly her voice, mirroring each word: *bonswa, bonswa, souple, pa fe sa . . .* Watching this woman gives Avis such pleasure—the rhythm of the woman's voice, the filigree of birdsong in the trees, the atlas of breezes carrying jasmine, vanilla, and gardenia—even the sweetness of the rotting mulch and briny air bewitches her.

That Thursday, Avis leaves the kitchen the moment Brian departs, wiping her hands on her apron, and goes to the place in the fronds. She presses against the avocado trunk, hidden under a screen of leaves. Rain begins misting through the fronds: the cloud cover turns the morning sky into a emerald post-dusk hue, mixing things up. Soon she sees the back door nudged open by a brown foot, a flicker of pink toenails: the woman emerges in an old lemon-colored shift— bateau neck, sleeveless—beneath an apron. She places a metal pot on the ground, then sits beside it on the cement step, just under the eave of the house. There's a pile of leaves in her apron, as usual, and she sets to work, stripping pieces of greenery, tossing part, throwing the rest in the pot. After she has worked methodically for some minutes, the woman begins to sing. Avis strains to hear: it's a syrupy old tune she's heard somewhere before. *Mon amour, je t'attendrai toute ma vie . . . Oh mon amour, ne me quitte pas.* Her voice is thin but on-key. Avis releases a breath and the fragile sounds of air and insects are part of that diastole. She is so relaxed she is almost drowsing.

Out of the corner of her eye then, just breaching her peripheral vision, she spots a movement like a brush of premonition. Lamb's orange form creeps past her, belly low, warbling and chirping—his gray eyes on the mynah.

The woman spots Lamb nearly at the same time and gets to her feet. "Hsst. Bad, bad!" She kicks in Lamb's direction, the cat flattening but not retreating. The mynah releases a piercing *awgh* and lifts its black wings like a villain's cape. Lamb freezes in mid-stalk, the bird puffs up larger, hopping forward, shrieking *aawgh, aawgh!* Certain her cat— which had once belonged to Felice—is about to be eviscerated, Avis bounds from her hiding place, fronds and leaves flying, into the neighbor's yard and scoops up the tabby, simultaneously catching flashes of the flapping bird, the woman's hand fanned at her throat. Avis hurries back through the leaves, across the yard, through the French doors, and tosses the cat so it yowls, midair, and falls on the couch.

Avis stands with her back to the French doors, shaking and out of breath. Slowly, she risks a glance and sees the woman has followed her through the palms and now stands in Avis's yard. She is rigidly furious, arms akimbo, fists balled. "You are watching us!" the woman shouts, her voice elongated. Avis wavers in the door, her hand trembling on the frame. "I'm terribly sorry," she mumbles. "I'd swear I'd pulled that door shut—they swell up in the rainy season . . ."

"Who are you, lady?" The woman is implacable. "What do you want?"

Avis takes a few meek steps outside. She clasps her hands at her waist. "Oh, I'm so—I was just—I was doing some—I was in my garden—and—I heard some voices. I heard you, I think—and I—and I—"

The woman's eyes dart around the overgrown yard. She squints at Avis, chin forward. "How long you been watching me?"

Avis lowers her head. She feels breathless and woozy. "A while."

"*A while*," the woman says in her contrapuntal way. "A while, yes." Something relaxes in the filament of the woman's eyes. "You aren't altogether in possession of yourself, are you?"

She looks different here, in another context. Avis sees she is very small—a good head shorter, possibly thirty pounds lighter than Avis. Her yellow dress, kerchief, and gold-beaded earrings glow as if absorbing energy from her body. The woman's eyes tick over her, inventorying, then she turns her head slightly and backs away. She moves toward the palms, shoves them aside, and walks through.

THE NEXT MORNING, Avis draws a comb through her wet hair and the tines fill with strands. Under the bathroom light, she stares at her reflection; her skin looks depleted and she believes she can divine the round shape of her skull through the hair. A dermatologist had told her last month that her hair would quit falling eventually. Probably hormonal, she'd said, adding with the condescension of the young: Our bodies change. Her mother had warned that Avis would get fat from baking. Now Avis looks at her hard little wire of a smile: Geraldine had said nothing about going bald. Avis scoops her remaining hair in one hand, tilts the scissors in the other, and snaps away furiously. "Here you go!" she says to the mirror with a big smile. "Happy Birthday, Felice! Happy Birthday to you!" It takes just a few minutes to lop it all off, so what remains—about two to four inches—juts from her head in a tufted silver and brown corona. She pushes it back and tucks what she can behind her ears before tying a slim silk band around her hairline—loose hairs a disaster for baking. She sweeps the bathroom floor and wipes the sink, listening to the neighbor's bird chatter in the other yard.

Avis returns to her desk, skin still humid from the shower, her left hand combing the blunt ends of her hair. With her right hand, she browses through the rest of the day's orders: *cinnamon palmiers; pistachio-cocoa 12-layer torte* . . . She gazes at this order a moment, her pulse elevated, as if she's been drinking too much coffee, and she begins jotting notes on a new pastry: *For this cake, I want to mingle the womanly and masculine foods—sugars and meats in particular. The walls must come down. Must temper, must balance. Add the leeks to the chocolate, vanilla to the turnip. Tear away the sacred walls between the sweet and savory worlds.* She stops and rereads what she's written: what does it mean? Again she hears the mynah singing in the neighbor's yard.

Avis lowers her head, runs her fingers into the new perimeter of her hair. She tries to think her way through this: the link between death and sugar. Stanley sends her nutrition newsletters with reports on diabetes and obesity. It seems to her that sugar is a metaphysical problem: each occasion of eating asserts its own needs. Her fingers wait on the keyboard as her vision glazes out the east windows, unfocused. All the glorious pastries of the world are baked and eaten and gone forever, and there is only the fiery moment of the *now*. Minds and bodies tell one story: I tasted; I loved; I was young. But the *now* burns everything in its oven. Her mother said that heaven was "the unattainable." The mynah's cry tears at the air, sailing over the trees and hedges and songbirds. She thinks: Perhaps the neighbor hates me because I work with sugar.

Suddenly it simply isn't a choice: Avis feels she must explain herself to the neighbor—it's unbearable that the woman might think Avis a fool or insane or not "in possession" of herself.

The grass feels hard against her bare feet and she pushes through the thicket of the palms, scraping her arms, the fronds like pastry knives. The bird in its cage becomes agitated when it sees her, and Avis nearly stops, startled by its keening. The sun is up, but the woman hasn't come out yet. She taps, then raps her knuckles against the wood-framed screen door: the back door is open. "Hello in there!"

A shape emerges behind the dark screen. *"Dieu."* Pure exasperation. She tilts open the door. "You are here again?"

Avis tries to smile, her lips tremble. "I brought you . . ." She holds out the white bakery box.

The neighbor steps outside and gives her a long look—less caustic than before, but still full of irony. Finally she says, in that contrapuntal accent, "So I am never going to be rid of you."

Avis touches the lid of the box. "Do you like chocolate and hazelnut? They're petits fours. They have a little layer of marzipan and a layer of meringue. Some berry." As long as she stays focused on the box her voice is steady. "I wanted to apologize."

"You did, did you."

"I wanted—" Avis turns slightly, gestures toward the trees. "I was just peeking," she says hopelessly.

"Yes, like a spy."

"No, no, please. The—your bird was—singing—making its sounds. And I just came to see. I work at home. I'm a baker." The woman's face registers nothing. Avis soldiers on. "And I came—just to look. And you looked so pretty and the bird was so sweet with you, and so . . ." She trails off.

The woman's obsidian eyes are pitiless. "How many times you watch me? More than one?"

Avis clears her throat lightly.

"Spying," the woman says matter-of-factly. "Where I come from, you know what happens to spies?"

"Nothing good, I'm sure," Avis mumbles.

Then she seems to think of something. "You know how long it took me to polish that tray? An hour and a half. Just to get it clean."

Avis almost says: You're not supposed to clean it. Instead she opens the box and offers it again. "Please. If you would accept these? It's just something small."

Finally the woman consents to look in the box. Avis can smell the sparkling *fraise des bois* essence. She sees a lilt, like sadness, in the woman's face as she touches the box. "These are marzipan petits fours?" She lowers her face, inhaling. "The lady who owned the house where my mother worked—almost every day she ate these. This style. My mother smelled like these berries. Every day, the cook made twenty petits fours."

"That would have kept her busy!" Avis smiles carefully.

The woman gives her a cool look. "Yes. The lady ate two, the son ate four, and the husband possibly one or none. They threw the rest to the pigs. All the food in that house was so beautiful. The house was like something from heaven—much grander than these around here." She looks up and Avis senses something conjured, shifting between them. "I learned to mistrust beautiful things."

"Your yard is beautiful," Avis says softly.

She looks around, both of them taking in the orchids in the trees, the fountains of greenery, creamy blooms of gardenia and emerald shrubs that seem to Avis to have sprung up in a matter of days.

"It doesn't belong to me," the woman says. But something in her has relented. "*You* were the one who made those black cookies? With your own hands?"

Avis holds the box in her left hand and lifts her right. The woman studies it, as does Avis: the skin thickened and dry and loose as a work glove, the fingers crosshatched with fine white scars from nicks, thicker pink and red scars from varying degrees of burns, white crusts of flour along the nails and knuckles, the powerful wrist, the wiry, defined muscles of her forearm. "Not a white woman's hands," she says slyly. "Do your neighbors know you have hands like these?"

"I have no interest in the opinions of my neighbors."

"In that case . . ." She places her hands on the bottom and closed lid of the box. "I shall accept your beautiful things. Perhaps even eat one or two." She looks up from the corner of her eyes. "I won't throw any to the pigs."

She begins to move back toward the house and Avis follows, reluctant to lose her so quickly. "May I ask—"

The woman sighs, turns, mouth downturned, eyes liquid disapproval.

"What is your name?"

She lifts her black eyes. "What is *yours*?"

"Avis. Avis Muir."

"Then I am Solange."

"Solange." It's not as musical when Avis says it. Her breath is high and thin: she wants to ask where she came from, if she will stay, why she is here in this neighborhood. But the woman's face recedes into a powerful remoteness, dismissing Avis. She waits another long moment and notices a flutter of red: a cardinal quivers in the bushes against the woman's house. Avis wants something from her. There's a space inside of Avis like a cookie form, which seems to be the very shape of the thing she wants from this woman. Heaven is the un-haveable, her mother said. She remembers Geraldine's soaps that looked and smelled just like caramel cakes. Avis ate one when she was very small— then, aghast, spat it out. Her mother had said, That's what make them so delightful—you want to eat them, but you *can't*.

Still, Avis refuses to believe that she only wants to want: that was her mother's illness, not hers. She rubs her knuckles over her lips thoughtfully and finally says, "I'd like—I would hope—we can be friends."

The woman laughs, revealing beautiful, bright teeth. "Hope all you like, but I may not feel the same."

Brian

AT THE INTERSECTION OF BIRD AND U.S. 1, BENEATH the shadow of the Tri Rail overpass, the Dominican woman in the peaked straw hat sits on the concrete divider beside her little array of mangoes and string bags of some sort of nut or pod. She also has a carton filled with bunches of small purple flowers. Brian waves a few bucks out his window as he pulls up to the light. The regular homeless man, skin burnt beyond race, is there as well, on the other side of the street. He notices Brian's gesture and starts to move toward him, but the woman hustles over. They make the exchange and Brian is out of there—pulling into the stream of Benzes and junkers and Hondas—before the homeless man can come close.

At the Ekers Building entrance, Brian notes the way Rufus averts his gaze from the bouquet (he feels conspicuous, with a leather briefcase in one hand and the flowers—so small they're almost a corsage—in the other). "Hello, Rufus," Brian says as he enters.

"Hello, Mr. Muir."

It's a relief to have the elevator to himself: he and his flowers might just escape further scrutiny. Several mornings in a row now, he's awakened with an uncanny sensation, as if he is turning into another person: an old, well-loved, and polished carapace breaking open, odd imaginings seeping in. He wakes from dreams of fighting with his son who becomes Brian's old man. Or nightmares in which he wanders unlit marble corridors, footsteps in a dusting of powder, searching for something. He thinks again of how numb and distracted Avis has seemed this week. It's Felice, of course. The missed meeting. Just days before her eighteenth birthday. He'd awakened early that morning to a metallic sound—swishing and clicking—through the bathroom door. When he went in, later, to take a shower, he found a dark swath of hair in the bathroom trash bin. He'd lifted it out of the trash, held it for a moment in the palm of his hand, some lost, tender thing. Quietly, he stole some thread from the sewing kit, tied up a lock, and slid it into his briefcase. What does he suppose a lousy bouquet can achieve in the face of this—slippage? He senses a kind of global slide, as if the material nature of his world is losing its integrity. The sight of his wife's discarded hair was so painful in the moment, almost nightmarish: like a dream of spitting teeth into the sink.

Up to 32 he glides, ears popping. He starts to regret the flowers. Old-lady flowers, the sort his grandmother would've cultivated in her wheelbarrow planter. Dark lavender petals and bright yellow centers. It occurs to him that he should at least have waited to buy them on the way home. Now he will have to keep them fresh somehow. As he nears his office, there's a sound of voices: Fernanda and Javier round the corner laughing, Javier's hand slipping over the curve of Fernanda's shoulder.

Javier spots Brian first. "Here's the man now!"

"How are you, Brian?" Fernanda asks. He sees them both notice the bouquet; Javier's forehead ticks back. Fernanda glances at her Cartier. "You know, I think I really can't spare the coffee break right now, Javier. Rain check?"

Javier's face darkens. "Fine," he says coolly, already en route to the elevator. "I've got to get back to it myself."

Brian watches him go. "That Javy," he shoots for a humorously deprecating tone.

She glances at him, then laughs and says, "Oh, I know."

Brian walks her to the door of her office, holds it open, and she looks at him over her shoulder. "Will you come sit for a few minutes?"

A little twist in his heart, he follows her in. The office smells different. Gone is the executive mosaic of leather, metal, and aftershave. He thinks he identifies gardenia and dendrobium—their neighbors the Regales grow them. He takes in the redecorated room: there is a journal bound in a speckled coral cover; a languorous yellow ceramic mug; a small jade ring. On the desk, beside the computer, he spots a figurine and a stone-colored disk. Fernanda sees him looking and picks up the figurine. "It's Erzulie?" She turns the piece in her fingertips: beads and bits of feather and cloth. "She's very powerful, this lady. A force of nature. My grandmother was from the Islands—she gave her to me. Erzulie was supposed to help me with my grades. Ha."

"Like a saint?" Brian glances at Fernanda. "But I thought you were—"

"Jewish?" She smiles. "Don't you think you can be more than one thing?"

"Oh, I, of *course*—"

She waves it away. "And of course, this is the *other* thing my grandmother gave me." She holds up the white disk. "It's a mud cookie. She said to remind me where I come from. Sort of a *Don't get too big for your britches, missy*." Brian had been about to reach for it, but she slides it to the edge of her computer. "I grew up in a very modest home. I like to think of it as a reminder of what I'm never going back to."

She looks so self-possessed, Brian can't help but admire her: the secrecy, the flecks like gold leaf in her irises—old bloodlines. It seems to Brian there is an untouchable quality to her. A veil laid over her features. As with Avis. He glances at the goddess. "Your grandmother sounds like a genius."

"That would be the nicest way of putting it." Fernanda laughs softly. "Listen, I wanted to thank you—again—for the other day. Javier can be a bit, well . . ." She lifts her eyebrows. "*You* know." She taps a sky-blue pencil against the edge of her desk. "Ever since I moved into this office, he's been coming around. The way he stares . . . Like I'm a penthouse unit and he can't wait to make the sale."

"I'll have a word with him." Brian glares at the view through the swooping glass wall. Beyond the glass, the ocean looks like molten nickel. "It's unprofessional. Javier has no business coming around, pestering you when you're trying to do your job."

"Oh, please don't." Fernanda hunches forward. "You've been so kind—terribly kind. You're the only one who—the others—" Then Brian watches, dumbfounded, as Fernanda lowers her head and starts to cry. Her breath catches and she hides her face in her hands.

He is paralyzed. The last real tears he remembers seeing were from his daughter, the long nights after her returns: how she'd sob in her room, while Brian hung back in like ghost in the corridor, bewildered and angry. He feels impossibly clumsy: he tries to behave—as best he can—in the manner he thinks a compassionate person would. He bends toward Fernanda, placing one hand on her shoulder, and says, almost inaudibly, "Oh, my dear . . ."

She sniffles and lifts her face to him: her eyes and nostrils are barely inflamed, rimmed faintly pink. "I'm in a . . . some kind of situation . . . I don't have anyone to tell."

"Well." He hesitates. "Can you tell me?"

She shakes her head, then looks at him, smearing away tears with her fingers. "How could I? I wouldn't want to burden you—of all people. You're overloaded as it is."

He draws himself up, making fun of himself. "If it helps at all, I am a lawyer. I'm a professional at keeping secrets."

She laughs and sniffles again. "Well . . . maybe . . . if you swear . . ."

He draws an *X* over the front of his suit jacket.

She nods and lowers her head, then murmurs something so quietly he has to ask her to repeat it: "I'm seeing Jack."

"Jack?" he echoes, so relieved that she stopped crying that he barely registers her confession.

"You know. *Jack*."

Brian smiles apologetically: it sounds like the name of some kid at UM.

"Parkhurst."

He stares, still uncomprehending.

"Jack Parkhurst."

Suddenly it feels as if his heart is swelling beyond its natural dimensions: it's difficult to breathe. *What?* "How did you—" He doesn't know what to ask. He shakes his head dumbly, an empty, horselike motion. Jack Parkhurst, company president and CEO, head of his own pseudo-dynasty of developers, free-trade cronies, and rich, Old Florida Bubbas. But even so—even considering the flotilla of wealth and influence—change-jingling, seventy-four-year-old neglector of wife and children—*that* Jack Parkhurst? "How did—how could—"

"He was very attentive," Fernanda says stiffly.

"I'm sure he was—is?" Brian amends. "Are you still . . . ?"

"Is—I suppose. I want to end it, though. It's not right for either of us."

"*No,* well . . ."

"I'm sure I sound awful. It's so hard to explain about Jack . . . He can be so charming."

Brian has been upper management too long to be surprised at the hidden seams of the business world. Still. He can hardly believe that Jack Parkhurst has laid his crepuscular hand on *Fernanda,* caressed her shoulders, that his cottony mouth has gone anywhere near her neck. "Oh, my dear." Outside the window, a replica of his own office view—a perpetual motion of cars, chips of light flowing along the causeway a mile away, heading out over the water—now sapphire brilliance under a break in the clouds.

Fernanda seizes his hands. "I feel like, sometimes, more than anything I just need a really, really good—I mean, a wonderful *friend,* you know? The sort of person who's so close to you that you can say anything." A shadowy dimple appears at her left jawline. "Brian. You're just—you're a real guy. The old-fashioned kind—like Jack likes to think he is."

Brian lowers his head. He notices her glance fall on the violets again and he stares at them a moment himself. Slowly, he lays them on her desk. "For you."

"Oh Brian." She holds them to her nose. "They're just . . . they're lovely." Leaning forward, she slips them into the carafe of water on the corner of her desk, and Brian notes, with embarrassment, that the flowers are dwarfed by the container.

"I must—I should get back to the millstone—" He half rises, half bows out of his seat, and eases out of the office.

THE TELEPHONE; the glass walls; the gray condition of office light. The day has passed into afternoon and outside Miami is burning like a scarlet orchid, bursting into flame. Brian sits motionless at his desk. If he turns to the west, he will see at least thirty-eight cranes and rigs grinding away, and almost all have some connection to PI&B. A stack of ever-renewing contracts to review and assign to his underlings; proposals for still more deals, piled in folders a foot high. He picks up a folder labeled *Bonsai Towers* and attempts to browse through it, but the pages smear into each other. He attempts to stack them, tapping the pages against the desktop, but they splay against the glass. He drops the paper: *Who does he think he is?*

Randy old Parkhurst. Past company rumors—insinuations of sexual bullying, intimidation, advances—rise to the surface of his memory. It's one of Brian's tasks to make bad things go away, and he usually shuffles these cases to his underlings, each of whom is authorized to bestow modest settlements and severance packages. As Jack's counsel, he thinks, he should personally warn him away from Fernanda. He winces again at the thought of them together. Jack, he will say, the liability exposure—it's not worth it. What if things go sour? How can they not, eventually? Thus saving both the company and Fernanda much unhappiness. Win-win. He stares at the slippery image in the darkened screen. *Remember where you come from.* He imagines the young Fernanda, her hair in two braids, a wise grandmother from a Caribbean place.

He decides to take a break, wanders down to the lobby and finds himself in the gift shop, chatting with the high school kid about Stanley and Felice as if they both still lived at home: "I can't believe where the time has gone. My boy Stan's got a serious girlfriend now. And it's going to be my daughter's eighteenth birthday . . . big one, right? What do you get for an eighteen-year-old girl?"

As he strolls back toward the elevators, the lobby doors open and a phalanx of upper-mid management enter, fresh from a four-cocktail investors' meeting, heels clicking on the marble. Brian halts as if pelted by buckshot. There's Parkhurst blowing hot air while the others double over with laughter. Esmeralda is stationed at his side, aloof as Eva Perón. "So Warren calls me—" Parkhurst's voice booms all over the lobby. "Fella brings me out in the jet to *Omaha*—have you ever been to Omaha? God-forsaken place. Middle of nowhere—to a restaurant with animal heads, all staring down at us. Steaks as thick as my arm—they're hanging off the plate—lying right on the god-damn table. And Warren leans over and says to me, I bet you don't get that in Miami!" The last line is delivered in a thrombotic bellow and everyone around him breaks up.

Brian considers escaping with the elevator, but Parkhurst spies him, calling out, a feeble old bleat, "Brian, hang on!" Brian's gluteus locks up. In the past, he would have asked Jack how the Bentley was handling. How Jack Jr. was making out at Penn. Parkhurst moves his soft body in its Armani threads onto the elevator, eschewing the separate penthouse car: he enjoys riding with the "people."

"Counselor. How in the hell are you?" He slaps Brian on the back.

"Jack. How's this weekend looking? Gonna get out on the links at all?"

The elevator stops and opens. It's two stops before Parkhurst's floor but all three of them exit.

"Brilliant weekend, really, really brilliant," Parkhurst mutters as Esmeralda walks off headed east. As Brian watches Esmeralda's receding back, Parkhurst leans into him. "Stay tuned—there's a sweet little old deal coming up I want to get your eyes on. *Real* nice, Old Florida real estate. It's in this spot downtown—we're gonna call the whole area NoDo. Like it? North of Design District."

Brian jams his hands into his pockets; he's wobbling inside himself. His head gets heavy and suddenly he's watching himself and Parkhurst from twenty feet down the corridor, saying, "Yeah, Jack—I've been wanting to talk to you about one of those projects myself. Northeast Fifty-sixth Street? I think there's issues."

His employer turns his big, white-haired head in his direction. "Don't tell me—it's the hippies again? Goddamn freaks—what're they doing in Florida? Let them go hump the trees in California."

"No—no—nothing like that." Brian brings his hands together, trying to take hold of himself. He hadn't prepared for this sort of confrontation, but suddenly it feels crucial. He's had it with Parkhurst, his office with the elephant's-foot wastebasket, the walrus-tusk letter opener. Sick to death of self-satisfied arrogance, the way he treats employees like possessions, his little insinuations that Brian *needs* him, strutting around as if his company were some version of the Isle of Dr. Moreau. "I was looking again at the neighborhood specs for the Little Haiti deal—there's questions."

Parkhurst stops mid-corridor. "Didn't you sign off on it?"

"I did, sure, but new issues have come to light."

"Like what?"

"Like I don't think we did sufficient market feasibility study on the area."

Parkhurst crosses his arms, tucks his spotty hands under his biceps—a thick-brained, obstinate gesture—preamble to one of his development pitches. "What issues? The whole Design District region is going insane, Brian. You can't even get onto Northeast Fortieth anymore. I think Conrad put his finger right on it. All those nice fruity restaurants and furniture stores, a performing arts center—some fucking day. Stryker's chomping to redev that Caribbean Marketplace. And city center, man—the midtown development deal is phase two now—all that new urbanism crap—two minutes' walk to the dry cleaners. It's gonna be the Italian fucking Renaissance around here in a few years."

"Yes, yes. I'm not questioning any of that."

"Didn't even need a feasibility study, if you ask me—just look at it. And NoDo *North* is pre-gentrification—really young, super sexy. Our building's gonna be red-hot—top architect, and Valente and his boys are laying the bricks for us. A big fat block of condo towers that'll blow the place out of the water. Fifty stories, Venetian marble. Conrad wanted to call it the Tom Perdue. Dumb fucking name—after some nobody. I had to persuade him out of that. We're calling it the Blue Topaz."

When Jack gets excited about a project, it's like watching kindling smoke: this is *the* deal. The one. Brian presses his hands into a kind of praying fold, lowers his face to his fingertips. His law school friend Dennis thought Brian was nuts taking a job with a developer, said that he was entering "the belly of the beast and taking an office in the colon." Supposedly he'd be pushed into a servant's position—devoting his energies to subverting contract wording, excavating loopholes, massaging bylaws, and generally clearing the path so his boss could proceed with the greatest of ease. But how was that different from any other corporate hired gun? He lifts his head. "Jack, I'm not sure we shouldn't take a pass on this one."

Parkhurst blinks slowly. The more their business has grown, the more Parkhurst likes to give outsiders the impression that his attorney lives next to his skin. Brian has never before tried to get in the way of a PI&B project, but he remembers vividly the night he'd visited that art gallery; the sound of neighbors talking in the night: a particular mood of serenity and contentment. He knows the essence of the city is its neighborhoods, most of which are being systematically broken into by developers—their constructions driving out the old homes and families, ushering in nonresident owner-investors, anti-communities made up of transients and tourists—no personal history or investment in the place where they've landed. He thinks of the little brown-faced doll on Fernanda's desk. For all they know, her grandparents live on that very street. Now he takes a breath and begins listing worst-case scenarios. "It's old, Jack, like historic old. The street in question doesn't even border the District—it's deep, old neighborhood. According to our new intelligence," he lies, "there will be a citizens' turnout that'll make those hippie tree-huggers look like a tea party." He shakes his head. "We could be tied up for years." And you, he thinks, vain old man, do not always get want you want.

Parkhurst studies Brian's face. Over the years, he's come to rely increasingly on Brian to help guide projects. Still, the old man thrives on resistance, derives jolts of inspiration from roadblocks. "That could be fun," he says. "Haven't seen a goddamned crowded zoning meeting in years. 'If you know the enemy and know yourself, you need not fear the results of a hundred battles.' "

Sun Tzu. One of Jack's favorites. Brian nods. "Right, right. But then there's plain bad decisions. Remember the publicity nightmare when they gutted Overtown to put in I-95?"

"Terrible move."

"Disastrous." Brian folds his arms as they stop before his office. "We've got to be smart about risk-reward ratio, take another look at cash flow. There's no parking, no infrastructure, and frankly, I'm concerned that the downtown corridor is approaching saturation."

The recessed lighting makes a nimbus of Parkhurst's white combover. He looks down the hall past Brian for a long moment. "Brian, I hear you." Parkhurst's tone is modulated now; his white brows lower. "At this point, we're more than three-quarters in. Tony Malio did beautiful work greasing the zoning board and we have an initial clearance there. I met with the Aguardiente group and shook on it." He lets the glass corridor partition swing shut behind them as Brian turns. "So here's what we're gonna do: we'll send Tony back out in the field—the Citizens' Action Corps, is that it? Have him grab a paralegal, go visit the natives, shake some more hands, throw another third, up to double, onto the payouts. Make everybody happy."

The two men gaze at each other a moment. Finally Brian lifts his chin, smiles. "Of course, Jack, excellent plan."

Parkhurst slaps Brian on the arm. "Good man, Brian. Thanks for speaking up. Honestly. Solid gold."

He watches Parkhurst turn back down the hall, lifting his eyes

to the embedded ceiling lights as if gazing toward heaven. The glass
partition whispers shut. Brian taps the glass corridor wall to his
office, then lets his head tip forward, gently, until the top of his forehead touches the closed office door.

SLUMPED IN HIS CHAIR, Brian coughs, tries to clear his head, his
spiraling disappointment. He has hours yet to go: phone calls to the
Latin Builders Association, the Planning and Zoning Board, and the
Regional Planning Council; a polenta Bolognese from the executive
dining room; a spirited visit from Javier, his voice booming over Brian's desk, talk of another gloriously named project.

There's a call from Stanley. He listens in the dilated office light
as his son tells him about *difficulties, girlfriend, money . . .* Stanley
says he wants to arrange a *meeting*. Like a client. Brian's concentration hazes into a reverie of throttling Parkhurst.

"So Dad?" his son is saying. "That okay? Yeah?"

"Did you talk to your mother?" he asks reflexively.

"Mom?" Stanley sounds irritated; then he sighs. "She'll just say
the same thing."

Brian pushes his fingertips into his temples, rubbing.

"How about can we just agree on meeting at the house?" Stanley's
voice is rigid. Brian finally realizes that his son is under some sort of
duress; he tries to pay attention. Brian must've said something appro-
priate or reassuring at last because Stanley sounds happier now. "So,
cool. We'll come over. It'll be good."

Brian spots Fernanda on her way out, a gray naiad rippling in the
glass wall, and he's struck by an ancient memory. Twelve years old,
feeling dizzy and sick, stretched out on a pew in a tiny mission chapel. He had visited this place with his family. The church was white
as snow, the ceiling ribbed with timber, and an immense golden Jesus
was pinned to the wall above the altar. The church, the dry hot air,
the smell of sage, the sight of a black-eyed girl with dimpled feet and
a black velvet ribbon around her hair. It comes back to him in finely

etched detail—the sweetness of mariachi ballads and Mexican Spanish and the clear air. Suddenly he is asking his son, "Stan—have you ever heard of such a thing as a mud cookie?"

There's a brief silence, then breath—almost a laugh. "Well—yeah. I guess so."

"What is it exactly?"

"If we're talking about the same thing . . . it's pretty much what it sounds like. Maybe they add some lard to hold it together, but it's basically dirt. People live on them, in some countries."

"God," Brian murmurs.

"Well, if it's that or starving to death? You take the cookie. Why you asking about that?"

There it is, Brian realizes, the reason he'd tried to deflect Parkhurst from the one neighborhood: he imagined telling the story to his son, how he'd stood up to that greedy Goliath, on behalf of all those poor and dispossessed. Score for the other side. He'd imagined the approval in his son's face, at last. "Oh, just something I saw," Brian murmurs. "Nothing important."

Avis

Avis RUNS HER HANDS OVER THE UPHOLSTERY on her chair arms. Back and forth. New girlfriend: her husband had tried to warn her. She registers, in her peripheral vision, the girl, this Nieves, gazing around her dining room, tipping her drained Villeroy & Boch cup—peeking at the manufacturer. Brian sits in the matching arm chair to her right, Stanley sits at one end of the couch, oriented toward them, watching Nieves—*awaiting her command*. Normally Stanley comes to their house only on the holidays. Avoiding his sister's ghost, Avis supposes. And herself.

Avis pours a half-refill of tea for the girl. "Did you inherit your china?" Nieves asks. Acquisitive thing. "It looks valuable."

The girl really is quite striking. She has the translucent face of that starlet . . . The actress's name has flown right out of Avis's head, but she can't help noticing the way the girl wears her dark hair in similar long, smooth twists. Her skin is a satiny caramel with notes of mocha and chocolate, her eyes black almonds. Avis wonders if growing up with such a cinematically beautiful sister has made Stanley too vulnerable to beauty. The young woman leans back, still clutching her cup, and Avis notes the fullness of her breasts and a certain thickness about the girl's body, as if she were older than Avis initially thought. She stretches, bending slightly, then finally smiles. Stanley says, "Mom bought it on a trip we took to Germany. Years ago."

Avis is pleased that Stanley would remember—they were on a sort of family vacation. While Brian attended a contract law conference in Frankfurt, Avis had taken the kids on a day trip to a medieval town in Bavaria, its narrow streets crowded with porcelain shops. The children helped Avis pick out the paper-fine china, its intricate webbing of cracked glaze, a sprinkling of rosebuds along the rim of the saucers. Now she smiles thinly at Nieves, thinking about the pieces she'd smashed on the patio after Felice had left for good. Avis had worked methodically, a piece or two a day, destroying her prized possessions, the satisfying crunch, like flinging robin's eggs. Until Brian quietly suggested that Stanley might like to have them someday. She stopped in time to save the cups and saucers.

"I like old things," Nieves says. She contemplates the cup again. "But these are lovely."

"I'm so glad you approve," Avis says.

Nieves looks up at her as Brian and Stanley rush to interrupt, Brian saying, "This tea is from—" just as Stanley says, "Mother made these meringues." *Mother*—not Mom—Avis catches the remonstrance and she knots her hands together: *Behave*. Nieves puts the meringue in her mouth, as if to stop herself from speaking, and Avis knows what she's tasting: a crisp folding air, then melting bits of shaved chocolate. Nieves's mouth softens into a sigh. "Oh," she says quietly, as if talking to herself. "Wonderful."

Avis stands, her eyes hot, and hurries into the kitchen.

THE OTHER DAY, Avis had been in the kitchen preparing a batter when Stanley's deliveryman had come to the door. Along with her usual baking supplies, Eduardo carried a cooler full of organic produce. She followed him back into the kitchen and watched him remove chilies, onions, garlic, and tomatoes from the cooler. A whole chicken. He opened the refrigerator and slid in cartons of milk and eggs, a wedge of lemon-colored cheese, bunches of lettuce, broccoli, and cauliflower. He closed the fridge, then flipped the cooler shut. "Your son doesn't approve of your eating habits."

"No kidding." Avis sighed as she filled a pastry bag. Once or twice a month a supply of unasked-for items.

"Risky, though—giving someone a bunch of food they don't like."

190 ... DIANA ABU-JABER

"He knows I won't be able to let it go to waste."

The mynah started its shrieking: a fierce, shattering *braaaah*. He swiveled toward the window. "Wow. What the hell."

Avis piped tiny *quenelles* of tea cake dough onto a cookie tray. "He'll settle down in a second." She slipped the tray into the oven, then looked over Eduardo's shoulder: they watched Solange walk down the steps, hair tied in a faded turquoise scarf, a teal dress fluttering with the air.

"What's the deal with her?" Eduardo asked. "She the house-keeper?"

"Of course not." Avis pulled out a tray of scallop-shaped molds for madeleines. "I don't think," she added quietly, pouring batter into her molds.

Eduardo didn't speak for a long moment. "Haitians were the first ones—you know—to throw a revolution, kick out the colonizers." He lifted his chin, apparently at the neighbor. "Those kidnapped Africans—they'd adapted to Haiti but they never forgot who they were—they knew they were free people."

She slammed the cookie molds on the counter, settling the dough. "Huh." She set those aside, then stooped to pull a ring of strawberry *génoise* from the lower oven.

"Though, of course, it's kind of funny . . ."

She glanced over, took in the slight asymmetry to his face, flattened lower lip, shadowy outlines of the tear troughs beneath his eyes. "What?"

"Well. Just. Here you are, still a slave to the French."

Avis straightened, hands on her hips. "I work for myself. That's hardly slavery."

"Hey, we all choose our own masters." He turned to the window. "Have you seen anything magic going on over there yet?"

She laughed and placed the springform pans into the cooling rack, bits of parchment lining jutting up like feathers around the edges. On the top rack is a cooled and decorated seven-layered *opéra* cake. Her client—the Peruvian ambassador—had requested a "tropical" theme for a dinner party dessert. Avis had based the decoration on the view through the kitchen window, re-creating in lime, lemongrass, and mint frostings the curling backyard flora, curving foliage shaped like tongues and hearts, fat spines bisecting the leaves.

Eduardo edged closer. "You don't believe it?"

She began pouring chocolate *pastilles* into the bowl of her double boiler. "I thought you said voodoo was just another type of religion."

"It is. Religion with extenuating circumstances." He leaned over the stove.

"Uh-huh." Avis adjusted the flame.

Eduardo moved to another corner, trying to get out of the way. "Let me tell you something. About ten years ago? I was a production assistant for a crew that was filming on Haiti. It was supposed to be a documentary called *Flowering Heaven*—about home gardens in the Caribbean. I just went to hang out on the beach. Anyway, when we were there, we met all kinds of people who went to witches—like, instead of doctors? They had curses broken and got cured from all kinds of weird diseases and problems. We met people who used those little dolls, and spell-casters . . ."

Avis hummed and stirred the melting chocolate, watching it turn black and glossy as it liquefied, seeding it with bits of chopped *pastilles*. "Oh right," she murmured. "And the people they cursed, they'd get weird aches and pains, right?"

He lifted his eyebrows. "Hey, you really think there's an explanation for everything?" His voice was intent and confiding. "You think the world is only what you can see and feel?"

Avis dipped the tip of her spatula into the melted chocolate and brought it close to her lips, checking the heat. "Our senses tell a lot more than we realize."

"All I know is we saw things there . . ." He shakes his head. "All kinds of people said they'd attracted their husbands and wives with charms."

"Sure, love potions." She scraped a few more bits of chopped chocolate into the liquid to bring down the temperature. "Do you know what I do for a living?"

"One man told me he woke up in the morning with this woman's face in his mind. He'd never seen her before in his life, but he became obsessed with finding her. It turned out she lived miles away, in another town. She'd seen him once, at a market, and made a love charm to call him to her. A few days later, he was knocking at her door."

Avis looked up at the wobbly reflections in the stainless steel cabinets lining the walls. Sometimes when she baked, she thought she caught sight of some odd movement in the corner of her eyes—but it was always this reflection flashing from surface to surface. "So how did this guy feel about that? About the fact that she'd used a charm and tricked him into it?"

Eduardo shrugged. "They got married. He loved her. I don't think anyone particularly cared how it happened."

STANLEY IS GOING ON about work, how they might have to expand— the property developers circling Homestead like vultures—a reproachful look at his father. She observes the formal way he holds his cup on a saucer—letting everyone know that he too is a guest in this house. His voice has a buzzing tonality that irritates her. Makes it hard to listen to him: buzz, buzz, buzz. Whenever they visit him at the market, she's noticed his customers and employees hang on his words as if he were some sort of saint or the head of a cult. People tell her: "Your son is amazing, Mrs. Muir. How did you do it?" She rubs her thumb over her knuckles, listening to Brian making chitchat, quizzing them gently. Nieves crosses her arms, lets her head tip back, watching Brian.

"When did you two start seeing each other?" Brian asks.

The girl smiles. "Seeing each other?"

Stanley takes her hand. "Actually, Dad, Nieves and I are living together."

Brian gives a sort of huff at the same time that Avis feels something tighten, a bone pressing against her heart. "You're *living* together?" he asks.

Nieves's crossed leg bobs up and down. Stanley has an odd, guilty expression now, his cheeks flushed. "She just moved in. This month."

"To your apartment?" Brian is openly astonished. Stanley lives above the market in a bleak one-bedroom in downtown Homestead. Attached to the apartment is a small studio he uses as overflow for the market's storeroom. Brian and Avis used to joke about Stanley being married to his work. How quickly things change, Avis thinks. Brian squeezes her limp hand. "Now, but don't you think you kids—"

"We're having a baby," Nieves interrupts.

"What?" Avis is breathless. "You mean *someday*?" But of course—it rushes in on Avis—she doesn't mean "someday." At last Avis understands what she's been seeing all along—the blue shadows under the girl's eyes and her puffy face. Avis turns to Stanley—who is staring at Nieves—and it's like peeling back a series of transparencies. There are the sloping bones of his adult face; there is the sugar-milk skin of Stanley at four. "Stanley?"

Stanley lowers his gaze to the floor, forearms balanced on his knees. He's the picture of remorse and Avis feels an almost pleasurable impulse to scold him. She reminds herself, he isn't much younger than she'd been, barely twenty-seven, pregnant with him. "Obviously the timing isn't the greatest," Stanley mutters. "With the business taking on all this new debt, plus the tax hike . . ."

"How pregnant, or, I mean—far along—are you?" Brian asks Nieves. Avis hears a bounce in his voice. "Are you taking folic acid? Have you seen a doctor?"

Folic acid! Now Avis reaches for her husband's hand. She wants to protect him. Nieves looks at him warily. She's dressed in low-rise jeans, shiny sandals with just a filament of leather over the toes, a satiny, clinging top that looks like underwear, and a pair of sparkling loop earrings. "I'm probably due in the winter I guess."

"It was pretty, you know, unexpected," says Stanley, as if he's learning all of this for the first time. "We're still figuring things out."

"It's marvelous!" Brian blurts; he turns to Avis: his eyes are damp. "We think it's wonderful, of course," he says. "Congratulations, you two."

"But we need money," Nieves says. "Stanley was supposed to tell you? We really do. Right away."

Stanley's face is a dark putty-color.

"Oh. Yes," Brian says.

"You already knew about this?" Avis releases his hand.

"No, no—not the baby! Nothing about the baby."

The baby.

"Stanley was supposed to tell you," Nieves says.

"What?" Avis's voice wobbles; her neck feels hot.

Brian puts his hand on Avis's arm while addressing Nieves. "Remind me—"

"One hundred twenty-six thousand dollars," Nieves says. "We have to get that much, or it won't work."

"Oh, this is ridiculous!" Avis says. She doesn't care for this girl. She places her hands square on her knees—they feel knobby; the bones in her back feel sharp as piano keys. Already a querulous old lady. "A hundred twenty-six *thousand*? My God, how do you expect *us* to come up with that sort of money?"

Stanley starts shaking his head heavily. They've bailed him out a number of times in the past with small gifts, disbursements, a few thousand here and there; one loan of twenty-five thousand, which he'd partially paid off and they'd forgiven the remaining seventeen. But this sounds like extortion to Avis—this dreadful girl, using the threat of a grandchild. Another thought comes to her: could they even be sure that the child is Stanley's? She must discuss this with Stanley in private. But he's looking at her now as if he were embarrassed or disappointed. "Mom, I talked with Dad—I mean we thought we could get away with eighty thousand before but our other investors— their money's tied up—"

"It's true, dear," Brian interrupts, his hand curved around her forearm. "We did discuss this—Stan and me. I'd been meaning to talk it over with you—well, we've both been so busy." He lowers his head, touches the back of his neck reflectively. "It's hard to know exactly the best moment for these things."

"Stanley—*tell* them," the girl says.

Stanley's gaze rests a beat too long on Avis. "I didn't want to worry either of you." He rolls forward to put down his cup. "The thing is . . . the owner of my property keeps getting approached by commercial developers—I guess Homestead is getting kind of hot all of a sudden."

"I knew it," Brian bursts out. "Dammit. Goddamn gold-diggers."

"He's a good guy—Calvin Mails, the owner. He's trying to work with us, but there's all these sorts of crazy numbers flying around and he's ready to sell."

"We can buy the building and land for five hundred K," Nieves cuts in. "Basically, that price? He's doing us a huge favor because he loves Stan. He could probably get almost twice that. But it means we've got to raise twenty percent just to qualify for the loan. Plus a little extra for closing costs and expenses."

"Of course, of course . . ." Brian mutters, glaring at his lap.

"All our money's been going right back into the business—it's been strictly subsistence living—for both of us," Stanley adds, linking his fingers with Nieves's.

"You remember?" Brian chides, brows lifted. "I warned you!"

"Dad." He sighs through his nose. "I didn't have the money to buy the place five years ago any more than I do now. Twenty thousand or a hundred. It might as well be the moon."

"Well, but twenty is a whole other—"

"Dad, believe me—we've tried—literally—everything we could to avoid coming to you. But once we're owners, it'll be different. The market's really healthy. I don't know exactly when, but—I swear—we'll pay you back soon. With interest."

"Interest isn't the point here, son. And actually, interest rates on business loans—"

"It doesn't matter!" Nieves erupts. "What matters is that if we don't buy the building we'll lose the market. We can't even afford to relocate—there *is* no place cheaper."

Avis's body fills with adrenaline tremors. She holds the lapels of her blouse closed in her fist, presses the silk against her throat. It is intolerable. The *problem,* as she sees it, is this—this *Nieves.* Where did she come from? Look at her, slouching, her tight shirt, the blebs of fat just beneath the corners of her sulking mouth. She thinks she can just waltz in here and take their son and their money? And now she'll produce a child to torment and blackmail them with—threaten to never let them see the baby unless they do as she says. The first grandchild. *Their* feelings are immaterial: Avis and Brian will have to dance to this girl's tune. It is unbearable, absolutely unendurable.

Avis stands. She is gratified to see a spark of anxious curiosity on Nieves's face. "No," Avis says, her voice ridged with emotion. "It's not fair. This isn't right or fair."

"Dearest." Brian's hand lingers on her wrist; she yanks it away.

"I won't do it—I won't do any of whatever you think you're cooking up," she says to Nieves. "I've been tortured enough already, thank you very much."

"Cooking up?" Nieves looks at Stanley. *"What?"*

Stanley's expression opens to incredulity; his eyes flick between his parents.

Avis's pulse is pounding so hard it seems it must be visible. In some way, this girl is the reason that things aren't right. Because that's what a girl like this does—breaks into a family, sets them against each other.

Brian stands beside her now, sliding an arm around her shoulder. Is he shaking? "Oh . . . She doesn't mean that at all! Avis hasn't been feeling well," he says lightly. "There've been these—disturbances—in the neighborhood lately . . ." Was that a chuckle? "Please—kids—we *do*—we want to help you—your mother and I both," he says to Stanley. "We just haven't had a chance to discuss any of this between the two of us. It *is* a lot of money. And—well—now a baby coming! It's all just a bit overwhelming, you know? I think Mom's just in a state of, like, shock—aren't you?" He gives Avis's shoulders a squeeze. She lowers her eyes and finds she's staring at the navy polish on the girl's toes, the thong of a silver-sequined flip-flop.

Stanley rises as well. "Well," he says quietly. He clears his throat. "Well I guess this wasn't the way I expected things to go."

Avis interposes herself between Stanley and the girl (which isn't difficult, as the girl remains seated after Stanley has risen, Avis notes, as if it's all a matter of supreme indifference to her if they stay or go) and puts her imploring hands on his chest "Stanny..." She is reassured by the solidity of her son's chest, his familiar smell of toothpaste and grassy earth, his boy scent. "You're trying to replace her. Felice turning eighteen—a little like losing her again, isn't it? I think it is. Almost worse in a way..." Her eyes darken. Brian clears his throat as if about to speak and her focus returns. "I have—just a suggestion. Why don't you and your girl try staying *here*—with us, for a while? We'll give you some money and we can cover your living costs while you figure things out with the market. Would that be nice? Let's just try being a family together again," she says quietly, ignoring Brian, who keeps trying to cut in. "My goodness, Stan, you're practically still a baby yourself! Let us take care of you. I mean both of you, of course. We'll help with the money. But just come home for a bit." As she speaks, Avis feels buoyed by this idea: Stanley needs to come home! They would make it up to him—whatever he thought he'd been missing. It wasn't too late—they could show him. And if he insists on bringing this girl—fine. "It's a bit of a mess," she says as gently as possible to Stanley. "No, of course—this baby is wonderful news. But you two don't have any idea what you're in for. You're going to need us."

Only then does she realize that her son's face is growing remote, sealing up, just as he used to do in his childhood. And Avis can feel her insides start to crumple, a fernlike twisting-in. "Oh—I. I'm sorry." She steps back, as if she could pull away from the words. "Just—never mind. That didn't come out right, maybe."

"About a thousand years late, Mom." His voice parched. Stanley sidesteps Avis and offers his hand to the girl to help her up. They behave so formally, like children impersonating adults. Avis finds herself admiring their gravity as they move to the door, a regal height to the girl's shoulders.

"I'll call you later," Stanley mutters to his father as he ushers his girlfriend through the door. Then pulls it quietly shut.

Avis stands alone for a moment, staring at the door, not moving.

"Ah," Brian says.

She wraps her arms tightly around her middle. She doesn't want to talk. All the words have left her. How many times is a person supposed to lose her children? Is this why she went through motherhood? The morning sickness that lasted all day, the swollen ankles, the all-night feedings, the fevers and crying and vomit? The anxiety and the waiting up, and on and on. All for what? A moment where you stand there and watch your child close the door in your face.

BRIAN FINDS AVIS OUTSIDE, sitting in the backyard on a teak folding chair. He sits beside her and for a few minutes neither of them speaks. Finally he reaches for her hand. "You're in shock. I know you're in shock. We both are. It's a lot to take in. For both of us. But— just imagine, sweetheart? A *grandchild*."

Avis stares at the fluttering palms. "Not my grandchild. You can have her."

"You don't mean that! You're just overwrought." He attempts a new, lighter tone, "How do you even know it's a her?"

"Don't you see what he's trying to do? He's trying to replace Felice. He was cheated of his old family—we all were—so he's trying to make a new one. Just like he was always running off to his gardening and his market."

"Sweetheart." Brian presses her palm between his fingers, his voice thin and trembling, as if running through a wire strainer. He sits unusually upright, his face so alert he seems almost frightened. "Isn't that a good thing? Doesn't everyone eventually want a family of their own?"

Avis frowns, smoothing back the short ends of her hair.

"Maybe we should just give them the money."

"It's too much!" She wraps her arms around her elbows. "Who is this girl he's with anyway?"

"Well, the mother of our grandchild, at the very least."

She is touched, briefly, by an awareness of her husband's anxiety, but her own preoccupations are overpowering. She doesn't respond. The late-afternoon sky is a green watercolor. Everything in the world seems bound to the screen of fronds; everything is breathing, subtly, quietly, barely moving.

TUESDAY MORNING, AFTER BRIAN—finally, blessedly—leaves for work, Avis leaves her rounds of dough to rise and goes straight outdoors. She'd listened to the mynah's chatter all through the early morning while kneading the puff pastry ("I swear it—I'm going to report those people to animal control," Brian had said at the door). When Avis steps through the fronds, pushing aside the nodding spindles, Solange is sitting in the grass, legs folded under, as if at a tea ceremony. She doesn't exactly smile at Avis but she nods, her face relaxed.

Solange hands Avis an old-fashioned silver peeler and they cut tiny zucchinis into strips that Solange collects in a pot beside her on the grass. Then they hunt around for a shrub buried in the thickets at the west corner of the yard. It has a frilly, dainty leaf that Solange calls *"vervain"* and she tells Avis that it's good for strengthening the "female systems." She hums as they collect, and the bird grows still, then she sings a few fragments of song, shreds of music, the words floating away like confetti, like tearing a letter into pieces. The long, patient labor reminds Avis of the externships she did in culinary school—visiting different pastry shops and kitchens, listening to the bakers' philosophies about their work, their approaches and aesthetics. Only Solange speaks little, her thoughts seemingly embedded in the small movements of her hands.

"My son would be shocked," Avis says into the silence, vaguely smiling. "Me, in the dirt. Outside! He would be amazed." She glances at Solange.

"You don't go out of doors?"

"Almost never."

"You close yourself in on purpose. It's not healthy."

"I don't like vegetables, either." She continues to smile, enjoying the feeling of confession. "I don't like growing them, cooking them, or eating them."

Solange finishes cutting a zucchini. "When I was growing up, there were two worlds—one was inside the great house and the other was outside with my mother. Inside was very fine and very clean, and a lot of black women to keep it so clean. The lady of the house— Myra—she was light-skinned, but she wasn't pure white. There were a few drops of Africa in her, so we knew that was why she hated us so much. She worked the women like slaves. But my mother would steal outside when she could. She changed us out of our good house clothes into the old castoffs, and we would go tend to the vegetables and herbs in the patch the gardener gave her." Solange wiped at the edge of her forehead with one hand. "Sometimes she went foraging too. Inside, I learned the alphabet, but outside, I learned all the plants." She looks at Avis, holding the peeler aloft.

They work easily together through the silent hours and heat. A few times during the course of the day, Avis hears the phone ringing inside the house and she knows she should go back inside: she imagines the dough overinflating, the orders unfilled. But there is such rare pleasure in sitting in the grass and sweating, skin pearly with humidity, the sweet chlorophyll stains on her palms: she can almost understand why someone would choose not to live inside a house. She thinks about the hours, whole days on end, Stanley spent working his garden. Outdoors, nothing but the scent of the air. Midafternoon, Solange goes into the house while Avis dozes in the shade near the birdhouse, sweat curling down her neck. After a while, she brings out a soup with a cloudy, briny broth, dashes of the peeled vegetable and chopped greenery they'd collected. They eat it, sitting together on the back step of the house, holding white porcelain bowls. It is ineffably good and restorative. Avis's knees and back are stiff, but she finds that she's so hungry she barely notices. When they finish, they put the bowls on the cement step.

Avis sighs, sitting back. She rubs her hands on her jeans and says, "I guess I'm going to have a grandchild."

Solange sits back as well, placing her hands flat on her knees, her stern gaze seemingly drawn into herself. Avis watches her and begins to feel that the other woman is looking at something invisible—a sort of communing—and that the slightest movement could cause her to fly away. Eventually Solange turns her attention to her empty bowl. Her face is hard, her teeth an unearthly white against the purplish color of her inner lip. "It's a strange thing, how life can roll out in front of you, so nice and welcoming. Like you been promised a trip to a beautiful island, where the trees and gates are full of flowers and the roads are like shining paths and the air smells like sweetness, and all around the ocean's like a bright blue marble. You reach out for it . . ." Solange lifts the surface of her palm, uncurling her fingers. "You can almost touch it and smell it, you're practically almost there. And then, just at the moment before you arrive . . ." She closes her hands into a fist, skin over her knuckles turning pale. "You have to understand— after something terrible—*insupportable*—happens to a person, it's hard not to feel like the terrible thing is out there, everywhere, inside of every single thing you see and encounter. And it's hard not to feel this sort of rage against everyone. Sometimes it takes everything a person has, not to let everything turn black, not to feel like everything you touch is scraping off your skin."

Avis swallows. She wants to say, I know, I know, I know this, I do. But she doesn't speak, sensing the size of what Solange is talking about: an enormity, bigger than anything she has known. Too big to look at directly.

Solange shifts her leg so the mynah steps up onto her knee, its scaly talons carefully opening and curling around her leg. It hunkers like a child in her lap and she strokes its head for a while, humming, its neck feathers ruffling up between each stroke. "A grandbaby," she says at last, "is a stroke of luck."

Avis blinks and shades her eyes with her hand. She lowers her chin onto the palm of her hand, studying Solange. "Yes, thank you," she murmurs.

Solange lowers her shining lids and runs one finger down the back of the bird's head. Avis eyes her, afraid that she thinks Avis doesn't deserve a grandchild, as if believing a thing might be enough to keep a grandchild away.

For the rest of the afternoon, Avis digs rows of shallow furrows in which Solange drops tiny seeds. They cultivate a garden plot at the far western edge of Solange's yard—a spot which probably cuts into the Martinezes' property line next door. Solange amended the soil with her own compost, raised beds sparkling with minerals. From time to time a ghostly ringing from Avis's house reaches them in whiffs through the trees.

"That's Miami, calling for its sugar," Avis says.

Solange's face is traced with dark trails of sweat. She pats mounds of earth carefully over each seed. "You don't care? You can afford to laugh at your patrons?"

Avis drags her fingers into the black soil, reviving a scent memory, distant scrap of childhood—the pleasure of digging in dirt. Does she disdain the people she bakes for?

Solange pats some of the raked bands of soil. "You might just poison someone that way. If you don't care very much."

She gives a thin smile. "Have you ever done that? Sort of lost your place in things?" She knows she *should* be worried: there's a tower of pans growing in her sink, all sorts of tiny unfinished chores: separate eggs for a soufflé; place orders for nutmeg and coconut—tasks Nina had performed, efficiently and automatically. Avis rakes open another seam in the dirt and gestures for a seed, not ready to face her kitchen.

Solange raises her eyebrows without looking at her. "No, I don't forget where my place is. I bide my time."

Avis shakes her head. "I forgot what this was like."

"Myra—the lady my mother worked for—she had no children of her own, so she tried to win me all the time." Solange cast a sidelong glance at Avis. "She would give me bonbons and treats and dresses. She never wanted me to go outside. I was the only child there and it was a lonely place. The house was built on tall rocks above the water. Miles away from town. Sometimes it was so quiet we heard cars and voices—sometimes shooting. Once I thought I heard a man screaming. Mostly there was the sound of the waves, water the color of blue beads. I learned about France all the time, in the books the lady gave me to study. I read Dumas, Hugo. Later, Proust. The only thing I knew about my own home was what my mother taught me when we were outdoors together. Myra did everything she could think of to keep us apart. She told me terrible things about my mother. She said my mother had tried to smother me in my sleep, after I was born, but that Myra had saved me."

Avis fingers the short, curling hairs at the nape of her neck, reflectively. "Do you think it's true?"

Solange's eyes seem to harden, as if she'd forgotten she was speaking out loud. She pauses and there is the wind's liquid swish through the palm spears, the dark interstices between the fronds. A big sea-green anole watches them, frozen on the Martinezes' loquat. For a moment, Avis has the oddest feeling, more tangible and familiar even than déjà vu, that all of this—the leaves and Solange and the lizard and the wind—has happened before, in just this way. The sunlight is brassy and lower now, cutting across their faces, and Avis scratches at her wrists: the mosquitoes will be worse soon.

"You know what I think?" Solange asks coolly. Avis sees again that slim crescent of teeth, her dark purple underlip. "I think my story is not something to wrap up with a bow and hand over. Not to you and not to anyone."

THAT EVENING, WHEN AVIS goes back inside, it feels like a deliberate act, a small attempt at return. She moves through the house, switching on the lights and closing the shutters against the evening. Lamb follows her, twining between her ankles. She opens the front door and Lamb comes out on the front step with her: the neighborhood is falling into a velvet green darkness, the advance of the tropical night. A few people—high school students and domestics—are still out, strolling home, most of the commuter cars tucked in their driveways. It's been a long time since she's last stood on her front step, watching the neighbors come in.

Avis goes in to take a shower. While she's toweling dry, she hears Brian's key. He's home early for the first time in ages and this, she realizes, makes her happy.

Avis pulls on her thin cotton bathrobe and pads out to the living room, barefooted. At first he doesn't realize she's there, and she has a moment to observe his unguarded expression as he sorts through the mail. The lines in his face, the pensive eyes—and now he wears glasses—are all stimulating to her. How easy it is—when one lies beside another person for years—to forget to look at them. In the beginning, she'd thought she'd never stop looking.

Brian glances up; his eyes light on his wife, and there is a moment of hesitation. Then he gives way to a full, helpless smile, and says, "Can you believe it?" Just as if this were an ongoing conversation. And she says, "I *know*."

Brian moves closer, takes her hand, then closes his arms around Avis. She inhales his plain scent, then places her hand at the center of his chest and presses the side of her face against his body. She thinks about the story that Solange almost told her and feels grateful now that Solange had held back from it. Avis wants the world to be clear.

Felice

WHAT COULD SHE HAVE BEEN THINKING, LIS-
tening to that fool? How had she become so easy to dupe? *Oregon.*
She shifts her weight forward on her board and feels the salt air on her
face and eyes. She is happy—delighted even—to be free of Emerson
and his dumb plans. *This* is the special world, right here. Emerson.
His parents gave him that bizarre name to try to make themselves
seem clever and special: which is always the sign of the dumbest,
most un-special people. She pictures him, the clayey whiteness of his
skin, the pink of his scalp showing through his stupid Nazi haircut.
Who's he kidding, anyway? That strongman stuff? How lame and
sad. Like that proves anything.

Felice rolls down to Lincoln Road, then hops off, flips the board
up and carries it as she walks along the mall. She doesn't need to
be cautious anymore. The police haven't eyed her very closely in a
year or two, and several times now she's spotted kids from school—
at bars, stores, and the beach—whose eyes glazed over hers without
a glimmer of recognition. She turns right onto Washington to Seventeenth Street, past a cloud of Japanese girls with auburn hair and
fuzzy animal backpacks, and strolls into the tattoo shop. Recently
Duffy's has been her main source of income. She'll put her feet up
in one of their dentist chairs by the chrome sinks while Kaiyo and
Frederick airbrush ornate, brightly colored designs on her back,
arms, shoulders, and legs. They pay her two hundred bucks to sit
out in front of their store in a halter top and shorts, sipping Frappuccinos and flipping through magazines. German backpackers,
Brazilian and Gulfie rich kids all get snagged on her look. She sees

them out of the corner of her eyes, blond college kids daring each other to go talk to her—as if she were someone famous. Some go to Duffy's for the stupid spring-break airbrush that will start to streak off as soon they wade into the surf; most of them get permanent ink. They come out and show her the new illustrations on their skin—tramp-stamps with stock designs—butterflies or boys' names. Sometimes Felice feels kind of bad about it.

She's been scouted by Ford and Elite—real New York agencies. Micah, the agent for Elite—a tall black guy in silver eyeliner—said that Felice was "heart-stopping." Everyone says that Felice looks like Elizabeth Taylor—all pleased with themselves, as if she were hearing this for the first time. It used to bug Felice: she pictured that squat, henlike woman in her wig and jewels, holding hands with Michael Jackson. But one day, Duffy brought over an old movie magazine while Felice and Berry lounged at their café table. He opened it and jabbed at the photo. "There. Look. You kids really are morons. You really don't know anything, do you? *That's* Elizabeth Taylor."

Berry craned over the page. "Wow, you really kind of do. Look at her. You guys could be related."

A little nearsighted, Felice held the magazine closer, startled to see the resemblance—the straight brow bone, glimmering eyes, the fine jaw; only Felice's straight hair was self-hacked below the shoulders and Liz's hair was a sable bob, thick as a paintbrush. She finally realized what a compliment this comparison was.

Now Duffy smiles at her from behind the front counter. "Hey, Felix, where you been hiding?" She knows she's his favorite model. He opens the picture notebook, extricates an envelope and pulls out a wad of bills, then starts peeling off twenties: he does this for her once in a while, whether there's work or not. "Here, scram, go have fun."

She tucks the bills into her front pocket. She's actually disappointed. "Can't you use me?"

"We're closing up tomorrow night—there's a hurricane watch. You got a place to stay?" He looks over the crowded little store. "Could've used you this morning. Bunch of scouts here, talking about another reality show."

Felice balances her board on one hip. "*Here?* How many shows do they need about tattoo stores?"

"A lot, I guess." Duffy says, running his petal-tattooed knuckles over his bare scalp. "They do it, this place'll go nuclear."

"Awesome," Felice says, unaccountably glum.

"You shouldn't be working tonight anyway. Isn't it getting to be your birthday?" He taps at his grubby keyboard. "Yup—there you are," he says, pointing at the screen. "You and my mama—the same day—August 23rd. Tomorrow!" His lips move silently as he reads. There isn't a lot on the screen, just a couple of fake names—Felix Moreno—a fraudulent Social Security number and address, some other odds and ends he helped her invent. Apart from the year, the birth date information she gave him is accurate. "Your big two-oh girl! Here." He peels off a few more bills. "Get indoors and have champagne. You can have a hurricane party."

On her way out, Felice slips through a clot of Danish tourists, six-footers with hair the whiteness of candle tips and lashless ice eyes. She notices that fifteen-year-old Irma (pronounced *Ear-ma*) and her thirty-two-year-old mother-agent, Pax, also happen to be there. They started showing up on go-sees last year. Pax sits on the love seat with her gray-tipped bulimic's teeth. She clutches on her lap a lavishly ugly double-buckled Fendi croc purse. Irma reclines in one of the store's hiked-up dentist's chairs and gazes into the distance as Maurice spray-tats a ten-color Hawaiian Tropics Betty Page down the length of her leg. Felice feels a flash of anger: since when is Irma getting Felice's modeling work? Duffy, still at the front counter bantering with a couple of guys in navy and white Lauren, notices her glare, "She got here first." He shrugs.

Pax smirks and singsongs at the ceiling, "Somebody's getting street-kid skin."

Felice's mind darkens, her thoughts turn into ropy strands; she thinks of pointing out Irma's speedball shivers. Then she notices that

Pax is hunched forward, holding her daughter's knobby hand. Felice stares a moment. She turns away, pushing through the shop and out the glass door.

LINCOLN ROAD GLITTERS with reflections—display windows, doors, kiosks. As she walks, the street becomes a flicker book of images. In sixth grade, Hannah taught her to let her eyes unfocus and detach herself from the public gaze: "Don't ever look at people—they have to look at *you*." Felice has always relied on her reflection for consolation—beauty her only certainty. She walks up to the rectangular mirrored column flanking a gelato store. There's a faint shadow ringing each eye, a crease at the corners of her lips, and her neck juts forward at an unappealing angle she'd never noticed before. Plunged into a black mood, Felice stares down the length of Lincoln Road: everywhere, it seems, are girls and their mothers. She passes the tables at the bookstore café, where a waiter in an ankle-length half-apron stops and watches her. Annoyed, she returns his look. Then she feels the bottom of her stomach drop: The date with her mother. Felice looks at the table where her mother probably waited for hours. How could she forget? She squeezes her eyes shut, presses fingertips against the corners so hard that white phosphene ghosts leap inside her eyelids. Stupid. Stupid.

She feels she is falling into a canyon of vaporous sadness. She walks deeper into the shopping corridor, the jangle of voices, electronic music broadcast from the boutiques, and the hooded wash of trade winds and palms. She becomes angry with herself for her sadness. Sorrow is a luxury, like that of home and school—like living in the gentle, indoor world.

SHE USED TO FEEL concerned about keeping up, knowing things like who the prime minister of England was, or what war was happening where. For a time, she tried going into the libraries—for the comforting quiet, the soft furniture—as well as for the books. But librarians were more eagle-eyed than teachers or police. They knew instantly who was actually working on a school project and who was just another street rat.

Two sisters used to run the small south branch of the Miami Beach library, Ms. Vera and Ms. Hoff. They let Felice stay and read all day long. They tolerated a limited amount of napping in the padded chairs. Ms. Hoff showed Felice how to set up an email account and how to browse online for news and current events. Ms. Vera gave Felice novels: *Dubliners; Pride and Prejudice; The Sun Also Rises; Catch-22; Beloved.* One day, Felice came across a novel on the Recommended Fiction shelf. It was about a man who was obsessed with young girls—*nymphets.* Hannah had used that word. When they had Mr. Rendell for orchestra, Hannah had said, he loves nymphets— watch out. As Felice read, the book began to bother her. She was angry with the show-offy language, some of which she couldn't follow. But the story—about this babyish girl who fell into an old man's clutches—captivated and horrified her and filled her with near- sensory memories.

"The kids at this school think they're so great," Hannah drawled. It was a week before Thanksgiving—Felice's favorite time of year. They were lying in the east field, the air vibrating with late heat, the grass warm and crackling under their legs. "I can't stand this place—I can't wait to get the hell out of here."

Felice held her hand up so sunlight glowed peach and gold in the web between her fingers. Recently Felice's friend Bella told her, with affected dismay, about a rumor going around that ever since she'd met Hannah, Felice felt that she was "too good" for the rest of them. They were starting to feel, Bella sniffed, that Hannah had a real "attitude." Felice lowered her hand and squinted at Hannah, "So where you gonna go that's so much better?"

Propped up on her elbows beside Felice, Hannah toyed with a ribbon of Felice's hair. "Nowhere. Were you aware, by the way, that Rendell is madly in love with you?"

"Okay, that's gross." Felice clapped a hand over her eyes. "Lizard-Face. Yucky-do."

"Oh yeah?" Hannah breathed, leaning so close Felice could smell mint gum. "Well, guess what? You *own* that dude."

"Still grossing me out."

"Maybe we should have him killed," Hannah said speculatively. "It's really pretty scummy, the way he checks you out. You know how they did it back home? Some guy starts giving a girl the eyeball . . . and *schlerp!*" She dragged a finger across her throat.

Felice giggled, repeating the motion. "Yeah, *schlerp* to the music man!"

"Serious," Hannah said, her face suddenly deadpan. "I saw it done. Ask me what happened to my big sister sometime."

"You did not."

She just stared hard at Felice, then rolled up to her feet and walked away, throwing back her hair and brushing off the grass, so Felice had to run after her.

THE BEACH GLISTENS before Felice as she heads down Fourteenth, board banging against her hip. The water looks like melted light, flooding above the horizon. She wades through another berm of afternoon tourism along Ocean Drive, then she's on the footpath to the beach. She thinks of Emerson saying when you live at the beach, you have to remember to keep looking. She wishes he was there, then turns away, quickly, from the thought.

Berry and Reynaldo are in their place at the Cove, sitting with Heinrich—a model and crackhead—and Tracey, who looks spent and ugly from too much crystal, and mostly makes her money from stripping and hooking. Felice has seen her sleeping under picnic tables in the early morning—the hour when the craziest, most broken-down people drag shopping carts along the beach walk, trolling the garbage for empties, rinsing themselves at the freshwater showers. The kids sit on ratty towels and jackets, protected by a bluff of beach grass.

They're hunched around a popping, greasy-looking joint. Heinrich sucks smoke through his teeth, shaking his head, exhaling through his nostrils like a dragon. Felice joins them, folding herself onto a shared towel.

"Got any candy?" Berry asks, eyes watering. "I'm super hungry."

"I wish," Felice says.

"So you're hanging out with the Young Aryans now?" Reynaldo asks her. "What's up with that?" He tilts back his head, the joint hooded under his fingers, cupping a curl of smoke.

"No Aryans allowed," Heinrich says. "Not on the beach." He must have come from a shoot—the woodchip curves of his hair look like they've been sprayed with a glittering resin.

"Whatever, you guys." Felice shrugs. "I think we broke up or something."

A skinny tourist kid in a pair of board shorts leans over the wooden rail. "Hey." His teeth are very white. "You guys know where I can get some junk?"

Reynaldo looks at the joint in his hand as if it had suddenly appeared there. Tracey lurches at the tourist. "Fuck off, *surfer dick*." She has two vertical lines etched from her nostrils to her lips like parentheses. Everyone but Felice laughs. "Go the fuck back to Cheese-ville," Tracey adds morosely. "Fuckhead *surfer dick*."

"Jesus, fine, fuck you too," the tourist says, backing away, then stops and shouts, *"Bunch of no-job losers!"*

Reynaldo sighs a wisp of pot smoke and watches it curl in the air. Berry takes the joint, pinching it between her thumb and index fingers. "This isn't so bad, Heinrich," she observes. "I'm getting a buzz. I just wish I had some Twizzlers."

The tourist stalks off toward the crowded south end of the beach. Felice sees him stop short once or twice, as if struck by some new, cutting remark to fling at them.

"So what's happening, baby?" Berry asks Felice. "I feel like we never see you anymore." Her heavy-lidded eyes lower, examining Felice. "Is your skinhead nice?"

"I'm here now, aren't I?" Felice says, then adds, "Tomorrow's my birthday."

"It's your birthday, baby?" Reynaldo asks. "That's insane."

Berry kisses the side of Felice's head. "We're going out, for sure. We're getting loaded."

"Birthdays," Tracey says scornfully. "Fuck me."

"How old are you?" Heinrich asks Felice.

She smirks.

"Old lady," Reynaldo sings. "Eighteen."

"Fuck you," Tracey says to Reynaldo. "That's the same age as me."

Felice sucks in a breath, on the verge of a laugh. Is she kidding? She studies Tracey. Her skin is mottled and creased and browned, her hair is matted but thick. Tracey sleeps outside, she reminds herself.

"I'm sixteen," Heinrich says. "I'm going to be in Milan—or L.A., I guess—by the time I'm twenty. My agent says I've got the spring cover of *GQ* in the bag. But I can't wait to get into film. I'm done dicking around with modeling."

"Sucking dick, more like it," Tracey says.

"At least I've got a fucking life."

"How about I'll beat your fucking brains in you don't shut the fuck up," Tracey says, and takes a long, crackling hit on the joint.

Felice stays out on the beach, stoned and half drowsing, watching a bar of sunset glowing like a heated ingot. For a second she sees a gleaming bank of blue color, then a flash of green. It vanishes instantly. She curls up on her side on one of the beach blankets—a fuzzy synthetic with the remnants of a satin border: the sort of blanket that used to lie on a child's bed. Felice wonders if Emerson saw that green sunset; she closes her eyes, listening to the stoned voices and the rising, gravelly wash of the waves.

Brian

THE RIGHT FRAME OF MIND IS LIKE A BETTER ANGLE
of light, Brian thinks, it changes everything. Last night, he and Avis
sat on the couch, talking about the coming grandchild, ruminating
over this newcomer. She put her feet in his lap. For an hour, he had
intimations of an earlier life. The first evening in ages that they'd
spent together. Old times. The only off note was when he'd raised,
again, Stanley's request for money. Avis had crossed her arms and
looked displeased—as if it hurt her somehow. Again she'd said that
awful thing, How do we know it's ours? And Brian had almost said,
At this point, I hardly care. He'd dropped the topic. He thought: She
doesn't believe we can afford it.

He slides his hand along his butter-colored leather briefcase.
Downtown Miami glows in his windshield, the morning sun gild-
ing the vines and fronds that border the highway. He strolls from the
garage into his office building, hums in the elevator. He taps on his
computer. Among a pile of messages from Agathe and Malio, three
new emails appear on the screen: *Parkhurst@PBI.com,* subhead:
Acquisitions.

The sparkling mood dissipates. Parkhurst. Brian considers trying to get in touch with that group—what were they even called?
Citizens' Action Corps for Little Haiti? To say what, exactly? *Run?*
Brian glances up: the lights are on in Fernanda's office. He tries to
direct his attention back to the laptop. To the right of the email box
is a stream of news items: *Housing Market: Bubble Trouble? 2005:
A Bigger Boom Ahead? Competing with Foreign Investors.* He clicks
over to the live-feed weather channel to see the latest foaming white

spiral flicker back and forth over the ocean. A tropical system like an Indian mandala, moseying toward the Caribbean, an announcer saying, "Climate analysts warn that this one looks like a doozy . . ." They always say that.

He smoothes his hands over his face and tries to imagine some sort of career escape route. Retirement holds no attractions: he's a mediocre golfer at best, a duffer, and no good at working with his hands. Perhaps he should taper off from head counsel, shoot for something less front-lines, bury himself in the research libraries. He's secretly imagined hanging out his own shingle, practicing on his own terms—but there is something daunting there. The sort of thing, he imagines, that would keep him awake at night, worrying about those billable hours. He lightly beats at his lowered temples with the flats of his open palms, a dull pressure building behind his eyes, the contents of his skull expanding.

A warble of corridor sound and Brian looks up to see a splinter of light. Javier in his door. "Aha, you're here." Javier taps a folder. "Got a little somethin'—somethin' to talk to you about."

"Not a great time, buddy." He rubs his forehead.

"Good, for me neither!" Javier drops into the chair across from Brian's desk. "In which case, let's dispense with formalities. Here's my question: Are you ready for your next million?" He slides the folder on the desk.

"The what?"

Javier laughs. "The latest million, bro. To add to the pile."

"Pile? You've got me confused with sales. I'm a paper-pusher."

"Ay, man, listen, I come bearing glad tidings."

Brian pushes back against his chair, the apparatus tilting. "Parkhurst send you? About that Blue—whatever—Topaz place?"

"*Coño*, man, nobody fucking sent me." Javier bounces his fist on the padded chair arm. "I'm here because I care about your gringo ass."

"I'm sorry to hear that."

Javier holds both hands high, a big shrug. "Just got these listing details on my desk this morning. It's a little extracurricular something, so no telling on me, okay? I heard about it from Brooksie Martell."

"That guy!"

"Relax—Brooksie's not attached to this. These guys are new."

"What's the name?"

"Prescott and Filson."

"Never heard of them."

"They were one of the groups in the big Bank Towers. Silent partners. Focusing on prestige projects." Javier fishes in his suit pocket and draws out a ivory-gray card like a chip of enamel. He hands it to Brian. "They're working with Shaquille O'Neal and Tom Hanks on a midtown restaurant package."

"Hollywood money," Brian sniffs, tossing the card on his desk.

"Who cares—old, new, Hollywood—long as it's green, right? Listen." Javier rolls forward, resting his forearms on the desk. "This is the real deal, Bry. They're keeping the offer small and sweet. I know of two other top realtors buying in. Tippy-top." He cocks his eyebrow. "Sales are limited to eighteen investors total. For the whole damn building. You gotta be invited."

Brian smiles, despite himself. Javier has attempted to lure him for years. "Ah. So they're doing the chosen ones a big favor—*letting* people hand over money?"

"What can I tell you? Have to pay to play." Javier spreads out his hands, a lavish shrug. "They're gonna call it the Steele Building—nice, huh? They snagged Ira Huntington—he designed it so it'll look like a solid piece of stainless steel. It's near the Indian Creek—non-oceanfront—they nabbed the property practically gratis—*stole* it from the Miami Beach geriatric crowd, and"—one hand tilts—"passing the savings along." He picks up the folder. "You won't believe the plans—cathedral ceilings, wet and dry bars, private theaters, tiered terraces. Each unit gets its own maid's quarters."

"Maid's quarters. Jesus."

Javier flips the folder open, one finger tracing the floor plans, tapping the brochure. "The units are going to be a-freaking-mazing—I just read the specs—the floors are getting this pink marble quarried right from Carrara. Viking ranges and Sub-Zeros—the real stuff, not the mass-market crap."

"Heaven forbid," Brian says. "And what are these miracles going for?"

"You get in for two point three, deep-deep preconstruction discount."

"Two point three *million*? Are they dipped in gold?"

"You're buying *floors,* man. Two units per. Two-floor minimum per investor. And you'll be able to sell each unit separately. We'll turn them around, I kid you not, for five, maybe six *each*. And *that* buyer's gonna get a screaming deal and make a bundle. Come on, Bry, you know the game. I'm not telling you anything new here."

Brian sinks his chin onto the heel of his palm. "Where's that three million supposed to come from?"

"*Two* point three," he says, "You don't *have* two point three? Are you shitting me? You need me to open a home equity line for you, Brian?"

"Who else is buying in?"

"A few local big shots, some overseas clients."

"What? Like, Saudis?"

"The client roster's almost full. You want in, you've got till close of business tomorrow. Latest."

Brian drops his hand on the *Times* and sits back, regarding Javier. He's worked late hours with this man for sixteen years; they've whacked racquet balls and trudged across greens together; their families know each other, they have annual shared rituals: the Miami Ballet's *Nutcracker* Suite; Mango Festival at the tropical garden. Brian leans forward, his weight resting on the desktop. "Everything's tied up in other investments. And yes, Jav, it'd be quite a feat for me to get ahold of that much."

Javier's expression fades slightly. "What're you saying? You can't be bothered to move money out of those products getting you— what—ten—hell, say *twenty*—percent for a deal that'll bring you maybe even a hundred percent return? Listen, *hijo*—there's already big wallets getting in line behind the first buyers."

Brian works his jaw; a popping sound. "*Now?* There's already a second wave?"

"And *they* will have people lining up to buy. Couple weeks turnaround, maybe."

"No waiting period? No ninety days?"

Javier shrugs. "Come on—things don't apply to some guys the way they do to other guys. I don't have to tell *you*. You got enough cheese, you write your own rules."

Brian feels breathless; dismayed by a sense of his own collusion: for years he's ignored such items as the company's practice of issuing complicated investment IOUs to overextended clients, Parkhurst's love of tiptoeing up to the financial line, overextending himself on costly architects, building materials, bribes for political candidates. Brian rubs one hand over his face as if erasing each feature. "Don't like it."

"*No problema*. But—you ask me? The thing is? You're walking away from the sweetest, easiest bundle you'll ever make in your life."

"Please. Do not patronize me."

Javier laughs. "What patronize? Life is beautiful! Let yourself enjoy a little. It's only top, top, top players in on this one. We'll have the deal in the bag and the money spent practically before morning."

"What about you? You going in on this glorious deal?"

"Yeah, just a little, little strapped right now." He runs his tie between two fingers. "Hey, I make a couple of the commissions on your excellent investment, I'll be right in line myself." Javier's voice lowers, smug and cagey. "You've got to have faith."

Brian gazes at Javier. His mouth feels papery, even the tips of his fingers seem desiccated. "This would be funny if it weren't so . . ." There's that tremor again in his hands. He holds them in loose fists, and sits back. "If I didn't want to buy one of those townhouses in the Grove for two hundred sixty K, why on earth would I go for this spaceship?"

Javier spreads out his fingers on the desk top so they seem to float on its green glass surface. "These guys are young and lean and hungry. They want to make their mark and they're being smart—" Javier ducks, lowering his voice to a hiss. "This is the kind of discount you'd never see from Parkhurst. Or any of the other *viejos* around here. Not in a billion years." He gives Brian a narrow look. "This is the jackpot, buddy. I'm not talking to you as your realtor here, I'm talking as your *compay,* your *compañero*. I haven't seen a deal like this in forever."

Brian locks his arms across his chest: he can envision his son's face so clearly, eyes downturned in disapproval. "Then it's too good to be true. Or it shouldn't be true."

Javier nods slowly; moving closer; his hand is on Brian's arm and Brian straightens, terrified Javier might try to embrace him. "Man, I am worried about you, you know? You're being weird at work, you're being weird about your kid . . ."

"*Kids*—I have two children."

Javier closes his eyes. "*Hombre*. I know that."

"What do you want me to say, buddy?" Brian's hands come together then separate on his desk. "I don't even know . . ." He looks as if he's holding something broken open—a nut or a shell. "Your kids—it's okay between you and them, right?" He squeezes his hands back together. "After Felice—you know . . . I think I did it wrong. I mean, should've come home more. Something." He tries to speak conversationally, but his voice is humiliating, jagged and bouncing. "And Stan . . ." He shakes his head. How does it work, this process of rethinking things?

"Stanley's a great, great kid," Javier says softly. "He grew up to be fantastic. He knows you love him, brother."

When Brian smiles this time, it really does feel as if something on his face must be cracking. "Why does he know it?"

Javier shrugs again, but cheerfully. "I don't know, man. Seems like kids just kind of love their parents, right? One way or another. No matter how crappy we are. Crazy system, huh?"

Brian's face has gone numb. "Really crazy."

"Fuck, man." Javier stands, scooping up his files. "What do I know? I'm a realtor. Forget the stupid deal—I get carried away. Just. Don't worry so much, right? You can't be a lawyer every second, you know? You can take it easier than that."

As Javier scrapes together his papers, Brian's hands and face relax. He clears his throat and says, "Tell me again—about those condos?"

IN THE STILLNESS following Javier's visit, Brian paces his office, circles the computer stretching his arms and neck, checking on the cityscape below. There's a stinging hum through his body: if he still had a bottle of single malt in the filing cabinet, now would be the moment for a belt. Instead he leans forward, allows himself a glance down the corridor to Fernanda's office: through the glass wall, he catches the gleam of her hair as she bends toward her screen. He feels, in some way, off-kilter. All these years of working for a developer, yet simultaneously holding himself aloof from participating in development: as if, he thinks with a great inward roll of the eyes, he could remain unsullied, untouched by the flow of money beneath his feet. Just as he'd once believed that Avis carried within herself some proof of Brian's own innate decency. Because Avis had married Brian—because she loved him—*ipso facto,* he must be a good man.

He holds a contract folder and gazes mournfully at his immense blue-gray view until he realizes that he's staring at a reflected face. He turns and Fernanda is there, standing over his visitor's chair. Had she seen him spying? Her eyes cut toward his, an amused, slippery glance. "Can I steal you for a second? I'd really like to get away from this place."

"Away—out of here, you mean?" He puts down the folder.

"I don't care where—just anywhere. You pick."

As soon as they leave the parking garage, she turns to him. "First of all, I'm so sorry." He glances up from the traffic. She is gazing at the dashboard as if she were fond of it. "I acted like an idiot the other day. That's just—that's not how I am. All the tears. It'd been a long day and I haven't been getting enough sleep."

"My dear," he starts, but Fernanda cuts in. "Wait, please. I'm so embarrassed about the things I told you. About me and Jack."

"But you shouldn't!" He tries again. "I'm *glad* you told me. I've been thinking about what you said."

"Oh, please don't," she says with a laugh. She glances at him from the corners of her eyes. "It's all fine. I'm learning a lot from Jack— we're having a great time together. We get each other. It's a very simple relationship."

He frowns at the road. "I don't see how you can say that."

"Why not?"

"Why not!" He lifts his hands from the wheel. "The power dynamics. He's too old and rich and you're too smart for this kind of thing."

He turns into the South Miami shopping district: UM students jaywalk in front of the SUV, apparently convinced of their immortality. Brian turns down a side street and pulls into one of the diagonal parking spaces in front of the Whip 'n Dip. This was the place his children had wanted to go when they tired of pastries.

Fernanda's eyes darken with laughter. "Ice cream?"

He feels the back of his neck grow hot and wonders if he should pretend to be making a joke. But she's already pushing open the passenger door.

Fernanda orders a small cup of vanilla and Brian asks for a black coffee. They walk down the block to the small park and settle on a wooden bench She smiles and faces him. "I'm flattered that you've been worried for me. Really. But things are good. I don't want to change any of it. And I don't want to leave my job."

"Oh, I don't think that you—"

Fernanda sighs, a subtle lilt, instantly raising apprehension in Brian. "Do you remember Vicky Asafi? She used to work in H.R.? Really cute blonde, late twenties?"

Brian watches her a moment, nods slowly. "Her husband got transferred someplace. To Atlanta?"

"Did you ever meet Vicky's husband?"

Brian doesn't answer. He studies Fernanda's eyes.

"Because, you know what, she didn't have a husband," Fernanda continues. "That was just a story they cooked up. She was having an affair with Jack and when she decided to break things off, she was 'let go.' "

He lowers his eyes. Of course. "She could've brought charges against him."

Fernanda shifts back on the bench and gazes into her ice cream. "Yes, gone through an ugly, protracted sexual harassment trial, the full legal weight of PI&B, leading to uncertain results: no job references, that's for sure. Or she could just start her life over somewhere." She tucks the spoon in her cup. "Be done with it." Her voice, in trying to sound untroubled, seems to trip. "Thanks but no thanks, Brian. I need my job. More than that, I *like* my job."

Brian takes a sip of coffee but it's sour. He walks to the wire trash container and tosses the Styrofoam cup. His head is filled with coppery echoes. He gazes at her as he returns to the bench: her eyes seem heavier, like a sleepy child's, her lips are plum-colored, sulky. She places one hand on the elbow of his jacket, an infinitesimally delicate touch. He inhales strands of perfume and vanilla ice cream and recalls the Regaleses' yard—the white adobe house, its front lawn filled with waxy starfruits, their sweet, sweat-ish funk, and the nodding gardenia blooms. She frowns and looks patient and sympathetic. "Brian, if it makes you feel any better—I do think you care about me and are trying to protect me."

There's a flicker of warmth at the base of his chest as he watches her. "But you see—you understand—" He opens his hands. "That story you just told me? That's exactly why all of this—with Jack—it has to end. It just—it isn't right for you."

Her smile is almost transparent. She looks different out in the natural light—younger and plainer and more lovely. "How exactly do you know what is good for me? What do you suppose you know about me?"

"Well, I'm pretty sure I know what isn't good for you." Brian lowers his gaze.

She sits back against the bench, a honeycomb of tree-filtered light illuminating her hair, the dot of silver sparkling at the center of her clavicle. "My father says, To know the person you have to know the tribe."

"So he'd say I have to know your family? To give you advice?"

"Something like that." She lifts her face: the day is mild. Overhead, white smudges of cloud drift past, bits of steam from a teakettle. "My grandparents and my mother left Cuba with nearly their whole synagogue. My mother—for years, she told me—she used to cry over the little group that stayed behind—always worrying would they ever survive. Afraid Castro would just—" She lifted the flat of one hand, her fingers straightened, nearly curved backwards, her head slowly shaking in a kind of denial. "Mother used to think in ten or twenty years that there wouldn't be any of us—any Jews at all left in Cuba."

Emboldened by this bit of personal information, Brian asks, "And your father? Did he come with them?"

She drops her hand. "*Papi?* He's just Catholic. That's what he liked to say, just-Catholic. He came here before my mother did—with his family. My parents made a big scandal when they fell in love—mixing religions. *Papi* said—first my mother's people survive the Pharaoh, then Hitler, then they have to go out and find Castro—that's professional suffering." She smiles at her scraped-out cup of ice cream. "The truth is—my parents went through so much just to be together, I think it burned most of the religious feeling out of them. We didn't go to any services when I was growing up. There were just a few things—the silver candlestick holders. Sometimes my mother lit them and said the Friday blessing. Sometimes, braided bread—challah. A pewter mezuzah by the door—I thought it had special powers. That's all. Oh, and *Papi* said he gave me his Catholic guilt."

"So if you weren't raised in a traditionally—"

She's already shaking her head. "There are some things that—go deeper. More than prayers. There's a way of seeing who you are that remains—after everything else." She says this delicately, like a doctor delivering complicated news.

Her clean hair falling forward and her back so straight and brave, Fernanda looks to Brian as if she could be twelve years old. He feels another twist of protectiveness toward her. Leaning closer . . . Ah yes. The silver sparkle is a tiny Star of David on a short silver chain. It rests there like an amulet, investing her with layers of private history. He should, he thinks, be able to draw on his education and experience—all those years of helping others in their restless goals, years of observing ambition and power—in order to help Fernanda. Did he learn nothing from losing his daughter? "I'm not like him," he blurts. "I'd never try to take anything from you."

"I know that!" Fernanda presses his hand between both of hers. "And I'm grateful for your friendship. Honestly, you have no idea. But, Brian, you know what? I'm *happy*." An indentation forms on the verge of her left jaw. She smiles, brushing away a wisp of hair. "I love adventures. I love men. All kinds," she says with a little laugh that stabs him to the quick. "I've learned from my parents that this world—well—amazing, impossible things can happen out of the clear blue sky. Dictators, pogroms. I don't want to marry Jaime Roth, who took me to my high school prom, and lead a pure, holy, traditional life keeping house and producing babies—as my mother would like. Oh, it doesn't matter that she didn't do it—that only makes her want it all the more for *me* . . . I want to have another kind of life. A life like my mother's." She pauses, scrutinizing him: Brian notices the lilac tint of her lids and looks down at his lap, subtle emotion moving in him, a roll of smoke inside a glass bottle. "It's very basic," she says. "Don't expect your kids to want the things that *you* didn't want."

Avis

AVIS PRESSES THE PHONE AGAINST HER EAR HARD enough to leave an impression. The sun is barely up, but Stanley has always been an early riser like his father. He answers on the fifth ring, "Yes, Mother?" He responds to her questions with one-word snippets—terse, but unable even now to cut her off entirely. So she learns: the baby is due late November, they don't and won't know the gender (Nieves doesn't want to know), Nieves feels *hurt* and *disappointed* in Avis. Stanley feels *whatever*.

She walks through the house with the phone as she humbly receives these tiny, wounding words. She fingers her chopped hair; peers through the French doors to the back. As Stanley confirms that, yes, they need the money, yes, the market really *is* in danger, Avis flicks on the TV, volume low. On the Weather Channel, a fleecy mass hovers due east of the Turks and Caicos, about to head for South Florida; an announcer mutters predictions in a dire tone: *wind speeds, organized system, making landfall . . .* Avis sits heavily on the couch only half hearing her son, imagining the food- and water-hoarding scene at Publix. It's been several years since the last real hurricane came through, but she remembers it well: the shuddering "outer bands" of rain, the hollow clap of the silver palms, the susurration of the fronds, archways of blowing branches.

"So if there's nothing else, Mom . . ."

Already dismissing her. She holds the phone with both hands. "You do know there's a hurricane coming? Thursday? It's on the TV right now. It looks big."

There's a pause just long enough for a muted sigh. "You'll be fine, Mom."

"No—I know, but I'd like *you* to come. Or—or at least—" she stammers. "Please—just be careful," she finishes in desperation.

THE SPIKING HUMIDITY is a disaster for her baking. She has to discard two batches of meringues that turn soft. She'd abandon puff pastry for the whole summer if she could, but the customers want their crisp, light crusts. Avis sets up her usual stations of flours and spices. At 7 a.m. it's already so hot she assumes Solange won't come out. But a half hour later, as Avis is stirring cocoa nibs into a vanilla batter, she glances at the window and spots her neighbor squatting at the edge of her yard. "Not in your usual place," she calls from the door.

Solange stands nimbly, and Avis sees her apron contains dark strips. "There are interesting things in your yard." She leads Avis to the stubby bushes in the far corner, a place their landscapers have elected to prune and ignore, instead of doing the more surgical work of weeding. "Here's a plant going to waste." Solange strokes the long, spiny branches between her fingers. "This is good medicine. You boil it for tea, for restorative properties." She picks the quills, adding them to her apron. "This is granny bush—you use it for women's trouble—pain and bleeding."

Avis looks around at the land she's inhabited for nearly thirty years. Years ago, when she'd studied the constructions of stem, blade, stamen, ovule, she loved the infinite possibilities of the plant kingdom—but she had been interested in color, scent, presentation: the beautiful names—cloth-of-gold crocus; ash-leaved trumpet, star-of-Bethlehem; meadow saffron—the loveliness of a blown field of asters or irises, a ring of roses to bed a wedding cake, the careful depiction of a peony in cross section on the page, a gentian constructed in icing. She knew all about beauty and almost nothing of utility. "All kinds of good things here," Solange says again, her fingers combing the weeds. "You boil that thistle to cure asthma—its sap will take away warts. The leaves of that lime tree are fine for the skin, the guava calms the stomach and nerves. Over there? The bark on your lignum vitae regulates the system." She stands, one hand holding up the pouch of stems, the other pointing out plants.

Avis plucks a stem of a pointed, glossy leaf that's established itself in that far corner. Solange says, Wild coffee. Avis holds it under her nose, studying the musty green fragrance. "Could I bake with this?"

"You roast the seeds, to make a brew."

Avis smiles, twirling the bit of twig. "My son would love this."

Solange lifts her head so the sun turns her dark irises amber. "I told my son that there used to be one flavor only. Everything was pressed together. The universe, the people, animals, vegetables, dirt, water—everything—in the smallest seed. That's what people try to do—eat and touch small pieces of the world to try and get back into the whole thing again. Sweet and sour. That is how bush medicine works."

Surprised to hear about a son, Avis glances at her. Solange lifts her fingers to Avis's hair, a spidery touch at the side of her head. "Come here." She leads her to the step to the French doors. Just beside the step is a squat weed. Solange touches Avis's head again—it's almost painful, the shame of her thinning hair. "This . . ." Solange bends and pinches the shoots between her fingertips. "It's called Braziletto. You boil the leaves and sip the tea. It fortifies the blood. Your hair will stop falling." She places the leaf in Avis's palm. "Will calm your pulse as well."

Avis stares at it. Then she notices Solange's stillness. She follows her gaze to the empty windows of the house, the black reflections, as if the building were filled with stormwater. She picks some of the little shoots. "Where is your son now?"

Solange smiles, her eyes untouched. "I had to leave him. He's back home there."

Avis needs to creep into some shade, out of the blistering heat, but now she can't move; the breath rushes in and out of her. "How old is he? Is he with family?"

"Yes. All the family is there." Solange sorts through the herbs in her apron, running the twigs between her fingers. "His name is Antoine and he's the very best in his class. He is wonderful with a soccer ball too, but he can't keep hold on it." Her lips part. "He's too softhearted and he gives the ball away. He's the fastest and strongest, but no one wants him on their team."

"That must have been so hard." Avis's voice is low. "For you and your husband—not to be able to bring him with you." Solange closes her fingers around another sprig and doesn't say anything. Avis says, "I have a daughter who—she doesn't live with us. She hasn't, for years. It breaks my heart, every day."

Solange looks up from her sorting. "Oh yes." It seems she doesn't say this so much in sympathy as in acknowledgment of a basic truth. "Of course."

"Is there a remedy for that?" She means to say this lightly but she sounds serious.

Solange's eyes flicker to her face, examining and curious. Then her thin fingers wrap around Avis's wrist. "I don't know. We'll see about it."

Avis follows Solange across the yard, following the path she'd taken on the day she'd felt so furious about a noisy bird. Weeks ago: it seems like years. They go up the rough cement step and enter an enclosed back porch which contains another birdcage: this one is smaller, made of silvery metal; it hangs from a hook in the ceiling. The bird rests there purring as the women enter. Avis glances around as they go into the house, but the shades and curtains are drawn and the windows behind them are open, so the interior is dark and sleekly sultry. The kitchen seems to be the only room lit with natural brightness: the slats of the blinds are turned open, so the room has a clear, marine light. Solange seats Avis at a table on metal pipe legs with a Formica top and Avis cannot help an evalu-

ative scan of the kitchen: no appliances beyond an enamel refrigerator and stove—small and clean. The dainty refrigerator like an
old-fashioned icebox.

Solange holds a cast-iron pan under the tap, then places it on the
stove's coil. "There are varieties of pain . . ." She begins removing
jars from the cupboard. "It's simple fact, not sorcery. I don't believe in
spells—I only know in some way the idea of a spell is powerful. You
have to be careful—that kind of stuff leaves a residue behind."

Avis holds her forearms propped on the table. On the counter
across from her, tiny green chilies float in a clear liquid, as if suspended in light. Stacked beside the jar there are bundles of sprigs and
leaves bound together with a kind of raffia. The unfamiliarity of these
objects give them an allure, a glistening touch of the unknowable. On
the opposite counter, Avis notices several small woven grass effigies—
birds and squirrels—of the sort that were tied to the trees. Solange
plucks one up and places it before Avis. "These are just things that I
make. Ideas. You may have this if you like."

Avis picks it up. Woven entirely from waxy green blades of grass,
its upper half appears to be that of a woman, her arms outstretched
in a U-shape, as if calling to someone, her lower half tapering into a
fishtail. "You made this? It's beautiful."

"Avis," Solange pronounces her name with sharp emphasis on the
second syllable, *Ah-vees*. "It's only grass." She pours a steaming pale
yellow tea into two strained mugs, then she places a mug before Avis
and sits in the other chair, its cracked vinyl back patched with cel-
lophane tape. "The lady of our house had me baptized and raised
me with Catholic instruction. My mother taught me that the world
is crowded with gods—they live in all kinds of places and you can
call on them. It seemed to me that both systems believed in slicing
through." She moves the edge of her hand through the air. "To reach
worlds beyond the world. Using prayers to carry us."

Avis lifts the hot mug, enjoying the sensation of heat in her palm,
thinking of her mother's heaven of completion and return. "What do
you believe?"

Solange inclines her face toward the surface of her tea. "I try never to believe anything at all. If I start believing things, I might believe that the universe is a dead door, that we all get crushed."

Avis thinks of her mother's last days in the hospital: a shared room with a plastic room divider, a scrape of dry coughing on the other side of the divider. She felt brutal as a captor, refusing to bring her mother home to die. In her last days, her mother wouldn't eat anything more than ice chips. She railed in one of her old languages, muttering over and over some sort of imprecation, something that sounded like *haya kharra*. When Avis noticed the way a young orderly turned his face away from Geraldine's ranting, Avis stopped him, "You understand her, don't you. What is she saying?" The young man hesitated. When Avis pressed him, he finally said, "Life is shit."

Solange's hand sweeps across the Formica as if straightening a tablecloth. "I believe in small rituals: cleaning dishes, minding the plants. Other such processes."

Red-black petals, a wooden pencil case, a small purple satin sash, a string of beads with a delicate white cross. Solange moves around the house collecting and placing these items in a canvas bag. She asks Avis to take her to her own kitchen. They cross the yard again; Avis shyly leads Solange through the French doors and then the door to the right. She feels self-conscious over the cool beauty of the room, afraid she'll be offended by such a display of wealth, and watches Solange as she turns, looking, not touching anything. But she simply asks, "Where are your husband and son? This would work better if they were with us."

Avis imagines their reactions to Solange and her spell-casting— if that's what this is. Brian, she's fairly certain, would be mortified. And Stanley, it seems, would be curious, polite, and distracted. She extracts an old photo of herself, Brian, and Stanley on some sort of excursion. Solange studies it a moment, then includes it with the other items. "Now, what would you make for your daughter—if she were to come home tomorrow? What would it be?"

For a moment, Avis is motionless, intimidated, studying the

cold tang of the stainless bowls, their perfect emptiness. Solange picks a small bowl out of its nest of bowls and hands this to Avis. "Don't think so much," she says—the voice of someone used to ordering a staff.

Avis takes the bowl, coolness on her fingertips. She has no *mise,* no utensils; she reaches into the flour and sugar with clean hands, running her fingers through powder. Her palm warms the butter; she pours in a drop of almond extract, then splits a vanilla pod with her paring knife, scraping in the seed caviar. One of the simplest cakes that she knows. Solange leans against the counter as Avis stirs wet ingredients into the dry, making the batter. "Where I grew up," she says, "sugar is a luxury. Though I didn't know this until I left the great house. Then I discovered—the people where I'm from, they live and die in these magnificent cane fields." She idly turns one of the bowls on the counter. "Sugar is like a compass. It points to trouble. My husband used to travel to plantations across the border—the other side of the island. Until the new man came to power and then people began to find the cutters' bodies hacked into pieces."

Avis is afraid to look at Solange: the air is tinted with sugar vapor: it is, of course, the one irreducible element in her work—no matter what else is added or taken away. "Which is what makes it such a strong thing." Solange's tone is almost conversational. "Sweet in the mouth, terrible to the body. The cane cutters never get to taste it. Never like this." She draws one finger through the sparkling crystals in the bin.

As she works, Avis feels as if the woman's voice has set something loose in her, a private mourning. Her spoon turns a long, continuous ribbon through the batter: heavier and heavier. Avis's private tragedy with all its pain seems to shrink. She begins to wonder if there's any point at all to pastry work—it's irrelevant, even absurd. Ease and comfort: lotus-eating, Stanley called it. Escapism, gluttony, corruption, self-indulgence. He never adds sugar to his coffee. Avis isn't stirring correctly; her hands feel weak. Finally Solange takes the bowl and pours it into the cake pan. She slides it into the hot oven and lets the heavy door rumble shut.

WHEN THE CAKE IS cool enough to box, they take it to Avis's car, Solange on the passenger side. She says, "Where is the last place you saw her?"

Avis places her hands on the bottom of the steering wheel. The first time she saw her daughter after she'd run away for good, Felice was taller and slimmer, her hair longer: she'd been away from home for six months, long enough to be physically changed. A deep shaking began in the quick of Avis's bones. She was torn between the need to touch her daughter, to hold her tightly, and the sense that even the lightest touch might cause her to flee back to her underworld. There was a new downturned shadow to Felice's mouth and her lowered eyelashes cast crescents of shadow on her cheeks: she had a faintly exhausted quality which trickled through her posture. She could have been fourteen or twenty-eight—she was poised, self-possessed. As soon as she folded her long limbs onto the café chair across from Avis, she'd said, "I'd like to make a deal with you."

Avis sat motionless, staggered by the moment, barely able to hear or think, while Felice explained the "deal." Felice would agree to more of these meetings—occasional, entirely at her whim—but in exchange, Avis and Brian had to agree to *stop*.

"Stop?" Avis felt so slow, the word blurred and heavy. Here was her daughter before her, talking to her, as if nothing at all had changed. Here was Felice.

"Looking for me. Trying to make me come back. Hiring people to find me. You have to give up now." Felice's tone was like a chip of ice. "Because I'm happy with the way things are. And I am never, ever, coming home again." Felice gazed at her mother with an expression so entirely frank—so separate—that it seemed to Avis that she felt a wave of particles rising and twisting; each particle was a bit of memory, every second that she'd held the child between her arms, inhaled the scent of her scalp, kissed her shoulders, pressed the drowsy face to her chest as she tilted a bottle to her lips, the consummate intimacy of feeding a child this way, all of it rising, curling, as this extraordinary face told her: *stop*.

Could it be that she'd always been a little afraid of her own daughter? That she simply didn't know how to fight her? The terrible fact presented itself: Avis had no choice but to accept.

"THE LADY OF THE HOUSE—she did all she could to take me away from my mother. She told me my mother was ignorant and dark black like an African. But I saw how my mother knew every plant in the gardens and forests, like the lady of the house knew the words in her books."

There's rain on the streets and occasional ripples of light, high up overhead. Avis can only steal glimpses of Solange as she speaks, her profile nearly invisible beside the rain-streaked glass. "I was seventeen when I met Jonas. The lady sent me into Cap-Haïtien with the driver for some dried hibiscus for tea. We could have picked it right in the field, but she said that kind wasn't good. Back then, Jonas worked in the market in town, selling spices in big cloth sacks. When she found out about him, the lady said, of course, that he was filthy and uneducated—same things she said about my mother. She wanted me to stay in the house. She said, 'You are almost a daughter to me.'" Solange gave a laugh like a sniff, her head bobbing slightly. "My mother told me—If you're lucky enough to know what you want, then you must chase it. I left the house and the gardens and the stone verandah that overlooked the ocean—places I'd known all my life—and I went to live with Jonas in a house with a cracked cement floor and a patched tin roof, no electricity. We had to take our waste out in pails and pour it into the alley that ran behind the house." The rain tapers off as they approach Miami Beach; trails of water stand in the street, a mist thrown up between the cars, rows of bronze streetlights glow overhead, already coming on in the late afternoon. "It felt like my life's door had opened. When my son was born, I began making my bush teas and medicines, to help him thrive. Jonas said these brought him even more customers at market than his spices did. My mother came to visit one time to see her grandson. It took her six hours to walk to us. She said the lady of the house was ill and she couldn't stay away for very long. I understood. The lady was like a difficult family member—you might dislike, or even hate them a little—but you can't leave them."

Solange is silent as they cross the causeway, the bands of traffic curving and rushing high over the diamond water. "I've never seen this before," she murmurs. "Only from the airplane."

They drive into town and park in the city lot, then walk to Lincoln Road. It looks different to Avis, so late in the day—wilder, somehow. She edges toward Solange, turning from the spill of shop lights and electrical music. Girls in skimpy, ruffled shirts look stiff-legged and robotic. Beside Solange—seeing with her fresh eyes—Avis feels as if an unacknowledged horror in things rises more forcefully to the sur-face. But Solange swings her arms as they walk, looking around: she says, "I wish the lady of the house could have seen *this*—she wouldn't think she was quite so fine as she did."

They make their way up the street: as far as the fans' whirl of shadows on the sidewalk; Avis stops and gestures to the heavy tables, wrought-iron chair legs and bases. "There. That's where we meet." There's a desolation about the place now, though it's crowded with customers, legs crossed, hands resting on iced drinks. Avis senses a weight, as if all of it is gradually sinking into the earth with all those empty hours of waiting.

Solange takes in the tables and diners: the scene is washed in late, limpid sunlight. Avis wonders what the diners see when they look at them—a pale, middle-aged patient and her young attendant? She feels a flash of trigeminal pain across one cheekbone and inhales sharply. Solange plucks at her sleeve. "Come away. Let's see some more."

They weave through the crowds, Avis hurrying to keep up with

Solange—a slip of aquamarine skirt. Avis holds a shopping bag that bounces against her legs and bumps into passersby. She feels sweat at her temples and under her arms. The sky is hazy blue with clouds like fine scratches; bisecting the walkway are rows of date palms, full as pom-poms, with powerful, corrugated trunks. Solange hovers at the busy edge of Ocean Drive, waiting within a small crowd for the light. Avis doesn't think she's even aware that she's behind her, but then Solange turns and reaches between two girls to take hold of Avis's hand. She keeps her strong fingers on her as they cross the street and make their way toward the beach.

Avis doesn't come here. She hasn't been this close to the water since she'd agreed to Felice's terms, years ago. Avis had gone home and told Brian about Felice's demand. For the first time in months it seemed they were too drained to fight each other. Brian shook his head, saying, "That's ridiculous. Just let her go? No. No way. There's got to be something else we can do." And Avis said, "Please tell me what it is and I'll do it." Anything. Anything. She felt the fight slipping away from them, talking about it was running through sand, trying to stand in breakers, the sand swiping away from under their feet. Gradually they stopped speaking with police and school officials and neighborhood watch groups, and Avis never went to the beach again.

She is surprised now by the residual warmth she can feel in the sand; she slips off her clogs, stepping through it, bits of shell and stone and cigarette butts. The late-afternoon-near-evening light is tinged with mauve and it wavers across Solange's face in pale bands. "The water smells different here," Solange says.

There are still small groups of college kids on towels, but most of the tourists and families are packing up, lugging folding chairs, a pleasant weariness rising from their burned shoulders. Solange sweeps off a patch of sand with the flat of her hand, as if dusting a piece of furniture, and sits, knees bent and gathered to her chest. Avis hovers uncertainly beside her, finally sitting, the bag with its boxed cake between them. Solange stares hard into the widening band at the far edge of the water. It is hard to tell in the lowering light but Avis suspects that her eyes are rimmed with tears. Avis shifts her gaze to the sand—a cream-colored shell, a stone, the delicately ridged exoskeleton of a horseshoe crab. "It's been so long since I've visited the water," Solange says. "I grew up beside it, but after so many years I thought I might even forget it." She rakes her fingers through the sand. "It's good to feel like this now."

"Like what?" Avis shades her eyes.

"Like nothing." She smiles. "When I came here, I came with nothing. Just that bird in a cage. The one you love so much." Another smile.

"And your husband," Avis prompts. "You came with him."

She glances at Avis. "Yes. And him." She begins unpacking the items in her bag then. She touches each one to her forehead, then hands it to Avis. "Think about what you would like to say to your daughter now."

Avis takes the small jar with its clear fluid, but she can't think of anything to say. Mostly there's blankness, as Solange puts it—like nothing. Still, she touches the things—the scissors, the satin sash, the prayer book—and hands each back to Solange.

"Good," she says. "Fine. And now what you need to do—you take the cake and break it up, scatter it on the water for the birds and fishes." She points over the shadowy waves. "You talk to your daughter as you scatter it."

"The cake—you mean, just break it up?" She feels a kind of flinch.

Solange's face is impassive. "However you can do it."

Avis stands and reaches into the bag, into the white box, carefully lifting the cake with her fingers. She holds it in both hands and walks down the incline to the water. The sand looks beige against the dark foam of the surf and Avis hesitates a moment before wading in. The water is warm and easy and the bottom smooth. She is able to make her way through the small breakers with little trouble. She doesn't look back at shore; she walks until the water approaches her hips, her work pants balloon around her, the houndstooth check darkening. The thought comes, how she might have viewed all this in the past:

sentimental, maudlin. *Happy Birthday*. Bitter little words. Avis holds the cake then digs in with her fingers. It crumples instantly and she has a memory, not of Felice, but of spreading handfuls of her mother's ashes into Cayuga Lake, so cold that March it was still frozen in spots, and she had balanced on the steeply banked shore, almost doubled over from the cold, flinging the ashes with stiff, red fingers. Now she tosses the crumbs everywhere, her breath chugging as if she were sobbing; the sound bounces over the water. She knows that this ritual is not for getting her child back. There's a sparkle of efflorescence on the water's surface, just a few feet away; she wades in deeper, toward the bubbles, then feels an uncanny shimmer against her exposed calves: a school of fish is swarming her, feeding on the crumbs. She watches them, minute flickerings beneath the surface. A bit of cake bobs on the water, rising and falling. She sinks to her chin, then lifts her feet and lets her head dunk under so the echo of the water fills her ears, the thrombotic pulse. She opens her eyes to an indigo blur and considers the pleasure of opening her throat and lungs—the scorch in her lungs and the release of it.

Avis tilts her head back, pushing off the sandy bottom. She breaks the surface to see a ragged shadow plummet—a seagull snapping up the cake, lobbing back into the sky.

SOLANGE TURNS TOWARD the passenger side window as they pass over the causeway, the water a navy field trembling with lights. "I'm going to come back here."

"I'll take you anytime," Avis says.

Solange looks at her again with her cool, curious gaze, then something seems to release in her eyes, as if she were looking right through Avis; turning back to the window she says, "I have to go get him."

Avis glances at her, but a kind of heavy, silencing drapery seems to have fallen over the car, separating the two women. She drives Solange back to her home, pulling into the driveway behind a black sedan. The house lights glow and a form moves behind the curtains.

Solange doesn't get out of the car right away. She stares at her lap, then mumbles *"Bonne chance"* as she kisses Avis's cheek.

"Bonne chance?" Avis smiles, but Solange climbs out of the car in silence. Avis sits with her hands draped on the wheel, a wisp of melancholy in her chest as she watches the woman walk to the door of her house, enter, and close the door.

Felice

HEAT LIGHTNING FLICKERS IN THE NIGHT, FLASHES with a violet after-image. Felice walks the empty beach with Reynaldo and Berry, the three of them bumping into each other, their voices absorbed in the salt air. She feels light as the dry lightning, casting no shadows. She spent the day lying out on the beach with Berry, dozing and eating candy, just as if the two of them were college girls on vacation. Only the vacation doesn't end. If she were home . . . For a moment, she allows herself to imagine the sort of birthday cake her mother would make, the scent of baking, the rosettes sculpted in fondant. For all she knows, everyone from her old life could be dead—like Hannah used to say. Everyone that she's ever loved vanished.

They walk to the public restrooms, a squat cinder-block building, and enter the women's room. It's deserted and echoing at this hour. There's a grit of sand coating the sinks and masking the mirrors. They wash themselves with the trickle of cold water at the sinks under beige-green lights: Reynaldo's and Berry's skin looks mottled and scaly along the backs of their arms. Felice frowns at her own hazy reflection, tries to smooth her hair, but then Reynaldo shakes his head and says, "You're not allowed to look at yourself. You're such a freak of nature—it's disgusting."

Berry makes snatching gestures at Felice. "I'll take your eyes, skin, hair, lips, and body—thank you very much."

Felice grabs Berry's hand and they play wrestle. "What're you even talking about?" She laughs, pushing on Berry's hand. They dance around, stamping in the gray puddles on the floor. "You guys are way cuter than me."

Reynaldo snaps his fingers. "Do not do that. Do not even say that to me, bitch. I'm a have you arrested."

Felice feels hungry and good from all the pot they'd smoked and a little baggie of cocaine they'd shared with Heinrich—a couple of birthday snorts. They leave the restroom and walk up the cool carpet of sand in the moonlight, and Felice feels like they own the beach. She's put Emerson out of her mind: a distant figure, he might be one of the flakes of moonlight sparkling on the waves. Felice skips into a scissoring jump, throws down her board and tries to do a cartwheel. After a few attempts both Berry and Felice manage crude cartwheels. They laugh wildly and turn one after another, kicking up sand. Reynaldo sits on the beach, watching. Finally Felice picks up her board and they head toward town, shaking sand out of their hair and beating it from their hands.

There's the usual din of people parading along Ocean Drive. Felice can feel the throb of a bass a full block before she hears the music. It's hot out but there are still long lines for outside tables at the cafés; rental cars ease down the street, girls sitting on top, legs dangling into sunroofs; music blares out of the Versace mansion, the Time café, a row of expensive boutiques. Even just a year ago, Felice still enjoyed this scene, the stalk through the crowd with her friends, all of them long-legged, hair bubbling down their backs. Now she feels remote from everything. Some college kid in a T-shirt that says *no limitZ* lets an enormous plastic cup fall from his fingers to the sidewalk. Black fluid sprays everywhere. She has started to notice the garbage. When she was fourteen, the beach was enchanted. But now she sees that people come for a long weekend, a week perhaps, that it's a temporary enchantment, that people behave here in ways they never would back in Naperville and Houston and Scranton. Felice once talked to a girl at a bar who was amazed to hear that Felice had been born and raised in Miami. "No way, you're from here?" The girl's face was sun-scorched with pale rings around her eyes. "This isn't a place where people really *live*."

They leave Ocean Drive and walk over to Washington where

the sonic boom of the clubs intensifies. Velvet-roped lines stretch along the sidewalks and girls in lingerie dresses and towering shoes eye Felice with arch faces. The night swishes with languages: Portuguese, French, Russian, Arabic, intertwined with cigarette smoke and the smell of alcohol and perfume. Everyone awaiting the moment of entry. When Felice's friend William, at Cloud 9, stashes her board and unhooks the rope to let them pass, the waiting girls' eyes narrow; cigarette smoke streams between manicures. In their jeans and tank tops, Felice and Berry never wait for entry and never pay an admission fee. They enter the club's bolus of dancing, pulsating lighting and noise. The place is a Roman circus of floors and lobbies: there are circular metal staircases and semi-private nooks for snorting and smoking and screwing. A series of spotlights synced to the music strobes the crowd, so amplified Felice feels its throb in her rib cage. She's happy to be here again, inside the animating charge. The music pauses, shifts, and Felice watches the crowd pause and shift, as if jolted by a live current. Just the way silvery schools of small fish swerve in tandem. The dance floors are tidal—all movement and turbulence—swept into an internal sea.

They club-hop, visiting a series of dance floors, a series of velvet ropes unhooked. Berry tells their friends that it's Felice's birthday and Reynaldo crows, "She's *eighteen*—you believe that shit? She's one of *them* now." People buy them shots. They see kids from the beach, from the tattoo shop, from the Green House—including one of Emerson's skinhead friends, Anders. He tells Felice, "Emerson's really worried about you, man."

In the ladies' room at the third or fourth club, Felice and Berry are offered E, then something that's dripped on the tongue from an eyedropper. Felice nibbles at the sour edge of a pill and gives the rest to Berry. After Berry squeezes the eyedropper under her tongue, her pupils dilate to the outer rims of her irises. "Mmm. Yeah." She says to Felice, "Have you noticed how everyone here is super ugly?" She sits on the edge of the shelf of sinks, her body long and narrow as an insect's. Like Felice, she could make money if she showed up more often for shoots. "Don't you think they're such trolls?" She hunches over, hunting in her jeans pockets for a cigarette. A flurry of women rush in and out, crowding the long mirror, applying mascara, shaking out their hair, chattering, tugging at their clothes. Berry could say or do anything, Felice marvels, and they wouldn't notice a thing. Felice has lost track of how many Cuba Libres she's consumed this evening; there's a smoky tang in her sinuses and the floor seems to slope. She leans against Berry's sharp knees. "I think they're sweet," she says plaintively.

Berry exhales smoke. "Uggums. Big Chief Uggoos."

"We could be sisters, did you ever think of that?" Felice pinches the cigarette from Berry and takes a steadying drag. For a moment, she feels as if she and Berry are incredibly close. "Isn't it weird? All you have to do is hang around somebody long enough and you start to love them. Everyone in this club—we could all be one family."

Berry squints, trying to locate her cigarette. "You want to love an uggoo?"

"There's no such thing as the one perfect something or other," she says indignantly, as if they were arguing. "Anyone can be in love with anyone. Doesn't matter." She waves Berry's cigarette just out of reach. "Could be some drooling three-eyed dirt-bag out there—you could fall in love with him!" Felice feels unusually wise—as if the meaning of the night has revealed itself to her. Love is exchangeable, malleable: she traded one family for this other kind of family.

"Oh yeah?" Berry reclaims her cigarette. "There's this big fat nasty rich, rich uggum I saw at the VIP bar. I want to see you go in there and fall in love with him."

"You kidding?" Felice's voice clatters in the pink marble room. The sinks are stunningly white, like starlight. "Easy."

Berry slides off the counter with a whoop.

The club interior seems darker and damper now. There are several beach-rat kids out there, all dancing. Reynaldo is on the dance floor; Felice spots him rocking his hips, hands above his head; his face gleams, impervious as a totem. Berry slips her hand under

Felice's elbow and nods toward the penthouse bar. They climb the narrow spiral staircase. The throng upstairs has diminished to a ring of serious drinkers—almost all men—leaning on the bar, glass in hand, most of them watching the dancers. Felice spots the one Berry was talking about—a type that appears in all the clubs. Felice knows—guys like this are admitted because they're rich. He's short-ish with a thick neck and shoulders; hair sprouts from the opening of his creamy shirt. The man holds his bottle of beer around the neck with his fingertips, and he appears to be wearing clear nail polish. He's balding at the temples with a deep V of hair in the center of his forehead. His eyes are furtive, almost hurt, damp and animal. At first Felice shrinks back, but Berry hovers beside her, smirking, and Felice begins to feel untouchable, a deep, euphoric solitude. She's outgrown the sort of life she's been leading—alone and broke and afraid of things. This is it, she thinks. There's a volley of music, a thumping, computer-generated bass line, and a shift and surge roars through the dance floor. Time to be judged.

"I'm not afraid of him!" Felice shouts at Berry.

"What?" Berry cups her ear.

It's critical that she not back down from this man: if she does, then it's all been a waste and she's still just a weak, frightened, irredeem-able nothing. Felice is holding her breath as she approaches the bar, her jaw clamped, spine erect. Not afraid anymore. The man notices her immediately. He fixes on her with those eyes, as if she's late and he's been waiting. "Hello," she says, unable to smile, stopping a few feet away. There's someone with him, a nonentity in a business suit, half turned toward the bar.

"What's your name?" the first man shouts at her.

"What's yours?" she shouts back, edging closer.

He says something she can't hear. He shouts again, it sounds like "Marren."

She says, "Is that your first name or last name?"

He frowns and shakes his head, then he holds up his beer, lifts his eyebrows.

"Rum and Coke," Felice shouts. The man beside Marren signals the bartender for a round. Marren leans forward, extending his hand, Felice assumes, in order to shake hers, but instead he takes her by the wrist, his thumb pressing the bundle of nerves at her pulse, and tows her in. She takes awkward steps. Felice glares at her friend but Berry doesn't budge.

"Is your little friend watching us?" Marren asks, his mouth close to her ear, his breath warm on her neck. "Does she like to watch?" He holds her wrist, his thumb stroking it casually. He hands her a tall glass filled with crushed mint: it smells crisp and sweet. With her free hand, she holds the glass close to her nose, inhaling the fragrance. Energy whips across her body, wicking through the tips of her fingers. The air in the club takes on the ammonia tang of swabbed hallways and chalkboards and sweat and anxiety. The dance floor could be the commotion of the halls outside the music room.

That was years ago. She's another person now. Felice yanks her wrist out of his grip, hard. She's been on her own, making her own way, for five years—she's fed herself, bought condoms, learned how to deal with her monthly cramps, learned how to keep a roof over her head. She didn't get lost in the streets like other kids she met—unraveling into prostitution, alcoholism, meth, crack, their skin turned gray, faces sinking into skulls, their young teeth rotting away. Now she puts one hand on a hip, untouchable. Marren smiles, palms up—unarmed. His friend has turned back toward the bar. Hannah wasn't afraid of anything—even when she should have been. Felice comes closer to the man, daring him in some way. Marren looks exhilarated, his eyes wide, head lowered. She says, "Today's my birthday!"

He lifts his eyebrows and removes something from the breast pocket of his shirt, holding it up. A long silver-link necklace with a silver pear about the size of a marble. Felice is used to receiving jewelry from men—she pawns anything she can and gives away the rest. But this is unusual. For her thirteenth birthday, not long before she ran away for good, Stanley made her a baked pear in a *crème anglaise*. She no longer ate her mother's pastries by that point, but the pear flesh was soft as custard: she ate it sitting on the edge of her bed while Stanley watched from the doorway, and left only a stem and seeds. Now she keeps her face impassive, not letting on how much she wants the necklace. "I was saving this," the man is saying, his mouth again close to her ear. "This was supposed to be for another girl, but maybe I'll give it to you."

Eventually Berry joins them and together she and Felice flirt with Marren. The girls laugh, teasing each other, amusing themselves, dancing in place. It's late and there's an overripe, exhausted quality to the night. Felice doesn't want any more drinks but Marren buys them sugary mint cocktails. She accepts his beige tablets, then palms them, whatever they are, to Reynaldo, who gulps them down, then moves back onto the dance floor, eyes fluttering, his face blissful. Marren's friend J.T. barely speaks; he leans on the bar, his head pointed toward the corner of the room. But Marren is in no hurry: he laughs with the girls and fawns over Felice, calling her *princess*. After an hour or so, Marren produces the necklace again and dangles it in front of Felice. "It's yours—if you come with me . . ."

Felice slides a look at Berry, who grows alert, a tiny smile sharpening her expression.

"It's platinum," he says. "Pure platinum, from Cartier. You ever hear of them?"

Felice rolls her eyes. The music has deescalated—or her hearing has adapted to the noise—they can carry on something more like conversation. "Duh—I hope so."

"Platinum is the most precious metal there is. This is worth, like, ten times more than white gold." It ticks back and forth, a needle of light. "You know what this thing cost? You won't even believe it."

"It's low-class to talk about stuff like that," Berry says, delighted.

"Just guess. Who cares? I'm a low-class guy. Some girls like it."

"I don't know," Felice says. "Just tell us."

"Twenty-four thousand."

"Bullshit." Berry laughs.

"It was bought by an emir for his bride. You ever hear of the Emir of Oman?" He looks at Felice.

"So why doesn't she have it?"

"The bride failed to uphold her end of the transaction." Marren grins and nudges J.T. "And, like I said, I'd rather give it to you."

"Are you the Emir of Oman?" Berry asks.

Marren laughs into his drink and even J.T. turns around to look at her. "No, beautiful," Marren says. "He's just one of my clients."

THE CHAIN HANGS from her neck, the silvery pear between her breasts. Felice senses some sort of old ownership about it, which makes her like it even more. She touches the necklace again, then her hands move to the backseat upholstery of Marren's convertible. He drives with one hand slung over the tops of the seats, alternately watching the road and shouting into the rush of wind roaring over them.

Berry hadn't wanted Felice to go with them: at the last second, she'd come out of the club and watched with Felice as the valet pulled up in the forest-green Maserati, top down." Where you going again?" she'd murmured to Felice, eyeing Marren and J.T.

"I don't know—just one of the dumb places on Lincoln Road, I guess." Felice fingered her silver pear. She hadn't really wanted to go, but somehow it seemed like it would be worse not to do it. Letting the old terrors back in. Besides, she'd accepted the gift: she owed Marren another club, at least. "He doesn't even dance," she'd said.

"Just stands there and looks gross."

Felice hugged herself, one-armed. "Please come."

Berry's face flattened with distaste.

When Felice climbed into the car (J.T. took the front passenger's seat), Berry reached over the door of the convertible and gripped Felice's fingers, as if she were about to slide off a building. "Okay, look. You know what—don't go with these guys."

"I want to." Felice's voice was tiny. A late breeze was picking up and she barely heard herself.

"It was a stupid joke, what I said about hooking up with this asshole. Give him back the crappy necklace. Really—don't go. I don't want you to." Berry looked nearly frantic, her fingers clutching the window.

"It's no big deal," Felice said. "I'll see you later—at the Cove."

Marren pulled away, breaking their connection. Berry trotted after them, past the valet station, her silk wrapper shining.

Now Felice shivers a little with the ocean wind in the car. The motor hums as they turn the corner too quickly, whipping Felice back against the seat. From the sidewalk, young men look up, admiring the car. She finds a hair band in the backseat and scrapes her hair into a ponytail. Leaning forward, she shouts into the wind, "You guys—you don't ever dance?"

Marren smiles in the rearview mirror; the hollows under his eyes deep and gray. She feels something like the presence of ghosts, a breathing pressure on her skin.

"So what do you guys do, anyway?"

J.T. turns and says something. "What?" she shouts.

"He says . . ." Marren turns, streetlamps streaming past them, "that you talk a lot."

"What?" She leans forward, her shoulders tensing.

J.T. says something more and Marren barks with laughter. "He says he's feeling bad. Maybe we should let you go."

Felice takes a breath through her mouth.

"What do you think? I should just let you go now?"

He turns back, and as they drive several more blocks in silence, Felice realizes she's made a mistake. A torpor comes over her—the old feeling—icy and leaden, covering her, as she grasps that the situation has changed. *No,* she corrects herself. The situation has stayed the same: her thoughts have simply gotten clearer. Her limbs feel sluggish with a kind of dissolved terror. She sits back. They fly past the clubs.

They stop at a light and Marren twists around in his seat. "Now you're not talking at all. Can't you make up your mind?"

She blinks slowly, anesthetized by fear.

"Speak."

"Where are we really going?"

He flicks a look at her, sighs. "Downtown. That's where we're going. Now you happy?"

Downtown Miami: warren of back alleys, bodegas, hidden offices. She's heard the stories from the beach rats—how it's a place for the deeply crazy and dangerous, drop points for drug cartels, vanished children, human trafficking. The outdoor kids avoid downtown. She thinks about a yacht party she attended where guests whispered about the beautiful boys and girls with the deadened zombie faces. They didn't mingle or even seem to speak English, but they were willing to follow the older guests into chambers adjoining the staterooms.

"Maybe we should," J.T. says without turning. "I mean, let this one go."

"Fuck no—we're going to have *fun*." The light changes to green but Marren doesn't turn back or move the car. "That okay with you?" he asks Felice.

The car behind them gives a jarring blast. J.T. clicks open the glove compartment but Marren shuts it delicately, with his fingertips. "Don't." He returns to staring at Felice: under the layered ocean night, his eyes are wetly black. She could not have put herself in a worse place. For years she'd assumed that the worst possible thing had already happened; she tricked herself into thinking she would stay safe. There is no *safe*. Her mind, like her body, feels muffled and faraway.

Another car blasts behind them, and J.T. opens the car door and gets out. Felice lets her head fall back against the seat. The stars look close and bright. "Like soldiers," Hannah used to say. Felice wondered how stars could look like soldiers. Stanley told her that they turned pink before a hurricane. She stares hard at a cluster of stars.

"What're you doing now, crazy girl?" Marren is grinning at her over the seat.

Some old energy stirs in Felice, an impetus—half anger—and she sits forward, closer to the man. "Hey, can we stop somewhere first? Can we go to the beach? I know a cool place."

The man's eyes flit over her head. He turns around to face front, settling back against the seat. In a dizzying, reckless moment, Felice twists in her seat to face the car behind her. She waves at them quickly, silently mouthing, *Help, help me,* but she can see nothing beyond the glare of their headlights. She faces front again, quickly. Marren twists back, his hazy eyes gazing over the headrest. "Maybe. For a little while. What the hell?"

A knot forms in her throat, making it more difficult to breathe. "Cool, thanks."

J.T. gets back in and slams the door shut, shaking the car. "I told them to stop honking."

In her peripheral vision, Felice notes the other cars silently gliding around them as they remain parked at the light.

"Hey," Marren says. "Princess girl wants to go to the beach."

J.T. turns away to gaze silently out the passenger window.

"Hey asshole," Marren says to him, "when's the last time you been to the actual fucking beach? The fucking actual water and sand and shit."

"I know what the fucking beach is," J.T. mutters.

Marren turns and smiles. He looks uglier when he smiles—his face covered with a crosshatching of lines. His eyes rest on Felice's face. "The fucking beach. You never know what they're gonna say, do you?"

The light switches to green again. A car pulls up behind them and honks twice.

J.T. doesn't lift his head. "Fuck you, Marren, will you just turn around and drive?"

Brian

BRIAN SITS IN HIS HOME OFFICE LISTENING TO Avis's movements in the kitchen. His gaze skims over the computer out the side-yard window, to rest on a fat avocado, a bleb of green light hanging from a branch. Their tree is full this year, the fruit thud on the roof all night, but he doesn't like this varietal; they taste like old butter.

He stares at the numbers Javier gave him: there will need to be withdrawals, transfer of funds: he imagines giving the go-ahead to the agent: *Reserve me two floors*—muttering as if he were in some sort of TV thriller—anxious as his wife's shadow filters past the doorway. His eyes feel scorched. He'd lain awake all night, worrying over the deal—would they really be able to flip such expensive units—wasn't the condo sector always the first to lose value—affecting a deep, rhythmic breath when Avis came to bed, then staring at the subtle wavelength of her breath in sleep. Such a gamble, it seemed: he wouldn't be able to tell her. But he would be doing this for her, for their family. Toward dawn, he closed his eyes, thinking of the way his son's infant hands used to swim in his sleep, blindly sweeping over the blankets.

He studies the shadows fluttering over the window shutters—neighbors heading to work, as he should be doing—and marvels, with a detached, out-of-body calm, at how it's possible to arrange for one's wealth or destitution in a matter of moments. Every reserve, every last account would need to be emptied, every investment called in, penalties assumed; he would need an expensive line of credit and a new mortgage. Two point three million. Javier said it was possible—or did he say "likely"—that they would make double that when the units sold. He sits back at the desk, going over the numbers again, this time with the stub of a pencil on a pad of paper, as he might have done in grade school. If he makes the purchase, that will leave them a little over four grand in checking: almost exactly where they were when he was thirty-two, with a new mortgage, wife, and baby. The uncertainty returns: they could simply give Stan the money—as they had in the past. But Avis doesn't want to: she says she doesn't trust "that girl." Brian suspects, though, that she actually feels anxious about their finances. With a windfall like Javier predicts, Brian reasons, she'd relax.

Brian hadn't gone to law school hoping—as many of his colleagues had—to become wealthy. Discontent has been a gradual, almost metaphysical condition, seeping in, mineralizing his bones. The inevitability of salary comparisons, of spending one's life gazing up at the next guy. Still, he reflects, it's something of a relief to know one's net worth—even if it's about to be zero. At one point, early on, their savings and investments had mounted to nearly four million. But the debts accumulated: loans for the boat, condo, starting the wine cellar, a collection of antique botanical and zoological engravings—including a very old, expensive one from Paris, titled *The Types of Unicorns*. They'd gotten socked by the costs of starting and keeping his wife's business afloat. And he had to admit, didn't he, to some guilty relief when Felice had offered them her "deal," and Avis came home from that meeting saying, "No more private detectives, no more monitoring." Then, to cap it all, came the even greater costs of Stanley's market. He feels like a shrinking engine pulling the weight of endless boxcars. Can he live long enough, he wonders, to make enough money for everyone?

The shutters in his small office—formerly Felice's bedroom—are closed against the late-summer morning heat. Happy Birthday, baby girl, he thinks mournfully. Today, isn't it? The 23rd. Now the parent of two adults, Brian closes his eyes and mentally catalogs the physical ailments that have descended on him over the past few years: the aching hamstring and hip, the tender inner forearm, his inability to sleep through the night without one trip after another to the bathroom, the subtle abdominal pressure that teases and torments him—seeming to play tricks, eluding his doctors, frequently appearing coincident to the midnight bathroom visits, the occasional heightening (not quite *squeezing*) pressure on his chest. Is it possible to have such symptoms and still be considered "healthy"? Why does that one muscle in his back sometimes twitch? Why do his gums tingle? If you think you have *it*—if you constantly suspect and dread *it*—does that help keep you from actually getting *it*? Or does dread invoke *it* like an angry sleeping god?

The serrated cry of tropical birds pierces his window: he imagines their beaks like scissors, like the sound of anxiety itself: the world stabbing away. He realizes that he's been listening to a low-level warbling cry for some time. A baby's cry—that incessant register of complaint. Every now and then the cry seems to refresh itself, surging back with renewed vigor. The pattern of crying is, he realizes, regular as a tape loop. He moves nearer the window, peering between two slats in the blinds, finally grasping that it's the neighbor's damned bird.

AVIS HAS YET TO ASK why he's still home at 10 a.m. on a Wednesday. He feels like a poltergeist in the house of the living. He wears an old cotton bathrobe and walks from room to room of his not-quite-yet profoundly mortgaged home. Where is his nerve? What sort of man backs down from risk? He tries to calculate exactly how long the FOR SALE sign has been up on the Handels' front yard—four or five months? and he wonders if he can extrapolate from this the health of the condominium sales sector of Miami. He gazes at his own square coffee table, the Brazilian sectional couch and divan, the chestnut dining table that shimmers with polishing wax: artifacts of a previous life. Have their furnishings always seemed so cherished?

Brian calls work and tells Agathe he's preparing for the hurricane, then he goes to the kitchen door. Avis is leaning over the counter, her strong back to him as she rolls out a circle of dough. He admires the tidy crisscross of her apron strings, her narrow waist, her movements, so elegant and precise as he looks on, tentative as the sorcerer's apprentice. She turns, smiles, and looks at him, asks if he's feeling okay.

He shakes his head as if sharing a joke with her. "Just going to putter around on a few projects—want to get the place stormproofed. Supposed to be a big one."

She looks at him more closely now and he feels himself turning scarlet. They've ridden through several hurricanes in the past—including Andrew—with no special provisions. To his surprise, Avis nods. "Yes, that's probably a good thing to do."

Brian pulls on a pair of faded chinos and a soft old button-down shirt, then drives to the Home Depot in Pinecrest. It's so jammed he has to creep behind departing customers in the parking lot to get a spot in a distant corner. People mob the aisles of the cavernous store, collecting not only hurricane necessities—batteries and flashlights and distilled water—but also seemingly random items like plastic flower arrangements and Christmas decorations—all of the shoppers moving with the same taut urgency, their faces jutting forward, nearly running their carts into one another. Brian is astonished that so many people don't have to be at work at this time of midmorning.

He moves through the store with a sense of setting things to rights. Putting one's house in order. Time to get serious, he repeats under his breath. He looks for help, having come without any list, but the associates in their workman's aprons scurry through the crowds without stopping, like outnumbered riot police. Brian moves his cart forward, selecting things impressionistically: if something seems as if it might be useful, he takes it. Hammer, lightbulbs, hand-cranked radio help him to feel solid and directed, but increasingly isolated. He notices the other customers seem to move in and out of nebulous packs of family or colleagues, and everywhere, in every aisle, running currents of Spanish. He stands before bins of fasteners in graduated sizes, picks up one perfectly formed fastener—a miniature work of art in metal, its sides machined at exact right angles—and decides to buy this for Stanley.

He hurries toward one of the small mobs formed in front of a cash register. While people elbow and wave each other into the waiting crowd, Brian stands staring fixedly ahead, as if standing in a queue at a bank. He is fearful now of the thought that perhaps he isn't considering investing purely on Stanley's behalf, but in some small way, to impress Fernanda. He shuffles forward, his eyes glittering with preoccupation, a momentary fantasy. He imagines a pared-away existence—no difficult children, no painful history, no expensive house. He casts his gaze toward the far corner of the immense store and wonders: Where does a man in Miami run away to, anyway? Trenton? Omaha?

When Brian finally emerges with his hurricane-preparedness items, the sky over the lot glistens, brilliantly clear, a depthless turquoise. Pre-storm sky. He is unloading the bags from the car into the garage when there's a rap on the garage door. He opens the door to a short man holding two paper bags. "I knock and knock, but no answer," the man says stoically. "I almost give up. Then I see you drive in." Brian leads the deliveryman through the garage door into the house. Uncertain where the fruits go, he has him leave the bags on a kitchen counter. There are big covered ceramic bowls on another counter, but no sign of Avis, not even the scent of things baking: an unnerving emptiness in the air. "These are starfruit, lychees, and blood orange in the jars," the man is saying pointedly, as if he doesn't quite trust his goods with Brian. "Where is the Cuban girl? She don't work here no more? The boss answer the door last week. Now you." He seems openly mournful yet resigned to this turn of events. Brian studies the narrow tilt of his eyes, his expression evocative of years of patiently borne suffering and disappointment. Where has Nina gone? Brian realizes he hasn't heard Avis mention her assistant or seen her in weeks. How unfamiliar his wife's daytime life has become—a separate world, moving in an orbit barely adjacent to his.

After the delivery van pulls away, Brian walks through the house, looking for Avis. The bed is neatly made, all clothes are folded and put away. Back in the kitchen, he notices the dough seems to be outgrowing the ceramic bowls, strips, soft and pale as human bellies visible beneath each tea towel. A murmuring reaches him through the rear kitchen window. He peers through a dappled film of water spots to the backyard, its border of invasive bamboo and a messy thin palm he's been meaning to clear out for twenty years. He goes through the French doors, uncertain as to why he's moving so quietly; for some reason, his breath is knotted, caught in the top of his chest. Squatting slightly, he's able to peer through openings in the leaves where he beholds his wife sitting on the grass beside a young girl. He watches Avis's profile as she talks to the girl: they appear to be sorting some kind of weeds as they talk. He notices the dark bristle of Avis's hair: the girl's skin is a luminous coffee color, her back and neck upright. She stands and stretches and he realizes she's older than he'd thought, possibly the same age as his wife. A few feet away, the black bird purrs and babbles quietly. Brian feels cold with doubt, bafflement. When he was a child, his mother took him to a fortune-teller at a street fair. The woman fanned cards across a table. Those images: a hanged man, a woman on a throne, a fool wandering off a cliff, called up the same immutable feelings he has now, watching the women together. He feels a kind of terrible idea taking hold of him: that the reason he's started to act a little crazily is because, over the past days, he has sensed his family leaving him. He'd thought he was the one who made the decisions. But first the children went off and now, here is his wife in a scene of such utter contentment he feels he is looking into a future world, twenty years after his death.

BRIAN LEAVES HIS HOUSE in a state of ignominy. There are things to be done, he tells himself. In the past, whenever he's felt beset by nameless promptings and anxieties, he's always been able to hide in his work. Work rescued him and Avis both when Felice left. They submitted to hard labor: there seemed a genuine sanity in it. He lets his fingers ripple along the edges of the steering wheel, noting a greenish-gray haze at the edge of the sky. Brian picks up the phone. When Javier answers, he says abruptly, "Talk to me, man—that Steele Building—I've been thinking about it."

"Brian?"

Brian detects a flicker of sound in the background—a feminine voice? "Jesus, Jav, where are you? Are you alone or what?"

"Dude, what's your problem? You're the one I'm worried about."

"Worried? Why? Just because I'm going to put my goddamn house and my life savings on the line?"

"Listen, man, breathe—everything is fine—it's perfect, right?" Now Javier's voice is placating. "But I think maybe—look, we better slow things down. This isn't the best time right now."

Brian stares at the street. It occurs to him that he is, perhaps, losing his grip. His voice is half strangled. "Is Parkhurst gonna know about the Steele Building?"

"No, man, he doesn't know nothing. He's out of it. All he can think about right now is his Topaz deal."

For some reason, Javier's words make him want to weep or punch the steering wheel. "The Topaz Building. That thing."

"Buddy, hey, we need to talk. Now isn't the best time, though."

"You already said that. But the other day you said it was a beautiful life. So I've decided. I want to do it. I want in. Let's make a billion."

"That's good, Brian. That's really good." But there is something taut, almost compressed, in Javier's voice. "Just, relax yourself, all right? *Todo es fácil.* I've gotta go now, okay? But hang on—we'll talk very soon. For now, be easy. You do that for me, buddy? Just be easy."

HE TAKES BRICKELL, his usual route—joggers, bicyclists, green avenues, new cars, vertiginous high-rises on all sides. But it's midafternoon now and the light is all wrong: he's missing from his life and no one has noticed. When he approaches the turnoff to the Ekers Building, he drives smoothly past. Easy. He'll show him easy. He feels buoyant: he lowers the window and lets the air flood in: it smells like salt. Almost immediately, he hits lights and downtown traffic and he rolls the window back up. He has to jog to the east to skirt a construction site, trucks piled with plaster and lumber rumbling past in clouds of white dust. The entire city seems to vibrate with the roar of the cranes, as if its very core is being disemboweled. Brian stares at light skittering through the planks fencing off a work site and thinks of his son again: The wealthy need homes, too, he argues silently. But then he is haunted by some sense of revulsion: a soul rot.

Brian creeps through the city blocks then gets on to First. He rarely ventures this far north, past the Design District, its narrow wasteland of expensive furniture and home decor boutiques. But on First, the city reveals itself—a mess of check-cashing and pawnshops, Latin bakeries, and stunned, displaced tourists milling around. There are placards on a number of crumbling foundations, announcing, *The Future Site of . . . Developed by . . .* Everything is either falling apart or under construction. Even the people look different—darker skin tones, hair beaded, nails long and decorative, the cars dustier, rearview mirrors festooned with prayer beads, baby shoes, dice; there are dashboard saints and Virgins of Guadalupe, Cuban flags, flags of Colombia, Haiti, El Salvador, Lebanon. He makes a decision: he still doesn't know exactly where the Steele Building is, but he does have the address for Parkhurst's Blue Topaz. At the light on Northeast Fifty-fourth, he takes a left, following directions included in a folder from a commission hearing. It's a grimy, working-class city street with hand-lettered signs for local businesses: *Gonaïves Car Wash, Chez Italienne Fried Chicken, Bonjour Travel,* the battered *Église Haïtienne,* every window covered with bars and scrolls of ironwork, metal dumpsters covered with the sort of graffiti that looks like vicious slashes, rows of rusted metal spear fencing, sailing plastic bags, and weed-riddled torn-up lots. At the corner, pulled up beside King Stable Bar-B-Q Lounge, its sign faded to near-invisibility, he makes a right, passing a mural of Martin Luther King Jr. and Bob Marley and above them in sky-blue paint, *God Bless the United States of America.*

As he turns into the neighborhoods, he has a powerful sense of intruding: the blocks are tiny, without markers or sidewalks—the grass is thick with garbage—beer cans, used diapers. Children play in the street so twice he has to back out and go up a different block. He drives slowly, trying to see things yet not appear to be looking. A woman in a turban speaks to another woman in a tight caftan; a man climbs over a chain-link fence into a neighbor's yard; groups of people talking, sipping drinks, sit under rickety constructions covered in plastic tarps and canvas. There are taped car windows and houses boarded up with planks of wood, overturned shopping carts, yards of bare dirt, a flock of chickens scrabbling in a plot. He rolls through block after block. No one appears to notice him even though his car is so big there are sections where it seems wider than the street. He can't help thinking of how, when he bought this SUV—a white Mercedes-Benz G55—Stanley referred to it as his whitey-mobile. He's about to flee the area when he spots a billboard in another rubble field between rows of small wooden houses: *Future Home of Les Temps Perdu Condos Dev. by P.I.&B.*

Like everything else in the neighborhood, the sign looks provisional and decayed, as if it's been battered by the elements for a long time. He pulls up to the site and lowers his window. Beneath the bright yellow lettering, he can make out the pentimento of another earlier sign: *Future Site of À La Mode Hotel.* A thin column of despair rises within his chest. The problem isn't merely that the building will disrupt the neighborhood, he sees now. The problem is also that, in some sense, the neighborhood is undisruptible and unsavable. They bought the property from the Aguardiente Group, who apparently did little more than conjure up a name for their project. Brian frowns, running his fingers over the steering wheel. He'd heard rumors that the group itself had run into the usual tax and finance problems, dissolving after scarcely a handful of projects. It was easy to forget that so many of these groups were mere cabals, forming and disintegrating seemingly at whim.

There's no shoulder on the road and nowhere to park, so Brian drives the SUV directly into the lot, snapping twigs and crushing a swath of thorny green weeds. His company now owns the imaginary building in this field, and possession being nine-tenths of the law, he will inspect the empty space he's traded his honor in for. He climbs out of the car and counts off a hundred or so paces, stopping just before the field dead-ends in a chain-link fence and the back of a row of shedlike houses made of plywood. It's warm and the air swims a bit. On a kind of despairing impulse, he hikes up his chinos and squats in the weeds, then shifts to a cross-legged sit. The ground is sandy and covered in odd plants pushing straight up like fingers, and a bed of ground leaves, pods, shreds of plastic, cigar butts, and other unidentifiable, partially decomposed garbage. It's not an uncomfortable place to sit. In fact, as he reclines on one hand, he becomes aware of a softness in the air, a familiar scent of lighter fluid and grilling meat. Across the lot, on the other side of the street, he notices an immense woman in a dress of some stretched, shiny fabric, sitting on the concrete step in front of her house, staring at him. Her eyes look like punched-out holes, her fat arms rest on her knees. He waves at her and she doesn't quite wave back, but he detects an incline to her head. He thinks of his mother, her silent final months in bed, face shining with tears, watching her sons with a look of ancient disappointment.

There is sweet music from an invisible source: swaying reggae chime. He begins to imagine that the place is not all that bad, that there is, in fact, a pleasant sort of ramshackle quality about the neighborhood that he actually enjoys. He lets himself toy with an idea: if his investment in the Steele Building pays out, he will quit his job. They'll give Stanley what he needs and most of the rest will go to charity. They could keep just enough to buy a little house right here (this condominium—he senses vividly—will never get built), become the kooky white couple—greeted at first with suspicion, until—with Avis's baking—they manage to win the hearts of the neighbors . . . Or perhaps it's not him and Avis? Now he sees himself standing on a glass balcony overlooking the ocean: a younger woman wafts out; she is draped in silk, her hair like gossamer . . .

He is interrupted in these musings by a shout and looks up to see three lanky black men headed toward him from the opposite corner of the field. They wear tank tops and denim shorts halfway down their hips, revealing four or more inches of boxer shorts. All three of them are built like the figures on top of trophies, their arms sinewy with tight, round muscles, skin gleaming as if freshly oiled. "Yo, man!" the one in front calls. "What you doing out here? You lost or something. You gotta be lost." He wears a pair of aviator-style sunglasses on his forehead. "Guy's tripping," another one, in a red T-shirt, solid black tattoos engraved into his bicep, says. "He look lost."

Brian blinks at them. He thinks he should be frightened, but it seems he can't summon the energy for fear. How little it takes to make one's life jump its tracks. The phrase *put out to pasture* floats through his mind and he laughs. "Some pasture, huh?"

The men glance at each other. The man in red says, "Yo."

"How long you been sitting out there in the sun, man?" Sunglasses says. "Why don't we get you in your nice big car now and get you on your way?"

Brian points to the billboard. "You see that sign over there? That's me."

Sunglasses and the man in red walk to the sign while a third one in an olive drab tank top and a shaved head stays behind, watching Brian with his hands on his hips.

"That's me," Brian says again.

"Yes, sir," Shaved Head says gravely.

The two men study the sign, frowning, and Brian wonders then if they can read and, if not, if he's just insulted them. Sunglasses walks back with Red Shirt trailing by a few steps. "So you Pib?"

"Pib? Ah—PI&B. Yes. I work for them. They bought this property and they're planning to build here. Actually, probably they're just going to pretend to build and then sell before anything goes up."

Sunglasses tilts his head back and crosses his arms high over his chest, tucking his hands under his armpits. He gives Brian a long, dissecting stare. "Sorry to say it, but you don't really look like you work for nobody."

Rattled, Brian searches in his pockets, but he left his wallet in the garage with his new hammer and batteries. He extricates his cell phone and says, "Wait." When Javier picks up on the first ring, he feels a cascade of relief. "Hey, Javy! Buddy! Listen, I need a favor. I'm up here at the Topaz site and I need you to confirm for some people that I work for PI&B."

Sunglasses rolls his eyes. "Man, what does that prove? Just proves you got some homeboy who's crazy as you."

Javier, on the other end, says, "*What?* Who said that? *Where* are you?"

"The site. For the Topaz condo. Little Haiti, remember? Unless you want to call it North Design District. North NoDo? You take North Miami Ave—"

"What the fuck you there for? What are you doing? *Vámos,* get the fuck out of there, Brian. Don't tell me anything now. Just get in your car and go."

Brian wants to laugh at the creaking panic in his friend's voice, the way it intensifies his accent. "It's fine. I'm talking to these guys here—"

"What fucking guys? Do not talk to no guys."

"Too late."

"They right there? How many are there? Do they have guns?"

Brian lapses into silence. He senses his lovely, iridescent state of fearlessness start to wisp away. "I don't know," he says quietly as he eyes the way Red Shirt swings his arms impatiently, opening and closing his hands. "Possible."

"Brian, what the fuck. How the fuck did you do this?"

"I don't—I didn't—" His voice falters.

"Listen." Now Javier has dropped to a kind of broken rasp—the closest he can come to a whisper. "Do not move. Do not get into a car with them. Stay there. I'm coming. Right now. I'll be there in five minutes."

"Yeah. Yes. Good," he mumbles. He listens to the line disconnect and then listens to silence for a few seconds, wishing he could preserve the magical sense of safety he felt while he was talking to Javier. The young men shift and look around. Sunglasses says, "So what your boy say?"

Without meeting his eyes, Brian slides the phone back into his pocket. "He says he's coming here."

At this, Red Shirt throws up his hands. "Man, what're we hanging around this fool for? Let's leave him and go. I don't got all day."

Brian notices a look exchanged among the men and it comes to him then that they might not be the danger at all. Perhaps it's not necessarily a good idea for him to be sitting here alone in an open field. Danger—his sense of it—floats free of itself. Brian thinks of Parkhurst's contempt for "fearfulness," and what he calls its anti-dote—the "magnificence of ambition."

"Wait. Wait a sec." Brian carefully rolls on to his knees, then, bracing with fingers on the ground, pushes to stand, one foot at a time. "I want to—can we just . . ." He needs to catch his breath. "You seem like—like really good people—like—" He's shaken by some sort of emotion and has to let it subside: he doesn't have himself fully in hand today. "You remind me of my son," he says to the shaved-hair kid. "I mean, *he* wouldn't like any of this—the development. I just need to tell you guys something. If this project *does* get under way? These people—PI&B, they're going to try to destroy this place—everything you've built here. And you have to find a way—you have to really organize. The Little Haiti Action Corps—they didn't even come to meetings. I can give you the names of some good legal peo-ple—they'll do it pro bono."

Sunglasses holds the back of his hand to his forehead, shielding his eyes. "Whoa, man, wait a sec here. You're talking about the people you supposedly work for—is that right?" he asks. Brian wonders why he doesn't just lower the glasses to cover his eyes. And . . . why not a belt for those pants? Make life easier. Why not go to trade schools, learn some skills—like welding!—instead of wandering around like a pack of animals? That must not be the point, he thinks. So what is the point? He wishes desperately he could call Stanley right now, but fears these young men are out of patience—just when he could be on the verge of giving them some really useful advice.

"You dissing these people—you ain't even established you work for them yet." Red Shirt draws a finger through the air, limning his words. He's more compact and intense than the other two. "This muthafucka on crack," he says.

"You know what?" Shaved Head rests his hands on the striped fabric of his boxers. "These Pib boys? They come round here last month or two. These boys in suits offer my auntie money for that piece of junk she lives in—right over there, see? And then what, the other day, another dude come out, throw another pile of cash on top of *that*."

Brian notices again the flickering glance pass between the men: a kind of alert or caution. "What the hell, man?" Shaved Head cries: this is directed at Sunglasses, as if he'd said something. "It's no secret." His gaze swings to Brian. "They giving my auntie two hundred fifty *thousand* for her fallin'-down house. My auntie's eighty-two year old—her house smell like a hundred cats died inside it."

"Word," Red Shirt says.

"They're giving my mama and my granpapa the same," Sunglasses says. "You can trash the white boys all you want. That's some dollars. Shouldn't be messing with it."

Brian shakes his head, slow, wild energy entering his body. It's all around him, turbidity in the air, a humid swelling, like the curling of water before it boils. "Okay, so—they've already been here? I know that sounds like a lot? But if your auntie wants to go buy another place—she's gonna find out that—"

"His aunt is *eighty-two*," Red utters, his voice low and hot. "She ain't gone be buying no new house."

"She gone live with her people near Charleston," Shaved Head adds more casually. "My auntie is still cleaning houses for people, man. She gets six hundred dollars a *month*."

"My mama and granpapa and great-uncle, they live together and between them, they got nine hundred fifty dollars a month to live on. They pay taxes, too. You believe that?" Sunglasses says. "This money coming in mean some our old folks can finally relax."

Red Shirt spits into the field dust. "We're getting money too. And I ain't even gone discuss that with you. Yo, we don't even know who you are really."

A SLEEK BLUE BULLET of a car rolls in, stops beside Brian's SUV, and Javier springs out. Brian is touched to realize that Javier is afraid for him, that he did apparently manage to shrink the time-space continuum of downtown traffic and make it there in just over eight minutes. He jogs across the lot, taking in Brian, his dusty chinos, the three men, the scrubby, ruinous field. "*Hola,* boys. Greetings. What I miss? Bring me up to speed here."

Sunglasses snorts lightly, chin lifted. "This your homeboy, Habana?" he asks Javier. "'Cause he come up in here, get in that dirt you see right there, and start talking crazy shit about you people."

"Tell them," Brian says, vaguely sensing they're having parallel conversations. "They don't believe me. Tell them I work for PI&B."

Javier's eyes tick between Brian and the men. "Okay—yeah—this guy is my homeboy, and yes, he's on staff as our permanent, full-time *loco.*" He grabs Brian's arm and starts pulling him toward the cars. "Now time to get my friend back to work."

Brian lets himself be led forward, but as he walks his body feels pervaded by low-level trembling—his heart is beating in a strange way and it becomes harder to walk normally. Some vital thread in his fabric has been tugged away and he seems to be coming apart. "I want . . ." he says hoarsely, lumbering to a halt. "This isn't right. I want to help these men."

Javier's face swings around, eyes shining: he has the look of someone trying to carry a buddy out of a bloody battlefield. His jaw seems to have lengthened and his lips are pale. "Not now, Brian. Now is not a good time."

Brian pats his pockets, again coming up empty. "Damn, dammit."

"Listen, homes, you really work for these people? You already done plenty for us," Sunglasses says. Gazing at his patient face, Brian understands that the three men are just as eager as Javier to see him gone. He wonders if Jack Parkhurst assigned these three to keep an eye on this lot. Parkhurst had done something like that with an abandoned warehouse and parking area he'd acquired in a ravaged section of Liberty City. "What can I do?" he asks mournfully, already sensing defeat. "Is there something I can do for you guys? Do you have résumés?"

"Oh yeah, right here with our business cards," Shaved Head says.

"Yeah," Red Shirt says with a hard laugh. "Give us your car. What about that?"

"No . . ." Javier is shaking his head, eyes closed.

Brian looks at Red Shirt, wanting to do something to shock the smile right off his face. Something extraordinary. Reckless. He places his hand in his pocket, feeling the outline of his keys. *"Brian,"* Javier warns. "Stop."

"What does it even matter?" Brian asks, caught up in the euphoric jolt of his idea. "With that Steele investment, I'll be able to buy any—"

"It's not—" Javier snaps his sentence off, lowers his head, shaking it silently. "No, no. Bad idea."

"Why the hell not? You know what—I'll probably give a bunch of that money to charity anyway."

"Because," Javier hisses at Brian, "there isn't going to *be* any money."

"What?" Brian blinks.

"Fuck *you.* Charity." Sunglasses and Shaved Head have backed up as if Brian has announced he has plutonium in his pocket. "Yo—like, we don't jack people's fucking cars, man," Sunglasses says, and Shaved Head protests, "Fucking *charity,* asshole? The fuck outta here."

"What are you saying?" Brian stares at Javier.

"Later, man," Javier mutters, flicking a look at the young men.

"What in the goddamn hell?"

"You called me here." Now Javier's face is narrow with fury. "You drove in here due to losing your fucking mind, and I had to come get you out."

Red Shirt watches their exchange with interest. "Man, you think like giving us a freaking car makes it all okay, you really out your mind. You insane in the membrane all right. You talking about what your people done to my people? You give me your car, your house, your wife, and your great-granny, man."

"Word," says Sunglasses.

"But, okay, so if the dude is really feeling bad about shit, like I think he is . . ." Red Shirt turns to the other two. "I say why not. I mean, it don't change nothing, but if the cat really wants it so bad . . ."

"*Un momento, un momento.*" Javier holds up one hand. "What your people–my people we discussing? *You* people make your own mess in this country. My Americano here don't have nothing to do with *los Haitianos.*"

A visible physical tension rattles through the men as their attention turns to Javier. Shaved Head—the one Brian has come to think of as more restrained than the others—says quietly, "You fooling with me?"

The men murmur as Javier holds up his hands, backing away. "Hang on now. Listen, my homeboy here cannot spare his car. He really isn't right in his head, in case you haven't noticed that. This car—it belongs to his *wife.* You hear me? He gives this car to you, she'll be down here with *la policía* so fast. But look, okay—" He fishes two-fingered in the breast pocket of his shirt and flourishes a pair of folded sunglasses. "Do you see these? These are Leonards—and they're so exclusive you've never even heard of them." He nods at Sunglasses' head. "I see you have a nice pair right there."

The younger man lifts his head.

"I know those weren't cheap—those Ray-Bans." He uses his glasses to point.

Sunglasses snorts. "Cheap! Correct, muthafucka, these were not cheap."

"Yeah. But let me ask you—did you pay twenty-six hundred dollars for them? These"—Javier holds his own pair up again—"I bought when I made my first million-dollar commission. Remember the Olympic Hotel deal?" He nudges Brian with his arm. "These were custom handmade in Florence, Italy. German optics. Made of titanium—lightest substance known to civilization. Twenty-six hundred dollars, I shit you not. I had to make an appointment to come in and get fitted. I had to reserve them seventeen months ahead of time. And they're numbered—limited editions—you see this right here—what's this say?"

Squinting at the inside of the stem, Sunglasses reads, "Number 18."

"That's right—there aren't maybe twenty, twenty-five people tops, walking around wearing these. I happen to know that the Sultan of Brunei is one of them." Still smiling, Javier slides them off again with the tips of his fingers and hands them to Sunglasses. "Try them on. Go head. See what they feel like."

"Huh." The young man frowns, then takes the glasses, slipping them on. "Yeah, they all right."

"Nice, yeah?" Javier folds his arms in his smooth black suit. "You wanna trade?"

The man, stares hard at Javier, then removes the glasses. He holds them up to the light, tries them on again, keeping one hand on the stem. He looks around. He looks at Brian. The other two men each try on Javier's glasses, then the Ray-Bans, consulting with each other in low voices. Sunglasses cuts his eyes at Javier. "You didn't pay no twenty-six hundred for these. You wouldn't be trading for these if you did."

Javier keeps his arms crossed high over his chest, his head lowered, nodding slowly, judiciously. "Sure, yeah, that makes sense, obviously. I see that." He lifts his sharp face. "Now let me tell you why you might be wrong. Maybe I'm doing this because my *loco veridad* over here drove up your street and tried to give you his car and I'm just trying to get his ass out of here without anyone getting killed."

The men stare at him, their faces set, eyes glittering with hard, unamused stares.

"But maybe—and here's where I want you to pay attention—" Javier holds out the edge of one hand, just as Brian has seen him do at the dais in carpeted hotel conference rooms, pointing to the projected schematics of new buildings. "Maybe I just want your glasses, *hombre,* because, what the hell, I *bought* these glasses. Buying is easy. It's nothing, in fact. Anyone can get themselves a credit card—they can do the same damn thing." Javier snaps his fingers. "It just takes a little more green than usual. But *those* glasses?" He points at Sunglasses' head. "Well, those babies came from *you*—a badass muthafucka up in Little Haiti. It's like snatching the crown off the lion's head. There we were, alone in this crazy, broke-down field, surrounded. Dude was all set to fuck up my friend and me together. Instead we get talking? Next thing I know—he made a hell of a trade for himself. See, those glasses come with a *story.* And, for a sorry old *viejo* like me? Worth way more than some fancy store-bought crap."

The young men look at each other, their faces wary to the point of anger.

As Brian watches Sunglasses hand over his Ray-Bans—the exchange made in a kind of respectful silence—he has a sense of observing something like a primordial ceremony. Then Javier takes the fob from Brian, unlocks the SUV, and helps him up behind his own steering wheel, swinging the door shut behind him. Wearing the Ray-Bans, Javier salutes the three men and returns to his own car. He waits for Brian to pull out first. To make sure I'm going, Brian thinks. He doesn't dare even to wave at the men. The tall man is now wearing Javier's glasses, the curved lenses glitter blackly; the man looks unreadable and imperial.

BRIAN'S PHONE RINGS as he passes another mural of MLK—this one painted on the side of an on-ramp as he turns onto 95 southbound, hard to see in the lowering light. The evening is mottled and hazy. "You okay over there?" Javier, coming up beside him in his satiny blue Jag.

Brian looks at the car. "Were those glasses worth twenty-six hundred?"

"What do you care?"

"I want to know if I owe you twenty-six hundred." The roots of his teeth ache. "Because I can't really tell what anything is worth anymore. At least as far as you're concerned."

"Let's go to one of the hotels, we can have a drink, and we'll talk."

"No." Brian squeezes the steering wheel. "Tell me now. I want to know what the fuck is going on with that Steele Building project."

"No one's answering the phone at Prescott Filson."

Brian rubs the outer edges of his eyes: they feel gritty, as if there's a mineral residue. "Well, for how long?"

"Forty-eight hours. Give or take." There's a crackling rush of car echo. "They *split*. There's a *lock* on the development office door—the listing agent told me."

"Unbelievable. They actually blew town?" They slow down behind a backup headed to the beach exit.

"The FBI's already into it. These two guys, I guess they siphoned money from some project up in Delaware to try to get the Steele Building going."

"You're telling me I was about to give you all that money, and it was all just a big fucking scam? What, the developers took down payments and split to Grand Cayman?"

"Ah." He can almost hear Javier's shrug against the car seat. "I swear to you, Brian, I'm as blown away about it as you are. There's no way I would have taken that deal to you if I'd had the smallest idea."

"But you *did* know—why the fuck didn't you tell me the deal was crap?"

"What, when you called? I wasn't sure what was going on. The listing agent had just called me. He was freaking—he has clients who've already paid their money. He thinks the financing fell apart and the guys decided to hit the road . . ." Javier's voice seems to lose volume, as if he'd moved his mouth away, then back, ". . . distracted, a little. I took my eyes off the ball, I admit it and I'm sorry, man, *disculpe,* I apologize."

"Sons of bitches were a bunch of crooks! Or losers and phonies. And you're *dealing* with people like that? And dragging me in too?"

There's a silence filled with ringing highway noise, then Javier says quietly, "I fell for it—that's right—but there were plans and they did buy the property and they did develop other projects up north—I checked—and six other smart, rich *bisneros* gave them about eighteen million."

"Damn." Brian twists his hand on the wheel. "I guess it is what it is," he says. "But goddamn."

Javier sighs. "You are fine, man—right? Look—you didn't jump on it and *gracias a Dios,* eh?"

Brian feels ground down, too exhausted to do more than follow the bumper in front of him. He might just end up tailing this car to the Everglades or Key West. Simply can't think about it. He still doesn't know the truth about those glasses. After a moment, he squeezes his tear ducts and says, "Hey, buddy, I'm gonna head home, okay?"

"*Claro,* man, of course."

"I've gotta get things ready . . . with the storm and . . ."

"No, man—you gotta do it. Supposed to be nasty tomorrow. Get yourself home, get it sealed up. *Hasta la vista.*"

"Thanks, buddy. Really."

"No, no. For what? Go, get home. It's good to get ready for things, no?" Javier asks. "What do those Boy Scouts say? Be prepared?"

Avis

SHE THINKS SHE CAN FEEL A NEW WEIGHT IN THE AIR—
tomorrow's storm, but the first thing she'd noticed this morning was
a sense of tranquillity. As she showered and dressed it gradually
occurred to her that she was not hearing—for the first time in weeks—
the bird's racket. No deafening *braaah,* no singing, no little boy crying out to playmates; no mad laughter. Nothing. Avis had stepped
outside to look for Solange and found only the enormous birdcage,
still as an empty bell.

When she went back in, someone was at the front door. The man
seemed astounded when Avis swung the door open. He was well over
six feet, wide and solid in a square-shouldered black jacket and black
collarless shirt. Avis had the impression she'd seen him before. His
face was a mask of pain—coruscated, eyes burnt to crusts: consumed
in a way that was all too familiar.

He'd said, "My wife is missing—perhaps you might've seen her?
We live around the corner."

Avis's stomach tightened with dread: she wanted to shake her
head and flee into the house. She had her own private losses to con-
tend with. But he'd looked so stricken, his face shock-white, a livid
streak in each cheek—she couldn't help stepping back. She invited
him in and slipped from the room to fetch coffee and sugar.

Now the man hunkers over on their couch, taking up the center,
radiating loss. His jacket neatly folded beside him. For some reason,
he calls to mind her mother with her reams of poetry, slender chap-
books filled with her essays. Each one trying to get at Heaven. *Essayer*
means to attempt—she told Avis. As a girl, Avis imagined her mother

pulling arrows from her quill, aiming over her head, trying to hit the obscure target.

She's pleased with the steadiness of her hands as she brings coffee—the cups silent on their saucers. She has practice in panic—like an expert nurse or sponsor. She places the cup and saucer before him and watches him curl forward. He puts his hands on his cranium as if to hold it in place, stubble bristling through his fingers, and stares at the tops of his lace-up shoes.

"So, you live around the corner? On Camillo? Or Fluvia?"

He nods, still not lifting his head.

"Have you called the police yet?" She feels competent, almost motherly. In her element. "Do you have a photograph of your wife?"

He straightens, patting at his jacket pockets, produces a wallet, its edges white with wear, and extricates a curved photograph. He places it on the table between them. Avis stares at the familiar face: her face is plumper and milder, her hair is uncovered and glimmers in a close-cropped halo. "Ohh . . ." She leans in, taking the photo by its edges.

He looks up, hearing something in her voice; his face a beat of hope. "Have you seen her? She liked to work outdoors, in the back."

Avis holds the photograph in her cupped hand like a bit of eggshell. "You were—you're married to *Solange*?"

"You know my wife?" He straightens.

She shakes her head slowly, a sense of unreality rolling over her. "We've been getting to know each other."

"My God." His head lowers, his fingers push into his eyes.

Avis returns the photo to the table, as if it belongs to neither of them. She takes deep breaths—a technique she'd learned years ago from a grief counselor, to stave off panic attacks. "Have you contacted her family? When did you see her last?" Avis slides forward on the seat. She looks toward the windows, tries to will her thoughts into clarity.

The man seems stuck in some kind of maddening torpor. "Well, yesterday? Last night. I'm doing everything I can think of. She doesn't have any people here. I tried to track down her aunt and cousins, but it seems her family are all . . ." His head tips again, as if his skull is too heavy. "She wasn't happy. I always knew it. The police told me to write down everything—the details—what she was wearing, what she liked to do, the names of her friends. I'm at the ministries office all day—I worried about her getting lonely. I didn't know she had any friends . . ." His eyes flicker over hers hopefully. "I've been going from home to home—you're the first to know her name."

Something new occurs to her, a sliver of ice snaking down her center. "Is it possible she's been kidnapped? This city—things happen all the time." Avis stands and takes her keys and purse from the entry table. "We can go back out into the neighborhood to start. Did you contact both Gables and Miami-Dade police? You can't wait for them anyway—she's just another name on the roster to them."

The man shakes his head—that heavy movement again. I contacted all the hospitals—even shelters. "I've been looking all day, driving and walking. She doesn't have any money that I know of, and she doesn't know her way around. I drive her everywhere." The slow shake, the hands.

Avis feels hard, old energy welling under her skin. "It's too soon to panic—it hasn't been twenty-four hours? Perhaps she's just . . ." She moves briskly to the French doors, envisions a route Solange might've taken: Fluvia to Salzedo to Ponce de Leon. Perhaps a bus: a return to the beach. The imaginary escape routes fill her imagination, golden, bisecting lines. There are too many possibilities—the lines cross and recross, moving in opposite directions. Avis hears herself, the words she imagines for this process—*escape route*. Behind her, the man speaks as if Avis were still sitting across from him, saying desolately, "I think Solange doesn't want to be found."

AVIS TAKES HIM to the backyard and shows him the place in the shrubs where she used to spy, and then pass through, to visit with Solange. Now the wind is starting to pick up, so they pull the lawn furniture close to the house for shelter, and sip the cold coffee. The energy has shifted, crumbling away from Avis, creating a quiet passage, like a shared trickle of grief. He tells her his name is Matthew, he's from Vancouver, B.C. "Here is the true chapel," Matthew says wistfully, staring at the fronds.

"I suppose—it's a nice way to think of it."

"Not that different from Haiti. In some respects." His face is mild and quizzical. "I was a minister there—in Cap-Haïtien—for six years. A missionary—technically." Avis hears confession in his voice, sliding beneath the words. He keeps turning the china cup around in his fingers and she fears for it. "Somehow, over time, I lost interest in conversion. I started to feel that even in a religious community, faith is a choice made in private. Or should be." He breaks off, eyes lifted toward the fronds between their yards. "I've changed quite a lot, I guess."

"Was she in your church?" Avis tips the cup, watching the black slice of liquid.

"No." He rubs his temples. "Not at all. She lived nearby. She was famous for her remedies. We were in a rough patch, very poor, near Fort St. Michel. Lots of beautiful old colonial buildings around, but our area—mostly slums—shacks without floors. The poverty was mind-blowing. No indoor plumbing—not even in the hospital—sewage in the street. Kids washing in the gutters. TB was everywhere. And lots of the people preferred the old ways of treatment." His gaze moves from the cup to the feathery palms, the individual leaflets moving like fingers in the air.

Avis touches his arm and senses something dart through him, just beneath the skin, as if contact is unbearable. "Solange was different back then," he says, his voice breaking into a tremor. He clears his throat and waits, then starts again. "Well, for one, she was married. To someone else, I mean. They had a beautiful little boy," he says softly. "They were such a nice family—I used to see them. The three of them were always together. But in Haiti? In those days, there were militia—like street gangs. They took all the young men and boys—especially in the bad neighborhoods. The police were out of control.

Either you had to go kill for someone or they would kill you. Not to forget about American contributions—backing dictators is such an efficient way to shred the fabric of a culture. The Haitians have never been forgiven for demanding freedom." He carefully places the cup on the patio stone, as if that's just where it belongs. The porcelain a grace note against the brushed stone. "During my time, rebels targeted the churches because they thought we had hidden wealth and that we hoarded food. Obviously, ridiculous. There's always some theater of the absurd with these savage civil wars. It was something the boy soldiers told each other. In so many places, whiteness . . ." He holds out the back of his hand, tipping it up slightly so Avis can see the freckles and blue tracery of veins, "looks like wealth. But we didn't have anything—no matter how white we were. I had to turn all sorts of people away—friends, neighbors. What option did I have? We couldn't take everyone in—we could barely save ourselves. There was always shooting in the streets. Snipers and gangs, sometimes tanks came roaring up the lanes. Things just got worse and worse. I try not to remember too much. In Haiti, murder was very common— a pedestrian tragedy."

Avis bends forward, carefully shredding a blade of grass into her lap.

He smiles. "You'd think I'd have been better prepared. I've lived in four different developing countries—I try not to look at the politics of the place. It's always the same story at the root—colonialism sews its destructive seeds, and the more crowded the world gets, the more we destroy each other. People can't afford much compassion." He pushes forward in his chair, then stands and walks to the line of bamboo. "The thing about Haiti—with that sky and beach and mountains—from a distance, you think you made it to paradise." He holds his hands over his face a moment.

"We turned people away every day—the church wasn't any safer than any other place. Those soldiers—the boys—they had no respect for holy places. They'd lost the very idea of respect. Just like animals. Worse than. The things they did." He lowers his eyes. "But one day Solange showed up."

"Did you know her?" Avis clutches her elbows, now hunched over her coffee. "I mean—if she didn't go to your church."

"Everyone knew Solange. The doctors there were overrun, and missionaries—if they're any good—they wear many hats. We kept supplies of rudimentary medicines locked away—aspirins, penicillin, insulin, mainly. Some of my parishioners . . . I think they spent more time napping than praying in our chapel." He smiles thinly. "In any case—many, many people there—they just want bush medicine. They trust it. And Solange was brilliant—I saw it myself, with my own two eyes. I saw people recover from malaria, all sorts of fevers and skin conditions—that she treated. Those bush teas and poultices." He holds on to one of the segmented canes, his expression lost and abstracted as if he hasn't slept in days.

SHE COLLECTS A TRAY from the kitchen: arranges almond and mango cream puffs, brown sugar lace cookies, and miniature napoleons of vanilla and guava: fleeting breaths of *pâte à choux* and buttercream that dissolve in single bites. She places the tray on the low table between the folding chairs and pours fresh cups of coffee, aware of a kind of transaction taking place. He gazes at the plate of pastries, murmurs, "I couldn't—I haven't had any appetite . . ." But he picks one up, admiring the gem-cut layers of the napoleons. He places it in his mouth and Avis watches his lips tremble, his eyes close, the corners damp. He opens his eyes, staring at the plate, some desire settling into his posture. "I've never told this before—not to anyone—none of this story." He touches a cream puff and studies it as he speaks. "But there's no point to clinging to old secrets." He glances at Avis. "If there's anything left of my faith, it's my belief in confession."

Avis doesn't respond, hearing a wisp of her mother's laughter.

Matthew shifts the plate of pastries carefully on the table, not quite pushing it away. Finally he says, "Believe it or not, Solange offered herself. To me. She came and told me that—in exchange for her son's safekeeping at the chapel, she would spend the night with me. As many nights as I wanted. That's how she put it. She was desperate by that point. I'd heard stories about women bargaining this way, with their bodies—I was so mortified and sad for her and it was strange because you also think of such odd things at times like that. I remember noticing how well-spoken she was, how fine her English was. Well-educated."

He smiles, very slightly, at his coffee. "Obviously I said no. But Solange—" He shakes his head, smiling more openly now. "She really was something. Magnetic. She is who she is. Completely. I said both her son and husband could come work in my vegetable garden and sweep out the church. I thought perhaps if we took them out of the streets during the day the army would let them alone. Extend at least some symbolic protection of the church over her family."

Avis holds a sip of the warm coffee in her mouth for a moment, testing its bitterness before she swallows. "Did it work?"

Now his smile is automatic, vacated. "He disappeared. We heard later the husband was killed in the street fighting. That's what we heard. The rebels were trying to oust the president—poor Aristide. They were wild savages these guys—bloodthirsty, murderous. Underwritten by the Americans. They didn't care who they shot at."

Avis's throat feels dry; she studies the white star at the center of the coffee. "Her son—what happened?"

His eyebrow lifts. "He came to me. A very dear boy. One of these children who'd held on to their sweetness. Oh, a troublemaker too. He broke things and made a mess. Didn't matter. I became very fond of him . . . But he was only with us a few weeks. I should have let him spend the nights at the church. I didn't think." He hits his palm slowly, over and over, against the corner of one temple. A fragile, measured ritual. "No one could believe how terrible it would get." Now he looks directly at Avis. Avis drops her gaze: her hands go still on her cup. "He disappeared too," he says. She thinks about Solange talking about her son, saying, *I left him*.

Matthew re-clasps his hands. "Antoine. She never talks about him. They *must've* killed them—the husband and the boy. Did I already say that? She came back to the church again maybe two or three days after the boy disappeared. She was in shock. We didn't talk about her husband or the boy at all, though. They were two among hundreds. I think we talked about the garden. I wasn't entirely sure why she had come. Now I think she just wanted to be someplace quiet. She started to bring her herbs and transplanted clippings into my garden. She made her bush teas and dispensed them there, at the church. The fathers would've been horrified." He smiles. "And she offered herself to me again, for some reason, even though her—incentive—to do so . . ." He lifts his hands.

Avis feels a queasiness—soul-sickness—begin to steal over her. Her palms feel damp. She picks up one of the lace cookies, examines the filigree of chocolate, replaces it, clears her throat. She will remove the tray and thank him for coming, before he can say any more. But he raises his head as if he can will her to listen. "I didn't want her to stay—I swear—I argued with her! I told her to go home—every night I told her. It got to be too dangerous for her to go home. The rebels took over our street and there was shooting every night, tanks rolling over houses, tearing everything up. It was beyond deafening—a maelstrom. We were under siege. You can't imagine the feeling that you can't leave your house—that even your home is dangerous."

Avis feels a feverish shame creep over her skin, knowing she has to listen. She nods slowly, releasing the tea tray. She makes herself ask, "So . . . she stayed?"

He sits back on the folding chair. There is his off-kilter smile again. "When the fighters occupied the street, she slept in the chapel for a week. I stayed in my room on the other side of the wall. We listened to the tanks thundering, keeping everyone awake, till we were just so exhausted we all just learned to sleep through it. The gardener left and then the housekeeper ran away. Solange put on the woman's clothes and decided that would be her job. We nailed the doors to the chapel shut, but Solange begged me to leave the little stained-glass windows uncovered. And, you know, through that siege? Not one window damaged." He stares at the pastries. "Little miracles, right? Something to live for?" He seems to be mocking himself, but his smile fades. "After a couple of weeks of sleeping in the chapel, she came to my room. Like when she'd first arrived. I'd turned her away the first time, but you know . . ." He displays his palms. Something about the man seems innocent to the point of bafflement. "I felt truly helpless. We gave each other some comfort. I like to think we did. Of course I loved her—whether I wanted to or not. Sometimes I wondered if she'd put one of her hexes on me. I'd never been in love before and it was such a specific pain, so sharp, like someone had to be jabbing needles in a little doll."

"Then you decided to come back to the States?" Avis interrupts: she doesn't want to hear about how good or comforting Solange was.

The man rubs the inner creases of his eyes, his face pouched and swollen with shadows. He picks up the lace cookie Avis had touched and eats it, then two more. "Years ago, I had a church in South Florida and a couple of my parishioners were from a wealthy old family here. I traveled to the church offices at Port au Prince and called them to beg for help. I didn't care what happened to me but I was so afraid for Solange. I had to get her out of there." His voice diminishes. "The family rented the house for us. That's our backyard, right through the trees." He points.

"I know."

He nods and holds the smooth chair arms. "She likes to work outside. I can never get her to come in. Even when it's like this—like a jungle. This heat. I want to move us up north—I've been trying to get reassigned. Someplace like Vermont. I don't know if she'd like it," he adds hopelessly. "Now of course, I don't even know—" He breaks off.

Avis leans forward on the chair, wooden slats digging into the back of her legs. "She didn't leave a note? No warning at all?"

He reaches into his blazer pocket and withdraws a white legal-size envelope. He flicks it with the tops of his fingers. "This is from INS. It came the other day in the mail. Someone tipped them off. We were traveling so quietly. We moved a couple of times after her visa ran out, but I thought we'd be okay here for a while. I needed more time to get things in order—we'd applied for sanctuary status, but that was rejected. Maybe I kept her too isolated. My parish here doesn't even know that we're married."

Avis watches the way his fingers run along the outer corners of the letter. Already it looks grubby.

"I promised Solange we'd be okay. I said I'd go talk to them, that we'd just move again if we had to. I'd thought she seemed fine at the time." He holds his hand out, fingers extended. "Calm. She made dinner. I had my arm around her shoulders when we fell asleep last night. I woke at four a.m." His face slips.

Avis lowers her eyes, breathing shakily, slowly.

"She's always been so talented at hiding what she feels. Never seen anything like it. I'd never dreamed she would run away. She has no family in this country. No friends. She's totally dependent on me. I had to take her shopping. She wouldn't wear the new clothes I brought her—just the rags from the housekeeper. It was like she was biding her time. Just waiting." He lifts his eyes to Avis. "I'm so afraid she'll try to go back."

Avis feels cool throughout her body, thinking of the last things Solange said to her.

When he finally rises to go, he stops by the front door and holds out his hands to take hers. "Forgive me, please, for unburdening myself like this. In my line of work, it's usually the reverse. I feel embarrassed."

"I'm sorry not to be of more help," she murmurs. "I'm just sorry."

"This is the first time I've been able to speak—openly." He closes his eyes and squeezes her fingers; for one awful moment, she believes he's about to cry. He opens his eyes again. "I'm certain that the son and husband were killed. It's absurd to think otherwise. If you'd been there you could have seen for yourself. Just one ongoing massacre. If only we could have seen the bodies. She might have had some relief."

He releases her hands. "There were nights when the fighting died down and then there was such a silence. It seemed like you could hear the land and the ocean breathing, exhaling, if it doesn't seem too

strange to say. There were nights . . ." His voice falters and he clears
his throat briefly. "Sometimes we heard knocking. There were nights
that we could hear a child out in the street crying, *Maman, Maman!*"
His voice is soft and light. "Over and over, just like that, so sweet.
You couldn't tell if it was a boy or girl. Solange became certain it was
Antoine. Of course it wasn't. There were so many orphans—everywhere. I wouldn't let her go outside to look." Head lowered, he lifts
his eyes, their singed edges, to Avis. "It was the most dangerous at
night. Do you understand? There were snipers. There were children
with guns. They would use a crying child as a trick, to lure people
out of their hiding places. But still, Solange screamed at me. She beat
me with her fists like a man. I didn't let her go."

Avis stands. She picks up the plate of remaining pastries, takes
them into the kitchen, spills them into a paper bag, and brings them
to the man. "I'm sorry," she says, her voice jumping. She isn't sure
what she's saying to him. It occurs to her that he asked almost nothing about her friendship with Solange. Now she just wants him to
take his terrible stories and go.

He mumbles his thanks again and leaves her a dingy business
card. "In case you happen to hear something."

AVIS WATCHES THE MAN'S form diminish as he moves up the street,
the neighbors' lawns dark as old emeralds. She remembers how she
dreaded sleep in the months after Felice left. But her dreams were
light and oddly pleasant—heartbreaking only upon waking. There
were certain things she couldn't say or think or hear in those months.
Like *daughter* or *child*. Or *lost*. That was the worst of all, a sliver of
metal under her breastbone. She woke from dreams in which she
said it over and over, as if she were squeezing it from her body. She
remembers the way she felt when she finally understood that Felice
was not going to return, the sense of leadenness, the elemental weight
of it filling her bones.

She gravitates to the French doors, studying the scenery behind the glass. Her gaze falls on a pile of weeds heaped up on the patio and she remembers that Solange had told her they had some sort of special properties—like a witch's herb. The air riffles around her and it takes some minutes for her to remember why it feels so different. That quiet. There's a crosshatching of faraway bird cries and distant lawn mowers, last-minute yard work before tomorrow's storm. She finds she needs to sit down, flat on the cool rock. It feels as if steam is rushing through her body. She scoops up the piles of leaves Solange had left, gathering them into her lap. Her cell phone is in the front pocket of her cook's pants: she extricates it, her fingers tremble, misdialing until she remembers the speed dial. Pound sign. Three. A string of red ants cuts jaggedly across the stone, inches from her. She watches them in a trance, then scans the thickets of palms that border their property. Voice mail picks up. Peering through the scrim of trees, she glimpses the curved iron door of the birdcage standing open. "Stanley," she says to the machine. "Please. I'd like to come see you."

She hadn't felt—not in this immediate, personal way—just how much colder and sharper things could be, how planets could snap out of their orbits, how frigid, wasting blackness could come in a tide, erasing everything.

Felice

THE LOW CAR TURNS OFF ALTON ROAD ONTO ONE of the narrow numbered streets perpendicular to the ocean. Felice slides onto her back to gaze out the rear windshield. Usually the night sky is full of streetlights and sea mist, but once they turn, Felice notices a new clarity to the night; every scrap of cloud has dissolved and instead there are perfect constellations and a single red-white point of light sailing past like a space station.

It occurs to Felice that something about this man reminds her of Mr. Rendell. She wonders if she went with him tonight to take one last spill into her childhood, the sweet fever of old fear, making her feel so alive, sparkling. Everything smelled sharper and sounded clearer and the stars seemed to pop right out of the sky in those days. The smell of disinfectant and chalk and rosin and old instruments and Mr. Rendell's piney aftershave all made her feel awake and alert. They roll up to Ocean Drive and Marren doesn't bother with parking. He just stops in the street and puts on his flashers. "The cops know me." He slings a forearm back over the headrest and studies Felice. "So come on, fairy princess, we're here."

"This is stupid." The other man doesn't turn around. "Big stupid waste of time."

"You're the one wants to let her go." Marren's eyes look hollow and carved-out under the streetlights. "Anyone ever tell you—hey—" The man gives his friend a shove. "She looks like Elizabeth Taylor! Right? Anyone tell you that?" He chews on the end of a toothpick ruminatively, then works it between a couple of molars. "Those eyes of hers." He runs his fingertips along Felice's brow bone. "God, I feel sorry for you," he says abruptly. "What's a little girl gonna do with a face like that?"

They climb out and the night sand under her sneakers is dense and damp, wet cement, barely curving under foot. She smells the aftermath of rain—it must've come while she was in the club. Her skin feels like a finely woven gauze: the rain melts in the air in white flashes, flourishes.

The music room was supposed to be their sanctuary. She wasn't very good at violin, but she still enjoyed the rasp of the bowstrings, the cool tilt of the instrument under her chin—who knows why. The whole time she played, right from the start, she felt his eyes on her profile. Mr. Rendell's gaze, always there, hovering in the air. Even when he wasn't looking at her directly, he was still looking. Eyes hovering like bees. The music room belonged to her and Hannah. After class, they claimed the room for hours—supposedly to practice, Felice on violin, Hannah on clarinet—even though Hannah always said it was pointless—it wasn't like they were going to become musicians. They used to eat the *palmiers* and meringues Avis packed for Felice, and one day Hannah held up the scroll of a *palmier* and said in a languid, speculative way, "I wonder why your mother is trying to make you fat." She glanced at Felice, her dark, solemn eyes shining. "Do you ever think about that?"

Felice smirked. "You're crazy. She's a *baker*."

Hannah sniffed a meringue, then tossed it into a trash bin. "You ever wonder if she's trying to poison you? Because, seriously? I think she might be."

Sometimes Hannah would light a cigarette. She'd hand it to Felice, who held it up between two fingers, admiring the thin white trickle of smoke. She didn't puff on it, though: Stanley was contemptuous of smokers. She and Hannah lounged on the gray upholstered couch pushed against the wall. One day Hannah talked about her older brother Simon (Semir) who'd killed himself by drinking the cleaning fluids stored under the bathroom sink. She talked about it in a casual way, as if she were describing a shopping trip.

"Why? Why did he do it?" Felice was breathless: she couldn't imagine losing her brother.

Hannah looked disoriented: she touched her hair, which fell around her shoulders in pieces. Finally she said, "It was years ago. I hardly remember. He kept talking to himself a lot. And not to anyone else. I guess it was sort of like he forgot how to be happy." Then she smiled briefly and said, "I hope that never happens to me."

"Me either," Felice said, chilled and heartbroken for her friend.

Late on a Tuesday afternoon, after class, Hannah told her she had to get home early that day to help her mother "have her usual mental breakdown." This entailed, apparently, Hannah doling to her mother just the right number of Vicodin. "So she doesn't go haywire again," Hannah said, tugging on the sleeves of her thin black sweater. Then she and her mother watched TV together, but when Felice asked what they watched, Hannah admitted her mother generally slept through all of it. "I think the only reason she's still working is for the drugs."

Felice had never heard stories like this before. "Aren't you worried about her? What does your dad say?"

She shrugged and pulled the sleeves over her hands. "They know the deal. I've already told them I'm out of here in a year or so."

"You're only fourteen years old!"

"So?" Her face was clear and cool. "And they're a million and I can already do a better job than them."

"Where would you go?"

"Europe. Spain. Basque Country maybe. You should come with me. We'll take over the world."

Felice smiled and her gaze rippled over her friend. But suddenly Hannah seemed to harden, as if she were offended, and she said, "There's no point anyway. All any of us are doing is wasting time until we die."

"So there's no point to doing anything?"

She turned her head. "Doesn't matter if you're president or a bum. Not in the end. It all goes back to zero."

"How do you know?"

"I know."

Sometimes it was easier to be friends with Hannah when she wasn't around. There was something perfect about school after final bell—the formal emptiness of the halls. Felice and Hannah had talked about all sorts of plans—how they'd make movies together and see things. But when Felice was alone she could sink into the feeling of the future—the delicious ache of it—just by pointing her thoughts into the distance.

Felice slipped into the music room, evading the custodial staff who sometimes patrolled the school's east wing. It was silent and the room was full of long shadows. She left the lights off: beyond the windows, she could see rain prickling the cement courtyard. She heard a sound then and, turning, realized that she wasn't alone in the room.

Two people. They appeared to be crumpled together on the couch. She gradually made out Hannah's straight, choppy hair, her blouse unbuttoned and pushed down around her middle. Her skin had a bluish-white cast like marble. She'd never seen her friend's body before. Hannah, for all her ironic, knowing ways, was extremely modest—she refused to disrobe in front of or shower with the other girls after P.E. Hannah's eyes were lowered, her arms coiled around a man's bare back—his shirt on the floor, his fly flapping open, though his pants were still pulled up. There was a sound like a sigh and a moan—they hadn't seen her come in. Felice watched them, frozen. The man released another awful whimper: it was Mr. Rendell. Felice ran out of the room, the double doors crashing shut after her.

She ran down the hall to the girls' bathroom where she burst into sobs, bent over the sinks. When Hannah came in a few moments later, she could barely look at her in the mirror. She kept seeing the small arc of her friend's right breast squashed under Mr. Rendell's chest, the careful, precise expression on Hannah's face.

"Please don't report him." Her voice was trembling; she patted at her shirt, buttoning. "It doesn't matter at all. It's nothing."

"You said you were going *home.*" This was the least of it, but somehow it was the thing Felice picked to say.

"I know. It's stupid. He doesn't even really like me. He just picked me because I'm friends with you." Hannah's face looked young and bare and frightened. "But he knew *you'd* never go with him, of course."

Felice was shaking all over; she rubbed her arms with her hands; she kept feeling little surges of nausea. "So horrid."

"I know." Her voice was high and faint.

Another sort of possibility occurred to Felice then, a chill entering her bloodstream as she whispered, "Did he force you?"

Hannah's eyes seemed huge in the dim light. "A little, the first time," she murmured. After a moment, she dropped her eyes and said, "Not really. I kind of was happy about it. I couldn't believe that he liked me. Even a little."

"The *first* time? How often?" she started to ask; she broke off in the middle of *often*. She wanted to comfort Hannah, to feel sympathy for her.

Hannah started trying to explain to Felice, to give her details, in their old gossipy way. "It was the time you had the dentist, remember? You missed orchestra. Rendell said he wanted to go over a new song with me. Such a skank. He locked the doors that time—but I could tell he liked thinking about getting caught."

Felice tried to nod and laugh, but then for some reason, Hannah faltered and said, "I'm really sorry."

FELICE STRIDES AHEAD on the sand and Marren lets her—she knows he won't let her get too far. At least she doesn't have to look at him. The moon is burning through the sky and there are gray shadows everywhere. She skirts the Starbucks beach entrance, passes the thick thatches of sea grass—half trampled by tourists, even in low season—and wanders toward the Cove. "Over this way!" she calls, trying to project her voice. She can hear him trudging behind, his breath coming in the asthmatic smoker's wheeze she knows well—lots of outdoor kids have it. He doesn't have to be fast, of course, if he has a gun. Felice hopes one of the kids might recognize her voice. Farther back on the sand, away from the water, she senses other forms shifting past them: street kids—staying silent and unseen.

But there's no sign of Berry or Reynaldo. Of course: they'll be out clubbing for hours yet. They won't return till the water starts glimmering. The ocean looks high and white tonight, as if there is a hidden engine churning inside: the waves rumble, a deep drumming, rolling over all other sounds. For years, she's thought there was a way to stay safe: when bad stuff happened to people, it was because they were crazy or stupid. She'd even thought that about Hannah. As she waits for Marren to close the distance between them, she thinks: There's no escape for anyone. Felice stops and turns deliberately into the moonlight, tiring of cat-and-mouse play, facing into the glassy darkness between herself and Marren. She feels the ghost of an old age she will never live to see settling over her, oxidation rustling in her bones, catching up with her. Marren moves toward her. The night wobbles over his shoulder, and she sees that she's walked farther ahead of the man than she'd realized. For a moment, the noise of the surf seems to recede and she can hear his breath, the little huffs, as if he's already getting winded. "Hey, girlie," he calls. "Slow it down now."

Felice can't see any sign of his friend. She glances ahead, up the beach; the moon lights the sand like a trail of silver minnows. She starts walking again, a bit more quickly, just to see what will happen next.

"*Fuck*, girlie. Don't test me now. Trust me on that." His voice is tense. Felice speeds up, moving faster, feet arched and silent, until she's running, heading toward the firmer wet sand. She moves well on the beach. Almost flying. Skating. Behind her, Marren yells, "God—fuck. *Fuck*. Stop. Fucking stop *now*." Her lungs broaden in her chest, her wiry arms whip at her sides: perfect, coordinated action. She can see in the dark, she can run like this forever, like the free divers who slice through miles of ocean on a single breath.

There's a sound: something breaking or snapping—metal on metal. Then the explosion is so loud the night seems to wang inside out like a steel drum. Stunned, Felice trips, pitches face forward, sand grinding into her mouth and eyes, her ears scorched with the aftershock of noise.

FELICE DROPPED OUT of orchestra. She couldn't bear the sight of Mr. Rendell, his shambling, apologetic manner, his way of glancing at the sixth-grade girls. And Hannah had allowed him—that slack, pale body, arms like rolls of baguette dough—to *touch* her. The next morning, Hannah came right up to her after homeroom. "Hey, pretty stupid last night, right? Thank God you saved me."

"Yeah," she mumbled. Bella caught Felice's eye as she slipped past them in the hall, her friend alerted to some crucial shift in Felice's posture. "I've gotta—I better go," Felice said, moving sideways, as if someone were tugging on her arm.

Hannah stared, her lips parted, then tightened, bravely. "We'll hang out later, right?"

Felice didn't speak to her again after that day, not once. Her old friends welcomed her back as if she'd been away on an ocean passage. No one mentioned or seemed to resent the way she'd abandoned them for Hannah, no one questioned the way that relationship had abruptly ended. They spoke of Hannah in vaguely sympathetic, sorrowful tones. "It's so sad, the way she is," Yeni lamented. "It's not her fault, really."

"She's kind of pitiful," Marisa said.

"She could actually almost be pretty," Coco chimed in. "Like, if she straightened her hair and lost six or seven pounds to start."

"Quit slumping!" Bella proclaimed. "That's what I always want to say when I see her. And wear some actual colors for once. Enough with the black sweater. But she's just so *scary*?" She darted a glance at Felice.

At the lunch table, Felice ducked her head. "Did you know about her and Rendell?" There were gasps. And then a look—such a look—of sumptuous pleasure came over the girls' faces, like biting into éclairs.

All week, Hannah tried to approach Felice between classes. Felice moved to a desk near the front of the class in French. She felt Madame Cruz's scrupulous gaze take in the change. Then there was a substitute music teacher—no one knew what had happened to Mr. Rendell. Felice's friends traded rumors. Bella speculated that Hannah might've threatened to report him herself. "That's pretty brave—I mean, if it's true," Coco said.

"But honestly, she should leave you alone now," Bella said. She sat up straight in her chair. Her features were so delicate they were almost miniature—a small nose, lips like cinnamon candies, and mild blue eyes—so she always looked a little prim. "The way she's chasing you around—she's just embarrassing herself."

Felice was relieved to hear someone say this. Hannah's longing gaze evoked in her a guilty impatience tipped with anger.

Someone came up with the idea of the letter—Felice could no longer remember who. A couple of the girls dictated, and Marisa transcribed it in a flowing hand on scented stationary. It was filled with observations and recommendations about Hannah's "attitude" and ways she could improve her hair and clothing. It concluded by saying that they, the undersigned, were warning her to stay away from Felice, that they were tired of Hannah and her "weirdness," and that if she didn't respect this warning there would be "consequences." Seven girls signed the letter. And then, in enormous, bold letters at the bottom, Felice's name. They slipped it into Hannah's locker on a Friday. Idana Demetrius, a ninth grader who wasn't even in their group, ran up to Felice and Bella to say she'd seen Hannah reading the letter in social studies. "Her lips were moving," Idana reported. "She must've read it like thirty-five times."

Over that weekend, Felice began to feel anxious; her sleep was filled with broken, crackling dreams. She woke early on Saturday, looking around the still-dark room, a profound sense of dread snaking through her, un-wellness like static trapped beneath her skin. At breakfast, the egg her mother had poached—to Felice's usual specifications—seemed to be staring back at her, a glazed eye. She mashed it with her fork, then scraped it all into the garbage. She helped Stanley clear the table and dried dishes while he washed, which was so unusual he frowned at her. "What's up?"

"I don't know—I like to dry. No biggie." She rubbed the towel over a glass, circling the rim, then holding it in such a way that, light-struck, it seemed to brim with some brilliant ectoplasmic fluid. She let out a little cry and almost dropped the glass.

"What is wrong with you?" He didn't say it meanly. Her skin felt hot. "I don't know how to do it right," she said, rubbing again at the glass.

"It's fine," he said. "No big deal." The window was open: it was a windy day; she stared at that light, bouncing white diamonds of it, and tiny bits of shadow like musical notes, and the fronds like splayed-open green blades. They moved, murmuring and waggling, then suddenly went silent and reserved.

Felice felt a little better on Monday. She'd forgiven herself for signing that stupid letter: someone as tough and smart as Hannah would laugh it off. She was almost glad that she'd signed it. Some-thing had to be done, didn't it? She couldn't have Hannah moping behind her forever. Stanley dropped Felice off—he'd recently gotten his license and their mother let them use her car while she was work-ing. As Felice walked up the wide stone apron to the main entrance, she noticed Ms. Muñoz, her guidance counselor, waiting just inside the door. She'd never seen Ms. Muñoz outside of the main office. "Felice," she said, "can you come to my office, please?"

The air seemed to evaporate. She stared at her and almost burst into tears, almost cried, I didn't write the letter! It wasn't my idea! She scanned the hallway, bustling with students, waiting for Hannah to appear, her look of justified hatred.

In the office, Ms. Muñoz did not get behind her desk but sat beside Felice on the soft cotton love seat. She looked frightened as she touched Felice's shoulder, saying, "I understand you were good friends with Hannah Joseph?" Felice didn't make any reply, she simply waited, frozen. So Ms. Muñoz said, "I'm sorry to have to—to be the bearer of such terrible news, but Hannah passed away over the weekend."

Felice rubbed her forehead with the back of her hand; her throat felt sore. She wasn't sure of what she'd just heard.

The counselor's eyes searched the walls of her office; she knotted a tissue in her hand, touched it to her nose. "It's terrible. Just awful."

"Hannah?" Felice echoed. She was still thinking about the letter. "What did you say again?"

"She actually . . . I'm so sorry, Felice, but she did it herself. I mean—she took her own life." The counselor leaned in so close Felice thought she might be about to kiss her: Felice could see tiny inflamed red veins in her eyes. "I'm sure you'll hear rumors—the way things get around in schools. I'm so terribly sorry, my dear. I understand you were best friends."

Felice blinked, her eyes felt hard and scratched. Nothing would come into focus. There was a sere gray light around Ms. Muñoz's face that blended into the walls of the office. "Hannah isn't in school?"

"Oh, darling. She's gone. She died, my dear. Saturday morning— that's when they found her."

Felice took a slow breath. "I think it's—it's a mistake. See, there was this really dumb letter? I don't know. We all signed it. But I'm sure Hannah probably got really upset about it—that's just how she is. The rest of this is—somebody got the story wrong. I'm sure she's fine—I promise you."

"Felice," she said in an awful, melting voice, "I'm so sorry. It *doesn't* make sense, I know. And I know how hard it is—to try to take in something like this. Someone so young. It will take you some time to process it. You have to give yourself time."

"It's not hard. It's just a mistake."

"No, dear. The police were here and I spoke with her parents. I know it's a shock. It is for all of us."

"Then how did she do it?" Felice asked, now challenging.

Ms. Muñoz seemed to pull up into herself. "That really doesn't—I don't think you need to hear about that right now."

"But wait, just tell me, so I can explain this. 'Cause I'm pretty sure I can tell there's a big mistake here. You just have to tell me how."

Felice couldn't stop chattering—she felt as if she were caught in a spell of talking—as if she could talk through this situation and make things right. "Please, please," she begged.

"No, Felice . . ."

"Then I'll just find out from one of the other kids."

Ms. Muñoz shook her head. Then, for a long, elastic moment, she stared at the wall, her eyes turning glassy. Finally she murmured, "She used a belt, actually."

"A *belt*?" Felice felt the urge to giggle.

"Her mother—that poor woman—she found her."

Things were starting to come into focus again. The gray light bled into the corners and clear, straight lines began to emerge, underlining everything with white rays. Felice put the V of her thumb and forefinger to her brow bone. She could feel sharp twinges there. "But that's not how her brother did it." She was confused, her voice weak.

"Oh. Oh no." Ms. Munoz pressed her chest. "Oh God, I didn't know about that. They're supposed to tell us. Oh my God. That poor family, my God."

Ms. Muñoz wanted to call Avis, to have her come pick up her daughter. But Felice managed to convince the counselor that her mother would be out all day, making deliveries. Recalling something she might have heard on TV, Felice said, "I'd rather be here, with my friends—it will help take my mind off of things."

Her counselor nodded and gave her a note she could hand to her teachers at any point, that would allow her to go to the nurse's office. For the rest of the day, Felice kept feeling as if the ground had turned spongy or that her legs were too long or the walls too far away. She sat silently through classes, registering nothing, the teachers' masked, benevolent presences at the front of the room. Her friends surrounded her, just as sympathetic as Ms. Muñoz has been. They kissed her and stroked her hair and behaved as if Felice and Hannah had stayed fast friends till the end. No one mentioned the letter.

After final bell, Felice told Coco, Bella, and Yeni that she wanted to be by herself for a while. They gazed at her, their eyes round, and made her promise to call and check in. But Felice knew they'd start to forget about Hannah after they'd gone to the mall, had dinner, and watched TV. Walking through the echoing corridor, Felice was drawn back to the music room. She pulled open the heavy double doors, peering in as if she expected to catch some phantom of Hannah and Mr. Rendell together on the couch. She entered, staring at the vacant room and the couch in disbelief; shaking waves passed through her. She thought of the letter: its ragged edge torn from a spiral-bound notebook, handwritten in green ballpoint, decorated with daisy petals, the words: *disgusting, pig, stay away 4-ever,* the list of signatures, the last one—growing larger in her imagination—set off with flourishes: *Felice Muir.*

Ms. Muñoz hadn't mentioned if there was a suicide note. Perhaps Hannah had responded to the letter. Maybe someone—her poor mother—would find the letter with Felice's prominent name at the bottom. And maybe the police would come to arrest her for murder. Was that murder? Or maybe Hannah had folded the letter and put it in her pocket. And no one had ever found it and they would bury her with it forever.

That was the most horrifying possibility of all.

OVER THE NEXT couple of weeks, Felice began to feel stronger again. She started to eat, foraging from the family refrigerator whenever Avis went out. She watched great, drugging amounts of TV. One morning she went into Stanley's room while he was at school. It was so still and solemn, the walls painted a clean ivory, the floor bare wood, a cotton sheet on the bed, a curved wooden desk that must have come from their grandmother. A bookcase filled with importance: Chekhov, Merton, Marx, *The Writings of Augustine.* And cookbooks—the *Moosewood,* the *Greens,* the *Chez Panisse Cookbook.* Stacked on a nightstand beside the bed were notebooks, clipboards, and pages of drawings and diagrams: his business plans for a variety of shops—bakeries, a deli, a fruit and juice stand. Mainly, there were ideas for an organic food market. Attached to one of the clipboards, under a big silver fastener, were curling pages inscribed in ink: *Stanley's Manifesto*. Felice slipped it out from the pile and sat on the side of the bed studying the document. Stanley had worked on this statement—essentially, a list of goals—for years, adding to it when things occurred to him. Bella, Yeni, and Coco used to roll their eyes when Stanley talked about his manifesto, but Felice was privately proud of him—the idea of a boy making such a document, attempting to think about principles to live by. She'd never wanted to actually read it before, but now she held the clipboard tightly between her fingers, her breath rushing through her head.

> To offer clean, healthy food.
> To make the food available. Affordable.
> To offer the food in a clean, appealing environment.
> To get the food only from local, small, independent growers.
> Grass-pastured meats. Cageless.
> Produce in season only.
> Sustainably-grown.
> No genetically modified foods.
> Heirloom seeds and produce.
> No Monsanto, no Dupont, no corporate food.
> Hand-crafted.
> No factory-processed.
> No transfats or high-fructose corn syrup.

The lists went on for pages, on scraps taped to larger sheets, papers clipped or stapled together. Toward the end, she found what she was looking for—his mission statement.

> Because all people, rich and poor, young and old, deserve
>   access to and education about clean whole food, we will
>   be teachers, leaders, and activists first, sellers and purvey-
>   ors second. These are the principles I commit myself to,

to live by, always in that order. To make people healthier, happier, and smarter by bringing them better food: to contribute to the restoration of the earth, to making it a better, safer place for all people, but especially for all children on Planet Earth, to live and play in.

Felice stared at the loops of blue ink: they blurred and twinned. She thought she was holding the one thing that could save her. Instructions for getting better. She pulled out a new sheet of paper and began writing, very carefully: *This is Felice's Manifesto.*

I have to find a way to make up, if I can, for the terrible thing
    I did to Hannah Joseph (Hanan Yusef). I confess that I
    killed her. I was horrible to her and I signed the horrible
    letter that made her do it. I have to try to make up for it.
    That means
I have to be judged.
I have to make sacrifices whenever I can. Big and small.
I have to be punished. It has to be the worst punishment
    there is. I have to go away and to leave everything and
    everybody.
I have to try to become a completely different person from
    who I was when I signed The Letter.
If there is a way to help someone in bad trouble, I have to
    do it.
If something awful is going to happen to me, I will let it happen, until the Judging is over. Whenever that turns out to
    be. Murderers get the death penalty, so maybe that will
    happen to me.
Signed: Felice Avis Muir

When Felice left—each time she ran away—she took almost nothing with her. The first attempt, a week later, was mostly an experiment. The police brought her home: she apologized to her parents, she went back to school; she pretended to be her old self, as best she could. But she kept her manifesto folded into a rectangle in her backpack. It took six attempts over the next year, but one day she left home for good: she made it stick.

HER HANDS SWEEP over her body, checking that she's still alive and unhurt. The feeling of relief comes in a burst, revives her, cascading through her system—her lungs ache with a ripping influx of air. She turns toward the surf, but there's another explosion—air shredding open, just inches past her shoulder; her hair lifted and singed.

Her magical grace broken, Felice stumbles and stumbles, clumsy and shaking. She can't get purchase on the sand. A hand seizes her ankle, the fingers digging in, and she flashes on the way Bethany went down on the sidewalk, how Felice knew she wouldn't get back up again. "Fuck, you stupid, fucking . . ." the man trails off, sounding almost rueful, as if sorry that this is the way things have to be. As he drags her upright, her hand touches the dimple in the sand, the nub of bullet.

She can't see his face, just a glimmer of teeth. His hand is heavy, pulling her to her knees. The pants unzip silently. Her eyes water shut but this seems to make the roar in her ears louder, so she opens them again. His fists are full of her hair, yanking her head. She clutches his legs as if she might drown. Her senses drown, her eyes and nose full of salt, taste of limp flesh: a moan shifts through his body. She feels a frigid metal pressed into her spine, pointing down into the path of vertebrae. Tears leak from her eyes in an inert, horrible way; his hands crushing the skin at the back of her neck. She can't breathe and she wonders if she were to do something like reach for his gun it might persuade him just to kill her more quickly. Instead she reaches carefully and cups the humid sack of the man's scrotum as if for a caress, then squeezes with all her might, crushing his testicles. He screeches and goes straight down, banging his chin against the top of her head. He rolls in the sand, retching. Felice staggers a couple of steps, stunned. She can hear the man trying to recover himself, moaning and gasping. "You—you're gonna die. You're just gonna—fucking—"

Felice manages a few more steps, but she's shaking so badly she keeps going down to her hands and knees. She can make out the man's form, rolling over and up onto his knees, sides heaving, he lunges at her. She feels hands on her shoulders, a fierce grip, and she gasps. Her scream sails through her as she feels herself falling backwards. Then nothing is holding her down. Forms like pieces of night come loose, a thudding, sand spraying: two bodies thrashing. For one protracted, surreal moment, she thinks that the other man has caught up to them, that he and Marren are wrestling. But then she hears a choked-off straining, then wheezing, a very soft, low, stifled gurgle. After a pause, from the deep seam of the night comes a rattling, warbling sound unlike anything she's ever heard before. She reclaims herself, trembling, curls her hands into her arms, chest hunched over her knees. There's the sound once again, dismal and chilling.

EMERSON. CROUCHING ON HANDS and knees. She senses his hands near her, hovering, careful not to try and touch her again. Maybe he knows how it goes, has seen it happen with other street kids—attacks and rapes. "Felice," he whispers. She wants to ask where he'd come from, how he'd found her. But shock has stripped the voice out of her, so at first she can't make a sound. It seems possible that he might dissolve like a puff of dust—a hallucination. Finally he risks his fingertips, then his hand on her back. "We can't stay here," he whispers.

"You—" The whisper scrapes in her throat. "What—happened?"

"He's done. I made sure."

Her mind is narrow and isolated, her senses heightened to startling clarity: she can smell the topaz wisps of algae beneath the rocks and hear the crackling scurf of mole crabs plugging into the sand. "There was another one. With him." She scans the area, but the streetlights barely reach them. Clouds twist over their heads; the beach is a dark miasma, a gaseous planet. Something rumbles low inside her, slick pain in her gut, and she runs over the sand, toward the water's edge, barely skimming off her jeans in time. Her bowels liquefy. The surf boils around her knees as she finds and yanks free the silver necklace, throwing it into the moonlight. She finishes washing herself off, the water warm and mineral as a desert sea. But then her stomach lurches, bringing up bile and a hot streak of old alcohol. When she crosses the strip of sand to rejoin Emerson, he peels off his T-shirt so she can dry her legs. She accepts, too numb to be ashamed. He takes the damp shirt and whispers, "Someone is out here—something moving—over there."

Her gut rumbles again, but she clenches herself. They wait in silence, looking: Felice can perceive the third presence which also seems to be soundless and motionless. Barely twenty feet away. The dead man's body seems to be deliquescing into a black pool on the dark sand. Nothing is clear. She strains her eyes but can't make out the other man. Finally Emerson murmurs, "Let's move." He helps her start walking, to orient herself along the ridge of unlit beach, to stay far from the streetlights, slipping away.

THEY STICK AS CLOSE to the water as they can—the only place on Miami Beach that doesn't glow all night. It roars and surges, higher than ever, and makes it impossible to talk or think. When they notice the first hints of gray in the sky, they cut up into the neighborhoods. Emerson tells her that he'd gone to the Cove that evening, looking for her. He didn't see Berry or Reynaldo, but some of the outdoor kids had seen her in the club, talking to Marren, and another had just spotted her walking out onto the sand with him. "She should not be with that guy." The kid had pointed in the direction that she'd gone. "You better fucking hurry." Now Emerson doesn't let go of her hand, nor does he ask questions about Marren, for which she is grateful.

They make it to Derek's house and throw pebbles up at the window they think is his bedroom. It turns out Derek's father is out again and Derek is hanging around downstairs on the couch, the light from the TV shuddering through the rooms.

Felice uses the toilet, sweating and trembling and hunched, while Emerson and Derek confer in the kitchen. She waits until the serrated pain in her gut eases a bit and everything inside of her seems to have streamed away in a thin liquid. After that, she washes her face and hands and she rubs toothpaste all over her teeth and tongue and the inside of her mouth with her fingers. She rinses, clutching the rim of the basin. She churns Listerine in her mouth and spits, then swallows a tiny, fiery capful. Before she goes out, she cracks the door. She hears Derek say "lose her." He's arguing for Emerson to let Derek and their friends take care of him. "She'll be okay. Girls are okay—people feel sorry for them and take them in."

"No, man."

"I bet she's still got parents somewhere. I hear she comes from some fucking house in the Gables. Fuck, your stupid temper anyway, man. What does she need with a maniac like you?"

"Fuck you, Derek. We're together now."

"You've gotta get serious. You don't know who the fuck that guy was—he could have been some kind of Latin gangbanger. Or the mob—you know some of the Gambinos got a nice winter house a few blocks from here. This isn't like the time with that scuzzball punk at the mall. Nobody would've even cared if he'd actually died. You need some serious lying low, for a good long-ass time. Some witness protection shit, for sure. I deal with shitheads like that, and man, they have got some scary friends."

"Don't talk to me about that asshole." Emerson sounds caved in, shrunken.

"Whoa, man—he needed to die. No doubt. That isn't under discussion. But *you* need to live, very much so. And you know how it goes, it's always the same with these chicks—she was cozying up to him at some bar—everyone saw them. Some rich asshole is gonna have associates. People who care about what does and doesn't become of him."

"Fuck that loser." Emerson says with little conviction.

"Your funeral, Sonny. I'm just saying. If you're sticking with her, then you're on your own. Count me way the fuck out."

Felice moves into the penumbra of the kitchen light, puts her hand on Emerson's shoulder. Derek gazes at something beyond the walls of the room. For a moment, silence fills the space, ticking from the cupboards, pans on the drain board. Now his flat eyes take in the two of them. "Anyone could show up here, anytime. Like my asshole brother, or Steve-o, or anyone. You gotta get as far away the better. I'm gonna call you a cab."

There's a fight over whether Emerson will accept a wad of bills from Derek. Finally Derek stuffs the cash down the front of his T-shirt. Emerson removes it, glowering, and pushes it into his pocket. Derek flops back on the couch. "Up to you now. Good fucking luck— I hope it's all worth it." But then he walks them out to the cab, hands the driver a black credit card and a small brown paper bag. Derek and Emerson clap each other in a brief embrace. Emerson turns away from him then, automatically reaching for Felice's hand. As they pull out, Felice turns to see Derek standing in the arc of the circular drive-way watching them go, his face hard and motionless.

The cab reeks of a fir-tree car freshener, Felice asks the driver to take them to Homestead. The young black man squints at them in the mirror. "*Where* you want?" His accent is so thick the words are nearly unintelligible. Felice repeats her request slowly, gesturing south. His eyebrows lift. He turns off the meter saying, "Good he give me the card number then." She slides down in her seat until the back of her neck touches the low, molded upholstery. The car bounces over ruts in the streets, beads and medallions swinging wildly from the rear-view mirror, and a drizzle starts, stippling the windows. Not until they're approaching downtown does Felice feel some inkling of the night before. She has spent so many years awakening in unpredictable circumstances that she is almost accustomed to the dreamy, stifling sense of things, the acceptance of any terrible possibility. Traffic streams by, shadowy in the half-light, and Felice cranes around, studying the swirl of cars. Twice, she becomes convinced that she sees the green Maserati, but all the convertibles have their tops up in the rain, hooded and anonymous. Each car that quietly passes them seems like another miracle.

Emerson gazes ahead, ignoring the cars, but he holds Felice's hand so tightly that her fingertips feel numb. Once they exit the causeway and start racing along the 95 drop, she feels another potent, mortal quaking start up. Another person has died because of her.

"You okay?"

"No." Felice hunches into the low spasms in her gut, elbows digging into the tops of her knees. She stares at the driver's ID: *Henri LaValesque*.

Emerson catches her hand again; he holds it in both of his. "Maybe we should try—just—letting it go. All of it. It could be like none of it ever existed at all? Like here, we're in this car, just talking about interesting stuff, driving to this new place."

"Like what?" She stares at the driver's head. "What're we talking about?"

"I don't know. Anything."

She frowns at the streaks on the window glass; pieces of sunlight filter through some of the low-floating clouds, drawing out prisms suspended in light. Felice pulls Emerson's hand into her lap—it's ridged with calluses: she'd never noticed before. "Okay, why did they name you Emerson?"

"My dad." Emerson glances at the bright, streaky glass. "He was into doing for yourself, growing your own vegetables, making your own soap and candles. His favorite guy was this writer Emerson. He wrote about really doing your own thing."

"That sounds like a good way to be," she says softly, but the deep molten quaking has entered her chest and she's humiliated by the way her voice shakes. Emerson puts his arm around her shoulders and folds her into his side. She clings to Emerson's midsection, comforted by his size. An intermittent rain spatters the cab, sluicing up between cars.

After a while, Emerson murmurs to her, "Dad said that self-reliance was such a big American idea, but so what? I don't think it's that great . . ." His voice tapers off. "It's just what people do 'cause they don't want to say thank you."

Felice watches the bruised sky; another volley of rain sweeps over the cab. It slants in curtains over the city, darkening the platinum high-rises. An olive cast seems to emanate from the deepest part of the sky and she can feel a shivering movement as gusts of wind hit the car. Felice thinks about the fierce summer storms she's weathered in the Green House, the steamy unlit rooms, tree limbs banging against the roof. "That man's face." The words seep out of her, dank heat rising from her back. Her breath feels like it's squeezed into the tops of her lungs.

"No, no, no." He gathers her closer. "You don't need to think about that now."

"His friends will come after us, won't they? Derek's right."

Emerson seems to also be studying the back of the driver's head; he says quietly, close to her ear, "We're going to be fine."

The cab bounces onto the exit to U.S. 1. "Stanley—my brother— he'll help us." Felice takes taut little breaths. "He always knows the right thing." She knows Emerson is holding himself still and calm for her, that he must have just the same trembling in his core. Or he will have. The cab slows on the exit, rolling into traffic on the narrow highway; Felice is startled by the number of cars, the way they skim within inches of each other. She stares ahead through the windshield, over the backs of the cars lining the road. Gradually, a small comfort settles in her. It's been years since she's felt the faint rising sense of the future. But there it is, inside the torn-out cab, the stink of old cigarettes and fake pine, and Emerson's arm curved to her ribs.

Brian

BRIAN WAKES TO A SHARP RAPPING NEXT DOOR. Josh Masterson is on a ladder tipped against the side of his house, installing clear hurricane panels. There are also sounds of Avis in the kitchen, the preparatory clashing and sliding of pans. He calls the office and listens to a recording saying that "due to Hurricane Katrina," all PI&B employees are asked to stay home. In chinos and work shirt, he goes to the dining room table and finds a place set: a plate with two poached eggs, buttermilk scone, and blueberry-lavender jam. Avis comes to the door and says, "The hurricane special." He lifts his knife. "I am strong like bull."

Brian labors through the dawn, already a welter of humidity, the storm's approach churning invisibly through the air. He'd meant to replace the panels with easier accordion shutters. The pieces of aluminum are heavy and the edges cut into his fingers, even through his cotton work gloves. Worse, the small holes refuse to line up with the brackets; there is much clumsy hoisting, dropping, and realignment before he can manage to twist in a single screw at the top, at which point the lower brackets no longer line up. In two hours, he's managed to install three panels, covering two-thirds of one window. He's sweated through his work shirt, his hand shaking as he drags it across his forehead.

Craving respite, he creeps back inside. On a cooling rack in the kitchen, he recognizes his wife's slim, buttery *langues de chat* and the plump *croissants aux amandes* filled with almond cream and Kirsch. The counters are wiped down and the kitchen gleams with emptiness. There is a sense of absence and self-sufficiency here that shortens his breath, a pointed ache in his chest. Perhaps Avis is back in the neighbor's yard, sitting with the young stranger. Attempting to ignore this discomfort, Brian consults the Weather Channel: the first feathery wisps approach the Florida peninsula. A couple of forecasters argue over the tropical storm system as if it were an upcoming sports event: "So is it still a hurricane watch or a warning?" "NOAA says watch." "Don't you believe it—people better get ready for this baby. They're predicting landfall by late afternoon." An ominous commercial sponsored by their local Publix asks if everyone's got their "Disaster Provisions" ready. Then the local newscasters appear, talking intensely about canned foods, dried beans, games to play with the kids by candlelight. Brian has managed only to partially cover one of their twenty windows; he thinks of the driving rain and wind that may come.

On the other hand, he recalls that Javier said he was going in to work today. And what if Fernanda goes in? What if Javier tells her about yesterday afternoon in the field? Or about the disgraceful real estate scheme they'd fallen for? Brian feels a wincing contraction in the pit of his stomach. He showers, returns to the bedroom, and puts on his charcoal-gray suit and the white shirt with the thin blue lines. His jacket creases at his elbows: it's one of his older suits. Now he seems to be shrinking within it. He sees a thread at the cuff—the softness of such nicely blended cotton and wool, the way it rests on him like a soul. Expensive, fraying thing. He notices he can tighten his belt by almost a notch. The clothes help him feel better—a certain haze that's lingered at the edges of his eyes, a certain tipsy sensation like that of sleep deprivation, seem to lift a bit. As he emerges, he hears Avis in the kitchen.

"There you are." He holds his car keys tightly as he leans into the kitchen door.

Avis blinks up at him. She is shaking pine nuts in a skillet, tossing them in an ellipse over the fire. She turns off the flame and wraps her hands in her towel as she comes to the door, frowning. Brian tells her he's going to work, he won't be gone long. She touches his left temple, which causes his throat to constrict. "Are you sure you're—". She hesitates. "Are you sure you want to? With the storm coming. Weren't you going to work on the house?"

Brian kisses the side of her face. He tells Avis that he has some last-minute document review, he'll be back well before the storm.

"Nothing you can do from here?" Her tone is mild but grave. It's almost enough to keep him home, but he lowers his gaze. "I won't be long. Promise."

HE HEADS OFF, driving through the first lashings of rain. The highway is crowded—everyone trying to fit in last-minute commerce. Images of Javier and Fernanda fill his head: he sees them laughing, heads tilting together. The rushing, chaotic highway, the backlit sky—white satin clouds outlined in black, the spray of rain, all have an altered, pre-apocalyptic quality. He feels increasingly doomed, assailed by a series of bad decisions, yet he's determined to be at the office. Captain goes down with ship, he thinks as he pulls into the lot. A private little sinking. He thinks about Mr. Christian and his mutiny. Was it Bligh who'd gone mad or Christian? His knees feel spongy and untrustworthy, his mind tugs, trying to float away from his body as he walks into the building. Rufus seems surprised by Brian's appearance; something like concern touches his face—as if Brian looked *that bad*. Rufus barely gets out the words "Mr. Muir," and Brian rejoins, "Yes, hello, how are you."

He unlocks the door for Brian. "Not supposed to be letting folks in today," he mutters. "Supposed to be sending people home."

The building is half lit with a tinny echo like that of a mausoleum. Brian stares at the painting of vivid, grassy everglades that hangs over the elevator doors. He'd never really noticed it before: it glows in the dimmed lobby. He considers grimly that this is probably an image of the place—glimmering green marsh, corrugated alligator backs, sweep of lazing trees—they destroyed to make this office building. The elevator opens and he wobbles outside himself, gazing upon the thin spot at the back of his head from the elevator ceiling. The corridors on 34 are eerily hollow; his footsteps bounce back, perfect replicas. He watches his own progress down the hall. A line from somewhere—a nursery rhyme?—bounces through his head: I grow old, I shall wear my trousers rolled . . .

Fernanda's office lights are out. Of course. What had he been thinking? Relief courses through him, expanding his breath; he's able to collapse back into himself. Safe. What on earth would he have said to her? He will check his messages, he thinks, and go home, and that will be that. Inter-office mail is piled up against his door. Brian watches himself step over it on his way in. Gazing around the cool solemnity of his office, he feels a distance from his surroundings— stacks of thick contracts, his yellow pad covered with the details of commission hearings, the water-blue surface of his desk. And the view: the causeway, the fields of admiral blue water in the bay. All seems frozen and remote, like a diorama. With a soul-emptying sigh, he turns to the computer, taps the keyboard to awaken it, and lets his eyes focus on the Financial News, the headlines, *High Gas Prices Fuel Fear of Financial Hardship* and FLORIDA GIRDS FOR THE NEXT STORM. He scans the websites, searching for some news of the Steele Building fiasco—there is none—then retrieves his mail and combs the papers. A few stragglers and die-hards pass Brian's office, shuffling folders, determined to work until the moment everything shuts down. The spell of the workday wraps itself around Brian. He flips open a file of recent motions and is able to work uninterrupted by calls or associates. Javier appears around noon, nodding, fingers knotted loosely at the knuckles as he drops into the guest chair. His face is the color of cinders and Brian can smell a waft of tobacco. "Hey, there he is! I thought you might show."

"You know me," Brian says. He notices a missed button popping open under Javier's tie. "The old soldier."

"You get home okay? You sleep okay last night?"

"Beautifully," he says, realizing it is true—after much sleepless- ness, last night was a luxurious blank slot.

"Ha. Tell me what that's like." Javier lowers the top of his head into his hands. "I had two other investors lined up with that goddamned Steele Building. One of them tried to make a wire transfer from his account straight to the developers. It was so much that his broker put a partial hold on it, thank the saints." Javier crosses himself. "He still gave them about three hundred K."

Brian wheels back in his seat. "Not too much they can do if they can't find the guys." He considers how close he'd come to doing the same thing.

"Their lawyer knows where they are, but he's not telling. They're going to declare bankruptcy, and their assets—whatever the fuck they can find—gonna be stuck in receivership. Perez Properties says they want to sue for consulting fees." He rolls his eyes. "The *cabróns* lied— they didn't have even half the investors that they claimed. The money fell apart and the *pingas* ran." Javier nods, elbows propped on knees, his head lowered toward his shoulders. He rubs his hands together, fingers spread. "Hell of a thing, man. You know, I had some friends this happened to. Very similar. This town, you hear all the stories, right? Figure that *mierda* is just for the idiots, old ladies with their sweepstakes, any *imbécil* who wants to believe in magic." Still sitting, he stretches his back, cracking his neck to one side, then straightens, his eyes wide and glittering. "I thought I was so smart. I thought nothing gets past this boy." His fingers run over his temples; he looks as if he's attempting a telepathic feat. "It's like—damn. Should've seen that one a mile away."

"No, I know. I didn't see it either, and I feel the same—like, I absolutely should have." Brian moves a file back onto the stack, trying to seem nonchalant, but he feels an icy chill. "Cautionary tale."

"Thank God, eh?" Javier says with a bleak laugh. He grabs his arms. "Like check yourself for the shrapnel."

Brian smiles at the window, its surface intermittently clear, then stippled with raining gusts. In the distance, the bay is driven with sheets of gunmetal swells and troughs. "I had this stupid idea about it—because Stanley needed money."

"Yeah, but that was a *good* reason to do it." Javier sits back, his chin sinking on his chest. "We'll find another project—a great one, I promise."

"No, no. That's not what I'm . . ." The sky is getting so dark that Brian can see a layer of reflections there: Javier's crossed leg, the computer screen filled with passing stars, the framed photograph. A photograph without Felice! He thinks of his mother saying, "A child splits you open." He turns back to his desk, picks up a stray pencil, teeth marks in its blue paint, and taps it on the glass. "It's really strange. Trying to be decent—I mean, with your kids? All I figured out is the only way to do it is to leave them. You got to go away. To work. That's how you take care of them. That's what I learned from my own father. But then you're away from them and they'd don't even care about it, because what good is it . . ."

"What is this?" Javier starts laughing. "You're kidding. You're the best father."

Brian taps the keyboard, glances at the live tracking site, the milky pinwheel of this incoming system, Katrina, poised between the Caribbean and the peninsula. He'd forgotten to turn on his lights, the day prematurely dim, clouds rolling in, heavy as volcanic ash. "Why do you think it's so funny?" he asks. "Am I that ridiculous?"

Javier's laugh dwindles. "Well, no, man, of course. It's just . . ." he says slowly. "My God. For one thing, I thought you were *happy. Ay carajo!* You of all people."

Brian looks at Javier then, startled by the complicated uncertainty on his face. He hesitates, sensing that, in some way, Javier is able to peer into some shadow self of his. He feels a cool contraction now, pervading his skin, as if this sudden unburdening has left him feeling overexposed. He touches the wall and all hard surfaces seem to tremble for a fraction of a second, a swipe of vertigo passes through him. The lip of curvy exterior window is inches from his fingers and his attention strays: the sky trails rain-vapors over the city. "Provide, provide," he mutters.

"What's that?"

Brian shakes his head, touches his temples with his fingertips, as if fighting a migraine. He excuses himself. In the executive washroom, Brian splashes water across his face. He cups his palms and spills a cool handful over his head. He holds the sink and inhales deeply, regularly. Tries to focus on his eyes in the mirror.

When he emerges, his office is empty. It's getting so dark outside the corridor light seems drained. He spots a twinkle of light in the glass wall, a glimpse of movement in Fernanda's office. He strolls down the hall, then for some reason he wavers just outside the penumbra of her office. She must have moved, because he notices her form slip through the surface of the glass. Unable to see in clearly at that angle, Brian leans toward the glass: he realizes there are two people in the office. A soft, illicit sense like dread passes through him: he wishes he could stop himself, but it's almost as if some force is compelling him to look. Outside, what sounds like another volley of gravel rattles the windows, rain, flung with enough force to leave tiny transparent smears on the glass for a second, like claw marks. It surges in volume, spattering, then subsides. Moving closer to the glass, he spots Javier, he's sitting on her desk. Fernanda is sitting before him, inside the V of his legs, her hand on his knee.

His heart expands and collapses: electrical sparks speed under his skin, his limbic system fizzing and crackling. Brian moves backwards, away from the glass; a wisp of laughter escapes him. He sees her sharp, dark glance, then the corridor lighting switches off and there is only the backup generator light: white beams every ten feet; a previously invisible EXIT sign glaring from the end of the hall. The glass walls reveal an enormous, tumid massing of clouds, banks of black and white like a winter's day in Alaska. Brian makes his way to the elevator: as the doors slide shut, he hears someone calling him.

HE STANDS IN THE gloom of the elevator, sees himself in a dark green glade, around him there are children and friends, tiny lights glowing on a narrow leaf. He lifts his hands, opening and closing them; he feels prehistoric. If he could just take hold of one of the lovely lights . . . His head tips until his forehead touches the metal of the doors. It is, he realizes, the posture of his existence: face pressed to a snow globe. How had he stepped outside of his own existence? He was jealous: he admits this to himself. But now he just feels like an idiot. The elevator car jerks to a halt on 11 and the doors slide open. Brian must make his way in the pitch black of the stairwell, clinging to the railing. It smells like paint and stale cigarettes; twice he stumbles. He believes he can hear the crackle of cockroaches on the walls, some whispering shuffle high above him. The marble plain of the lobby feels like an empty stage. Rufus is no longer at his post. When Brian opens the glass door, a wailing wind nearly wrenches it out of his hands. The row of royal palms surge, their crowns and necks bowing to the west. His hair whips sideways, his suit plastered to him, as he dashes into the garage.

Only a handful of cars remain in the garage—Brian's SUV, Fernanda's sedan, Javier's Jag among them. Brian climbs shakily into the truck, then he just sits there for a while, panting, his head dripping and pressed against the steering wheel. He'd bought the thing envisioning expeditions to Sanibel and Captiva, he and his family, the back a jumble of fishing rods and tents. The only trip they'd taken had happened because one day, with no warning, Javier had pulled up into their driveway, honking, his car loaded with his own kids. Brian went but he'd spent most of the time checking voice mail and returning calls. Even out on the chartered boat, he toted along a waterproof rucksack full of applications for zoning variances.

Something hits his shoulder and clatters to the floor. A pair of sunglasses. "Hey, *culo*." It's Javier, striding, dripping, across the garage. "I call your name and you don't even hold the freaking elevator for me? I had to walk down thirty-four fucking flights, man."

Brian squeezes the steering wheel, as if stuck in rush-hour traffic. He looks away from Javier to the frame of the passenger window. "Really, can you just not talk to me?"

"What the hell, man? What's your problem? You go tearing out of the building like I don't know what . . ."

Brian presses his palm over his eyes. For a moment, the wind drowns all other sounds, roaring past the garage ramparts. "How long?" he croaks.

"What?"

"You and Fernanda. How long?"

Javier doesn't say anything for a few moments and Brian turns to look at him.

"I don't know—a couple weeks, I guess," he says quietly.

"Weeks?"

"Man, what do you even care?"

"I don't know," he says honestly. He folds his arms along the top of the wheel. "What about her and Parkhurst?"

"Santa Madre Virgen de Dios," Javier mutters. "What are you thinking, Bry? It's all play to her. Me, Parkhurst, whatever. She's just messing around to make her mother mad. Maybe kick herself a little higher in the company. I know that. It only goes so far. I'm not Jewish—she's never gonna stick with some Latino Cristiano."

Brian stares at the top of his windshield. "What about your wife?" His voice is stony with sarcasm. "Does she think it's play? Is it all a glorious entertainment?"

Javier doesn't say anything for a moment: abruptly his hands fall to his sides as he starts laughing. *"Ay, compay!* You didn't have a choice, did you? You're one of these guys who had to become a lawyer. You just love your words." He rolls his eyes. "Listen, *chico,* here's the big difference between you and me—last month, my wife threw me out of the house. She found some girl's number on a matchbook in my pocket. So I been living up the street, in the Intercon. They give you a nice breakfast there."

Brian's mouth opens.

"Things between me and Odalis . . ." His mouth twists as if he were trying to smile. "She says I don't love her no more. Stupid. What does that even mean? So I get a little lonely. So sue me." He gives Brian a cool glance. "Why you look so upset? You just let me walk thirty-four flights, man."

Brian climbs down from the car. "You didn't say anything."

"It's the first time I've said it out loud, even." Javier sinks back against a garage pillar. "Even my *papi* doesn't know. But I did it—I left. To make her happy. You see how that works? You keep leaving, like *you* say, to keep them happy. You go to work, you keep working, you run away until you're all the way gone. Maybe even you shoot yourself. And the whole time you keep thinking—Are they happy yet?"

Brian picks up the sunglasses—the Ray-Bans. One of the lenses is scratched. He rubs them against the sleeve of his jacket, hands them back to his friend. Javier sighs and props the glasses on his head. He loosens his tie, then undoes it, lets it hang. "Who knows—the last kid just went up to Gainesville. Maybe Odalis and me will be back again by Thanksgiving?" His mouth twists again, approximating a smile, his brows lifted, a yellow sleepless cast to the bottoms of his eyes. Brian shuffles to Javier holding out his hands, then wraps his arms around his friend, clapping him on the back. Javier leans into him. It happens in a few scant moments, but in that time, Brian feels the scoured-out quality in both of them, the absence of tears, the shared, unspoken wish that at least one of them could remember how to weep.

HE SQUINTS THROUGH the dark core as he merges onto U.S. 1, the washed-away darkness at the center of his windshield ringed by taillights, traffic lights. The storm has begun in earnest—the thunder sounds like distant drums—but he cracks the moon roof to admit the moist, mild air. Javier used to tell him: Things begin and end with the wife. He imagines, as he sails under the sulfurous lights, through curtains of rain, how he will unlock the front door and go to her.

There's another hard lash of rain and wind. The car shimmies with it and the row of taillights glows red. Someone two car lengths up puts on hazards; they strobe in the cascade. The car is quaking with the wind, wipers going at a frantic slash. The streetlights around him seem to wobble and his head fills with oxygen, a mind-expanding release. What appears to be a ten-foot-long striped store awning sails past his car; there is another red stream of taillights as a pond forms on the Dixie northbound. Southbound traffic is starting to dwindle—it's all northbound now: the hegira, rushing off the Florida peninsula—if they aren't blown off the road in the process. A long section of palm frond skates over his hood and flies off to the next car. His hands tighten as he navigates what appears to be a branch of bananas in the road. Brian watches a coconut bounce mid-highway, a few car lengths ahead. Traffic is paralytic, creeping, then stopping entirely. A few cars disperse into the Grove, Shenandoah, making big round turns around the blocks. And then it's too quiet, the rain pooling over the highway, wipers unable to keep up, tires hydroplaning. It's like taking a trip, he thinks, tension filling him with clear, still ideas. Going toward the other person, beckoning them back. Hopefully, the other person, your wife, will come back. You meet in the road.

The rain comes in an opaque sheet, it's like peering into a wave. Lightning cracks horizontally down the length of the highway. He moves at a crawl, the car rocking, the palms belling like blown-out umbrellas. Seconds later, the wind goes slack and the rain hisses away. There's a lucidity to the air. A blanketing calm settles over him as he considers how ironic it would be if he were to spin into the path of an onrushing car now, and never have the ability to see his wife again, to tell her that she is his one and only, that things will be fine. For some reason, his mind feels so light, an ether, as he imagines the house at the end of his block coming into view, its lights burning with a low sheen.

Stanley

H E SITS WITH HIS CHAIR CLOSE TO THE REAR windows, watching them liquefy, then solidify in the rolling gusts of rain. The store is finally starting to settle down after they'd announced they were closing early. He feels glassy with exhaustion. Years of hard, daily, market labor—trucking bushels of produce, scrubbing the walk-in dairy storage, pressure-washing the entry— have given him the ability to rise early and work well into the evening, not thinking, his mind content with and diverted by *doing*. But today, the frantic preparations for the storm—one ear trained on the NOAA forecasts—have left him nearly inert, bones dissolved. Too many loose ends. This damn business. He's been stewing: if his father doesn't stake him the money, they won't be able to cover the reassessed property taxes—much less make a down payment on the place. There are rumors that commercial property insurance premiums are set to double. Lord only knows what kind of wind damage or flood disaster he'll wake up to tomorrow. They've been fairly lucky with tropical storm systems up till now, but he has no faith in the store's elderly drainage system, their stormwater basin prone to overflowing.

The tarp tied over a pallet of rutabagas still on the loading dock looks as if it will flap free, and someone—probably Stanley—will have to run out in the rain and lash it back down. *Rutabagas,* he thinks irritably, watching the pale knobs gleam as the tarp flaps. The lights in his office have flickered a number of times, which means the backup generator may be kicking on soon—its roar loud enough to annoy neighbors ten blocks away. Although he's not sure who's left to annoy—the shops closest to him, over on Krome, are boarded up with plywood, windows Xed out with masking tape like the eyes of dead cartoon characters, the town shuttered and half abandoned.

Hurricane Andrew struck Homestead in 1992. Six years later, Stanley came hunting for a cheap storefront: he was eighteen years old and had a $10,000 start-up stake scraped together from working in orange groves, farmers' markets, and nurseries, as well as shelving product and bagging and rolling at Winn Dixie and Publix. He'd dropped out—college was for dawdlers. Andrew had left a trail of devastation across Homestead, slashing it open before ripping up the rest of the state. The locals who remained (thousands fled north, north, north) bore a dazzled, sanctified light in their faces. Stanley could still see the residue of the hurricane everywhere—in torn-up fields, acres of downed trees, houses smashed to pieces. Humble as its name, set off at the lonely bottom of the peninsula, Homestead was home to farmers and Mexican migrant workers in straw cowboy hats, flooding the dance hall weekend nights. The little downtown had been trying to reconstruct itself, but back then property values were flat. A realtor whispered to Stanley that the owner of the building, a former bank, near the corner of Krome and Northwest Second, was frantic to move to North Carolina. So, at eighteen, Stanley had his space and a $50,000 small business loan.

His lucky break came with another price tag, which was that he would have to spend a portion of each late summer and early autumn in a state of free-floating anxiety—watching the sky, listening to the radio—haunting the store like a captain preparing to die with his ship.

Now, as the latest system approaches—hovering somewhere over the ocean—he hears the rocket explosion of a transformer blowing a few blocks away, and the lights go out for nearly a minute. He's certain they'll stay out this time; but then they're back. His chest is aching, his lungs compressed. They can't really afford to run the generator—a ghastly, anti-eco, energy suck—for very long, but they can't afford not to. He has Bosch-like visions of rotting eggplant, broccoli; swarms of fruit flies attacking the bananas; he imagines the expensive, hormone-free, dry-aged beef, the unpasteurized goat's milk, the yogurt from Greece, cartons of organic ice cream flavored with rose-water or cardamom . . . all sweating, decaying carnage. It would take days—weeks—to shovel out from under. Not to mention the pressure-washing, disinfecting, and hunting for molds, fungi, and spores. Past hurricane seasons, they've suffered partial (yet substantial) losses, but never a total collapse. Not yet. He is entertaining such visions of disaster when Nieves barges into the office, not quite six months along, already carrying herself sideways, the top two buttons of her jeans undone, twenty-three years old and unconcerned. "Stanley— what the hell? Get out of here. There's rain coming in the north win-dows and Gloria's trying to help me mop."

This is what's really different about this summer—Nieves—her difficult, bossy, magnetic nature his counterweight. Stanley squints through the door into the market. "Gloria's still here? Everyone needs to get home now."

"Oh my God, you're telling me." Nieves pushes aside a stack of orders and billing statements from local purveyors and sits heavily on his desktop, scowling. "Make another announcement—there're still *people* out there. They're buying out the store—the canned and dry goods stuff is, like, gone. Bottled water—gone; bulk foods—gone. Now they're working on the perishables."

A little over a year ago, Freshly Grown was expanding and adver-tised for someone to manage cheeses, chocolates, and coffees. Nieves banged on his office door. She painted cat's-eye wings at the corners of her eyes back then; there was a gold stud at her eyebrow, a dia-mond chip tucked above one nostril. She didn't want to talk about prior work experience—she wanted to talk about wine varietals, the dry little bubbles in a bottle of Krug, the best cheese to pair with a good chardonnay. She half smiled, smoothed her hair behind one ear, and told him about the bands she'd sang and played guitar in; she stretched out her long legs and toted the ethnicities she'd uncov-ered in her family background: "Oneida, Mohawk, some kind of Afri-can—maybe Senegal—French, oh, Moroccan, um, oh, Costa Rican, Dutch—or wait—Danish? There's more. Those are just the main ones." She smelled bready, like a kid who'd spent the day outside playing. Stanley's office was filled with stacked cartons of organic crackers, macaroni and cheese, couscous—mainly a storage room with a desk and chair in it. She'd eyed the half-crushed cartons and said, "You need to deal with that."

Stanley loves the smell of the back of her head, loves putting his nose to her scalp, inside the wavy dark curtains of her hair. He stands and leans against the desk, pulling her in so she reclines back against him—she no longer resists his embrace the way she did before pregnancy. His hands move over her shoulders, the inner curves of her arms, then wander over her breasts, which, he's noticed, have assumed a fuller, teardrop shape, like the new lobe of her belly. His arms cross over her chest, entwining her. *Mine,* he thinks. He'd never say it out loud.

When they'd first started seeing each other, Stanley wasn't sure it would last: Nieves's personality could be cold and steady as a flashlight. And she always seemed to him to be poised in doorways, always about to leave him, leave town, and assume a new existence—like all the other employees and volunteers brimming with stories about house-building trips to Honduras and cross-country bike rides. (Last week he'd reluctantly agreed to a showing of Eduardo's experimental video: an insufferable diatribe on the evils of Big Sugar, spliced with photographs of electric-green Caribbean mountains.) Now he's no longer sure why he'd felt that way. Unlike other employees, Nieves never spent her days rambling on about traveling to Prague or the Galápagos or applying to graduate programs in film studies. Stanley, on the other hand, could be intrigued, seduced by the stories—the home videos of diving the Great Barrier Reef or of hiking Antarctica.

Unlike Nieves, he is tired and battle-weary: after Hurricane Charley ruined their drainage field last year, the Internet and papers were full of reports that the bump in hurricanes was connected to global warming, rising water tables and the ocean temperatures—that things could only get worse as the ice caps melted away. It was hard to fathom how quickly the world could change: when Stanley first opened shop, there was nothing around but acres of agricultural land, orchards of sweeping palms and everglades, tidal and primordial, filled with swooping egrets, ibises, the creeks nosed up with alligators. Now, barely six years later, every time he drives out of town, he sees new housing developments growing in concentric circles around Homestead—townhouses uniform as barracks, a hospital like a penitentiary, and billboards advertising this construction at exorbitant prices.

Whenever he mutters about selling the market to GNC, taking time off and learning to surf, or taking the train across Europe, or, for that matter, just starting over in a new place—Asheville, New Orleans—where they *get* small-local-organic, Nieves smirks, her eyes narrow to a black line. She says, "These are your people, Stan."

She took to the market as if she'd found her missing home. Nieves worked the longest hours of anyone, often opening the store before Stanley himself arrived. She worked tirelessly—even at hard physical labor—pushing trucks, stocking, and swabbing. He admires her, afraid of the way she makes him feel. She'd claimed him at their first meeting, and the intensity of this claim seemed the direct opposite of the way he'd grown up—nudged to one side, overshadowed by his sister's beauty, then her absence. Standing now, pressing her warm back into his chest, his arms capturing her, Stanley gazes into his store and thinks about how oddly specific love is, how it must always seem to every person that he or she was the one who invented it, and that no one else's love could ever be as strong. Stanley feels this way. It would have been nice, he thinks, to have had more time to be just a couple. But her pregnancy finally gave him a bit of calm: the luxury of their mutual ownership.

"Oh for—" Nieves's arms fall flat at her sides as she stares into the store. "Don't these people have homes?"

Stanley spots the silhouetted form of a couple walking up Ethnic/Prepared/Mixes. They seem to be hazily looking around, not shopping exactly, and he shifts his hands back to Nieves's shoulders. He's about to call out, in some exasperation, *Hey, we're closed—get yourselves home!* when he hears a young, quiet, familiar voice say, "Stan?"

HE ALWAYS MEANT to tell the girls he'd dated about Felice, how her disappearance had left such a mark on his life, but it turned out that she was something he couldn't talk about at all—as if someone had rubbed out those years of waiting and anxiety with a pencil eraser and now it was difficult even to perceive faint lines left in the paper. Only recently had he revealed to Nieves that he'd had a sister, that she'd "left home," that he "rarely" heard from her. At the time, Nieves had scrutinized his face, listening quietly in the shadow of their tiny apartment. She touched his hand and stroked the back of his fingers with uncharacteristic tenderness.

Now Felice stands in his kitchen, eating a peanut butter and jelly sandwich. Stanley feels layers of disorientation and distance gathering around him like the folds of a cape. This is my sister, he tells himself. Nieves is motionless, holding a scraped-out jar in one hand, as she watches Felice eat. The boy—Felice's friend—barely speaks. He ate his sandwich in three bites, then politely declined offers of more. He hunches on the stool, one bulky arm resting on the kitchen counter.

But Felice.

The last time Stanley had seen her, she was on her way to another "party." He had just turned seventeen and no longer believed anything she said. She'd run away five or six times by then. Their parents had recently started allowing her to go out again with her friends at night: her new curfew was ten o'clock and up till that point she'd been relatively good—twice she'd come home by 9:30. But Stanley knew. He'd asked her again, that very night, What is wrong? Why can't you tell me what's happening? He didn't know why he still bothered at that point.

At thirteen, she was already five feet seven, a little hollowed-out by her growth spurt, her chest concave, her eyes with their ineffable violet light enormous, her bangs cut straight across her brow so she looked very young and serious. He realizes only now that as time passed he'd continued to think of Felice as that thirteen-year-old child, preserved like a geranium between the leaves of a book. She is still young and slim, yet changed. Her shoulders are straighter and more refined; the bangs are gone—her hair swings to her shoulders. Her eyes no longer seem overlarge: they are wide, almond-shaped. Nieves stares at her: he'd failed to mention his sister's beauty.

Stanley tucks his chin: inside, a ragged blank—the feeling that this couldn't possibly be his sister: *she* is still out there—a thirteen-year-old, who vanished into the night, a black orchid. There's no way to reconcile this adult with the lost child. She mumbles to the boy (boyfriend?) as they eat, the two brushing up against each other, casually but continually, a kind of ritual of reassurance. Stanley notices their exhaustion—especially in the boy, who scanned the room as they entered—as if they've been through some sort of ordeal together. Their clothes look creased with sweat and grime and there's a rancid whiff of unwashed hair and skin. Felice's eyes have an odd cherry-red wire of light at their centers—a glint of barely contained panic. Stanley—who hasn't been able to say more than a handful of words—now finds his fingers are growing rigid on his glass of water. Some sort of energy field has invaded him, starting when his sister came to the office door and said, "Stan—it's me." He carefully places his glass on the kitchen counter. Her extreme state catches at something in his chest, but he ignores it: he feels little more than a cold absence—perhaps, now, a few wisps of anger. All those years in free fall, living through plummeting fear, living through her inexplicable loss. Is he supposed to snap his fingers and be done with it? He regards her with some fascination: Apparently people are capable of things like that—of running away without a word of explanation, of leaving you to years of nightmares, images of them bound, beaten, tortured—and then they are capable of magically, brazenly reappearing years later to request assistance!

Stanley notices again the boy's shoulders as he leans closer to

Felice for one of their whispered conferences. He looks broad and strong, but he moves with restraint, as if to make himself smaller. Stanley feels an impulse to stop him, to say: Save yourself. Or perhaps he should say, more simply—It's time for you two to go. He crosses his arms, the tendons in his neck and shoulders tighten. Just ask them politely to be on their way. Above all, it seems imperative to keep his parents from knowing about this visit—to spare them, if possible, one more iota of pain. After furtive meetings with her runaway daughter, his mother used to return with the disconnected expression of an assault victim. Stanley found himself in agreement with his father: insist Felice return or cut things off.

Evidently sensing his unhappiness, Nieves begins to rattle around the kitchen, pouring drinks, wiping counters. "The bathroom is over there if anyone needs it. Hey—really—how about you let me make you another sandwich? There's plenty of food—we're practically living over a grocery store." Their dumb old joke. Ha-ha. She smiles and leans against the fridge, and Stanley's neck prickles as he sees, for possibly the first time, her hands slide unconsciously over her stomach.

Felice finally seems able to focus—her gaze grazes lightly over Nieves. Her eyes widen. "Oh. Wow. I just—you guys—there's a baby?" She turns toward Stanley. "You're gonna be a *dad*?"

With a despairing breath, some of that fortifying anger rushes out of Stanley. Nieves nods and fans her fingers over her belly. "Not everyone can see it yet. People aren't sure if it's a baby or just blubber." She smiles and glances at Stanley. "But yeah—we decided to have it."

Felice breaks into a radiant smile, as if Nieves has just uttered the loveliest, most sentimental thing she's ever heard. Stanley shifts closer and places his fingers on his sister's wrist. He says, "Feef." Carefully, he encloses her in his arms, and beneath the grime, catches a whiff of that thirteen-year-old kid—grass and air-dried jeans—still there.

———

OUTSIDE, THE WIND GROWS more intense. Wrapped in blankets on the living room floor, Felice and Emerson lie curled together. Stanley listened to their low whispers for a while. They fell asleep quickly, despite the lights left on, the rain thrashing against thin windows. In the small, darkened bedroom, he and Nieves sit up in bed, Nieves's profile glimmering and imperious as she watches the foul weather. "We should just put them to work in the market," she says quietly. "Put your sister in wine or cheeses—she'd bring people in off the street. And that boyfriend is custom-made for the stockroom."

Stanley stares at the clock radio, its luminescent numbers look watery, floating in darkness: 2:48. Ever since he'd learned that Nieves wanted to keep the baby, he's started waking up at 2 a.m., his heart skipping, his breath at the top of his throat. Tonight, he hasn't fallen asleep at all. "They want to go to Seattle," he says to her profile.

"Oregon, dummy." She hits his knee. Then her expression flickers in the dark room, wry and suspicious, "Why didn't you tell me about her deal?" Stanley assumes she's referring to Felice's vanishing, but Nieves says, "God, she looks just like that old movie star—you know who I mean?"

Stanley gets out of bed and moves to peer through the door. His sister is so slim she's barely a lilt beneath the covers. "That guy—is he her boyfriend? He says he wants to go train at some gym out there."

"In Oregon, I know." Nieves nods, an archness to her voice. She crosses her legs, a hand on her stomach.

"I can't believe it's her." Stanley's voice is low. "I really can't. She was just such a kid when she left." He tries to get a better look. His sister's face is partially obscured by blankets, but he makes out that it seems to be contracted in a wince. A sharp line runs between her brows, her eyes squeezed like she's dreaming of an explosion. Even though the apartment air is lavishly humid, tropical with night heat, the wall unit sends cool currents streaming over his arms, between his fingers; his extremities are all cold. He retreats from the doorway. Nieves gathers the bedsheet to her chest. "Stan?" Her free hand scoops the hair up from her neck. "I mean, I know that we're not even really parents yet—we haven't even *met* the baby or anything. But already it's like, when I think about what your sister did to her. To your mother, I mean." Her voice is subdued. "Stan—that can't happen to us."

Closing the door, he finds his way back to the bed in the dark. Nieves is warm and damp against his chest; he pulls her closer, glad for the creature weight of her. "It's not going to."

"*Why* did it happen?"

"I used to ask her—all the time. Seriously. I'd ask Felice just to tell me why she was doing it. Once, I even said I'd *help* her run away if she'd tell me."

"What she say?"

He shrugs slightly. "She said she couldn't." Back then, there were times when he almost thought he understood Felice. Stanley saw the devouring way their mother watched her—doting yet somehow swallowing her up. He, in turn, often felt cheated: there might even have been a small part of him that was glad when Felice first left. Mostly, though, he missed her. He'd heard about the girl at school who killed herself—Felice had never mentioned her, but Yeni and Coco told him that they'd been friends. When he'd said the girl's name to Felice, an odd blankness had dropped over her features, emptying her face. She denied knowing her: he'd pressed but could get nothing more from his sister.

They shift positions, uncurling to lie side by side. Nieves has never been much of a cuddler, preferring a minimal touch—sliding the tips of her fingers under Stanley's waist or hips. Now she curls her hand around his. "Are we going to help them?"

Stanley smiles in the darkness, pleased by the *we*—not always a given with her. His breath floats above him and there is that sense again—the feeling he's had, ever since meeting her, that something polished and solid, like a marble shelf in his chest, is very slowly softening, dissolving into the air. "I don't know if there's much we can do.

Honestly, I don't know what to say to them. They probably just need money."

"Well they can go ahead and get in line," she grumbles.

"Don't worry about the market."

"I'm not."

"You know—we *could* always move the business. I mean, if we had to. Find another location."

She stares at him. "Are you kidding?"

Stanley's eyes fall to the wooden floor of their apartment, once office space above the old bank. It took eight months and over a hundred volunteers to tear out and remodel the building: they repurposed the teller counters for cash registers and the vault became cold storage. They created that market from the ground up: its hand-polished floor boards, inlaid decorations, and the stained-glass figure of Persephone with her crimson pomegranate over the main entrance.

They don't speak for a few moments, separately observing the darkness. Stanley notes a lingering green scent from the baskets of fresh mint, basil, sage, and oregano they foolishly used to decorate the front of the store. All that work will be destroyed by the wind. He often detects notes of fruit or prepared food twining through the floorboards into their apartment, perpetually reminding him of all sorts of unfinished tasks. He doesn't mind: he grew up in the sugar-woven air of his mother's kitchen—it was the thing that kept her away and yet kept her close—the scent of a cinnamon *palmier* in the morning was like having her hands beneath his pillow.

Nieves moves onto her knees to peer through the window. She says, "I guess there's around six grand, just over, in petty cash."

Stanley frowns, trying to think what she's alluding to. Now he eases onto his side, head propped, trying to make out Nieves's face, but she remains ineluctable. Recalling the thread of the conversation, it occurs to him to be indignant, to say: Are you crazy? Give that to them? That's not even our money—that's payroll and repairs and

purveyors! But she already knows this. And she knows they probably won't get the loan from his parents. So there's nothing to say.
There's only the matter of coaxing her closer in bed, of rubbing her
shoulders and kissing the nape of her neck, and wistfully thinking of
sex: already both of them are so tired these days, and the baby's still
three months away. When people learn of her pregnancy, they all say:
Enjoy these precious last months! It seems that something in Stanley
is readying itself. Frightened as he is, there have been moments lately
when Stanley has glimmerings of unexpected longing—as if this
baby is someone he already knows and loves. Increasingly, he senses
the energetic thrum of that third presence, the additional heartbeat
rounding things out, expanding everything—their home, their lives,
even the air molecules around them. His hands slide along Nieves's
arms, once again folding her spine into his chest, folding their arms
in over her belly.

"But what if it *did* happen to us?" She returns to her earlier fretting. "Like it did with Felice running away. I mean—Stan—I would
die. I wouldn't be able to stand it." Her voice quavers. "I'm not that
strong. Not like that."

"You are strong," he murmurs against the side of her head, strands
of hair in his face. "And it won't happen,"

"But *how* do you know?"

"We won't let it."

"Stanley?" Nieves whispers, her voice sounds rawer and younger.
"I think we should give them the money—or whatever they want. We
need to help them out."

Over the past year and a half, he has learned that Nieves has within
her something like a pointing needle. It does little good to argue with
her, though his own heavy nature often impels him to. Stanley tells
his girlfriend, "Maybe. I don't especially want to and she might not
take it anyway. And I'm not about to beg."

Nieves takes such a long time to respond, Stanley wonders if she's
fallen asleep. There are low, continuous rolls of thunder in the dis-

tance. Then he hears her saying softly, "She doesn't strike me that way—as being so hard."

She doesn't know, Stanley thinks. Even now, he can't stop checking on Felice, looking toward the door which he's left open, allowing no one their privacy. And he will probably get up several times in the night to make sure that he hadn't dreamed it. At this point, years after the fact, he realizes that it's as if Felice's departure has become an essential piece of her—the price his family had to pay for his sister, for having her at all.

THE STORM HAD GROWN exponentially louder, thrashing windows, the nylon curtains lifting inside the apartment. The clock radio had died at 3:35 a.m. The rattling AC fell silent, ceiling fans stopped rotating, and the constant electric drone—not only of their apartment but of the market below them—ceased. Outside, wind rose in eminence, pounding the building in an oceanic surge. Half asleep, Nieves curled against his side and they listened to the roar as if they were trapped inside a small boat, whipped by rising seas. He wondered at one point if the unprotected windows would hold: something outside seemed to burst and there was a furious pounding racket against the building like that of a madman with a hammer.

When he wakes again at 6:28, according to his wristwatch, the storm has abated, rotating north and east toward the beaches. The apartment is stultifying; Stanley gets up and cranks open the windows, the blue porthole in the bathroom, and more tropical humidity swims into the place. His eyes ache with sleeplessness. The sky is scoured-out and bright; the heat will be terrible. Nieves rises and makes sandwiches for breakfast—tahini, organic banana, and local wildflower honey on whole wheat—her manner so surly and ferocious that no one attempts to talk to her. Felice and Emerson look, if possible, even more stunned and white-faced than they had the day before. Emerson studies the first section of the *Herald* with an impressive thoroughness, turning a page, then turning it back again to reread something. Stanley makes them coffee with the good Jamaican beans and dollops of unpasteurized cream (soon to spoil if power doesn't come right back). Then they go outside to survey the damage.

Remarkably, none of the store windows broke; but there are drifts of plant debris and enormous palm fronds strewn across the parking lot like wreckage, their ends curling and gray. Power lines dangle from a pole at the corner, a child's pink shoe lies on its side in the middle of the parking lot. The generator roars, loud as a jet engine against the west wall. Blinking, shielding their eyes, the four of them wander, moving around fallen branches, the stump of an upended ficus tree. They are quiet, startled shipwreck survivors. Abruptly Emerson grabs the stump. "Where do you want this stuff?"

Stanley and Emerson designate a plant trash heap beside the dumpster and begin the tedious, oddly exhausting work of clearing and hauling. Emerson—Stanley notes—is a good worker, moving easily: the more he works, the more relaxed he seems. Felice and Nieves clear the doors, mop up the entrance, and sweep the store's concrete perimeter. Then they carry out aluminum lawn chairs from the storage room and a thermos of passion fruit tea and settle in to watch the men work. Stanley is still waiting for the moment Felice will stand and stretch, put her hands on her hips, pace a bit as if rehearsing her exit. He'd dreaded it when they were younger—the preamble before she'd go out at night. But Felice seems content to be just where she is, reclining in an old chair, feet propped on an overturned grocery cart.

"This is a great setup," Emerson says. He and Stanley are at opposite ends of a black walnut branch, lugging it to the heap—now piled high with branches and coconuts. "Your market—it's awesome. Like a community-service-type place, but also a great store."

"Yeah, I don't know about the great part." Stanley and Emerson swing the branch into the debris pile where it lands with a thump. "What we're shooting for, just basically, is to make good food available. Like, affordable. Talk about a magic act. Dole and General Mills getting these major subsidies, and we're telling the local growers we don't want to charge more than the chains do for their conventional and processed crap. We do what we can—take food stamps, all that. We offer barter and volunteer discounts, whatever we can think of. Keep overhead low."

Emerson squints at the store, hands resting on his hips. "Well, you're still standing, right?"

"Barely." Stanley uses the thumb of his leather work glove to push hair off his face. "I used to work at a co-op—everyone kept squabbling and leaving—couldn't hang on to customers. Of course, when I bought this place the old hippie contingent said I was turning 'establishment.' " He sighs. "Anyway, yeah, with this place the employees can own shares in the business—they run their own sections. Decent benefits, vacations, workshops. Blah, blah. And we're *always* behind on the bills. This place has been smoking money since the second I opened it." He smacks the dust off his gloves and surveys his storefront. "Maybe it's not losing money as fast as it used to. I guess that's something."

"Sounds good to me." Emerson looks at Stanley, then at his own feet. Stanley realizes then that Emerson wants Stanley to *like* him.

They sweat through their clothes and have to take breaks at shorter intervals. Stanley drinks iced tea until he can feel it sloshing in his stomach. He and Emerson clutch the wet glasses, pressing them against their faces. By noon, the sun roasts the air and a vaporous steam shimmers everywhere. Stanley suggests they break until sundown. But Emerson pulls off his T-shirt (Stanley marvels at the fan of muscle radiating from his neck and back), soaks it with a garden hose, and wraps it around his head. "I'll just go for a little longer, if that's okay." His innate politeness catching Stanley off-guard.

Retreating, Stanley discovers both Felice and Nieves inside the apartment sprawled on the leftover bedding and pillows on the floor, watching cartoons. They're eating the "all-natural" toaster tarts Nieves persuaded him to carry.

"Hey, sweat monster." Nieves kisses him, a drift of sugary blue-berries on her breath. "Electricity's back on. Yay."

Felice looks at him mildly, almost vacantly, and once again there is the unreal sensation: Can she truly be here? He goes to shower and as the cool water spills over him, he considers unhappily that he's no longer as angry as he used to be. It was so difficult—almost impossible, really—to put her away emotionally, to stop wondering where she was or if she'd return—he doesn't want to relinquish all that hard work. And think of what she'd done to their mother! His stomach tightens like a fist beneath his rib cage. As he's rinsing off the layers of soap, a thought creeps into his mind: *She's going to slip out while I'm in the shower.*

He forces himself to not rush: he taps up the warm and shaves in the shower, then lingers a few seconds under the spray. He towels off thoroughly, combs his hair, his pulse rising in his throat, breath. *Is she gone yet?* He tells himself that he isn't being quite rational. Finally he wraps a towel around his waist and emerges from the bathroom: the TV is off; the bedding has been folded and stacked on an arm-chair. Something like a dense, dark pressure settles over him. It is res-onant with old emotional weight—the loneliness of his old bedroom, the backseat of his parents' car, staring out the window, eternally searching—no matter if they were just going to the store, to school, to the movies. He tugs himself away from the feeling. *No, I won't.* Even if his hands tremble as he pulls on his pants. Because she will not do that to him, or to anyone he loves, again. He is not that boy who drove through the neighborhoods, imagining the worst things in the world, his chest filled with a sagging emptiness, looking for a sister who, he believed, had to be injured or dead.

Stanley picks up some of the accounting paperwork and a note-book from the desk in their bedroom. He'll need to inventory any exterior wind damage and inspect the inside of the market. The thought intrudes again: *She's gone.* He instructs himself: *Then I'm glad.* Felice will always land on her feet. He lets the apartment door swing shut behind him and takes the wooden steps down to the landing behind the building. It occurs to him then to wonder where Nieves is. He considers that Felice could not have been a good influence on his girlfriend or future baby: like a free radical, unsettling the environment. He climbs over some bramble that had blown in at the foot of the landing and the chain-link fence encircling the sides and rear of the market. The air vibrates with a high-pitched whine; Stanley walks the perimeter, gathering the twigs and debris, then stops abruptly: Emerson is still there.

He's out in front with Noah Tibold, who owns Zone Ten exotics nursery, and Nancy Pegrum—one of Stanley's cashiers. Noah is using a small chain saw to take apart a bougainvillea that toppled over the lot's north entrance. Emerson and Nancy rake piles of twigs and leaves. There's such a settled, contented rhythm to their work that for a moment Stanley just stands there quietly, watching.

Stanley's joints and muscles seem to loosen, relief coursing through his body. If Emerson is still here, Felice must be as well. But relief is immediately followed by stern annoyance. Stanley enters the front of the market. The generator is off and the air-conditioning seems to be functioning—he'd been braced for the pungent effluvia that had pervaded the store after Hurricane Charley. There's some frost buildup on the dairy cases, the cut flowers have withered away, and the magazine covers of women in yoga poses or of gleaming plates of vegan stew (*New Vegetarian*) have all curled and buckled. But they appear to have come through the storm intact.

There's a noise behind him and Stanley turns to see Marco Braithwaite, another regular, halfway through the door. "Stan? You guys open today?"

Stanley gestures him in. "We haven't restocked yet, but if you see something you need . . ." He swings his arm open; he feels careless, expansive. "Go for it."

Marco salutes, heading for the near-empty cereal aisle. "I'll leave the money up front, how 'bout."

Light-headed, Stanley strolls down Vinegars/Oils/Pastas toward the office. He can hear voices: the low current is Nieves and the nervous, lighter clip is, apparently, the voice his sister has grown into. Their voices slip together easily. He's never seen Nieves warm to someone so quickly before. Felice is awkward, as if she's out of practice with conversation, but she keeps going—making up for lost time. What happened to her? He's employed enough people on various sorts of margins to recognize the bitten-away cuticles, the haunted eyes. He feels another surge of irritation: she should go. He doesn't need this: he's got enough to worry about without more turmoil, wondering about whatever ruins his sister is running from or the next time she'll vanish. When Stanley reaches the doorway, both women look up, startled. Then Nieves smiles. "Hi, babe." She reaches up for his kiss.

Felice seems instantly diffident. "Hiya, Stan."

The air feels high and tight in his chest, his lungs cinched like a drawstring. *Felice. Here.* A velvety black gecko appears on the wall behind the girls—it's trickled out of some corner and now rests mid-wall, its tiny throat beating, its body pointed like a dart. Stanley looks back at the women and he realizes that Felice is watching him with some anxiety, as if awaiting a decision. Arms crossed, her right hand absently circles her left elbow—a small tic he'd almost forgotten. He smiles weakly. Annoyed with himself, his lack of will, he sits beside Nieves and tips his nose to her hair. *Not yet.* He closes his eyes.

FELICE AND EMERSON spend that night and the next on Stanley's floor, and still he fails to ask them to leave. Then they discover the couch in the living room pulls out into a bed—Stanley mimes smacking himself in the head—he'd completely forgotten (though it was, in fact, the place he used to sleep before meeting Nieves). Nieves gives him a narrow look and smooths fresh sheets onto the hide-a-bed.

Emerson spends the next few days clearing the parking lot, sawing tree limbs, sweeping the cement patio, and swabbing the store. Then he and Noah go out in Noah's pickup and return with flats of wind-resistant coleus and aloe, and plant a decorative border along the front of the store. Nieves walks Felice through wines and cheeses. They officially reopen on the third day after the hurricane, and right away customers flash through the entrance. Still, Stanley can't stop watching Felice, uneasy about the way his sister and girlfriend have adopted each other. He can't understand how they can have so much to talk about so quickly. One day while he's in his office, the girls are restocking the cheese cave. Through the office wall he overhears Nieves mention her big family. Their voices are barely muffled. Nieves is estranged from most of her relatives, and is coolly off-handed about it—Stanley has heard her tirades against her tyrannical stepfather and humorless siblings, as well as her disaffection for the notion of "family." He's opening cartons of crackers and stacking them against the wall when he hears Felice begin describing her life to Nieves—her runaway life. Stanley drifts to a stop, his hands still pressed to the large carton, as he hears: "It was like a kind of a halfway house, I guess. The Green House. Lots of kids. Yeah, Emerson, too, sometimes . . . No, I claimed this crappy mattress in a back room . . . A couple years. I guess . . . pretty safe. Compared to, you know, anyplace."

There is the creak of a hand truck, a sound of movement, something tumbles, a flutter of laughter. Then, "We really can't—exactly—go back. You know? I mean, I was done anyway. But we got into, like, some pretty heavy—some trouble? . . . Yeah . . . I did. Some guys . . . Yeah . . . I don't know . . . I guess I probably shouldn't say too much."

Nieves's questions are just soft dabs of sound.

"Modeling, sort of . . . Yeah . . . No . . . It was dumb . . . Tattoos . . . Yeah! Not permanent . . . I know . . . Actually it sucked . . . You can't hardly eat . . . Not that I . . ."

Just like that, filling in the abysmal silence, the missing past, as if such a thing could be done. He stares at the carton in his hands: Finnish Flatbread: 48 count. The yellow walls of his office, the wet stain beside the coffeepot, a mug filled with pens, curling photographs of friends waving from canoes, rappelling up sheer cliffs. On his desk, an announcement for underwater birthing class, a flier for a tai chi workshop, stating: *Only this moment, right now, to see the possibilities in it or not.* Everything is so ordinary, yet he feels as if he's been teleported to another solar system.

Stanley lies awake that night replaying old fragments, bits of memories of Felice: her tidy bedroom with the translucent shell chimes; the poster above her bed—*Christina's World*—the back of a girl's wind-stirred hair, her oddly twisted recline in the field. Stanley recycles their last conversations: the way he was always trying to apologize for whatever was making Felice run away, then trying to make himself angry enough not to care. But that was Stanley's big problem—his anger was insubstantial—it wisped away between his fingers when he tried to grasp it. He even tried to provoke fights with her: once he snapped, "You need a shrink!"

She'd asked, "Would that make you happy?" What a thing for a thirteen-year-old to say! How could he be angry with her when so often she didn't even seem to *be* there.

Now Stanley cannot shake the sense that Felice and Emerson are recovering from something like a catastrophic illness. There's a lingering frailty, a delicacy in their actions and voices, especially in the way they treat each other, with such tenderness and solicitude. Felice talks about Portland, about the route they'll take, how much money they'll need, the sort of work she might look for. But increasingly, Stanley notices, Emerson responds with less enthusiasm, in a kind of gentle, pro forma manner. Every morning, Emerson is the first up, the first to unfold the paper, which he combs, reading it all the way through, subsequently refolding it so it appears nearly undisturbed. Stanley has seen him retrieve the paper from the recycling bin later, on his break, and start rereading—his finger tracing the columns. Once, Stanley said something to Emerson about the president's obsession with Iraqi oil fields and the boy looked at him a moment before saying, "Oh, right—what a mess, I know."

End of conversation.

They work well together, Stanley will admit: this is something he understands—the language of communal work, how cooperation gives rise to the best kind of friendships. Stanley is impressed with Emerson's capacity for labor, his endurance, and his ability to learn quickly—how to inventory, to build displays, to keep accounts. He doesn't say much—especially not about himself, but to Stanley, this is a positive thing, refreshing even, after years of loquacious, sensitive young men, guys in touch with themselves, drummers, poets, and political activists—each brimming with feelings, insights, and opinions. Emerson is steady: a quality Stanley prizes. Emerson will unload trucks or work a cash register for hours, until someone orders him to sit, brings him some food. At times, he and Felice seem almost shy with each other, the backs of their hands barely brushing. Stanley tries not to monitor them, but he's painfully curious: he's never seen them kiss, though they continue to share a bed and stay continually in each other's orbits, murmuring together on breaks.

Stanley also refuses to ask Felice questions. He talks to her, of course; he is friendly and cordial—he hasn't asked her to go or to stay; he will not ask why she left or where she went. He imagines that he's made himself smooth and cool—like a wax candle or an old pewter spoon, half melted by time and use.

Don't go/Don't stay.

One week after their arrival, Stanley is stationed at his desk studying the books—his most dreaded task and yet the best to lose himself in. He hears a rustling, shuffling sound, the creak of hand truck wheels, then a furious, intent whispering that sends icy goose bumps down his back and makes him wonder if one of their homeless locals is trying to set up a bedroll in the cheese cave (they once opened the market to find a bedraggled elderly man sleeping in Prepared Foods). He lowers his hands on the keyboard, then wheels his chair closer to the office wall. Gradually he distinguishes two voices—Emerson's and Felice's. He hears another crackling rustle (grocery bags?), then Emerson's voice, somewhat louder, saying, "—it's here—under the . . ."

There's a pause, then Felice murmuring: "they . . . unidentified? . . . not him . . . I mean . . . he said his name . . ."

Their intent, muted voices rise and fall. Emerson: "Must not have had . . ."

Felice, reading in a sharp whisper: "*In an accidental drowning . . .* know it was even him? And *drowning?*"

"It's the same beach on the same night . . . anything . . . tide and the currents . . ."

"*A white man, mid-forties . . .*" She is either reading this or conceding something. "What about the other . . . his friend?"

". . . why would he stick around?"

". . . God."

For a long while, Stanley hears nothing but a whir of breath in his ears, a pump somewhere in the building, the buzz of the overhead lights. His mouth is so dry it adheres to itself. He closes his eyes. Through the wall, he hears minute, inarticulate sounds—perhaps paper crumpling, perhaps crying. He lowers his eyes to the heels of his palms.

He once let a girlfriend cajole him into spending a few nights with her at a hotel in Islamorada. She'd insisted that Stanley needed a "vacation," that he was too young to be so obsessed with work. He went grudgingly, annoyed at the waste of time and money. The hotel had statues of grinning tiki idols out front and furniture that stuck to the backs of their legs. He'd awakened late one night and got up to use the bathroom. As he washed his hands in the darkened room, in the mirror he noticed something move on the floor behind him. After years of working in the food industry, he had a near-telepathic ability to detect vermin and pests of all sorts, and he imagined how satisfying it would be to tell the girlfriend that the hotel was infested with palmetto bugs.

He turned. As he stared through the purple darkness of the room, he noticed trembling movements, then the extended claws like a waiter balancing trays, then a tail curling up and over. He watched in a kind of dream-state as two scorpions made their delicate, rickety way across the bathroom floor. And the feeling of that moment—a kind of mild horror as well as a decision to leave the creatures alone and never to mention them—was virtually identical to what he feels now, eavesdropping, listening to his sister talk about drowned men, unidentified bodies—both a recoiling dread and placid neutrality. What had she gotten mixed up in?

He consciously relaxes his grip on his chair arms, seeing the scorpions' scrape in the darkness again. He's given up on issues like Justice and Global Peace—preferring, instead, to be kind and generous to his employees, to take good care of his girlfriend. Lately he barely sees the migrant workers who wait for jobs in the lumberyard parking lot or amble around downtown Homestead, the heels of their boots worn down to softness. He wonders, Can anyone help it? What's ever right? You contract with a local farmer, only to find out that Dow Chemical controls their seed production. You lose money because your vegan customers want to have papayas or avocados in November. You lose customers because the only oranges you can get in December are from South America, because Big Citrus pushed a ban on privately owned orange trees, citing citrus canker, because it's more lucrative for Florida citrus growers to ship their fruits halfway around the world than sell at home. Because an apple grower can't afford to take a bite of his own fruit. Who says the world is fair? You have to pick your loyalties and your causes, Stanley thinks, throwing his copy of the newspaper into recycling. In this way, at the very least, he picks his sister.

ON FRIDAY MORNING, ten days after Felice reappeared, Stanley wakes earlier than usual. He watches Nieves's belly as she sleeps: his talisman. Each day he has awakened with a bit less anxiety, less surprised to find his sister asleep in his living room. He recognizes the way she pouts in silence, folds her hair over one shoulder, her zippy,

near-enzymatic energy in the afternoons. He allows himself the pleasure of simply enjoying her presence. Nieves opens her eyes: it's still
dark, the two of them lie there, silently aware of the other's stirrings.
Their wall unit rumbles away, making its weirdly human moan, producing icy streaks in the air. She shifts, orienting herself toward him,
and murmurs, "Let's ask them to stay."

"Here? In this apartment?"

"Maybe. I don't know. Or in the studio—we're not using it. We
can put the canned junk back in the warehouse." She sighs faintly.
Stanley can make out the glimmer on her lower lip, an iridescence on
the swell of her belly. Increasingly, she seems to have less energy to be
irascible, less will for gruffness. Sometimes he worries that her personality is eroding, that she's being washed away by the pregnancy.
His hand closes tightly around hers. "I like them," she says. "They're
sweet. And I think they need us."

She speaks with a kind of exhausted resignation Stanley recognizes
in himself. He runs his thumb along the inside of her fingers. "If we
ask them to stay, it might remind them that they were planning to go."
He'd meant this as a joke, but it doesn't come out sounding that way.

Nieves props her head on her hand, "First, though—you should
take her to see your mother."

"Oh." Stanley shakes his head. He strokes the length of her inner
forearm. He feels cushioned by fatigue. "That's pretty much the last
thing she'll do."

"It's different now. She's relaxed—more used to things. Please,
just—ask her again?"

"She'll think I'm trying to force her." He eases onto his back.
"That's how it is with Felice. This whole thing now—it's kind of what
it used to be like—she held us all hostage."

But the longer that Felice is there, the worse he feels about not
telling his parents—more of an accomplice. It was as if, in the past,
they could have pretended her running away had been a sort of natural disaster—inescapable, and nobody's fault. But *this,* her avoid-
ance, seems personal. And the more he considers this, the more the

old anger returns, tightening his stomach. He thinks: *What gives her the right?*

THAT MORNING, STANLEY GOES into the market early: Felice is already at the cheese display arranging a pyramid of sepia-edged triple-crèmes from Normandy. When Stanley first opened the market, the only cheeses they carried were flavorless bricks of organic jack and a rubbery, casein-free, vegan cheddar. Felice touches the cheeses with care, as if they're infants, her hands hovering above each piece, placing it just so. She has arranged sprays of yellow dendrobium around the lightly refrigerated deck. She is actually humming. When she turns toward him, her expression broken open, Stanley catches a glimpse of natural contentment before the wariness resurfaces. Her lifted hands pause, then move to her chest—as if identifying or shielding herself. With dismay, he sees her eyes glisten. "You want us to go, don't you?" she asks.

No. He doesn't say anything. Stanley lowers his gaze, studies the speckles in the linoleum. He argues with himself, with his old, hard nature, that tight nut at his center, that makes him feel at times that he's lived longer than almost anybody. She got herself here, didn't she? he asks himself. She's doing the best she can. Stanley can't bring himself to speak directly, though. He can't imagine using a word like *trust*. He shakes his obstinate head—just as stubborn, it occurs to him, as his sister. "I don't know," he says finally.

"You can't." She turns back to the stack of cheeses as if something's been resolved: as if her life depends on achieving that perfect symmetry. Her fingers tremble. She won't look at him. "I know how you are, Stan. You can't deal with it."

He backs away from her, turning his face, and retreats to the office.

Nieves brings him lunch around two, looks at him closely. She says his name, stirs the hair off his forehead with a finger, then returns her hands to her stomach. "Whatever." She smoothes little circles around her small swell. "But I wish you'd get over yourself."

After she goes, Stanley cups his forehead with both hands; he rubs his scalp, wondering how hard he'd have to bang his head against the desk before he'd pass out. He sits back, kneads his side. His market should carry Maalox. The inventory sheets arrayed before him make no sense. There are notes from Eduardo: *Calvin needs letter of intent by next week—latest; The basmati full of flies; Garlic shipment rotted* . . . He sits that way, immobilized, incapable of following his thoughts to any sort of insight or solution. This is the one problem he'd never expected to have. He feels stupid and afraid, internally frozen, a mastodon, afraid to leave his icy tomb. The little red light on his cell flashes—another apologetic call from one or both parents, wanting to talk, asking how they'd come through the hurricane.

At some point, beyond his silenced body and thoughts, he becomes aware of a sound: a long, low rumble, then a scraping noise. He isn't sure how long he's been listening without hearing it. He knows what it is. The rear lot for delivery trucks was repaved last year: now it's smooth and slightly curved, lifted a few inches at one end, on the natural incline of the land. The elegant surface was discovered by the local skateboarders. They're a nuisance—occasionally a couple of them clatter around the front lot and startle the customers. Stanley has added to his list the fear that one of his purveyors' trucks will hit a skateboarder and everyone will get hauled into court. Still, it's hard for him to muster what Nieves calls the "authoritarian will" to chase them away. Their rumble and scraping have become such a familiar backdrop he forgets they're around until he hears the dairy deliveryman out in back yelling at them.

This afternoon, dispersing skateboarders seems a simple, appealingly tangible task. He stands on the loading platform and inhales the syrupy hot air, watching the boys racing and spinning—their crisp, airborne movements. It's a small group of teenagers: weedy hair, thin chests, shoulders like clothes hangers. They push off against a small retaining wall, their arms sailing up, parallel to the earth, a deep crouch, aloft. It occurs to Stanley, watching them, that his own baby—gender yet unknown—could grow into one of them. He

wonders—could he actually love *this,* the flapping clothes and hair
and bad skin? He realizes finally that the boy he's been watching snap
his board into the air, then neatly touch down—long, black, gleaming
hair, pale white skin—is Felice. He didn't know she'd learned how to
skateboard. He's never seen her like this before—so intently focused
and content—her beauty beside the point, merely part of the catalog
of effects—speed, balance, daring. He admires her athletic form and
feels moved in some unexpected way. The three boys with her—
neighbor kids, the Mexican-American sons of the migrants—call out,
their voices lost in the hot air and a distant whir of insects rising from
the fields beyond the lot.

Felice swishes to a stop, neatly twisting the board to one side.
She jumps down, stomps on one end, flips it up, and catches the
top, nonchalant as a gunslinger. Smiling, possibly at her show of bra-
vado, she hands it over to its owner—fourteen-year-old son of one of
the onion growers. She slides her hands into her pockets, straight-
armed and now shy, and slinks over to Stanley. "Hey, Stan." She
pulls back her hair.

"Pret-ty cool." He nods at the other skateboarders, who continue
rolling but shoot him wary glances. "Where'd you learn to do that?"

"It's not so hard," she mumbles. "Just gotta do it a bunch."

"Hey, Nieves is saying—" He stops himself, frowns into the sheer
light, a distant vista of date palms. "She's going to be upset, you
know, if you guys go."

Felice smiles and winces; she uses the flat of her hand as a visor.
"She told me we should stay." Under her hand her eyes look like river
stones. "We can't, though, right now. We're gonna take off in a day or
two. I mean, we got this plan, you know? Maybe we can—for a visit—
when the baby comes? If you want us to?"

"*Don't* say—" He cuts himself off again. Takes a deep breath he
feels in his ribs. This moment. "Don't say anything you're not going
to do," he says more gently. He pulls out a fat brown envelope from
his notebook—two thousand in well-worn tens and twenties: he and

Nieves have subsisted on lentil soup, hummus, and bread in the past. "If you absolutely have to go."

She pushes the envelope back at him. "No. No freakin' way." Her brows lift and he sees the glint of their mother's will in her face. "We have money. Emerson saved up."

"Goddammit, Felice." His chest tightens with a kind of radiant anger—he has a brief, wild impulse to tear open the envelope and shower the cash over the skateboarders' heads. "Jesus Christ, why not?"

She looks at him, then takes the envelope and removes about five hundred dollars. "This will be our escape plan," she says. "For when it's time to come back."

He stares at her: his chest sinks on a partial sigh. It would almost have been easier if she'd stayed missing. No rough, ragged edges. He takes the remaining money. "I want to ask you to do something. It's about our mother."

She turns her head toward the skateboarders. "There isn't time. To see them? Really. We've got to hit it."

"But what if I ask you to do it." He draws a low, even breath. "For me."

She squints toward the wind-shaken treeline. He knows her, he thinks, and he doesn't know her. He feels the unexpected touch of admiration: she created herself, nearly from scratch. "Don't you think it's important," she asks suddenly, "you know—to sort of hang on to your plan for things?"

"Feef, I'm not saying move back, just—"

"No, no, I know. I just mean. You make a decision. Even a principle for a way to live your life? Don't you think that needs to be, like, the main thing?"

He studies her for a moment. "I think," he says slowly, "that principles are important. Yeah, I think they can get you going. Sort of help you see what you want to accomplish . . ."

"And what you don't want."

"Right. Yes, absolutely. But I think even principles can change, you know? People keep changing all their lives. It never stops. But I think it's not like the old principles were bad or anything—just sometimes you've got to add some new ones."

"Huh."

Stanley walks out to the edge of the platform and sits and then Felice comes and sits beside him. The sun softens under high clouds, far away, a sound of thunder—some hope of rain. They stay out there, waiting and not speaking, watching the roll and zip of the skateboarders.

Avis

AT MIDDAY, AVIS WALKS AROUND THE HOUSE, switching on lights. She moves from the rectangular windows in the living room to the windows in her study, to the small panes of the French doors, each time turning away from the dark glass, the reflected oval of her own face, her eyes fretful and shadowy. She hasn't heard from Brian since his abrupt departure for work that morning. After watching for hours, she had to turn off the Weather Channel as their predictions and graphs—something resembling a fireball hurtling toward the peninsula—grew unbearably ominous. By late afternoon, the storm's outer bands have started to lash the house with dark, heavy rain. She shivers, drawing her arms in close to her body, drifting to the front door to watch the rain sweep up the street. Lamb slinks under the couch and yowls softly. Outside of the kitchen and her normal work rhythms, Avis feels the strangeness of the house without Brian, its emptiness intensified. In the past, he'd always hired someone to cover the windows before a big storm. He made up checklists, tested the flashlights, and monitored the bottled water: they spent the hurricanes together, watching forecasts as long as the electricity held, then listening to the wilderness of wind. How did this happen? She used to live with husband and children. How does life dwindle to such a place in which one is boxed up alone? Had she truly dreamed of a private cottage? Now she listens in misery to the drumming rain and tries not to let herself imagine Brian stranded, stuck in a highway wreck, or worse.

The longer he doesn't answer the phone, the more she feels a pressure in her chest, as if a hand were softly closing around her heart. As she watches from a front window, the sky goes from a bruised green to a deep eggplant, enormous columnar clouds wall off the sun, and the rain rises, slits sideways, slicing at the roof. Where is he? She goes into the kitchen, hoping that a bit of work will calm her, but her hands tremble as she tries to roll out baguette dough, and for once her mind will not be subdued by her hands. She worries over Stanley, aware that a storm this intense could destroy his entire market; the thought tears at her that their last real interaction consisted of her denying him money. And there is also, of course, the transparency underlining all her fears: her anxiety for Felice. Where on earth could her daughter be in this weather?

As the day goes on and the storm grows, her concerns melt into one steady pulse of fear for her husband. Twice she picks up the phone, about to call the highway patrol, but such a call seems like an admission that things have gone too horribly wrong. She feels the sheen of dread, a petrification, as if her insides might turn to stone: the sense that Avis could not survive—not as a whole person—without him. The fear of losing Brian subsumes and encapsulates all the rest, spelling out her world, her understanding of loss. She sits on the edge of the living room couch staring at the black street, and the feeling of it spills through her, thoughts disjointed and dark as syllables.

This hurricane seems worse than any she can remember—even Andrew, which they'd lived through as a family. The thunder sounds as if it caroms inside a metal barrel—the house shakes from its force. The hurricane wind, which usually drives against the south end of the house, seems wily and demonic, coming from one, then another direction. Power lines sway and snap free and rain skirts the street forming a minor river. The wind masks all other sounds as Avis calls Brian's cell again: its unanswered ring like a stone's echo in a well. The wind starts to drive needles of rain through the window seams and under the front door. Avis grabs bath towels and a bucket but she can't stay ahead of it. She blames herself for the mess of rainwater: she'd repeatedly complained to Brian that she hated the idea of encasing their house in shutters, "closeting" themselves in darkness: now the floor and carpets along the south side of the house are soaked. This happened in much the same way, she senses, that she's brought this isolation on herself—her chronic retreat, training him, in essence, to leave her.

Late in the afternoon, Avis sees a watery flash of headlights out front: standing quickly, she is almost faint with relief. Brian straggles in the door, rain streaming from his face and collar. He'd had to park in the driveway—the garage opener shorted out. "I tried to call—the cells are useless. Oh my God—you wouldn't believe—"

She wraps her arms around the compass of his back, filled with joy. He presses his cold face into her neck, then looks at her, his hair dripping. "I thought I'd left the office with plenty of time but the storm came up so fast it was like a bomb. Traffic was dead in the street. I've been stuck on the Dixie seems like days." Avis smells dampness on him all the way to the silk lining of his jacket. She peels off his jacket and shirt and drapes these over the shower door. She sits him on the couch and rumples a towel on his dripping hair: his face has that long, earnest sweetness she remembers from their lovestruck college days. Her thoughts flicker to the long-ago tutoring sessions in her apartment on North Aurora Street—how she tried to get Brian to kiss her, how he was so concerned that she master the principles of economic theory. An emotional history like a fire they'd carried between them, seeming to dwindle, then rekindling and leaping, all the gas rings on the stove turned up high.

Brian reaches up to her hands as she dries his hair: she bends and kisses the top of his head. They remain together on the couch as the lights flicker off, then on, then finally go out for the night. The terrible hollow booming and shaking goes on; at one point the door and windows rattle insanely, as if some gigantic force were trying to invade. Avis sits with her head tilted low against Brian's chest and listens to the storm within the walls of his body.

———

AVIS WAKES IN THE gray dawn and studies Brian, his face mild in sleep. She rises, dresses for work, makes her determined way to the kitchen, wondering again how her children fared in the storm. The windows seem to be washed in green light, glittering with heat. The hurricane knocked down enormous fronds, spilled the stripling palms over, punched open new holes in the canopy; sunlight pours through in solid cylinders. She scans the treetops, the delicate, rummaging fingers of palm leaflets—everything heat-stunned. In the emptied backyard, the iron cage is lying on its side, door flapped open, a body with its soul turned loose. She thinks again of Solange. The world seems filled with the beloved missing. Inside the marble kitchen, she closes her eyes and can almost imagine knocks on a chapel door in Haiti, the child's voice. Her skin is covered in dots of ice. A swirl of vertigo. She would have torn the planks off the doors, torn off her own skin. She would have murdered the man in his sleep to have answered that cry. With shaking hands, she moves away from her view of the cage, calls Stanley and leaves a message. She tries to suppress the pleading in her voice: "Let me know how you came through? Just a quick call. Anything. Your father and I want to know."

Now she rolls the waistband of her apron over, hitches her hands at her hips. There's a backup generator designated specifically for her kitchen—the stove and refrigerator hum in their stations, still alive. She begins to call customers, but half don't answer. From those that do, Avis hears of more power outages, learns that restaurants and stores will be closed for the rest of the week. Her fingers curl, riffling through her folder: the largest current order—*ficelles* with a core of nutmeg and chopped bittersweet—bread and chocolate—is for the Marine Academy on Virginia Key. But the schools are closed. A distraught woman at Endographics (bimonthly *dulce de leche macarons*) tells her, voice shaking, that a bougainvillea fell through the window, throwing purple-budded branches across her desk, destroying her computer and files. Everyone sounds stunned, in post-hurricane shock. Avis reaches her friend, the chef in Coconut Grove: he says he plans to set up his kettle grill on the sidewalk in front of his restaurant and cook the contents of his freezers for the locals: all contributions welcome.

Brian hovers near the door, dressed in his soft weekend clothes, and he gestures toward the front. "Up for taking a look?" They leave the house, stepping over branches, staring at their lawn and the broken trees. They walk down their street past the big intersection with LeJeune, scanning the neighborhoods. Miami appears to be shut down—the traffic lights are out, the storm drains matted with debris, the avenues swamped. There are heaps of wet branches blocking the streets, beautiful old trees split into pieces or just overturned, root ends up. Neighbors move slowly across their lawns, dazed. Blooms and fruits and leaves are stripped away, a kind of dense black vegetal and bark matter sprayed across lawns and sidewalks.

After an hour or so of wandering through the streets, they return to the house to escape the sun's blare. Their own yard is covered with bramble but neither of them feels ready to take that on just yet. "How would you feel about doing a little something in the kitchen?" Avis asks tentatively. Brian laughs. He used to assist her before they had children, before she hired helpers, but she was impatient with him: he made mistakes—forgot to time the roasting almonds, or failed to sift the cake flour, or let the chocolate seize. Still, he accepts an apron and ties it on, smiling at the sense of occasion. He rests his knuckles on his hips. "Ready as I'll ever be."

The first recipe is ancient, written on a card in her mother's sloping hand—though her mother never actually made it. A list: eggs, brown sugar, vanilla, flour, chocolate chips. Over the course of the day, Avis and Brian fill the cooling racks with cookies: oatmeal raisin, molasses, butterscotch, peanut butter, and chocolate chip. Humble, crude, lightly crisp and filigreed at the edges, butter, salt, and sweetness at the centers. Avis samples batches with Brian. They stand near each other, immersed in the good, clean silence of work.

That afternoon, as the sun points low, potent rays across the yards, Avis and Brian pack the cookies into bakery boxes, stack them on the backseat and floor of the SUV, and set off. The traffic lights are still out and intersections are chaotic, drivers interpreting traffic protocol at will. Even though it's barely a mile away, the narrow, rustic lanes of the Grove are even more backed up and flooded than the streets in the Gables: they have to reverse several times and hunt for a passable route. There's been a storm of mosquitoes since the hurricane, and the heat makes everything seem slow and elastic, like a recording played at the wrong speed. Several times, they roll down the windows and give cookies wrapped in napkins to people dragging shrubs and limbs, raking lawns, sweeping sidewalks, slicing and sawing through piles of stumps, vines, brackish rafts of debris. A man in a sweat-stained T-shirt drops his garden hose and accepts the cookie, looking as if he might cry. When they finally get to Commodore Plaza, they spot Jean-Françoise in a white butcher's jacket tending a series of smoking grills in the middle of the street. Before him, a subdued group waits with paper plates, humble as a soup line. People sit on the curb and in battered aluminum lawn chairs. Waiters hand out dinner rolls, assemble small salads, grill fingerling potatoes, onions, and artichokes. The marrow scent of grilling meat mingles with billows of wet leaves, hot tar—someone's half-finished roof roasting. A glass pitcher is on the pavement, stuffed with curling twenties and fifties and personal checks. Jean-Françoise's smile is a white spark in his silhouette; he raises the flat of his spatula in a kind of martial greeting. "She arrives!" The late sun fills the street, a translucent mesh of light. He looks almost devilish in the yellow light, turning steaks and guzzling wine from a spotted water glass.

The people waiting on line murmur, excited by her white boxes. Brian and Avis deliver their stacks and try to refuse dinner, but the waiters bring them glasses of burgundy, porcelain plates with thin, peppery steaks redolent of garlic, scoops of buttery grilled Brussels sprouts, and a salad of beets, walnuts, and Roquefort. They drag a couple of lawn chairs to a quiet spot on the street and they balance the plates on their laps. Some ingredient in the air reminds Avis of the rare delicious trips they used to make to the Keys. Ten years after they'd moved to Miami they'd left Stanley and Felice with family friends and Avis and Brian drove to Key West on a sort of second honeymoon. She remembers how the land dropped back into distance: wetlands, marsh, lazy-legged egrets flapping over the highway, tangled, sulfurous mangroves. And water. Steel-blue plains, celadon translucence.

She and Brian had rented a vacation cottage in Old Town, ate small meals of fruit, cheese, olives, and crackers, swam in the warm, folding water. Each day stirring into the next, talking about nothing more complicated than the weather, spotting a shark off the pier, a mysterious constellation lowering in the west. Brian sheltered under a celery-green umbrella while Avis swam: the water formed pearls on the film of her sunscreen. They watched the night's rise, an immense black curtain from the ocean. Up and down the beach they heard the sounds of the outdoor bars, sandy patios switching on, distant strains of laughter, bursts of music. Someone played an instrument—quick runs of notes, arpeggios floating in soft ovals like soap bubbles over the darkening water.

Now the wind comes up, fanning them with music, laughter carried up from the street, then washing them with silence again. The stars are very gentle, faraway as old thoughts.

"Good God," Brian says faintly. He sounds like he's just reached the life raft, climbed out of a cold sea. He takes a gulp of wine, then rubs at the inner crease of his arm. "I don't know how you do that. That kind of exertion. And every single day—my God."

It had been a long and intense workday, but there was something more to it, Avis thinks—the strain of the day itself, the aftermath of the storm. She's so tired she feels as if she's floating just above the chair. "Trust me—not typical. I didn't even know if I could still push like that."

"You are something else, kid," Brian says. "But as for me. Boy, you never really expect it. I mean, getting older. It almost seems like you ought to be able to imagine your way out of it. Do something."

"Ha. Right. Like what?"

"It's nuts. Try to push back against it." He tilts his glass of wine, then gazes over its lip. "You start to see the edges of your life. It's like being able to see the curve of the planet."

Avis fingers the bowl of her own glass. "I know. Like you always knew it was there but you never believed it?" The night is forming into a dark glittering sky: the world is a bright machine carrying them inside itself. Though she sees Brian every evening, it seems it's been years since she's heard this—the actual sound of his voice. Being with him like this is like watching a tiny boat far out on the water, slowly, slowly borne back to shore. Avis turns on her lounge chair and touches his hair with the tips of her fingers. He doesn't move or speak: his eyes seem open wide. She trails her hand across the nape of his neck. "Let's go home," she murmurs. He cups her shoulders, slides his palm across the wings of her shoulder blades; his lips are dry, they taste of sea salt.

DURING THE COURSE of that week, she avoids the kitchen. She stays outside with Brian, clearing and raking the grass, sweeping the sidewalk, then the street in front of the house. Their power was restored on the afternoon following the hurricane, and for days afterward they've been one of the few houses on their block with electricity. The Handels run an extension cord to their house; other neighbors come to fill their coolers with ice or simply to sit in air-conditioning for an hour or two. Ella Regale's father comes over to watch his favorite Spanish game show. They finally make contact with Stanley, who assures them that he, Nieves, and the market, are all fine—though his voice sounds a bit dark and compressed to Avis, and he rushes off the phone after just a few minutes, promising to call again soon.

After the front of the property is cleared, Brian and Avis go into the backyard, pulling out fallen branches and fronds. The local businesses have started to reopen and will soon send their bakery orders, for which she is glad. But she isn't quite ready to go back inside yet.

Avis starts cleaning out the sprawling, wasted gardens Stanley had built, gathering brush, then weeding on her hands and knees for hours. The next day she returns to drag a metal trowel through the soil, over and over, until she is turning up fine, dry furrows, the soil sparkling. She leans toward the narrow rows and imagines the warm scent of planted tomatoes—it drifts into her senses as if they grew before her. She remembers the way Solange sat in the grass, the quick flint of her eyes, scanning the earth. It comes to her as she works that gardening is a way of staying put. That evening, Avis calls Stanley again and before he can vanish, she asks, "But Stan? Do you have one more minute?" She tells him about reviving his old gardens, how beautiful the clean plots are, and how she'd imagined the scent of tomatoes. He chuckles. "Oh yeah. That's how it gets you. One second, you're fooling around in the dirt, next thing you know you're up to your ears in squash and parsley."

"Could I do that? Squash?" She realizes that is just what she wants to do.

Stanley is drawn into it, despite himself: she can hear him give way to his old love of gardening. His voice warms with interest as he tells her how to amend the soil, the importance of organic compost, how to determine the best sun exposure, the uses of earthworms. She gets out paper and takes notes. They talk for over an hour, losing themselves in the discussion of vegetables, berries, herbs, their voices running together, trading ideas, the way they did in the days when Stanley assisted in her kitchen.

Avis says, "I thought it'd be fun to start from seeds."

"Sure, sure, just to make it as hard as possible."

"Isn't that the whole point?" She's laughing. "Seedlings are for wimps."

Then Stanley says, "Yeah, well, why don't you come here. We've got good heirloom seeds at the market. I'll be around tomorrow. Bring Dad too, why not?"

When she gets off the phone, Avis is still smiling, excited to tell Brian about this invitation—a sense of being readmitted to Stanley's life. But that night, Avis sits up late in the kitchen, moon glowing in the window, fretting over what to bring them. She feels nervous as a teenager worrying over a prom dress. She lingers over the cards in her notebooks—scraps of recipes tucked behind plastic sleeves— an enormous collection she's curated for years. She turns the pages slowly, in an agony of indecision, wanting to make them something perfect and beautiful. She considers a tray of flaky *jésuites,* their centers redolent of frangipani cream, decorated with violet buds preserved in clouds of black crystal sugar. Or *dulce de leche* tarts— caramelized swirls on a *pâte sucrée* crust, glowing with chocolate, tiny muted peaks, ruffles of white pastry like Edwardian collars. But nothing seems special enough and nothing seems right. Nothing seems like Stanley. Avis brings out the meticulous botanical illustrations she did in school, pins them all around the kitchen like a room from Audubon's house. She thinks of slim layers of chocolate interspersed with a vanilla caramel. On top she might paint a frosted forest with hints of white chocolate, dashes of rosemary subtle as déjà vu. A glissando of light spilling in butter-drops from one sweet lime leaf to the next. On a drawing pad she uses for designing wedding cakes, she begins sketching ruby-throated hummingbirds in flecks of raspberry fondant, a sub-equatorial sun depicted in neoclassical butter cream. At the center of the cake top, she draws figures regal and languid as Gauguin's island dwellers, meant to be Stanley, Nieves, and child. Their skin would be cocoa and coffee and motes of cherry melded with a few drops of cream. Then an icing border of tiny mermaids, nixies, selkies, and seahorses below, Pegasus, Icarus, and phoenix above.

You are lucky, Avis's mother told her, if you know what in this life you're hunting for. Avis has always known her hunt. She believes that her work is hard and essential, like that of nurse, firefighter, carpenter: she'll be needed after the collapse of civilization. Not the same as building houses, but still a crucial grace note. Avis exerts herself wholly and physically to produce an evanescence of sugar and butter—a phoenix's wing. She's proud to bring people the reprieve of a slice of torte, a bite of scone: a sort of remedy. Just enough to keep everyone going.

But Avis doesn't move. She's sunburned from kneeling in the garden and her back and arms ache. She stares at the cake sketches, and now they look gaudy, almost baroque. None of this interests her son. The cake fantasies seem like an indictment of her career: she sees herself drawing sweet vapors through the air, outlining the contours of a sugar castle. A bare, dry place in which to live. Too much sweetness, it occurs to her, is almost worse than too little. Swept by remorse, she presses her knuckles against her mouth. The moon is so bright it seems hot and the streetlights outside burn like match heads. Her eyes film with tears. Finally Brian is at the kitchen door. "Avis?" He comes to her side and slides his arms around her. "Come to bed, sweetheart," he murmurs. "Leave the cake for now."

IT'S BEEN OVER A year since they've last visited their son's market. As they walk through the parking lot they take in a number of improvements. Brian admires the raised garden beds made of cedar planks that flank the sides of the lot. There are stalks of tomatoes, staked beans, baskets of green herbs—oregano, lavender, fragrant blades of lemongrass and pointed curry leaf. The planter of baby lettuces has a chalkboard hung from its side: *Just add fork*. A wheelbarrow parked by the door is heaped with bright coronas of sunflowers, white daisies, jagged red ginger and birds-of-paradise. Avis feels a leap of pride as they enter the market: the floor of polished bamboo, the sky-blue ceiling, the wooden shelves—like bookshelves in a library. And the smells. Warm, round billows of baking bread, roasting garlic and onions and chicken. The doorframe to Stanley's office is an inlaid mosaic of seashells—a surprise from three volunteers who'd worked on it through the night.

Still, Avis feels naked without a bakery box, her arms empty. This is not me, she thinks. Instead they come bearing a cashier's check: the full amount Stanley and Nieves requested. She feels diminutive and humble inside the vast green world her son has created; timid about making this late offering. At the back of the store, they hear voices through the office door, and for a moment Avis has an anxious impulse, a thought of simply turning and going home. But Brian knocks and calls, "Hey Stan?"

As they walk into the room, Avis senses something, a frequency of sound or light like an echo chased out of the walls. Before her, a young woman is leaning on Stanley's big, messy desk, her eyes like sea glass, her hair whip-dark. So lovely she seems impossible—dreamed-up. Avis gazes at her and experiences a rush of sensation as if a river flashed through her body, before she understands who this is.

Felice is talking with someone, joking, when she looks over. Avis thinks, Stanley hadn't warned her either.

Brian wavers beside her. "Oh. Daddy." Her voice is nearly inaudible as she moves away from the desk and hesitates before her father. Her face has a red, streaky quality. Avis is about to warn him: *Don't touch*. Because she might run away! But the dream of her seems to become permeable because he walks through it, right through the old rules, of distance and untouchability. He embraces and holds her for a long, silent time. And Avis realizes then that her daughter did know—she'd agreed to this meeting. Brian's face is tipped to the top of her head, her small hands high on his shoulder blades. Felice seems to be trembling, fragile as a star, and Avis hears her say, as if brokenhearted, "I'm sorry, I'm sorry." And seeing this seal or separation break between Felice and Brian, Avis understands that in some way the world has finally shifted.

The air feels light and insubstantial; time has pooled around their shoulders. Avis is trying to explain something or ask for something—what is it? She doesn't know where to look or what to do with her hands or how to speak. She and Felice never used to touch at their meetings: it had seemed like a rule to Avis—the only way her daughter would consent to come near—and now she is still afraid. But there is the light sliding along strands of her daughter's hair, the scent of lilac, and she can't help herself, her gaze and her hands are drawn as if by magnetized forces; she brushes aside pieces of hair, cups her cheek, revealing the small, pale face breaking into tears. She takes Felice and holds her as if she'd caught her plummeting out of the air, feels the force of her daughter's velocity in her arms and rib cage. There's a sudden, surprising strength in her daughter's grip—an adult fierceness. Energy runs through Avis, rippling. A rush of indecipherable breath in her ear—Felice is talking to her, trying to claim her in some way with the stream of language, talking too quickly to be understood. Avis tries to calm both of them, saying, "It's okay, baby. I've got you—I've got you now." Until Felice quiets, not letting go, the two of them hanging on, gently, gradually collapsing together into the mutual silence of return.

Felice

FELICE WAKES TO THE RISE AND COMPRESSION of Emerson's chest, the slow wavelength of his sleep in the early morning. She couldn't sleep last night, twisting, kicking at the sheets, the air like a blanket, pressing her into the thin mattress. It was so dark—so hard to get used to after years of sleeping in an urban light haze—the blackness sank onto her body, lowering from the ceiling. It made her think of the night of the hurricane: they'd spread out on the blankets and let Stanley think they were asleep. The storm was like nothing she could remember, bending the palms nearly to the ground and tearing tiles out of the neighbors' rooftops. Feeling the walls tremble, Felice thought the apartment was about to break apart, that they would all whirl into the black hammer of the wind. Emerson talked softly to her about the strength of the building, the fastness of old structures, the solid foundations left by the old bank downstairs. Eventually he fell asleep, and then she'd lain awake for hours, alone, listening to the howling in the windows, her eyes wide open in the dark.

Last night was another long passage of staring and thinking, and an awful feeling had come to her, how all these years, she'd clung to an idea of penance, the hope that someday she would be judged—her crime and her self-imposed punishment—and somehow absolved. But now the world seemed immense and lawless and she knew there was no judgment—not the kind she was waiting for. She'd felt a sort of dread, granular and heavy, like a half-dissolved paste; it tasted sweet, like souls, she thought, and she felt she would never be free of it.

But just the intimation of morning helps Felice to feel lighter. This is the day they've decided they will go, because she and Emerson agreed that if they don't go now, it will become impossible. "We're getting attached," Emerson said the other day in the warehouse, surrounded by crates of Valencia oranges. "It's all right with me if you'd rather we stay."

Felice waits in a bed a little longer, eyes burning, but can't fall back asleep. Eventually she curls out of bed, dresses quietly, uses the bathroom. When she emerges, the door to Stanley and Nieves's room is still closed, but she hears soft noises in the kitchen. Nieves is there, working at the counter. "Hey." She turns and pushes the hair from her face with the back of her wrist, a butter knife in her hand. "Go back to bed, weirdo."

"What're you doing?" Felice leans against the counter next to her, steals a piece of yellow cheddar from the cutting board.

"I'm doing none of your business. What do you think? I'm making sandwiches for your stupid trip."

"For real?" Felice leans in for a better view. Particles of light are just beginning to drift through the windows. She feels better. Last night Emerson held her closely against his ribs and told her to breathe with him, to be calm, calm, calm. Breathe in, wait, breathe out slowly. He told her: This might take a while. In that dark spell she felt as if she'd forgotten her own name or who she ever was. Now the light in the kitchen is clean and vital and the terror has lifted like lace from her body.

Felice has watched Nieves for two weeks and knows she can be sharp and moody, but other times so quiet she barely seems to be present, an entrancing remoteness. On the cutting board there are two peanut butter and red currant jam sandwiches for Emerson and two Serrano ham, shaved cheddar, and apricot chutney sandwiches for Felice. Nieves wraps them smartly in waxed paper, tapes them, and puts them back in the fridge. There's also a cooler Nieves opens: packed with trail mix, sliced pears and apples, and the lemon bars. Jarvis Firmin, another volunteer, is going to drive Felice and Emerson in his nursery truck as far as Pensacola. From there, a series of

Stanley's friends and former employees will drive them across country. Felice squints at the kitchen window, trying to imagine the network that will carry them. Nieves sighs as she fits the lid back on the cooler. "At least you won't starve before Iowa City."

"Really, thank you," Felice says. For a second she feels a bitter little bead like fear or anger, like a remnant of a nightmare, surfacing at the center of her chest. She studies the floor with its cheap mustard-brown linoleum, so ugly. After a moment, the feeling softens again.

"If I thought it would do any good, I would tell you not to go." Nieves stares at her. "Don't go. Okay? Don't do it."

Felice gives the floor an aimless smile, wraps her arms across her chest. Nieves pinches the fabric of Felice's shirt—which had until recently been Nieves's shirt—between her fingers. "You're not going right this second—come on outside with me."

THE EASTERN SKY is beginning to take on depth as they push out of the apartment. A block away, there's a murmur of light traffic on Krome Avenue. Nieves and Felice walk down the main street, the stores quiet, several still covered with plywood and storm shutters. The light is so gray and glassy it feels as if the two of them might be ghosts, as if they'd wandered out of someone's dream. There's a small square with benches where Felice has noticed a few homeless people, drifters, sleeping in the grass; but it's empty now. They settle on one of the benches and watch coral streaks brighten and expand in the distance, pink wisps of clouds over purple wells of darkness. A whorled landscape of clouds piled on the tabletop of green fields.

The two girls sit close, their forearms bands of color in Felice's peripheral vision—reddish brown and pale olive. Nieves slumps back against the bench. "You know, I used to be so pissed at my mother."

"Oh yeah?" Felice stares shyly at her knees. "How come?"

"Mmm. I still am, a little bit," she continues. "Though I guess these days I almost think, like, a good mother will let her kids be pissed at her, if they need to, you know?"

Felice smiles. "Ha. You think?"

Nieves slides one hand over the small globe of her belly. "It use to be like I practically hated her for drinking so much and feeling sorry for herself all the time. And going off on how horrible men were and then following home any giant loser who showed up. Like my stepdad." Her fingers stop their slow circles and pat gently in place. "And then—just recently this was—I was at the market unloading artichokes? And I suddenly kind of knew that I only hated her because she had five kids and I was second to last and I just wanted her to myself. I was jealous." She smiles lazily at Felice. "Isn't that funny? How you can just know something all along but not, sort of, tell yourself?"

"I guess." Felice glances at Nieves's stomach. "Do you think you know something like that right now?"

"That's the trouble. You can't know until you *let* yourself know." Her head falls back to rest on the back of the bench. "It's like my mother had this story—I mean she had like a thousand stories. But there was this one I really loved. I used to think it was true. About a girl—she was really pretty and nice and smart and she lived with her mother in Florida. Just the two of them. But there was this guy? He was like, he did construction work, I think. Welding. He was totally into this girl, but she wouldn't even, you know, even look at him. He was rough and tough, like this bearded mountain-man type? So one day she was walking by the construction site and he couldn't stop looking at her and suddenly he just went crazy and like stole her. He grabs her and takes her like to the coldest place he can find, this freezing tiny island way, way north. I mean it's so cold and so far away, there's no other people and nothing grows there but little gnarly trees and little seabirds, but way off in the distance, so you can't even hear them. And he keeps her there with him in this little cabin and makes her probably like his love slave."

"Right, right," Felice says, listening, her eyes closed.

"So of course her mother goes berserk. Just insane. She starts looking for her daughter everywhere. She goes all over the world, asking everyone she sees. And one day she spots one of those little sea-birds and she gets a hunch and follows it back to the freezing island and she finds her daughter."

"This is supposed to be true?"

"Don't worry about it. This is the short version, I'm leaving tons of stuff out. Anyway, the mountain man says he won't give her up and the mother begs and pleads with him. So finally they work out a deal—the girl can go back and be with her mother for part of the year, and the rest of the time she has to go live on the freezing island with the guy." Nieves sighs and smiles and adjusts her weight on the bench. "That's pretty much it. That's the story. I guess I just loved thinking about the mother going and finding her daughter and get-ting her back like that. But the part that I never got? Was why did the girl keep going back to the freezing island? You know, like why didn't she just stay and hide with her mom somewhere?"

"Maybe she really fell in love with the welder guy."

"Yeah. I thought of that. But I also thought, you know, I bet she liked going away to the little cold island. She liked being far away and hidden from everything. Getting a break from her mom. She loved her but she always thought her mom was going to eat her alive."

Felice doesn't say anything. It seems like a sad story to her—like the girl never gets to have anything of her own—trapped on either side of things, between the cold and hot places. Felice can remem-ber feeling when she was little that she might get burned up in her mother's gaze. She'd thought that's what love was—like a furnace. But yesterday in Stanley's office, her mother had stared at her. Then, just like that, she stopped, her gaze fell, and something tipped inside of Felice. She feels it there now, subtle as a gesture: it is still falling, looping through the air. Another memory comes to her—something that's been happening since she's returned, as if a chest filled with fragments of her childhood has swung open. She thinks about a handmade ceramic bowl—a wedding present to her parents from her mother's mother—enormous yet almost paper-fine, light as silk. It was painted lavender and sea blue and a ring of silver fish swam between its bands of color. One day, when Felice was six or seven, she was alone with the bowl, tall enough to reach its protected shelf: she picked it up, turning it, admiring its colors. But somehow she lost her balance and the thing dropped out of her fingers, shattering on the floor.

Felice gasped, then burst into tears, inconsolable. Her mother rushed into the room. Instead of scolding her, Avis knelt beside her, lifted the biggest shard, and smashed it on the floor. "See?" she said. "We broke it together."

That was what Felice had kept trying to say to her mother yesterday. Seeing her again in Stanley's office, the old memory of the bowl had returned to Felice: that moment of closeness. "We broke it together," she said, caught in some crosscurrent—angry and hurt and full of wondering, helpless love, afraid to let go of her mother for even an instant.

Felice sits quietly, feeling the looping circle, the remnants of long-suppressed grief. Now she misses her parents with a vividness she hadn't felt over their five years apart—as if she hadn't had to feel the loss as long as she'd kept them at a distance. She almost can't bear to go to Portland, but as much as she wants to stay she wants to see if these new feelings will remain with her, to test the edges and see if she'll still want to come back after she's been away. And she's gotten used to the rigors and energy of movement: she isn't ready yet to ease back into the comforts of a family. She'll return soon, she thinks, but not yet. There's a long, faint call of gulls, soft as if the cries were a gradient of the air, its streaks of dampness and old rain. She listens to the birds, an arm draped along the bench, and her eyes slip back to Nieves's stomach.

"You can touch her," Nieves says, and smooths her shirt down. "Lately everyone does. I think she's still sleeping right now, though. Or he."

Felice moves her palm shyly over the rising curve, brings her face close and says, "Hello in there, baby." There's a flutter under her hand and she sits up and looks at Nieves, who is laughing. "She heard you," Nieves says.

"For real? Did she?"

She shrugs. "Sure, I guess. Why not? They've got ears and stuff."

Felice gazes solemnly at her stomach. "Can I hear her?"

"That I don't know." She pats her belly again. "Try if you want."

Felice considers for a moment, then she turns on the bench and lies back, lowering her head to Nieves's lap. Her ear presses against her stomach, and as she watches the dwindling streaks of clouds she waits. Gradually she makes out small sounds, a distant riverine gurgle. "Oh. Oh my God. Is that her?"

"It's probably just that I haven't had breakfast."

Felice puts her hand on the top arc of belly and presses her ear in close and she's almost certain now she hears a low, steady murmur. "Hi baby," she says. "Here I am. It's Felice." She seems to hear tiny motes, a far-off pulse like the movements of fish. The clouds unravel over their heads and Felice shades her eyes with one hand. Beyond the sound of the traffic there's a noise, a rip in the air. Unidentifiable and syncopated, it lifts, voices torn from the high branches. Felice watches as a flock of birds rises over their heads and curls into the white sky. She watches its progress and she holds herself silent and very still, waiting for what will come.

Acknowledgments

For invaluable advice, assistance, and guidance, my deep gratitude to Nanci Lanza, Stephanie Pacheco, Jose Pacheco Silva, Yesenia Balseiro, Bertha Vazquez, Cristina Nosti, Adrienne and Frank Curson, Sara Fain, Ellen Kanner, Mitchell Kaplan, Daniel Kaplan, Barbara Goldman, and Sally Richardson. Special thanks to Alane Salierno Mason, Joy Harris, Sarah Twombly, Denise Scarfi, and Andrea Gollin, who were heroic and steadfast and made this book possible. And thanks most of all to Scott Eason, who read every draft, and thought about, talked about, and paced through this book right beside me.

BIRDS OF
PARADISE

Diana Abu-Jaber

BIRDS OF PARADISE

Diana Abu-Jaber

HOW TO WRITE ABOUT A BAKER

By Diana Abu-Jaber

First published in *Gilt Taste*. Reprinted with permission.

In our family of mostly-women, baking was the feminine form. There was usually something magnificent under the heavy glass cover on the porcelain stand, some pastry displayed like a Tiffany's necklace. We baked for the sugar, but for more than that: for the communal pleasure of working together, for baking's equal parts chemistry and alchemy, for the physical beauty of the baked thing.

And yet, even after years of food writing, I'd not once addressed the private, ecstatic rites of baking. I'm not sure why that was, but I suspect I might have dismissed it—as if I'd decided baking wasn't quite special enough. It had always seemed so familiar and intimate, even in some sense, private—which perhaps made it seem dull.

My grandmother, an early, furious, proto-feminist, held that "women's work" was lesser stuff, far beneath her daughter and certainly not for her granddaughters. It was important to her, in fact, that we never learn the tasks that she was raised to do, like ironing, sweeping, or typing, that we never be, in any way, associated with such menial labor. Baking, with its quaint sentimental quality, had a special category, however: it was a form of guilty pleasure.

Not despised, but not to be taken seriously. Further, she had given me to understand that even in the professional world, men were cooks, like my father, and women were relegated to the pastry work—a backseat occupation with lower wages and less fanfare—in second place, always trailing the main course.

One day I began writing a novel set in Miami. The main character was a woman named Avis and the crux of this story, as I imagined it, was that her daughter had run away and that it had driven her slightly insane. I felt I understood Avis's solitude and angst, her struggle to feel like a part of an unwelcoming community. But on reading the early draft, I could see that Avis lacked a sort of direction, intention. This listless character needed some vital spark—the sharp hook on which to hang a novel. I could make her a pastry chef, it occurred to me, but I recoiled from the idea almost immediately.

I was writing about the restaurant world for the Portland *Oregonian* in the late 90s and early 00s. Every week, restaurants shimmered in and out of existence like fireflies. During this time, there was an intriguing bit of gossip involving a pastry chef.

Formerly head pastry chef at Alain Ducasse in New York, he'd been lured to Portland to elevate the desserts at one of the city's best restaurants. His work was reputedly stunning, Babylonian: ziggurats of sugar and cream, temples, pyramids, erupting volcanoes and cooling streams. The paper had asked me to write a profile on him and his work, but when I went to the restaurant, he was already gone. Apparently, this mercurial genius, this Daedelus, had lasted all of six weeks before the head chef had shown him the door.

"It was merely time for a parting of the ways. An artistic difference," Chef purred in his French accent. "He's extremely talented and he'd learned all we could teach him." But when I put down my notebook, Chef slapped the top of his head. "He's like all pastry-chefs, totally fucking insane! He wants to take over the whole kitchen! He screams at all my line chefs and throws pans at the waiters! He will use only hand-churned butter! He buys maroon saffron threads from Kashmir—for one mousse! And he was ordering gold leaf from Austria to sprinkle over his puddings. Actual *gold leaf*. Do you know what that costs?"

Ah, but I loved the idea of such egregious behavior in the name of dessert. It seemed wonderful to me that someone would damn practicality, to demand baking be given its due, to assert the sweet could be just as vital as the savory.

The following day, I sought out this gold leaf baker. He'd already taken a job at an expensive "atmospheric" high rise restaurant where the kitchen staff seemed to scuttle around and stare at him from behind corners. All suave, feline charm, he came to my table dressed in his white jacket and baggy pants and tilted his head as if we were on a date. His pastries, which a series of cowed wait staff ferried out, were architectural marvels—paved slabs of chocolate and shards of nuts, cakes with doors and hinges: they were indeed glorious.

But was it all a little much? It struck me in the moment as almost egotistical, to spend this much time and effort on dessert, making something too beautiful to eat. I noticed tucked among the gorgeous pastries, a single ripe pomegranate: it was nestled in a bed of green grass made of spun sugar. I was struck by the ingenuity of setting off the pastries with a bit of fruit—a nod to the un-improvable beauty of nature. A spark of modesty that redeemed the chef in my mind. He plucked up the fruit; using a sharp little knife, he cut into it, revealing rows of glistening ruby seeds. I realized it hadn't torn apart like a pomegranate would but broke into shards: its red sheath was actually a berry-tinted chocolate. While the interior seeds were actual pomegranate seeds, they'd been painstakingly embedded by hand into an inner membrane of white chocolate. I looked into the chef's hooded black eyes and thought: Hello, Colonel Kurtz.

He leaned across the table. "That French idiot—he is totally insane." His eyes were over-bright, his hands flat on the table. "He thinks that his cooking—*his meat*—is what's important? I feel sorry for him. I feel pity. He doesn't know that everyone is waiting for dessert?"

I thought about this sharp, hot energy years later when I began to rethink my character. I wanted her to have the same sort of nature, with that blend of male and female, ambition and comfort. Still, I tried to imagine all sorts of other pursuits for her: teacher, nurse, illustrator, tour guide: nothing fit. . . . There seemed to be an obvious solution and yet I avoided it.

Perhaps the problem wasn't simply about gender bias or status symbols but my own familiarity with the subject. I became a writer out of a state of crisis: as a child, I was drowned out by my loud relatives. My family was too insistent, too restrictive, too traditional: the spoken truth was dangerous. But if I wrote things down, I could take risks, just about get to the truth of things, my own truth. Writing gave me a sense of creativity, openness, and audacity—which meant everything to me. I had a dread of telling the same stories over and over—worse, of being *expected* to tell the same sort of story. I'd already written a novel about a chef in a Lebanese restaurant and a memoir filled with family recipes. How could I write about a baker and not repeat myself? I feared the story couldn't possibly stay rough and strange and new enough. It seemed inevitable that those deep planes of discovery and emotional risk would be smoothed away, polished by repetition into familiar old ideas. And so few American novelists seem to lavish much attention on eating and cooking in their stories—perhaps there was something inherently limited about such a basic human function. Just how far could I get with a baker?

An editor told me: It isn't necessary to reinvent the wheel with each new book.

I found this thought both reassuring and terrifying.

My new novel was about parents and children: as I revised I started to think about the way children teach themselves the things their parents fail to give them. I knew several women with unstable, unavailable mothers, and these daughters had become wonderful cooks, as if to supply themselves with the essential nutrients for living. Was the corollary true, I wondered—if you grew up with an unstable father were you drawn to baking? It seemed to be true in my own family, with its several generations of erratic fathers and daughters who loved to bake. I considered: so much of baking is a meditation: resting, rising, measuring. In the absence of a steady, trustworthy breadwinner, do children learn to make their own bread?

I was skittish when I met Scott. I'd been married and divorced, twice, and at the time I no longer trusted anything or anyone—least of all myself. In the beginning, I thought of our relationship as a kind of play: Even though we were in our thirties, we were still children, the two of us, broke, without houses, cars, or savings. But one day, about a month into our relationship, I woke up and the apartment smelled soft and sweet: he'd made biscuits—pillowy rectangles to eat with jam and butter. These were followed over the next days and weeks by cookies, loaves of whole wheat bread, and a dense chocolate cake dusted with confectioner's sugar. A few weeks before Thanksgiving, Scott made an apple pie. He peeled, sliced, and layered the apples with cinnamon, nutmeg, and butter. He cut lard and butter into the flour and kneaded it just to the point of smoothness. As he slid it from the oven in a plume of fragrance, I noticed the lid of crust was topped with a pastry cut out: a heart-shaped apple sprouting leaves. Wearing two elbow-deep oven mitts, he held it up. I snapped his photograph: he appears to be ducking slightly inhaling the aroma, a trace of a smile on his face, his expression says: *come hither*.

I loved the measured pace of our courtship, like the waiting patience of baking itself. It seems Penelopean: kneading, braiding, weaving the dough, only to devour it later and begin again in the morning. My husband won me over, in part, through his baking. My grandmother, I think, would have been won over too. When he met my father, of course, Scotty avoided the too-gentle topic of baking; instead they talked about guns and knives, racehorses and whiskey. And cooking. Manly things.

If I were going to write about a baker, I realized, I would be writing very close to the bone. The greatest challenge became one of perception and interpretation: how to avoid the sweetness? The sentimentality of baking, of something drawn straight from childhood? My character would have to be someone who worked with the blackest of chocolate, the kind with the barest traces of sugar. She would work in bitterness. I wanted the desert of dessert. I knew there was plenty of darkness within the glittering whiteness.

Slowly, carefully, I began to research baking in much the same way that I researched the occupations of my other characters: visiting libraries, interviewing professionals, visiting workplaces. I haunted the floury kitchens of bakeries, studied cookbooks, and invited a baker over for dinner. He showed me how to fold butter into puff pastry and talked about the reasons he became a baker:

He liked to get up in the dark.

He hated offices.

He wanted to meet women.

I realized I needed to come closer to my subject, if I could. I'd been a fixture at my grandmother's side throughout much of my childhood, which meant that I learned how to use a rolling pin, a balloon whisk, a candy thermometer—all without her ever admitting to teaching me. It was just something we did together as we talked. She showed me how to fold melted chocolate into stiff egg whites, to keep every last speck of yolk out of the whites, to invert the angel food pan on to the neck of a bottle so it would hold its loft as it cooled. In this understated way, she showed me the connection between baking and identity: It seemed that our hands were innately shaped to the curve of the dough; the motion of our arms lengthening and folding was the natural movement of kneading.

In my summer before college, Gram took me to Europe. We went, she said, so I could get "culture." Looking back, it seems the actual purpose of the trip was to investigate French boulangeries and patisseries. We glanced at the Louvre and the Eiffel Tower on our way to bake shops. We entered tiny places with polished stone floors and wooden counters where customers lined up for a few simple yet indelibly delicious cakes. We crouched over cases glittering with bright fruit aspics and twirls of meringue like whipped hairdos and mousses shaped like birds and starfish. Both treat and art object, these delicacies seemed to have a presence, an enduring nature that savory food did not.

Now, years later, I started remembering as I began rewriting. And I knew I'd have to go just a little further: I'd have to start baking again. I wanted to feel the dough under my palms, to remember the scent of butter, the taste of a vanilla crumb fresh from the oven. It had been months since the last time I'd poured batter into a pan. I had a baby now; I was teaching as well as writing; it was hard to find the time to bake. Cooking dinner was a necessity but baking had started to seem a luxury.

I decided to return to flour by starting with chocolate gingered cookies. A friend in my writing group had introduced these to me—decorative little disks—pretty, laborious, gingery-hot and wickedly seductive: just the right balance, I thought, of light and dark. As I whipped the butter and egg, I thought about how writing is a bit like baking: assembling the ingredients, mixing them, hoping it will all turn out. With each step of the recipe, a bit more of the main character revealed herself to me: when I grated the hot ginger I sensed her anger, scraping out the vanilla bean I felt her compulsiveness and perfectionism. Once the pan was in the oven I felt her anguish, the loss of something dear, the faithless wait for the impossible. She would be, I knew, the darkest character I'd ever written. I hadn't known this before I'd turned the oven on.

But even as I write this I feel the ancient fear return, sense the danger in linking writing too closely with anything like "women's work"—the fear that baking is too sensual and sentimental. Verging, in a literary sense, on the immoral—rather than the immortal. Baking especially can seem reductive, relying on precise formulas and measurements, unlike the artistic flourishes and spontaneity of cooking: baking seems premeditated, calculating. But every character has their own sort of scent and flavor—unless, of course, they taste only of the ink and the paper where they're written. In which case, I think, there's a kind of absence or loss—of imagination or courage, perhaps.

What to do? Characters, like living people, also have bodies and appetites. Does it have to matter so much who does the baking? Characters must also want to lift the cookie from its plate, to bite and feel the sweep of mind carrying them far out, beyond the page, into the widening sky, into the broad fields of time and imagination. Let them eat, I think. Let them live. Let them bake.

DISCUSSION QUESTIONS

1. Avis and Brian show us how the responsibility of children—and in this case, of a runaway child—can transform a marriage. How does the entrance of children change the relationship between parents? How does it change the parents or parent individually?

2. What kind of a mother is Avis? Is it possible to trace her mothering style to the way she herself was mothered? Could she have been a better mother to each of her kids? Is it fair for anyone to judge?

3. What did you think of Brian's comment about not bargaining "with terrorists" in regards to Felice? Are Felice's parents too strict or too permissive? Did they let her go too easily?

4. Have you ever witnessed or been in a situation where the behavior of a "problem child" overshadowed the needs of his or her siblings? How might have Avis and Brian better handled their treatment of Stanley in the wake of Felice's disappearance?

5. Why do you think Stanley grew up to become so principled? What kind of a father do you think he'll be?

6. Did you feel sorry for Felice once you learned why she ran away? How about before? Do you believe that it was entirely out of self-punishment that she left the comforts of her home and family, or was she being selfish?

7. How does a child's growing up and leaving home affect his or her parents? And what if they face an extreme case of this departure, as with a runaway or a child who chooses to leave home too soon?

8. What do you think is the significance of the novel's focus on food, in terms of both Felice's baking and Stanley's organic market? Is it just representative of today's foodie obsessions, or is there a deeper meaning?

9. How do you feel about the fact that at least one other street kid in Felice's crowd comes from a wealthy background? Are these kids

just misguided rebels, or did you feel they must have had real reasons for choosing to live on the streets?

10. How does the author's fascination with Miami come through in the novel? How might the novel have been different if it took place somewhere else?

11. How did you feel about the fact that the real-estate scam was revealed right before Brian invested his money? Why do you think the author gave him a second chance? What does his particular situation say about the real-estate landscape in general?

12. Is there a dark side to America's reputation as paradise?

13. What do you make of Avis's friendship with her Haitian neighbor? Are their situations similar or impossible to compare?

14. In what ways does the novel show us how we might be creative? Think of how characters like Avis, Emerson, and Stanley demonstrate creativity in their own ways.

15. Does Felice "grow up" by the end of the novel? What does it mean to grow up, and is one ever finished doing so?

16. Does Felice's family really come together at the end? Or does it seem as though Felice is just continuing to run away from her problems?

Janette Turner Hospital	*Due Preparations for the Plague*
Pam Houston	*Sight Hound*
Helen Humphreys	*Coventry*
	The Lost Garden
Wayne Johnston	*The Custodian of Paradise*
Erica Jong	*Sappho's Leap*
Peg Kingman	*Not Yet Drown'd*
Nicole Krauss	*The History of Love**
Don Lee	*Country of Origin*
Ellen Litman	*The Last Chicken in America*
Vyvyane Loh	*Breaking the Tongue*
Benjamin Markovits	*A Quiet Adjustment*
Joe Meno	*The Great Perhaps*
Maaza Mengiste	*Beneath the Lion's Gaze*
Emily Mitchell	*The Last Summer of the World*
Honor Moore	*The Bishop's Daughter*
	The White Blackbird
Donna Morrissey	*Sylvanus Now**
Daniyal Mueenuddin	*In Other Rooms, Other Wonders*
Patrick O'Brian	*The Yellow Admiral**
Samantha Peale	*The American Painter Emma Dial*
Heidi Pitlor	*The Birthdays*
Jean Rhys	*Wide Sargasso Sea*
Mary Roach	*Bonk*
	*Spook**
	Stiff
Gay Salisbury and	
Laney Salisbury	*The Cruelest Miles*
Susan Fromberg Schaeffer	*The Snow Fox*
Laura Schenone	*The Lost Ravioli Recipes of Hoboken*
Jessica Shattuck	*The Hazards of Good Breeding*
	Perfect Life
Frances Sherwood	*The Book of Splendor*
Joan Silber	*Ideas of Heaven*
	The Size of the World
Johanna Skibsrud	*The Sentimentalists*
Dorothy Allred Solomon	*Daughter of the Saints*

Mark Strand and
   Eavan Boland   *The Making of a Poem**
Ellen Sussman (editor)   *Bad Girls*
Mary Helen Stefaniak   *The Cailiffs of Baghdad, Georgia*
Sara Stockbridge   *The Fortunes of Grace Hammer*
Brady Udall   *The Lonely Polygamist*
Barry Unsworth   *Land of Marvels*
                                Sacred Hunger
Brad Watson   *The Heaven of Mercury**
Jenny White   *The Abyssinian Proof*
Belle Yang   *Forget Sorrow*
Alexi Zentner   *Touch*

*Available only on the Norton Web site: www.wwnorton.com/guides